ASCENDANCE OF A BOOKWORM

I'll do anything to become a librarian!

Part 2 I'll even join the temple to read books!

Volume 1

Author: **Miya Kazuki** / Artist: **Suzuka**
Character Designer: **You Shiina**

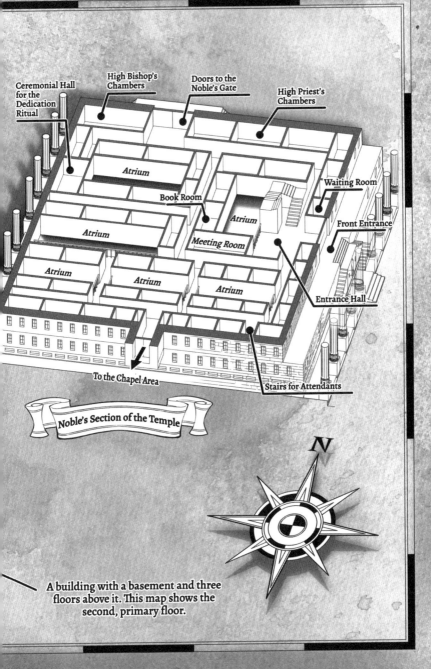

Ceremonial Hall for the Dedication Ritual

High Bishop's Chambers

Doors to the Noble's Gate

High Priest's Chambers

Atrium

Book Room

Atrium

Waiting Room

Front Entrance

Atrium

Meeting Room

Atrium

Atrium

Atrium

Entrance Hall

To the Chapel Area

Stairs for Attendants

Noble's Section of the Temple

N

A building with a basement and three floors above it. This map shows the second, primary floor.

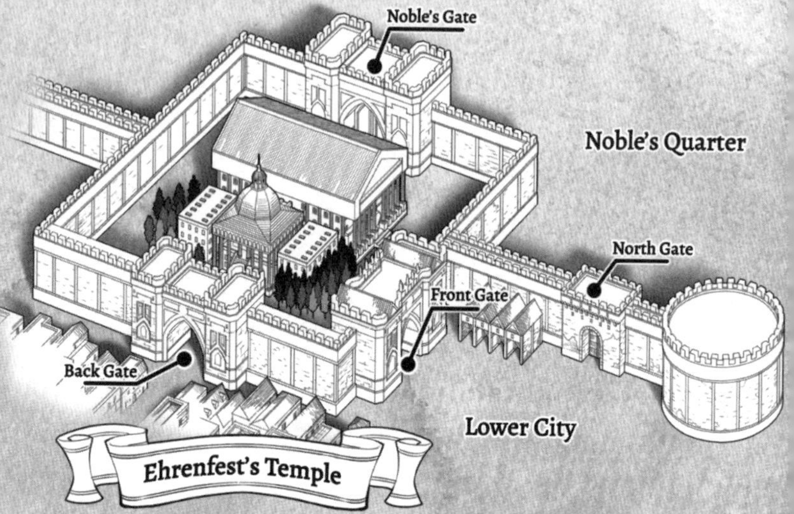
Noble's Gate
Noble's Quarter
North Gate
Front Gate
Back Gate
Lower City
Ehrenfest's Temple

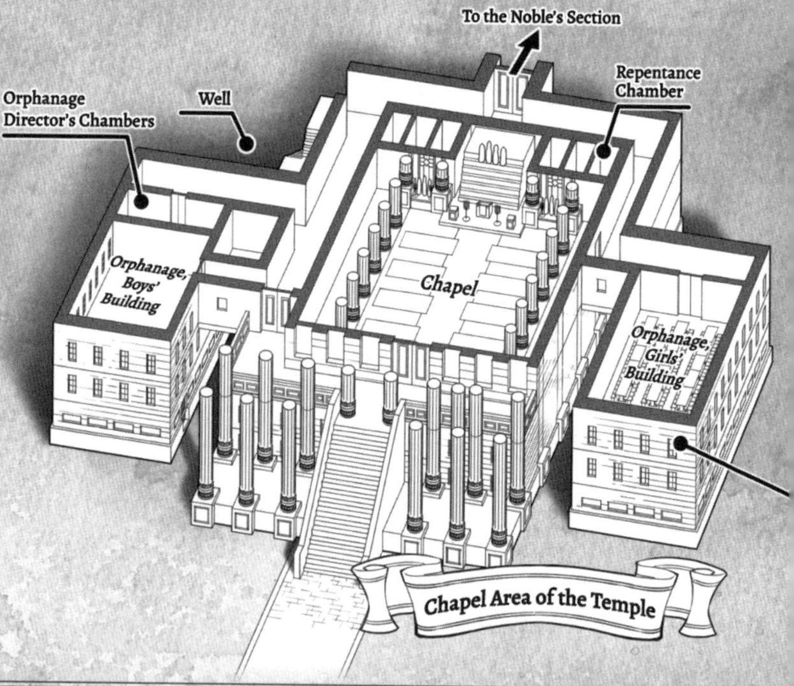
To the Noble's Section
Orphanage
Director's Chambers
Well
Repentance
Chamber
Orphanage,
Boys'
Building
Chapel
Orphanage,
Girls'
Building
Chapel Area of the Temple

ASCENDANCE OF A BOOKWORM
I'll do anything to become a librarian!
Part 2 I'll even join the temple to read books!
Volume I

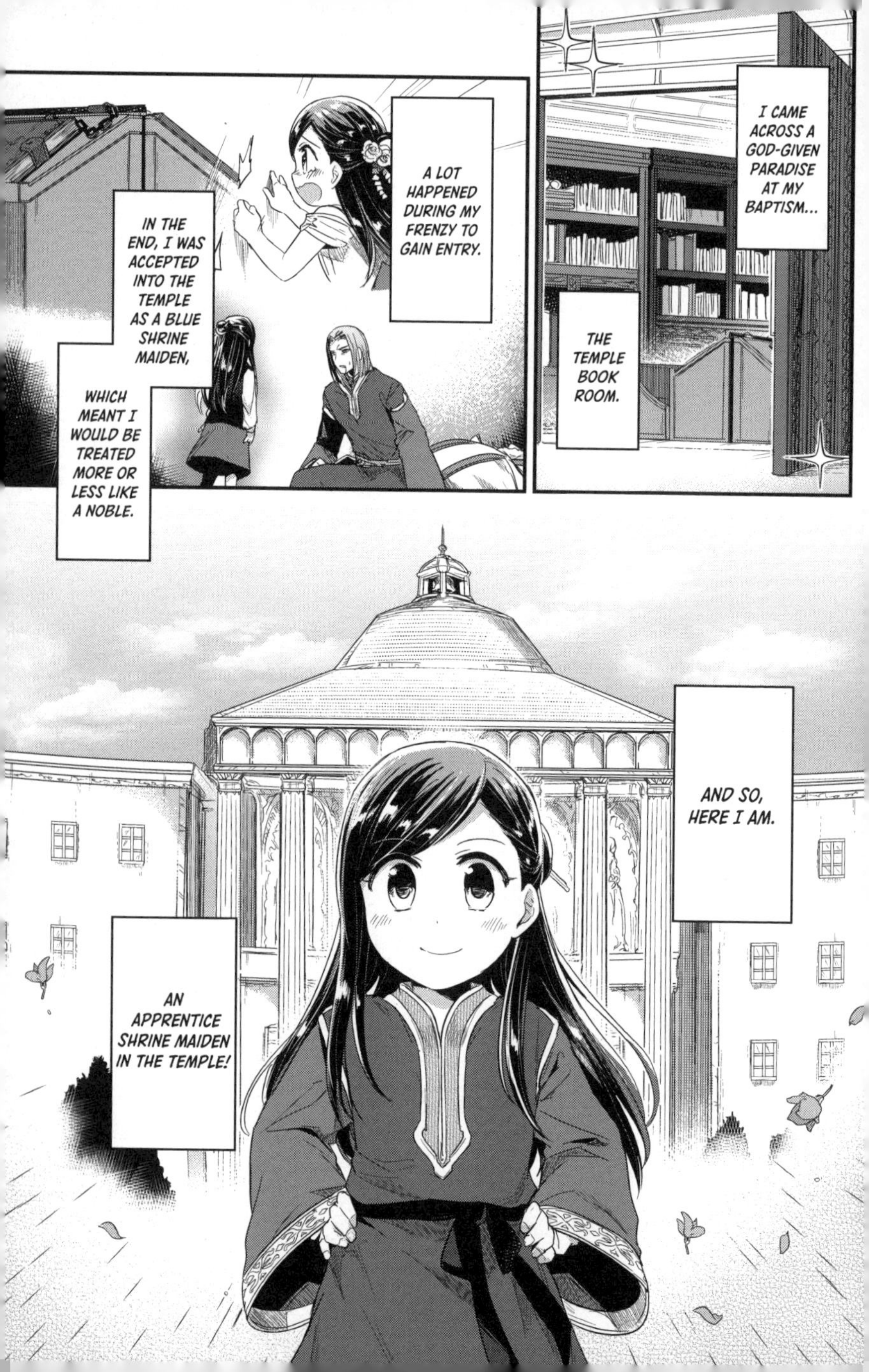
I CAME ACROSS A GOD-GIVEN PARADISE AT MY BAPTISM...
THE TEMPLE BOOK ROOM.
A LOT HAPPENED DURING MY FRENZY TO GAIN ENTRY.
IN THE END, I WAS ACCEPTED INTO THE TEMPLE AS A BLUE SHRINE MAIDEN,
WHICH MEANT I WOULD BE TREATED MORE OR LESS LIKE A NOBLE.
AND SO, HERE I AM.
AN APPRENTICE SHRINE MAIDEN IN THE TEMPLE!

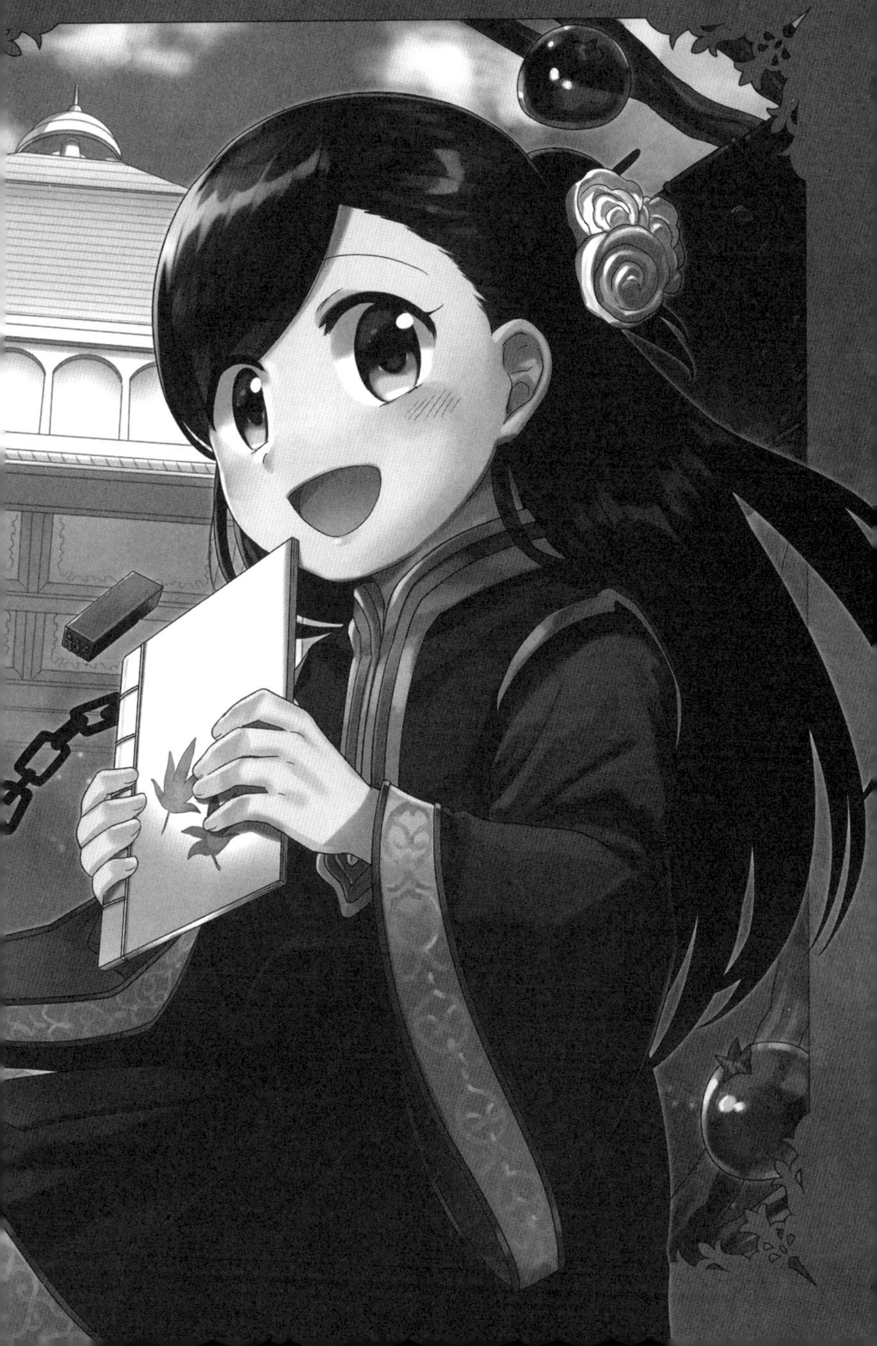

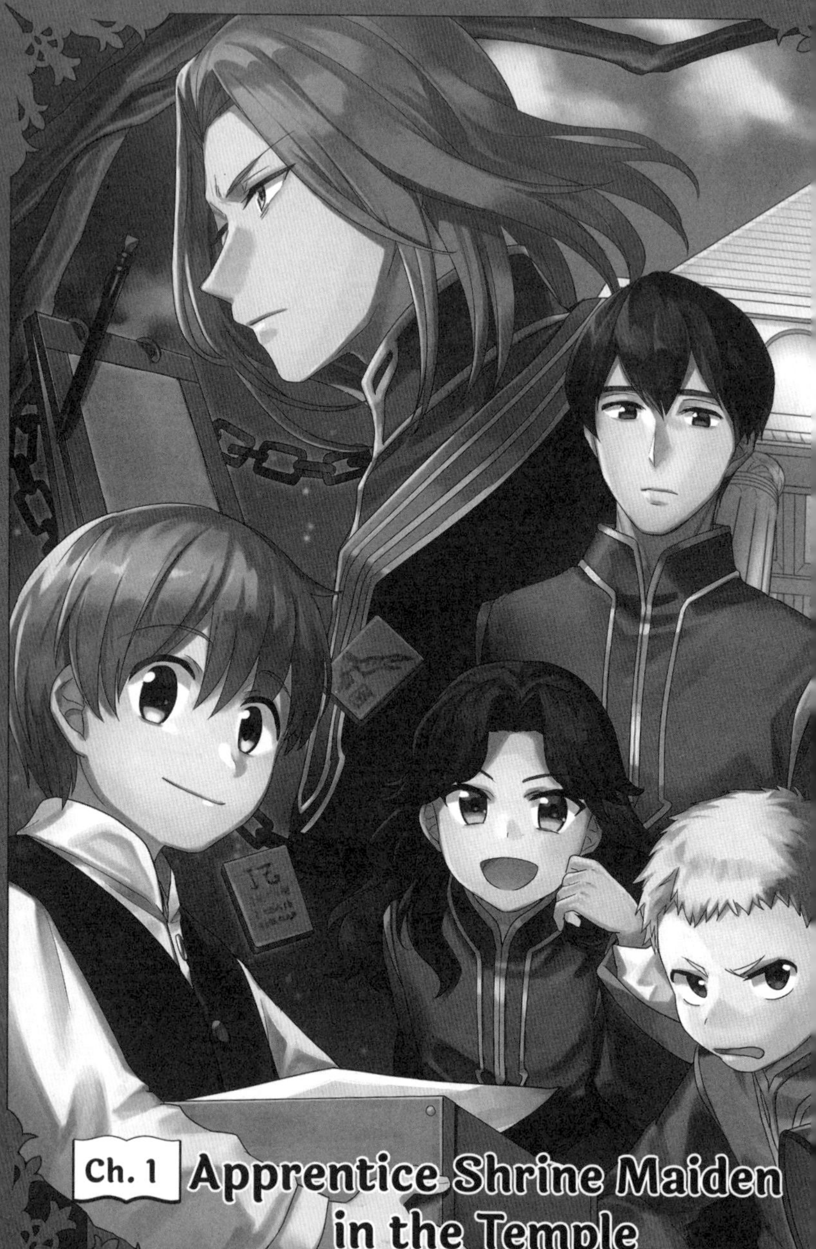

Ch. 1 Apprentice Shrine Maiden in the Temple

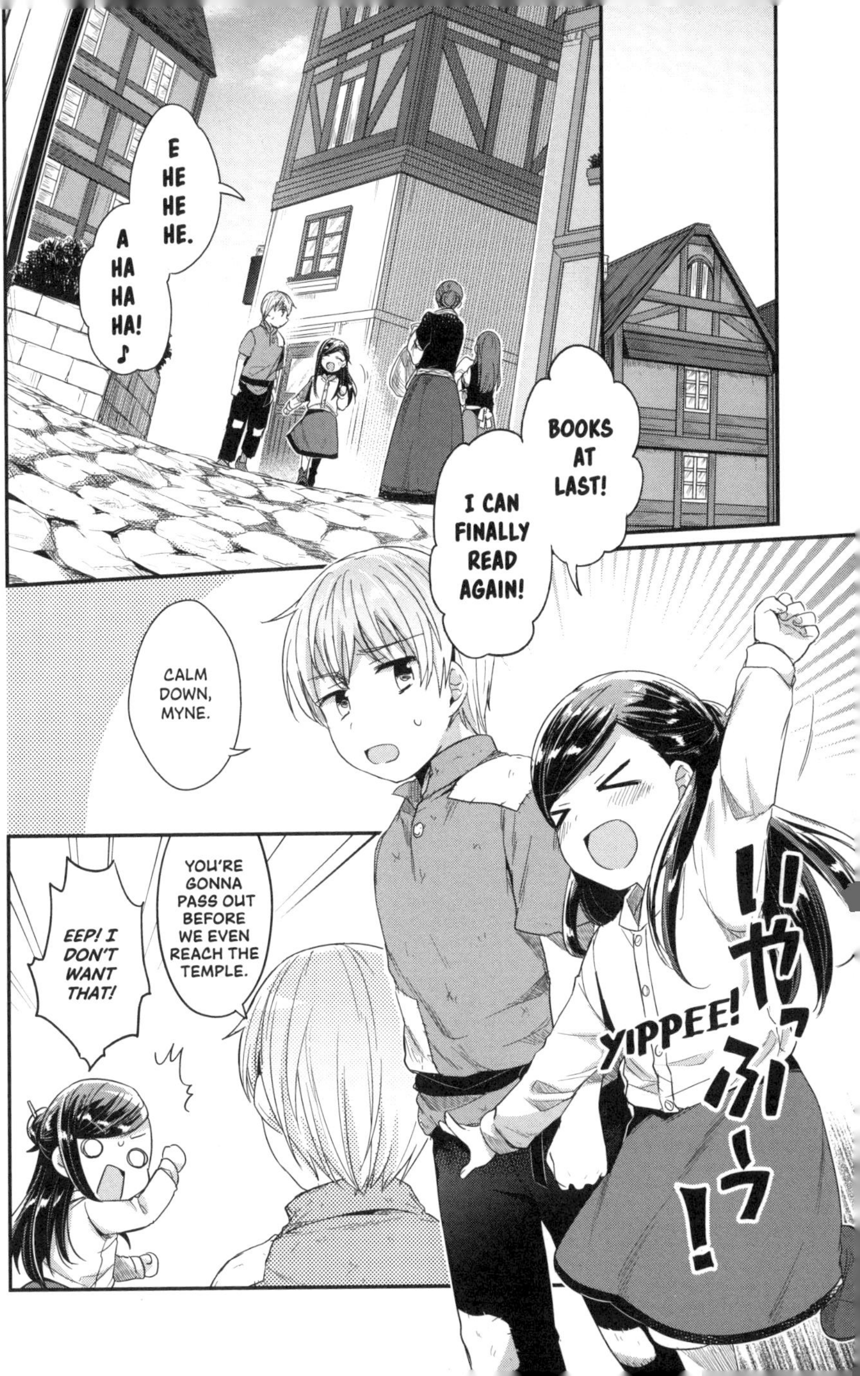
E HE HE HE.
A HA HA HA! ♪
BOOKS AT LAST!
I CAN FINALLY READ AGAIN!
いやっふーう!
YIPPEE!
CALM DOWN, MYNE.
YOU'RE GONNA PASS OUT BEFORE WE EVEN REACH THE TEMPLE.
EEP! I DON'T WANT THAT!

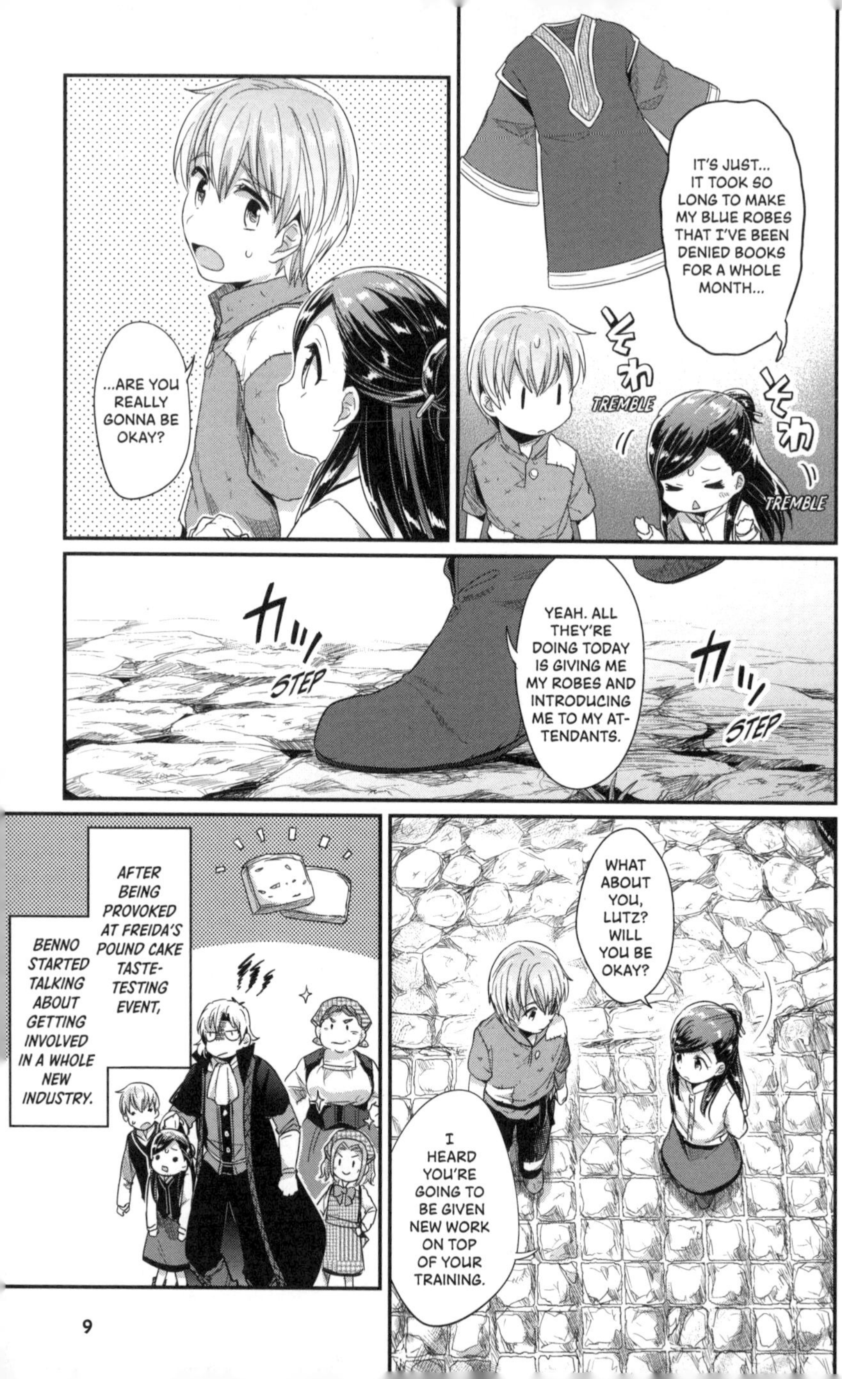
IT'S JUST... IT TOOK SO LONG TO MAKE MY BLUE ROBES THAT I'VE BEEN DENIED BOOKS FOR A WHOLE MONTH...
TREMBLE
TREMBLE
...ARE YOU REALLY GONNA BE OKAY?
STEP
YEAH. ALL THEY'RE DOING TODAY IS GIVING ME MY ROBES AND INTRODUCING ME TO MY AT-TENDANTS.
STEP
WHAT ABOUT YOU, LUTZ? WILL YOU BE OKAY?
I HEARD YOU'RE GOING TO BE GIVEN NEW WORK ON TOP OF YOUR TRAINING.
AFTER BEING PROVOKED AT FREIDA'S POUND CAKE TASTE-TESTING EVENT,
BENNO STARTED TALKING ABOUT GETTING INVOLVED IN A WHOLE NEW INDUSTRY.

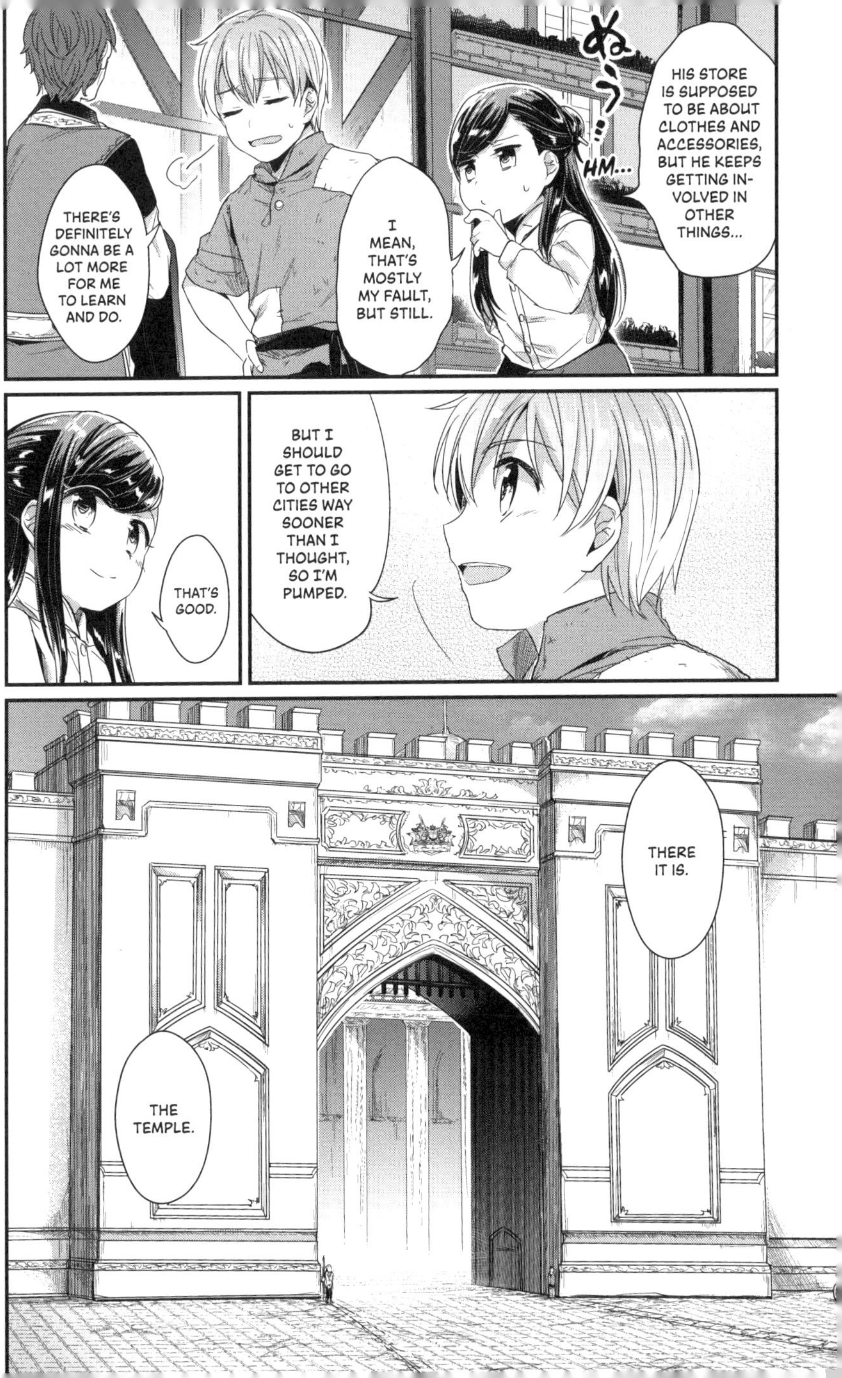

ぬう…
HM...
HIS STORE IS SUPPOSED TO BE ABOUT CLOTHES AND ACCESSORIES, BUT HE KEEPS GETTING INVOLVED IN OTHER THINGS...
I MEAN, THAT'S MOSTLY MY FAULT, BUT STILL.
THERE'S DEFINITELY GONNA BE A LOT MORE FOR ME TO LEARN AND DO.
BUT I SHOULD GET TO GO TO OTHER CITIES WAY SOONER THAN I THOUGHT, SO I'M PUMPED.
THAT'S GOOD.
THERE IT IS.
THE TEMPLE.

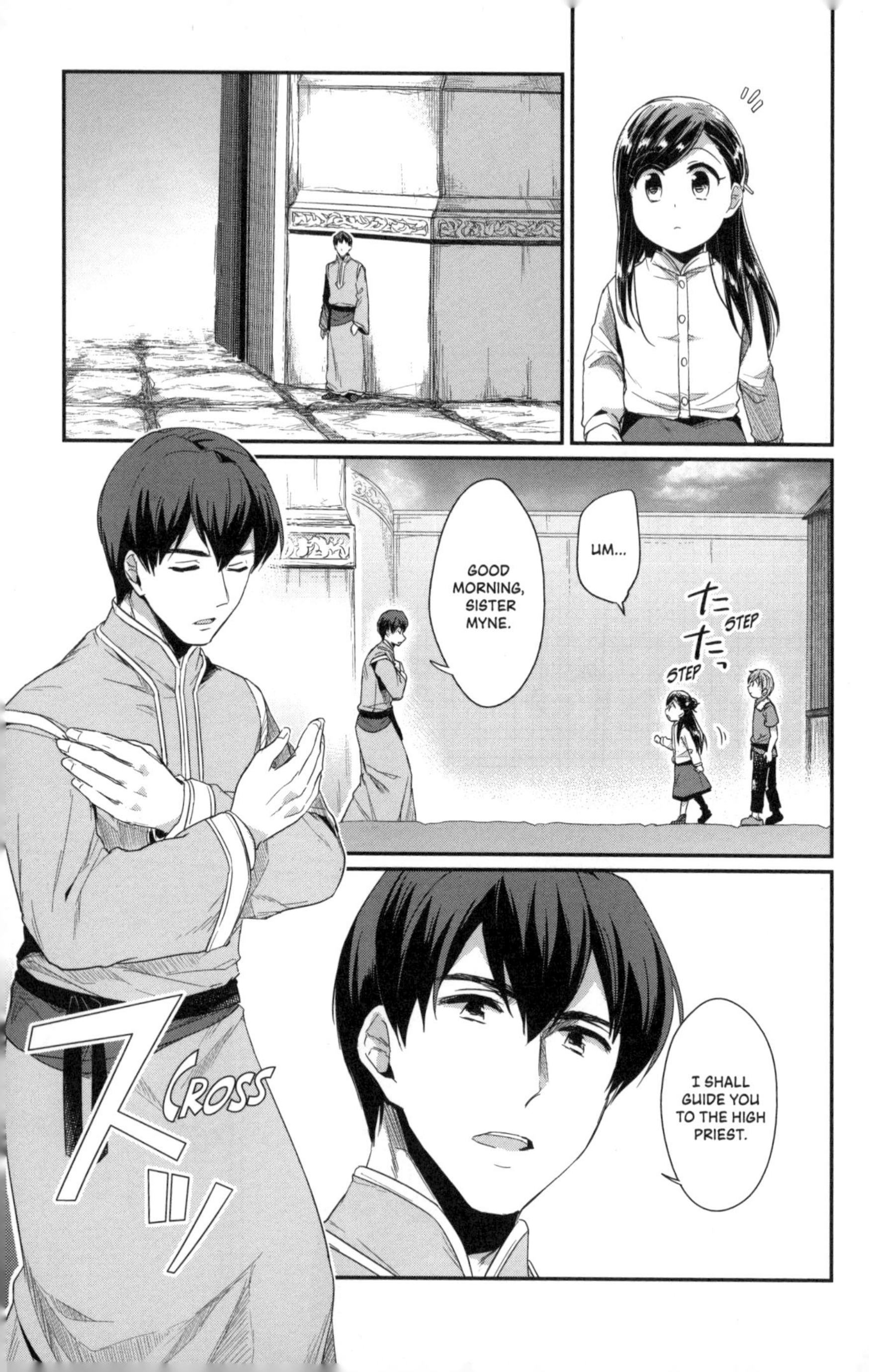
UM...
STEP
STEP
GOOD MORNING, SISTER MYNE.
I SHALL GUIDE YOU TO THE HIGH PRIEST.
CROSS

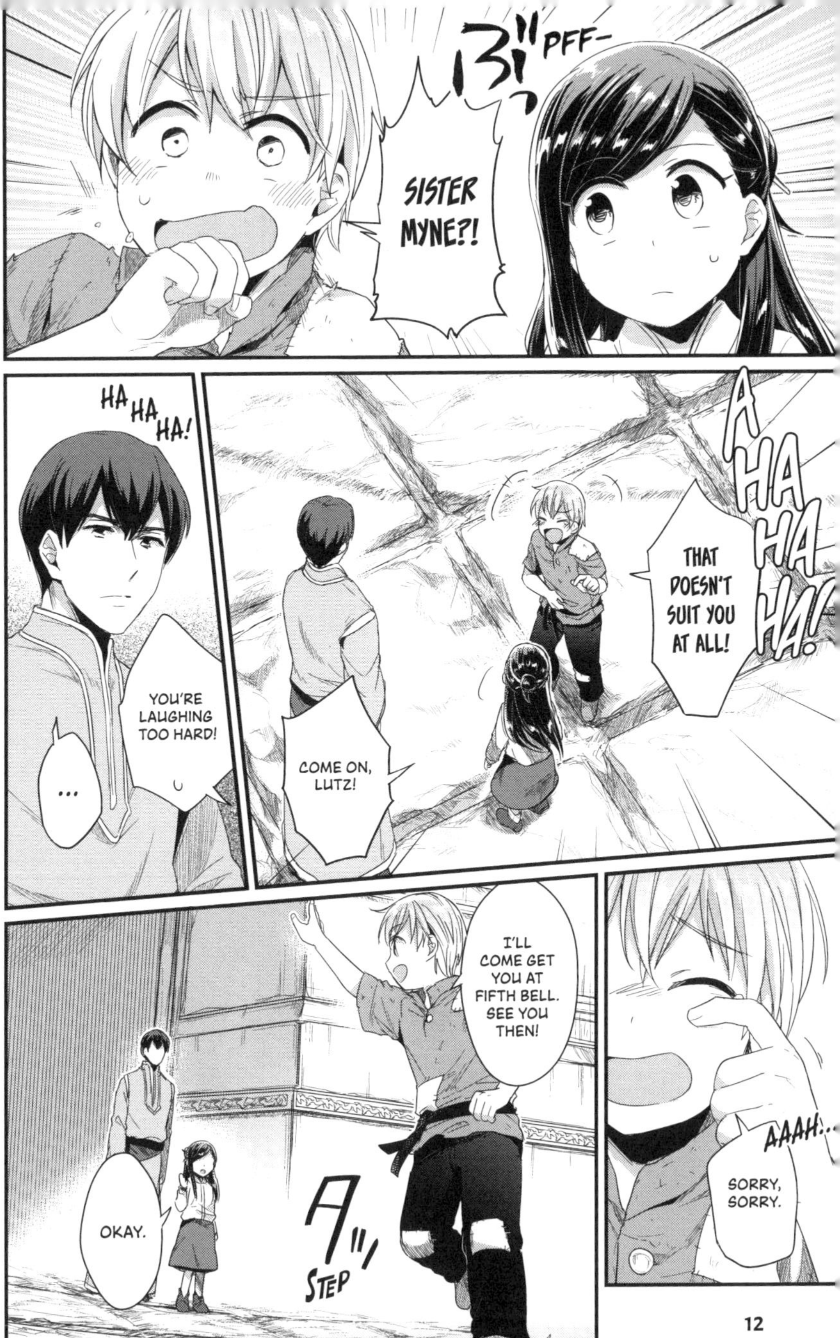
ぶ!! PFF-
SISTER MYNE?!
A HA HA HA!
THAT DOESN'T SUIT YOU AT ALL!
COME ON, LUTZ!
HA HA HA!
YOU'RE LAUGHING TOO HARD!
...
AAAH...
SORRY, SORRY.
I'LL COME GET YOU AT FIFTH BELL. SEE YOU THEN!
STEP
OKAY.

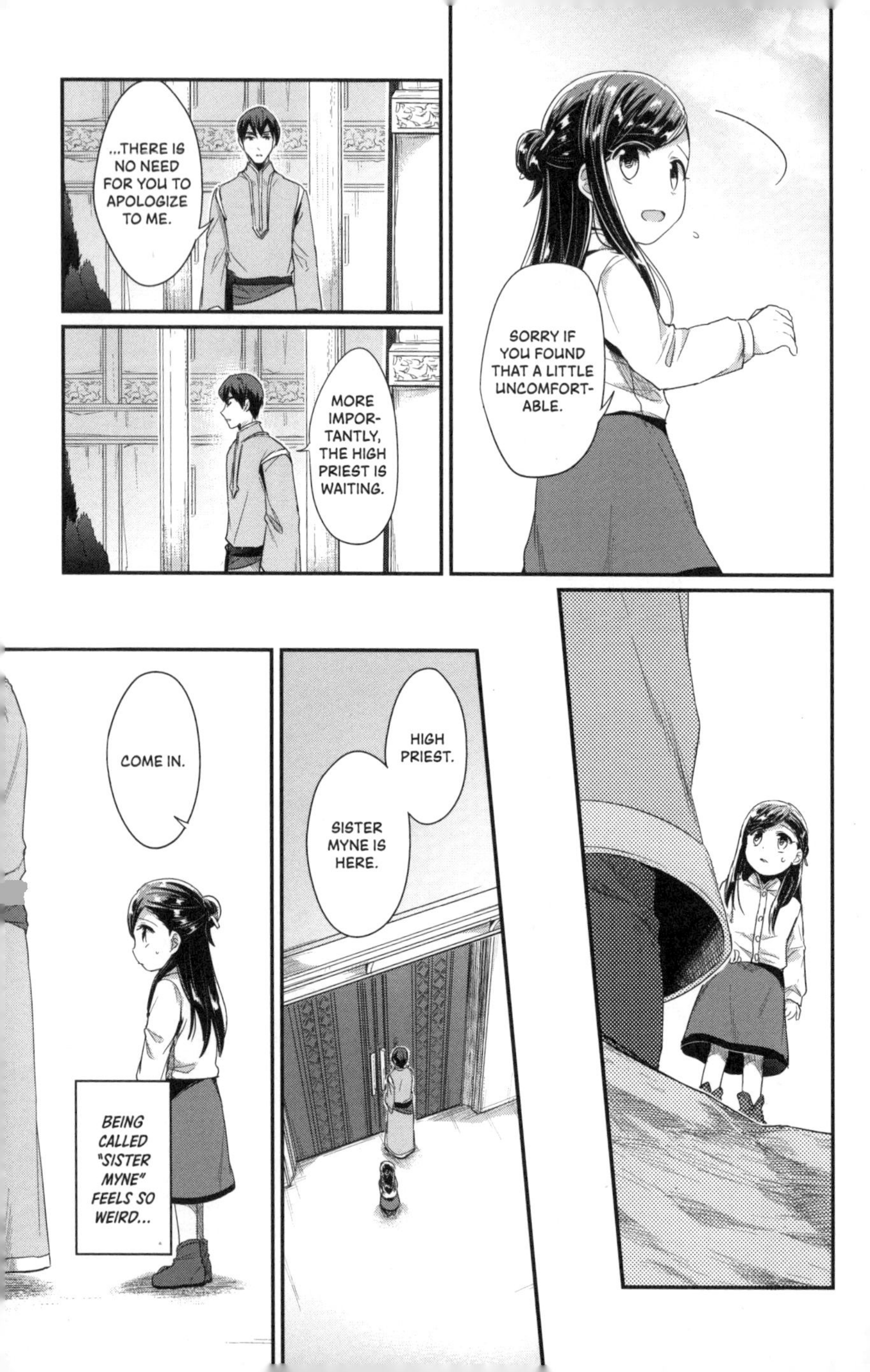
SORRY IF YOU FOUND THAT A LITTLE UNCOMFORT-ABLE.
...THERE IS NO NEED FOR YOU TO APOLOGIZE TO ME.
MORE IMPOR-TANTLY, THE HIGH PRIEST IS WAITING.
HIGH PRIEST.
SISTER MYNE IS HERE.
COME IN.
BEING CALLED "SISTER MYNE" FEELS SO WEIRD...

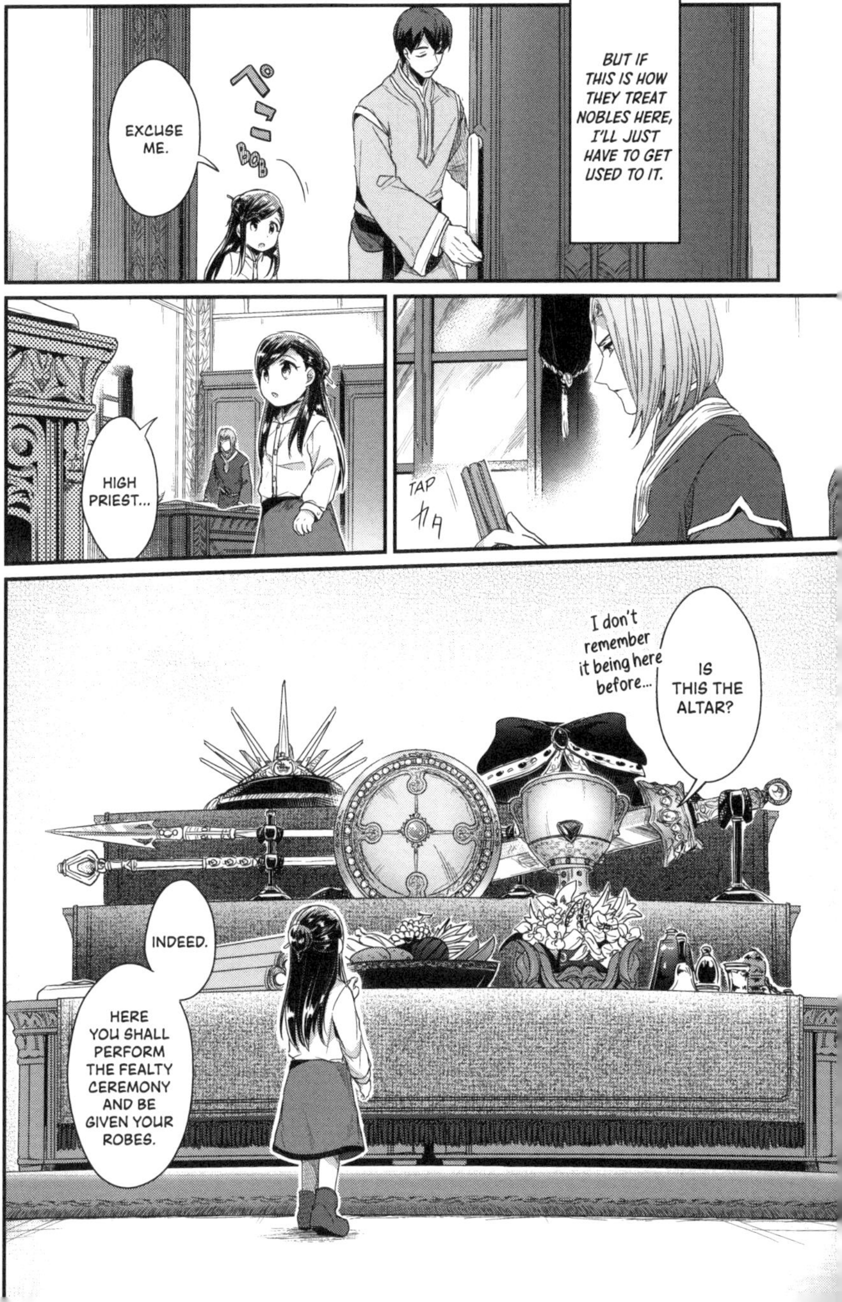
BUT IF THIS IS HOW THEY TREAT NOBLES HERE, I'LL JUST HAVE TO GET USED TO IT.
ペコ
BOB
EXCUSE ME.
TAP
カタ
HIGH PRIEST...
IS THIS THE ALTAR?
I don't remember it being here before...
INDEED.
HERE YOU SHALL PERFORM THE FEALTY CEREMONY AND BE GIVEN YOUR ROBES.

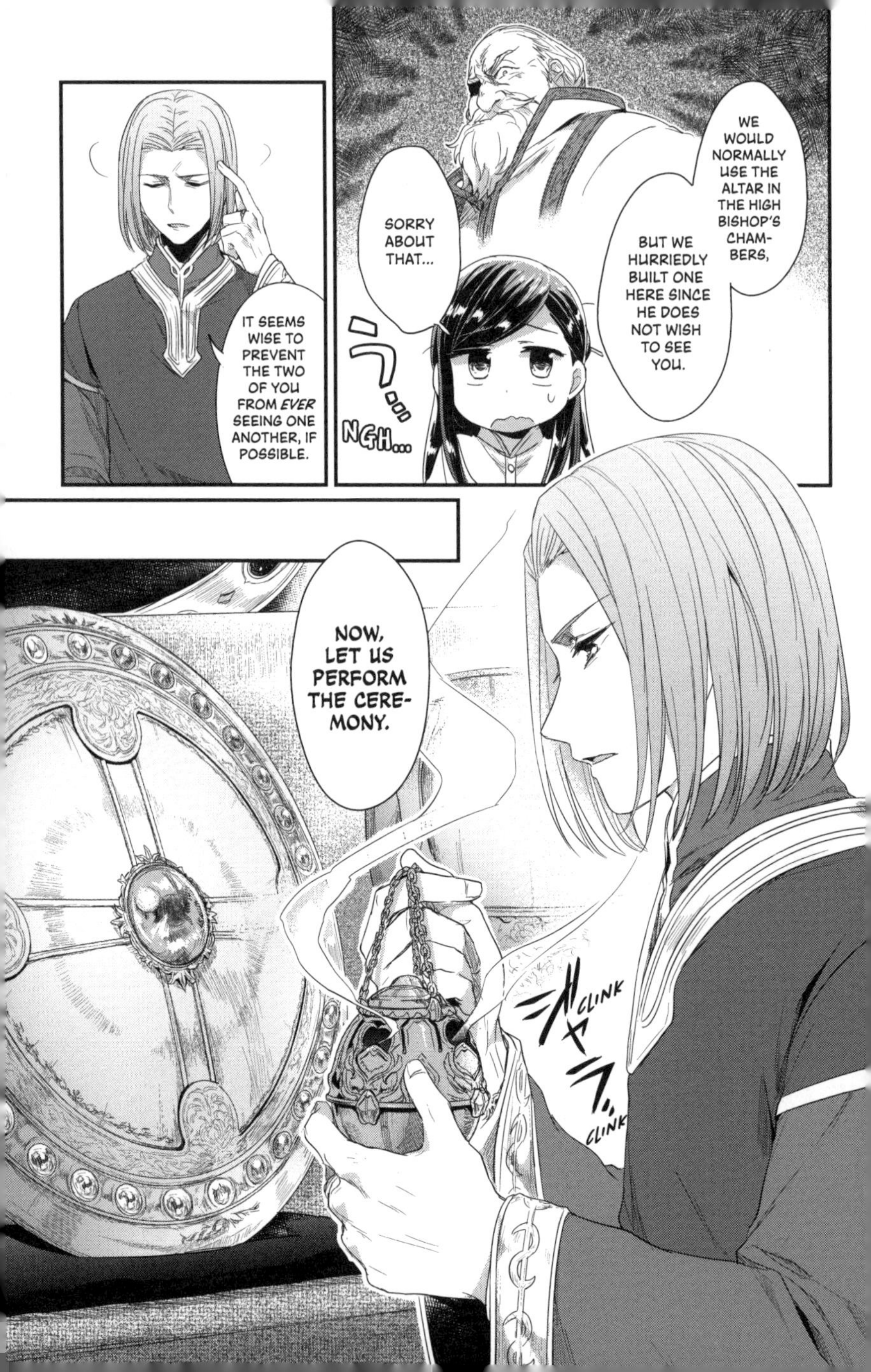
WE WOULD NORMALLY USE THE ALTAR IN THE HIGH BISHOP'S CHAM-BERS,
BUT WE HURRIEDLY BUILT ONE HERE SINCE HE DOES NOT WISH TO SEE YOU.
SORRY ABOUT THAT...
NGH...
IT SEEMS WISE TO PREVENT THE TWO OF YOU FROM *EVER* SEEING ONE ANOTHER, IF POSSIBLE.
NOW, LET US PERFORM THE CERE-MONY.
CLINK
CLINK

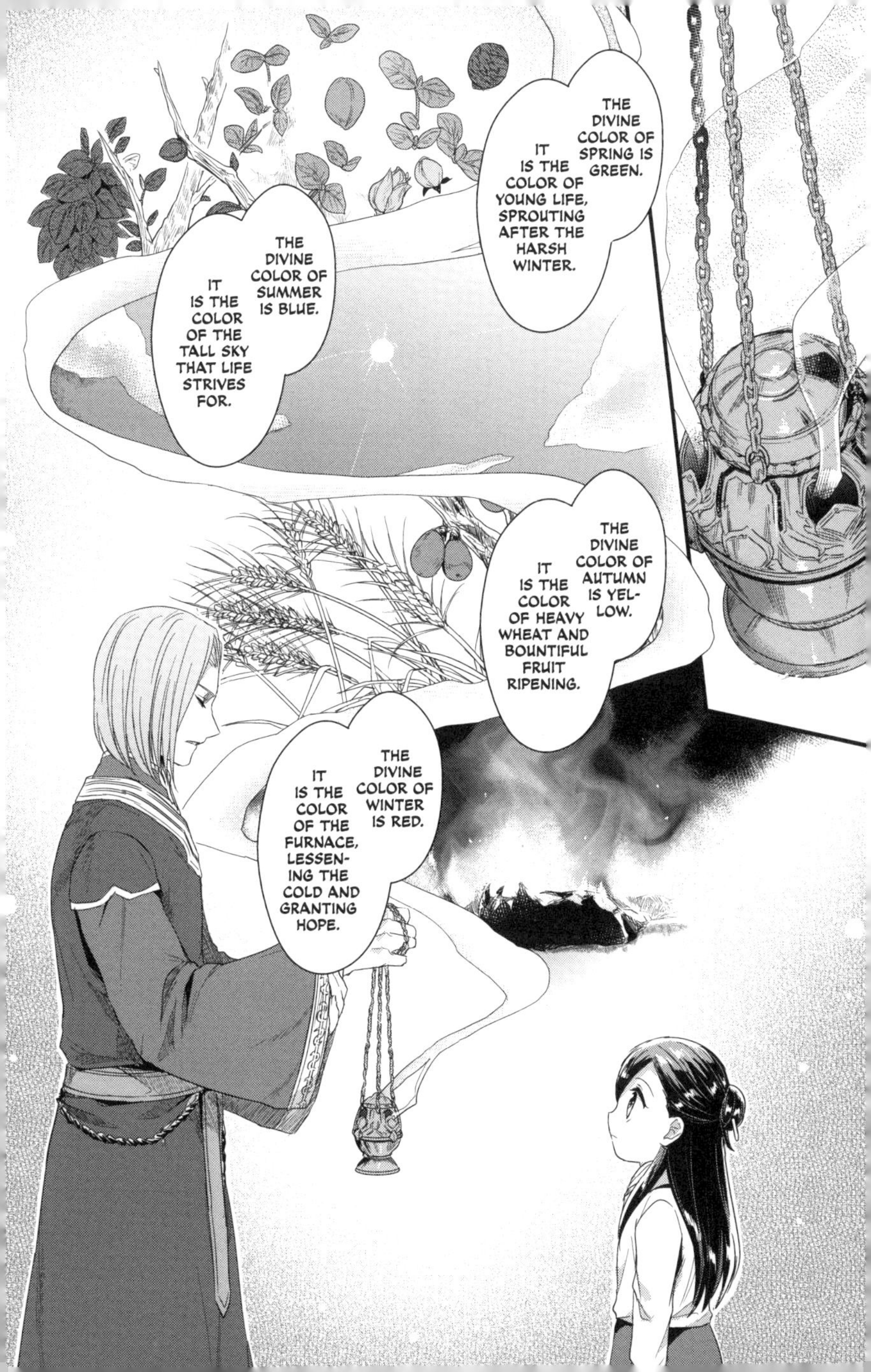
THE DIVINE COLOR OF SPRING IS GREEN. IT IS THE COLOR OF YOUNG LIFE, SPROUTING AFTER THE HARSH WINTER.
THE DIVINE COLOR OF SUMMER IS BLUE. IT IS THE COLOR OF THE TALL SKY THAT LIFE STRIVES FOR.
THE DIVINE COLOR OF AUTUMN IS YEL-LOW. IT IS THE COLOR OF HEAVY WHEAT AND BOUNTIFUL FRUIT RIPENING.
THE DIVINE COLOR OF WINTER IS RED. IT IS THE COLOR OF THE FURNACE, LESSEN-ING THE COLD AND GRANTING HOPE.

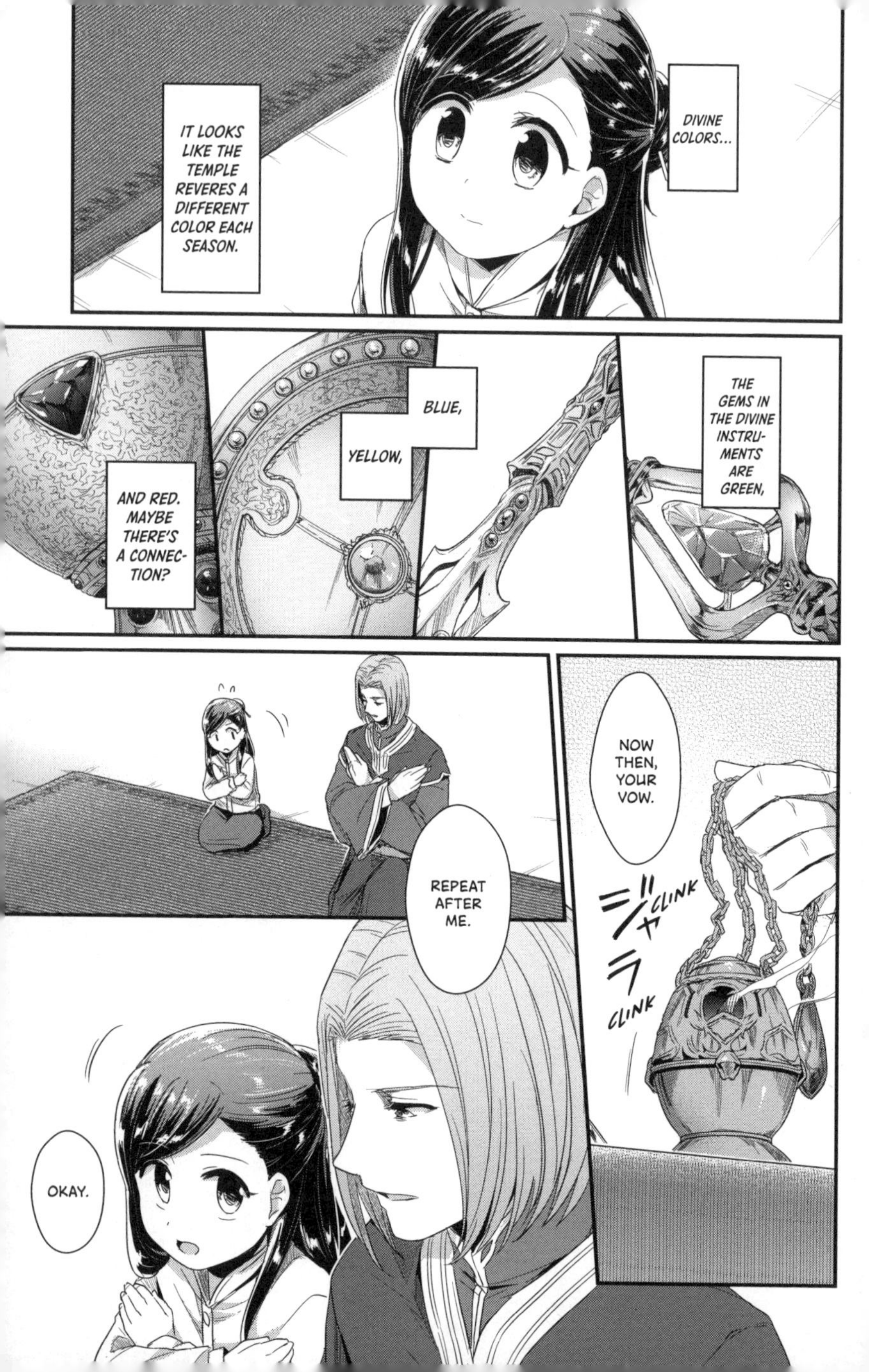
DIVINE COLORS...
IT LOOKS LIKE THE TEMPLE REVERES A DIFFERENT COLOR EACH SEASON.
THE GEMS IN THE DIVINE INSTRUMENTS ARE GREEN,
BLUE,
YELLOW,
AND RED. MAYBE THERE'S A CONNECTION?
NOW THEN, YOUR VOW.
ジャ CLINK
ラ CLINK
REPEAT AFTER ME.
OKAY.

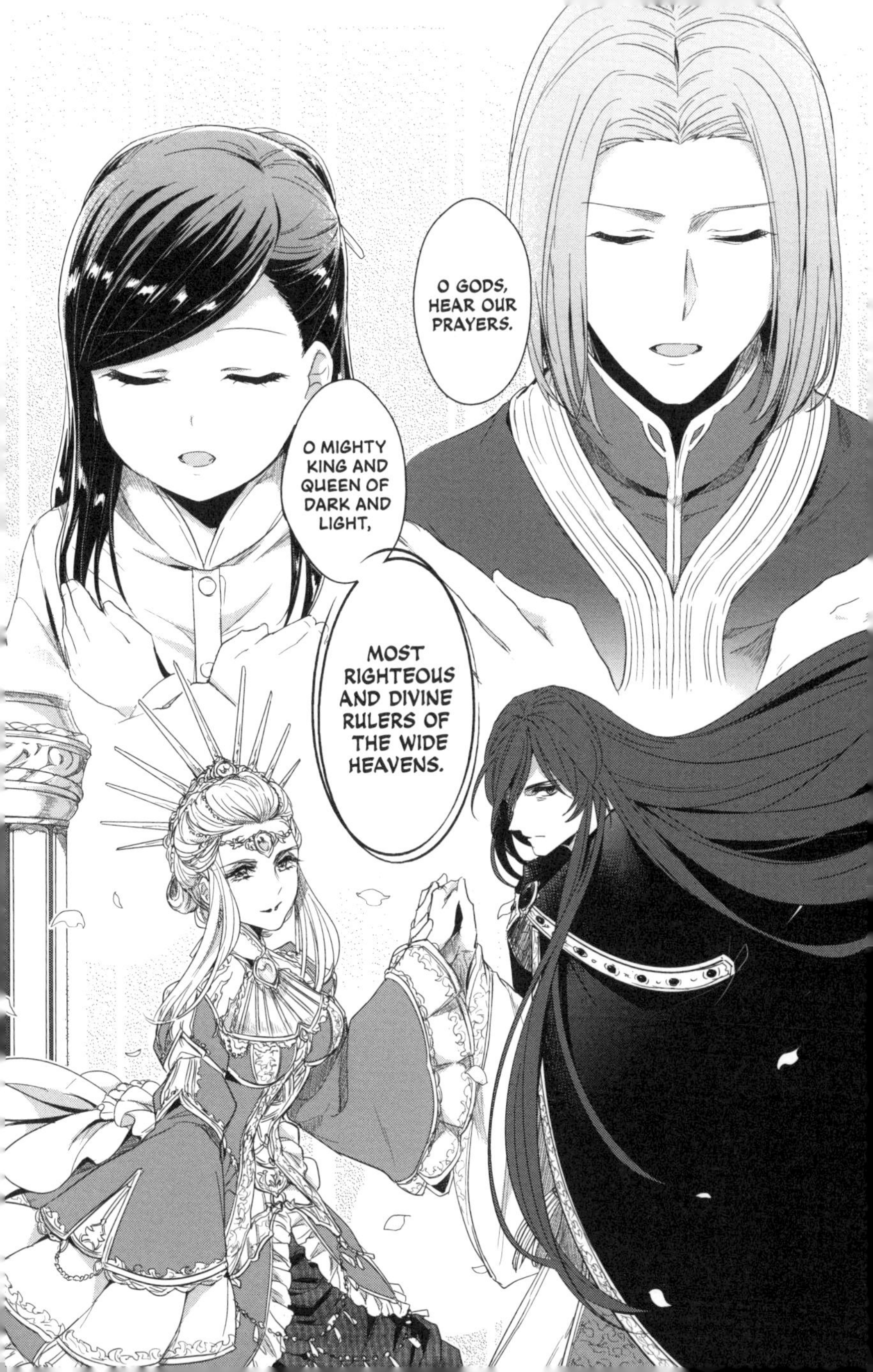
O GODS, HEAR OUR PRAYERS.
O MIGHTY KING AND QUEEN OF DARK AND LIGHT,
MOST RIGHTEOUS AND DIVINE RULERS OF THE WIDE HEAVENS.

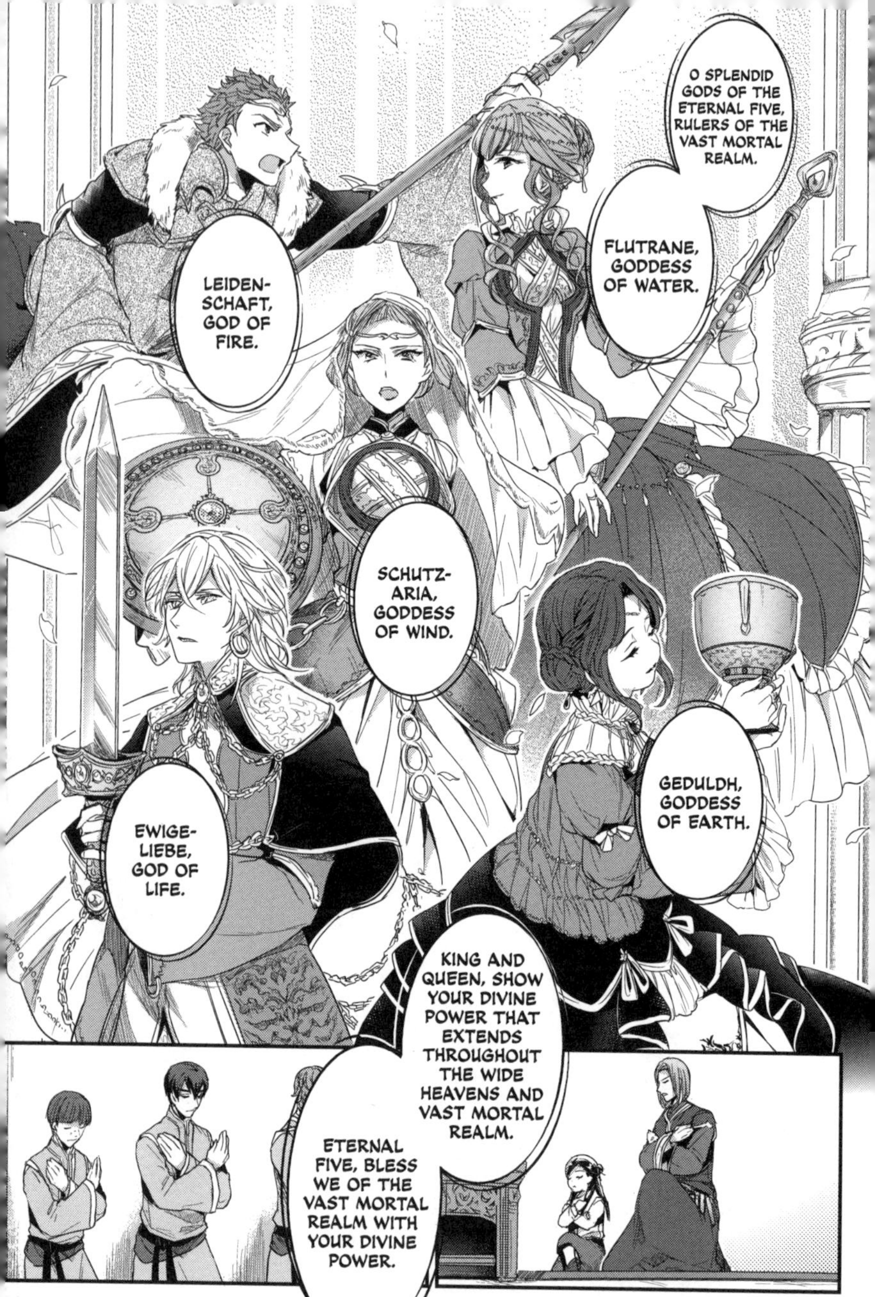
O SPLENDID GODS OF THE ETERNAL FIVE, RULERS OF THE VAST MORTAL REALM.
FLUTRANE, GODDESS OF WATER.
LEIDEN-SCHAFT, GOD OF FIRE.
SCHUTZ-ARIA, GODDESS OF WIND.
GEDULDH, GODDESS OF EARTH.
EWIGE-LIEBE, GOD OF LIFE.
KING AND QUEEN, SHOW YOUR DIVINE POWER THAT EXTENDS THROUGHOUT THE WIDE HEAVENS AND VAST MORTAL REALM.
ETERNAL FIVE, BLESS WE OF THE VAST MORTAL REALM WITH YOUR DIVINE POWER.

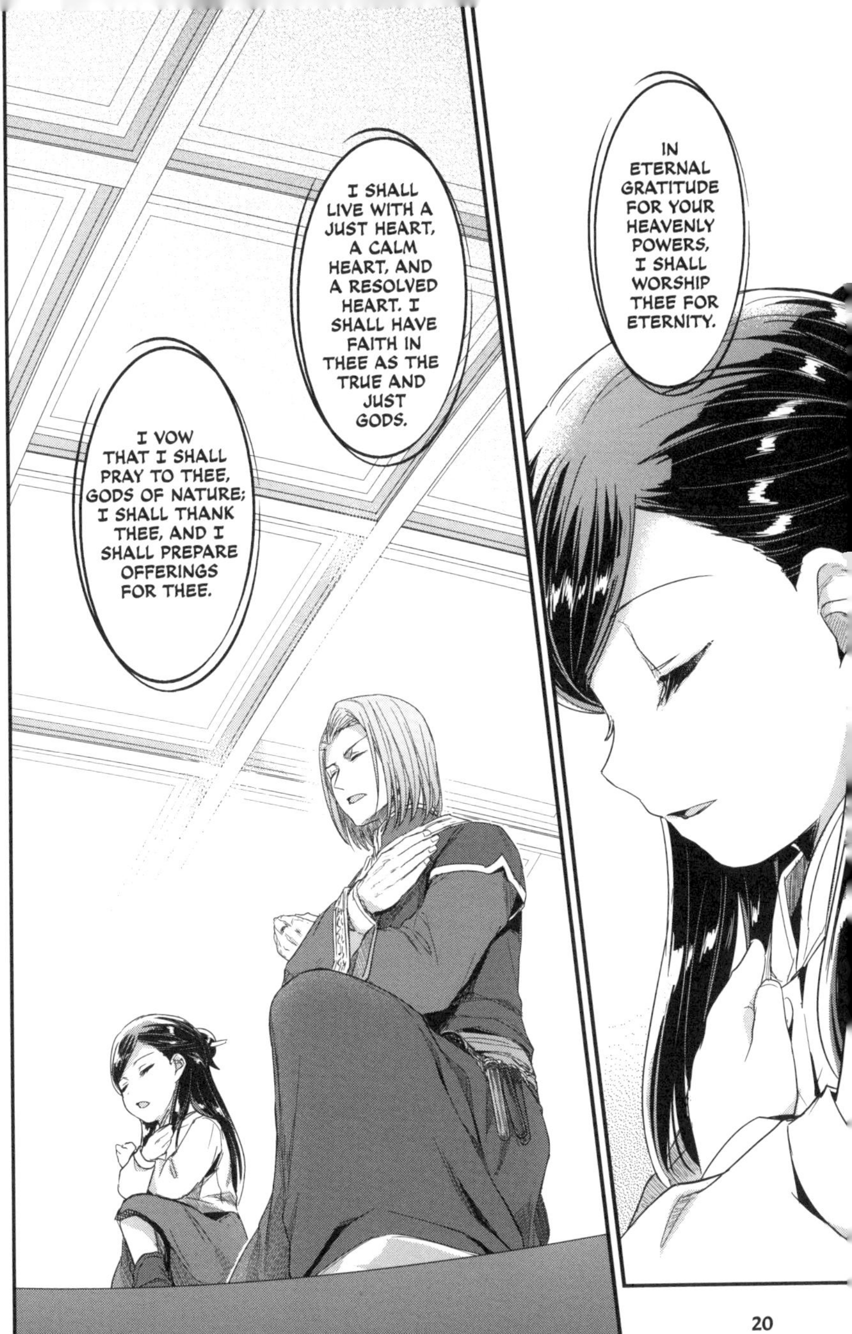
IN ETERNAL GRATITUDE FOR YOUR HEAVENLY POWERS, I SHALL WORSHIP THEE FOR ETERNITY.
I SHALL LIVE WITH A JUST HEART, A CALM HEART, AND A RESOLVED HEART. I SHALL HAVE FAITH IN THEE AS THE TRUE AND JUST GODS.
I VOW THAT I SHALL PRAY TO THEE, GODS OF NATURE; I SHALL THANK THEE, AND I SHALL PREPARE OFFERINGS FOR THEE.

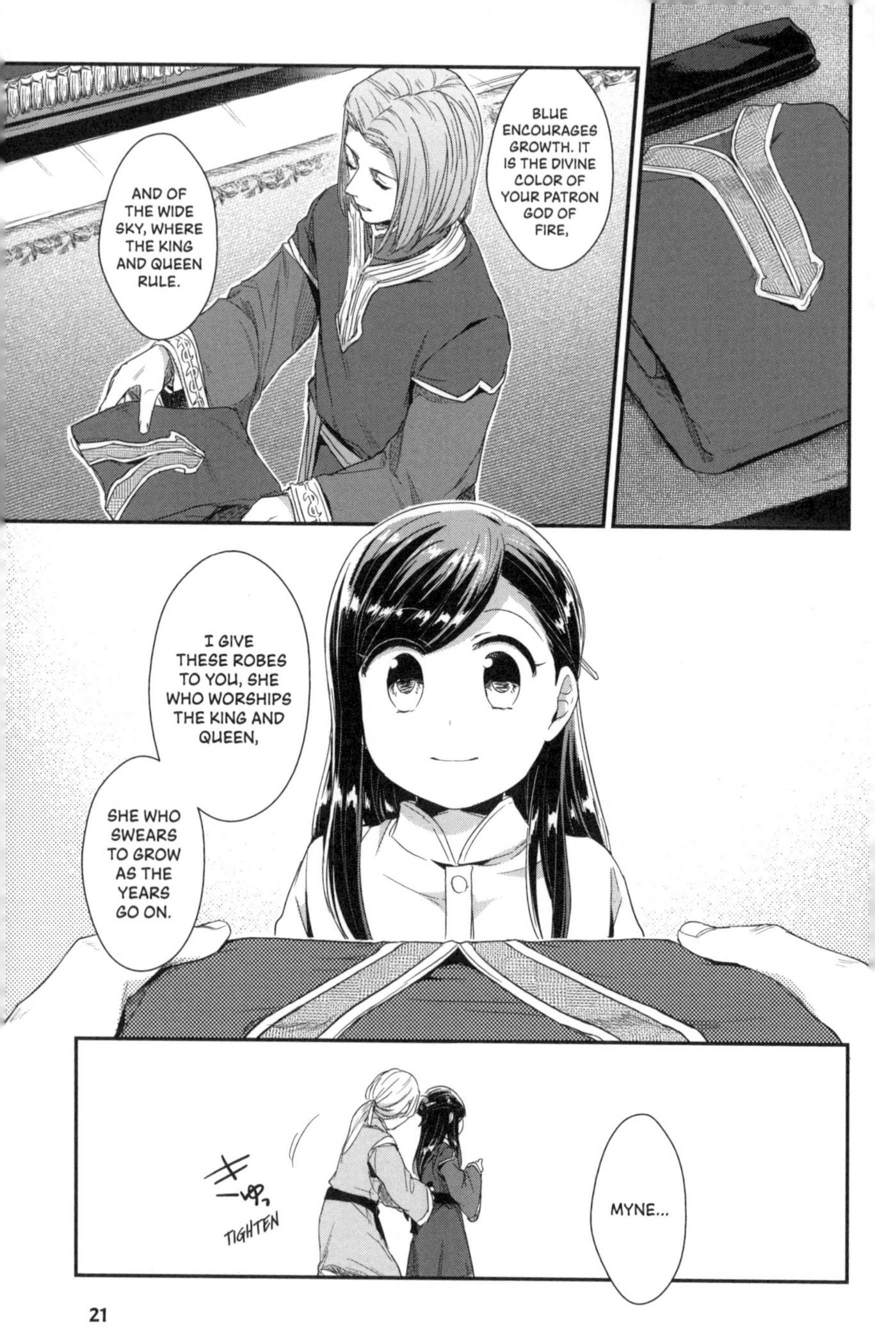
BLUE ENCOURAGES GROWTH. IT IS THE DIVINE COLOR OF YOUR PATRON GOD OF FIRE,
AND OF THE WIDE SKY, WHERE THE KING AND QUEEN RULE.
I GIVE THESE ROBES TO YOU, SHE WHO WORSHIPS THE KING AND QUEEN,
SHE WHO SWEARS TO GROW AS THE YEARS GO ON.
MYNE...
TIGHTEN

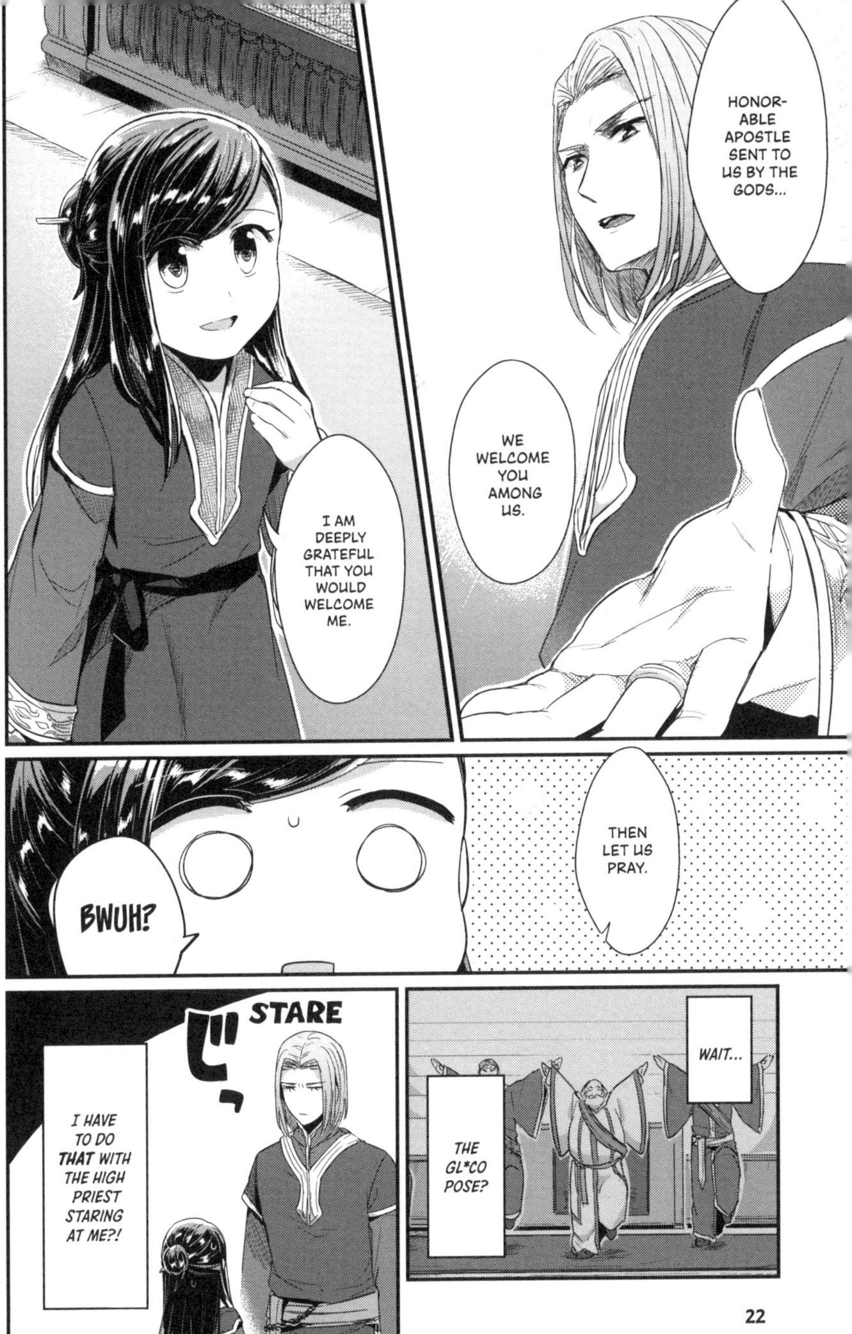
HONOR-ABLE APOSTLE SENT TO US BY THE GODS...
WE WELCOME YOU AMONG US.
I AM DEEPLY GRATEFUL THAT YOU WOULD WELCOME ME.
THEN LET US PRAY.
BWUH?
WAIT...
THE GL*CO POSE?
STARE
I HAVE TO DO **THAT** WITH THE HIGH PRIEST STARING AT ME?!

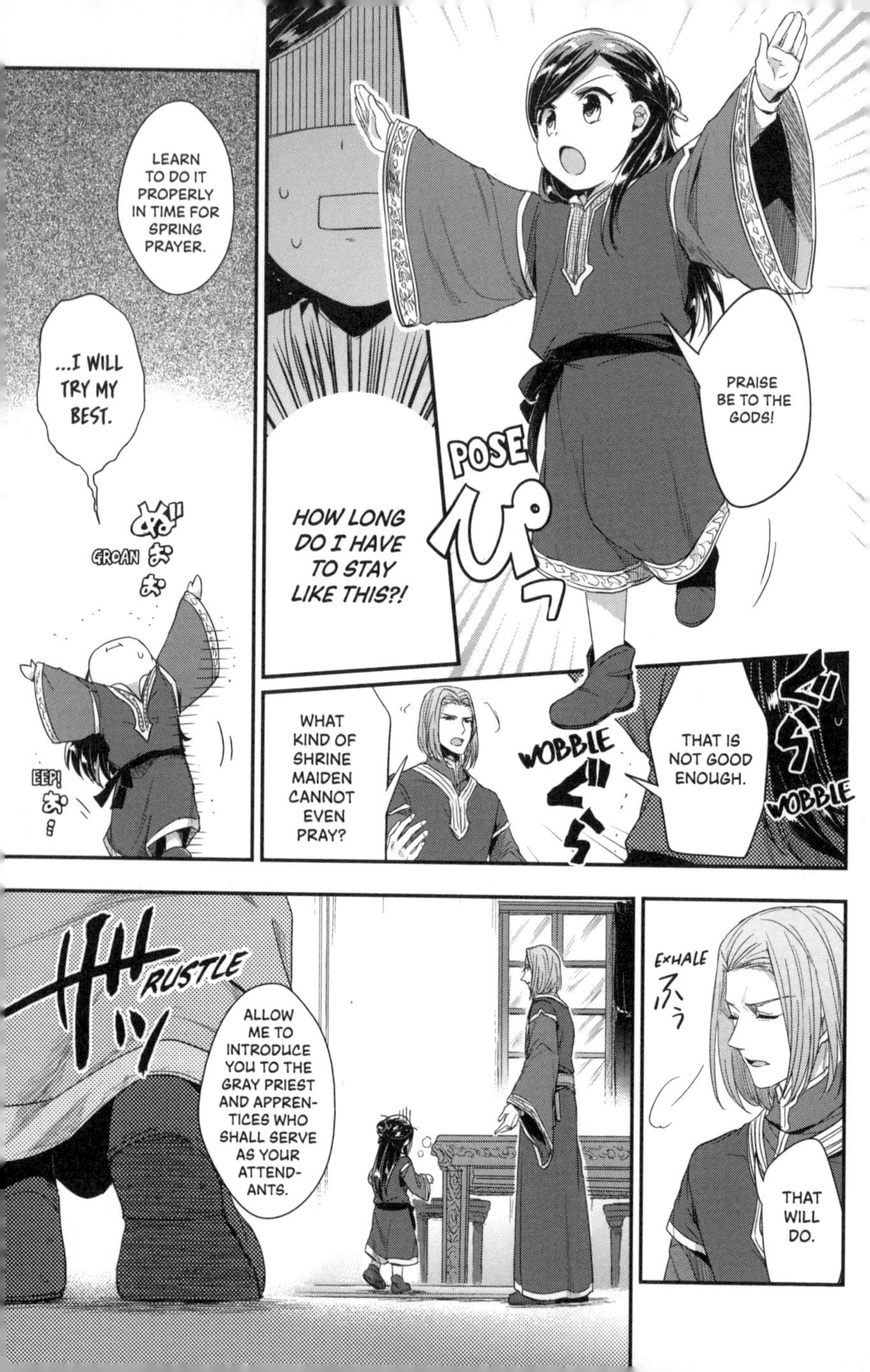

PRAISE BE TO THE GODS!
POSE
HOW LONG DO I HAVE TO STAY LIKE THIS?!
THAT IS NOT GOOD ENOUGH.
WOBBLE
WOBBLE
WHAT KIND OF SHRINE MAIDEN CANNOT EVEN PRAY?
LEARN TO DO IT PROPERLY IN TIME FOR SPRING PRAYER.
...I WILL TRY MY BEST.
GROAN
EEP!
EXHALE
THAT WILL DO.
ALLOW ME TO INTRODUCE YOU TO THE GRAY PRIEST AND APPRENTICES WHO SHALL SERVE AS YOUR ATTENDANTS.
RUSTLE

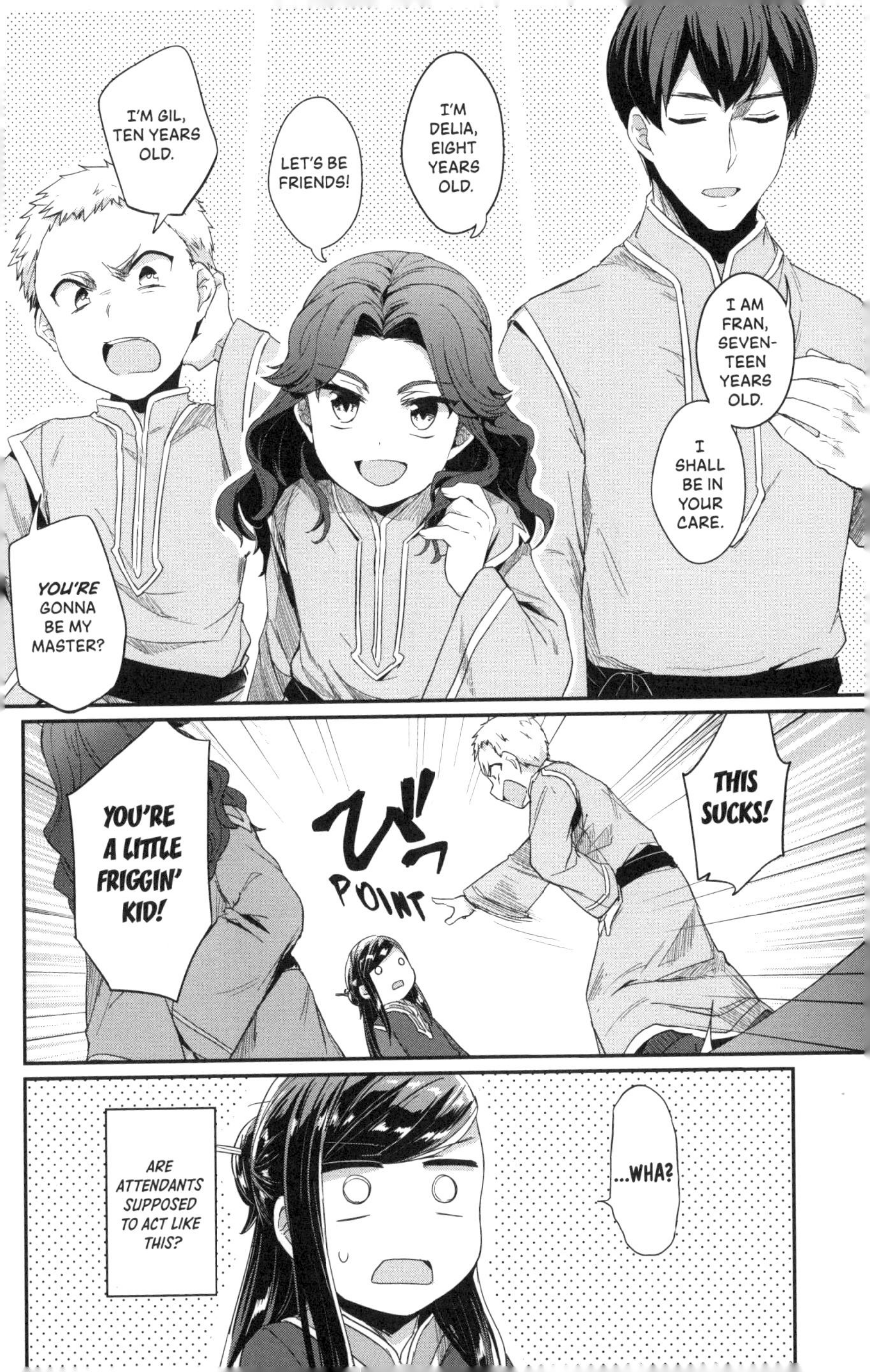
I AM FRAN, SEVEN-TEEN YEARS OLD.
I SHALL BE IN YOUR CARE.
I'M DELIA, EIGHT YEARS OLD.
LET'S BE FRIENDS!
I'M GIL, TEN YEARS OLD.
YOU'RE GONNA BE MY MASTER?
THIS SUCKS!
POINT
YOU'RE A LITTLE FRIGGIN' KID!
...WHA?
ARE ATTENDANTS SUPPOSED TO ACT LIKE THIS?

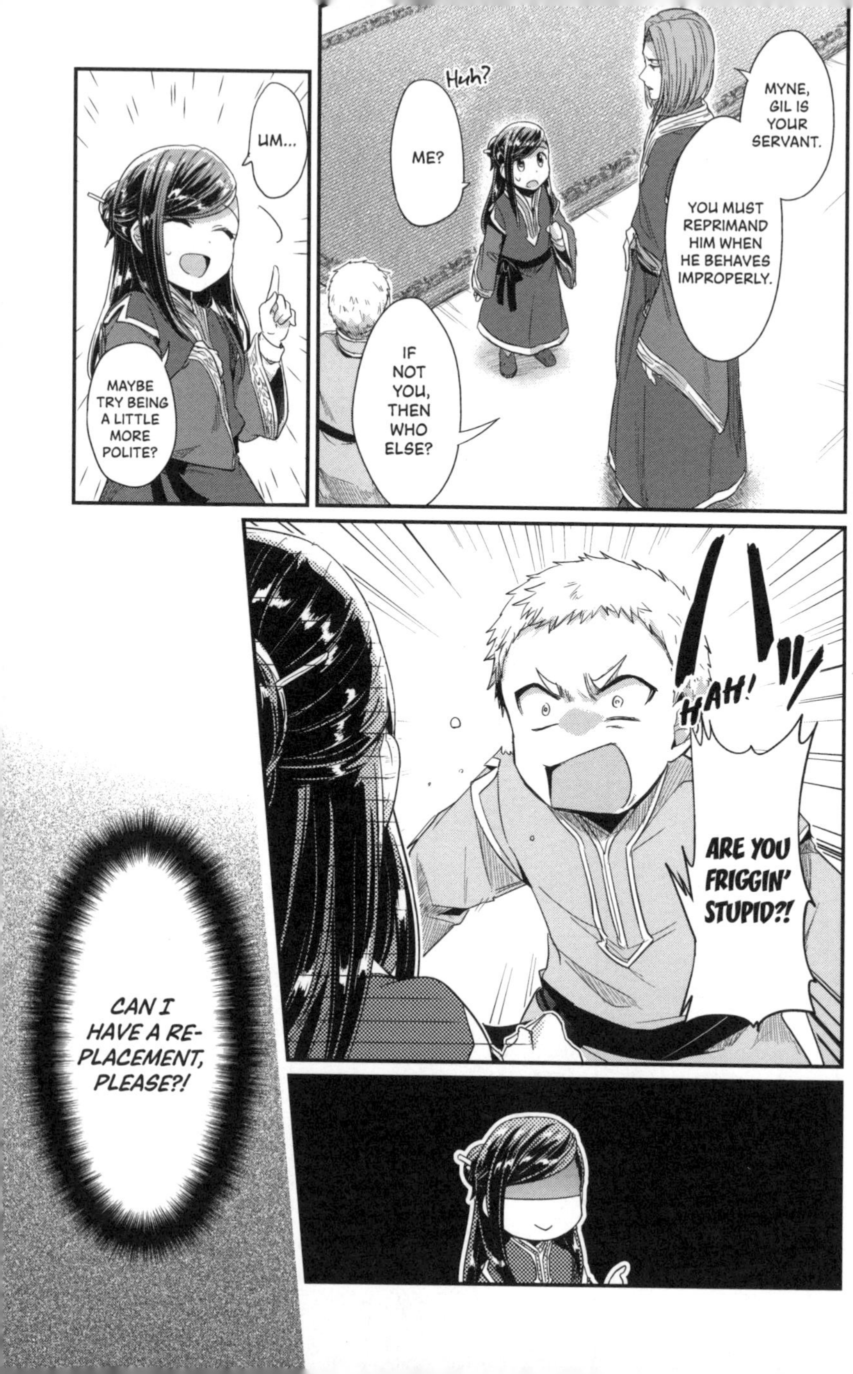
MYNE, GIL IS YOUR SERVANT.
YOU MUST REPRIMAND HIM WHEN HE BEHAVES IMPROPERLY.
Huh?
ME?
IF NOT YOU, THEN WHO ELSE?
UM...
MAYBE TRY BEING A LITTLE MORE POLITE?
HAH!
ARE YOU FRIGGIN' STUPID?!
CAN I HAVE A RE-PLACEMENT, PLEASE?!

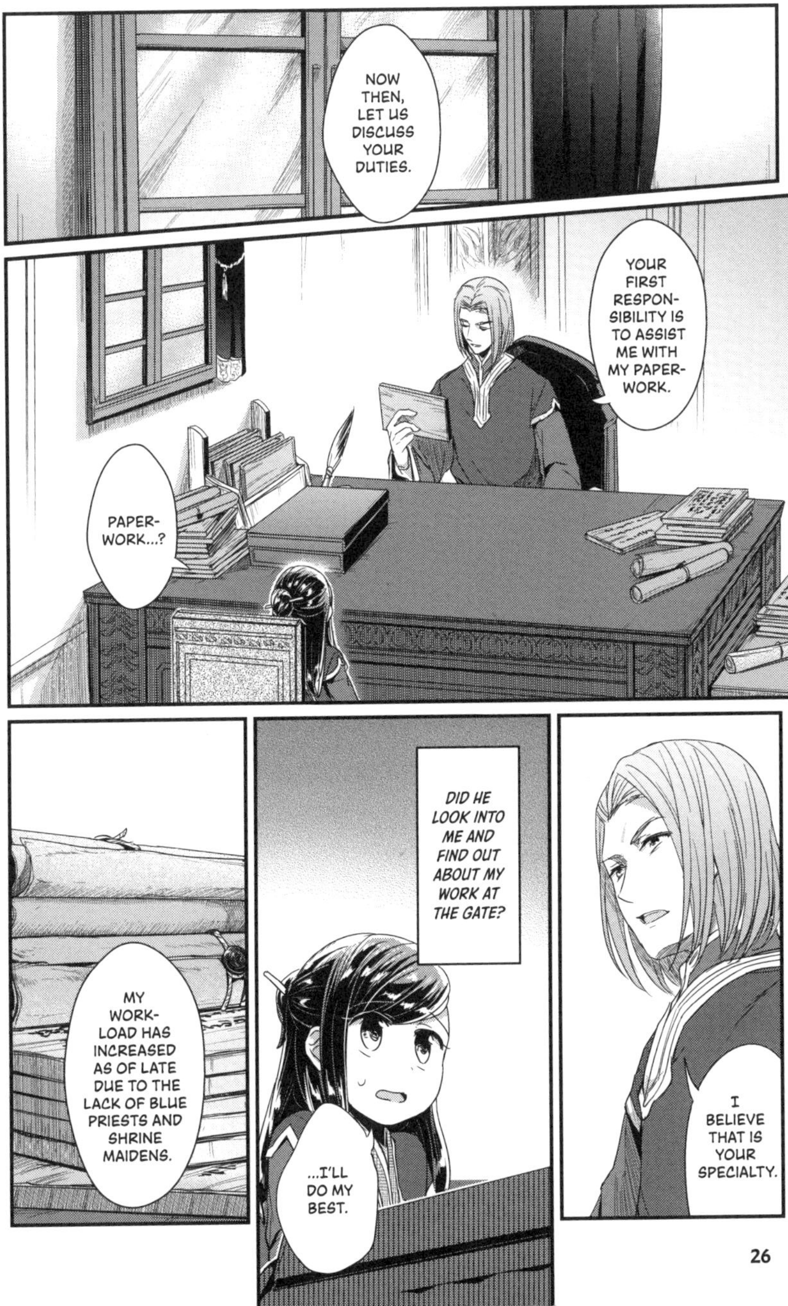
NOW THEN, LET US DISCUSS YOUR DUTIES.
YOUR FIRST RESPON-SIBILITY IS TO ASSIST ME WITH MY PAPER-WORK.
PAPER-WORK...?
I BELIEVE THAT IS YOUR SPECIALTY.
DID HE LOOK INTO ME AND FIND OUT ABOUT MY WORK AT THE GATE?
...I'LL DO MY BEST.
MY WORK-LOAD HAS INCREASED AS OF LATE DUE TO THE LACK OF BLUE PRIESTS AND SHRINE MAIDENS.

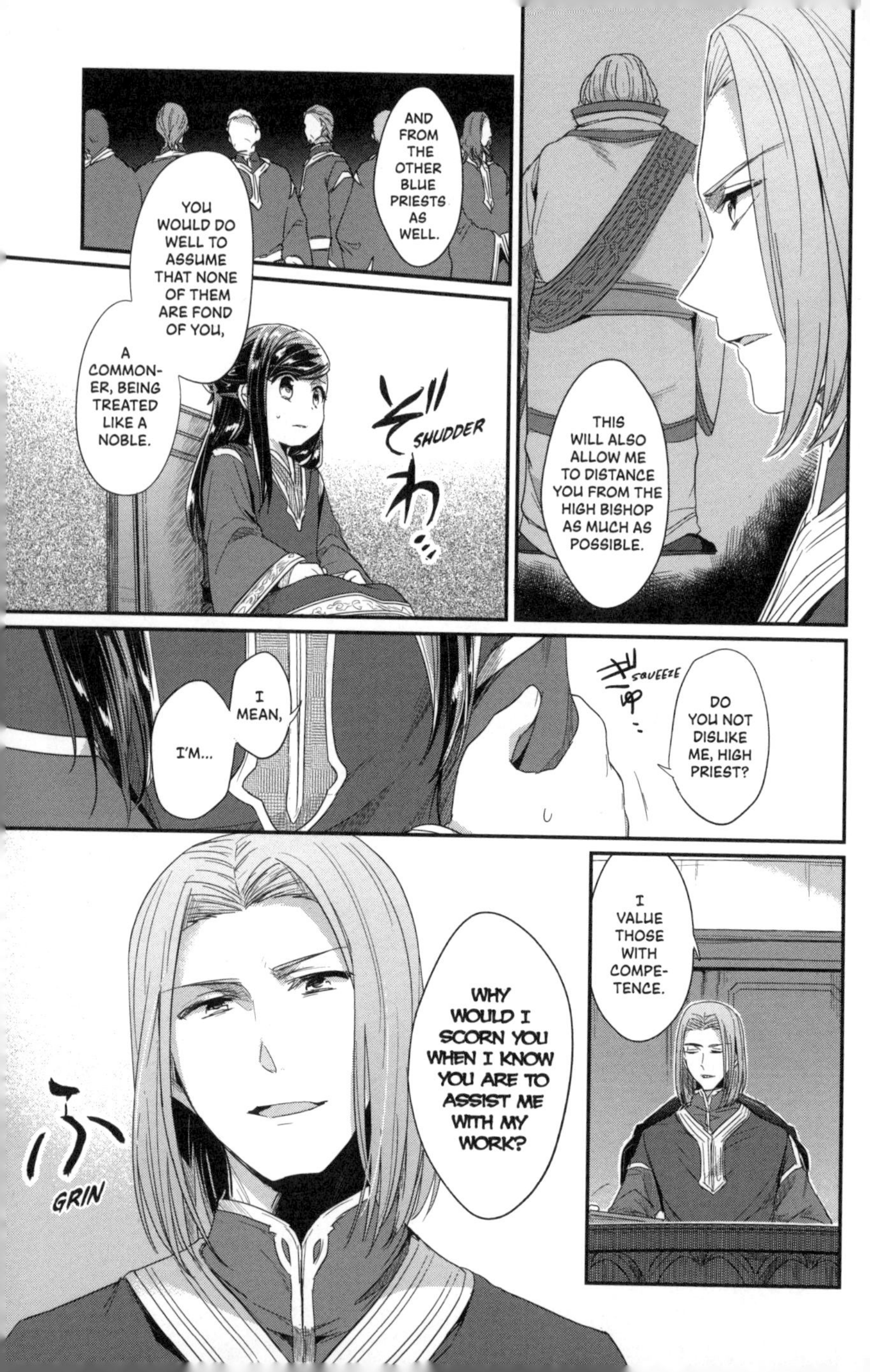
THIS WILL ALSO ALLOW ME TO DISTANCE YOU FROM THE HIGH BISHOP AS MUCH AS POSSIBLE.
AND FROM THE OTHER BLUE PRIESTS AS WELL.
YOU WOULD DO WELL TO ASSUME THAT NONE OF THEM ARE FOND OF YOU,
A COMMONER, BEING TREATED LIKE A NOBLE.
ぞわ
SHUDDER
DO YOU NOT DISLIKE ME, HIGH PRIEST?
SQUEEZE
I MEAN,
I'M...
I VALUE THOSE WITH COMPETENCE.
WHY WOULD I SCORN YOU WHEN I KNOW YOU ARE TO ASSIST ME WITH MY WORK?
ふ
GRIN

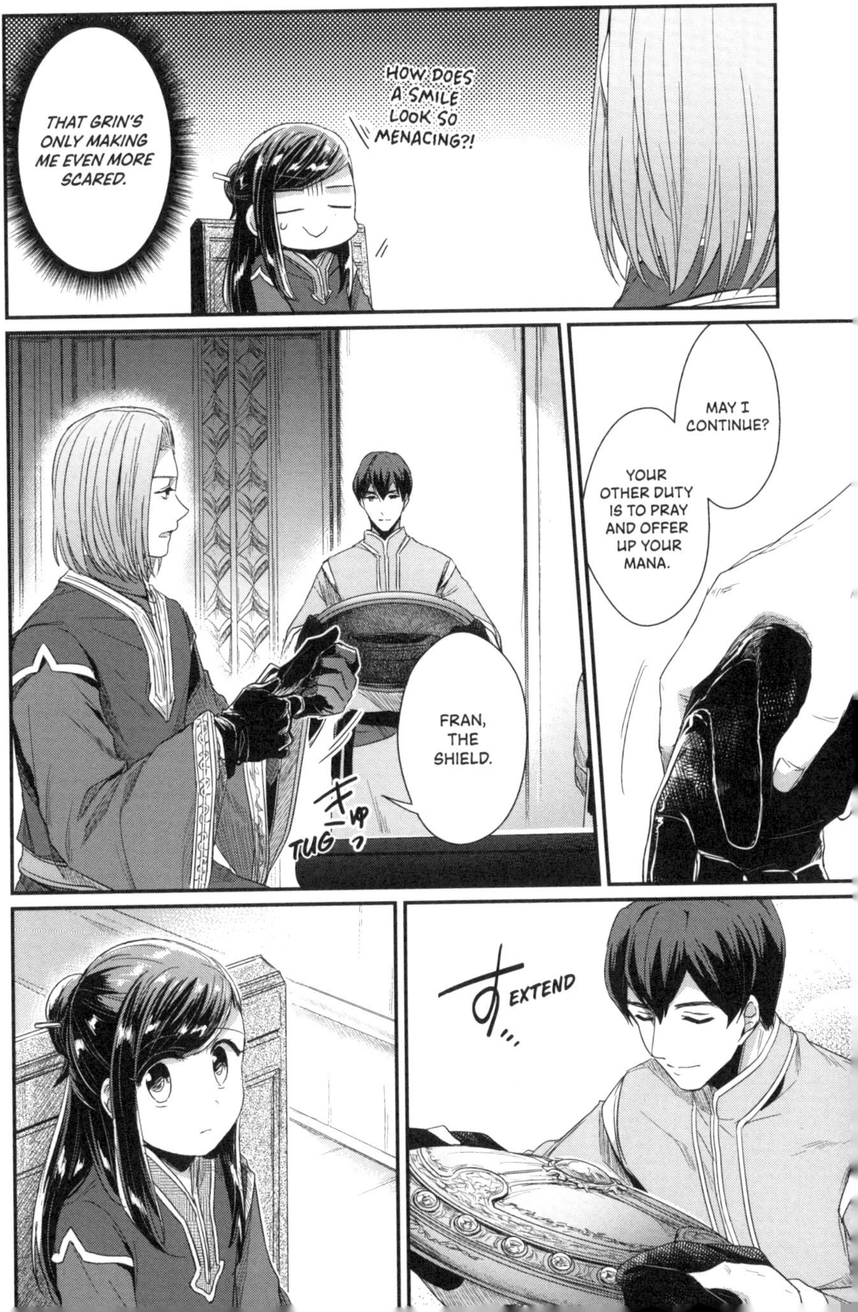
HOW DOES A SMILE LOOK SO MENACING?!
THAT GRIN'S ONLY MAKING ME EVEN MORE SCARED.
MAY I CONTINUE?
YOUR OTHER DUTY IS TO PRAY AND OFFER UP YOUR MANA.
FRAN, THE SHIELD.
TUG
EXTEND

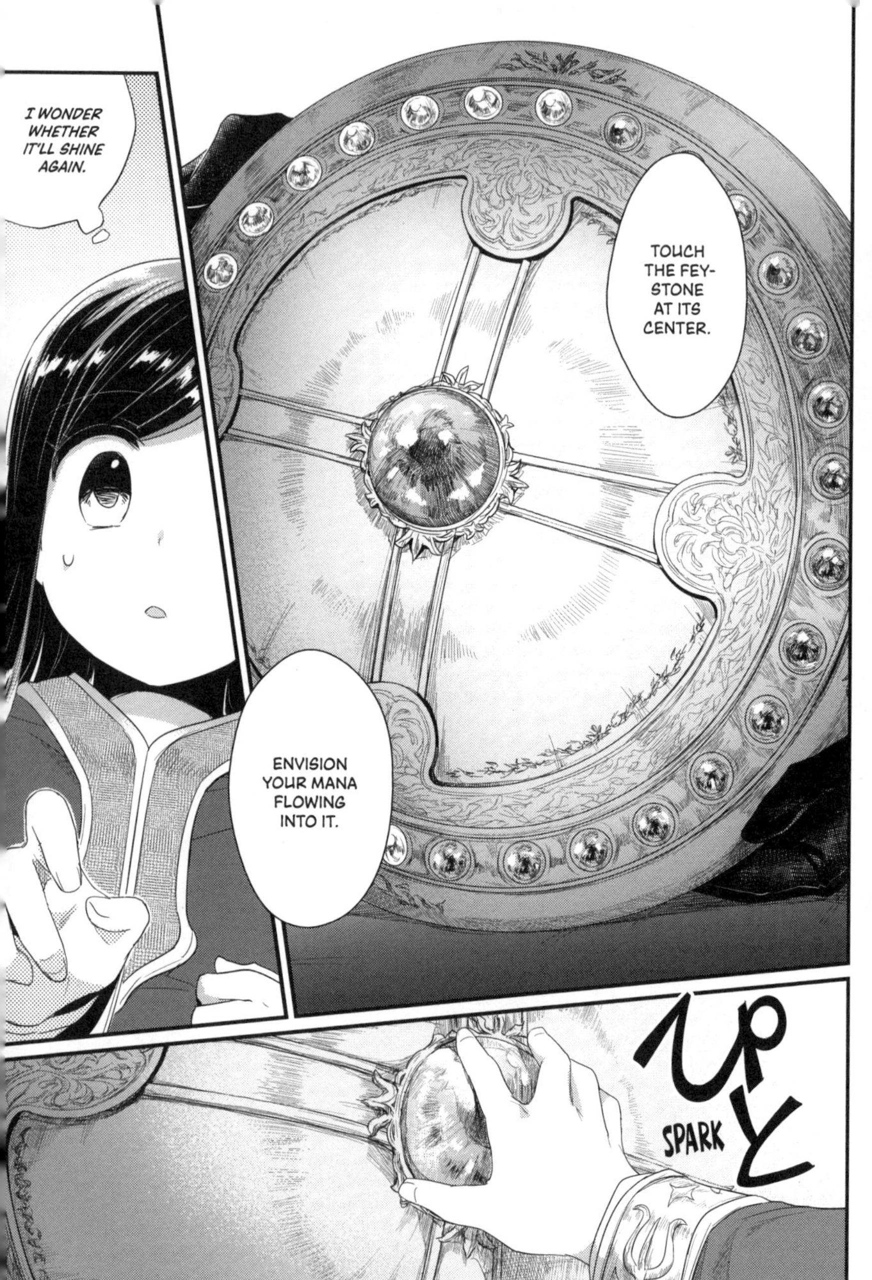
TOUCH THE FEY-STONE AT ITS CENTER.
ENVISION YOUR MANA FLOWING INTO IT.
I WONDER WHETHER IT'LL SHINE AGAIN.
SPARK

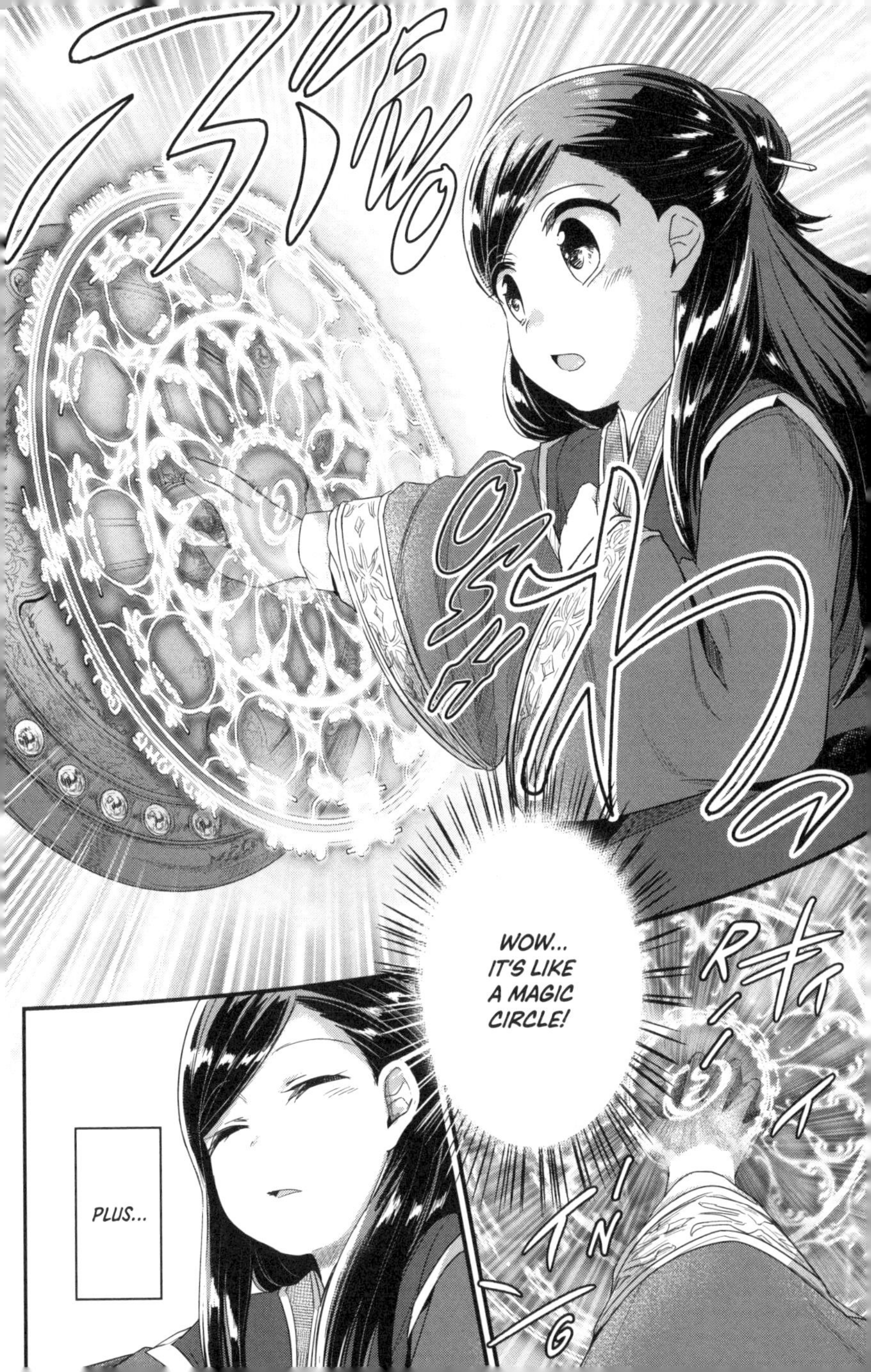
WOW... IT'S LIKE A MAGIC CIRCLE!
PLUS...

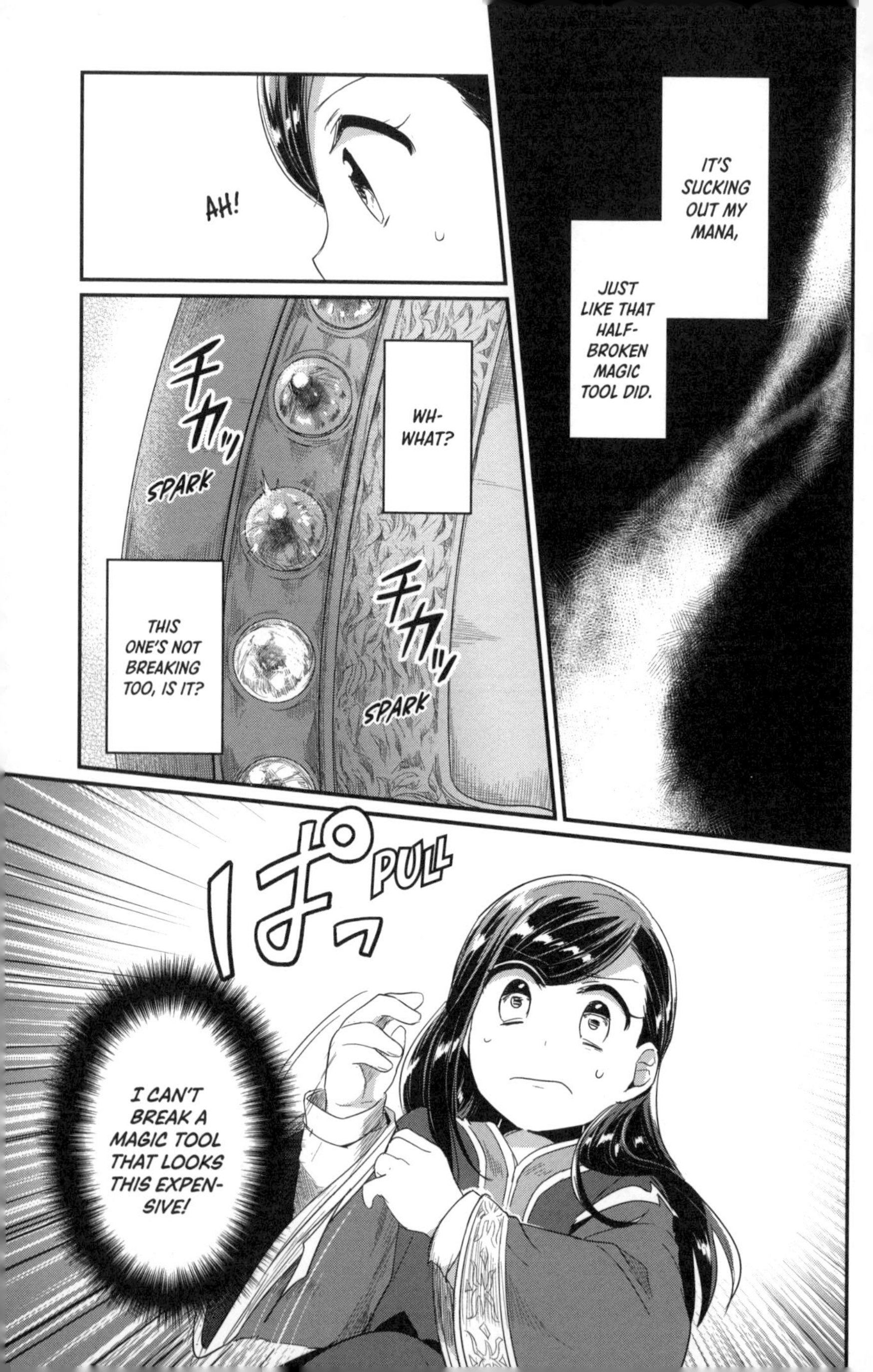
IT'S SUCKING OUT MY MANA,
JUST LIKE THAT HALF-BROKEN MAGIC TOOL DID.
AH!
WH-WHAT?
チカッ
SPARK
チカッ
SPARK
THIS ONE'S NOT BREAKING TOO, IS IT?
ぱっ
PULL
I CAN'T BREAK A MAGIC TOOL THAT LOOKS THIS EXPEN-SIVE!

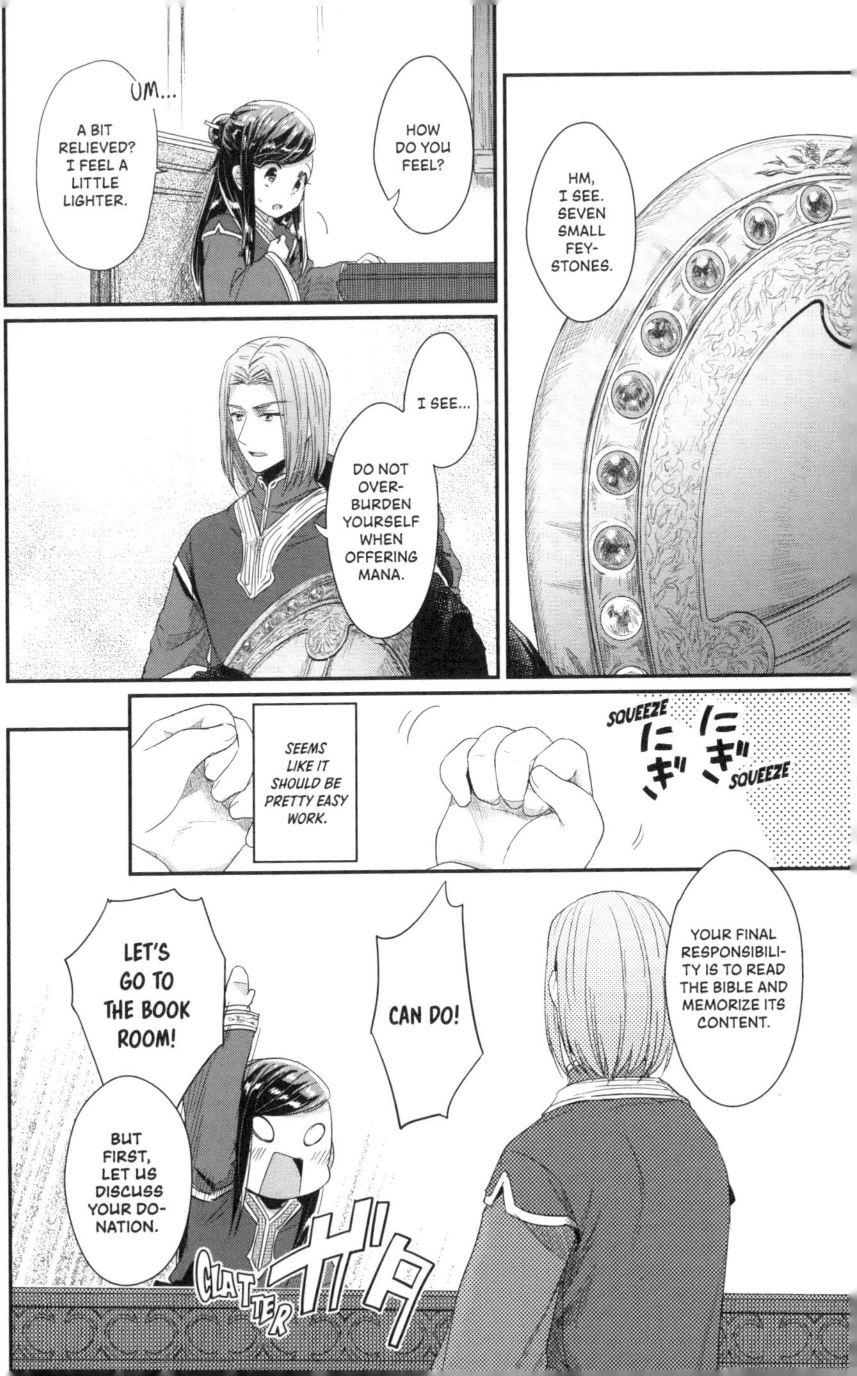
HM, I SEE. SEVEN SMALL FEY-STONES.
HOW DO YOU FEEL?
UM...
A BIT RELIEVED? I FEEL A LITTLE LIGHTER.
I SEE...
DO NOT OVER-BURDEN YOURSELF WHEN OFFERING MANA.
SQUEEZE
にぎ
にぎ
SQUEEZE
SEEMS LIKE IT SHOULD BE PRETTY EASY WORK.
YOUR FINAL RESPONSIBILI-TY IS TO READ THE BIBLE AND MEMORIZE ITS CONTENT.
CAN DO!
LET'S GO TO THE BOOK ROOM!
BUT FIRST, LET US DISCUSS YOUR DO-NATION.
CLATTER
ガタ

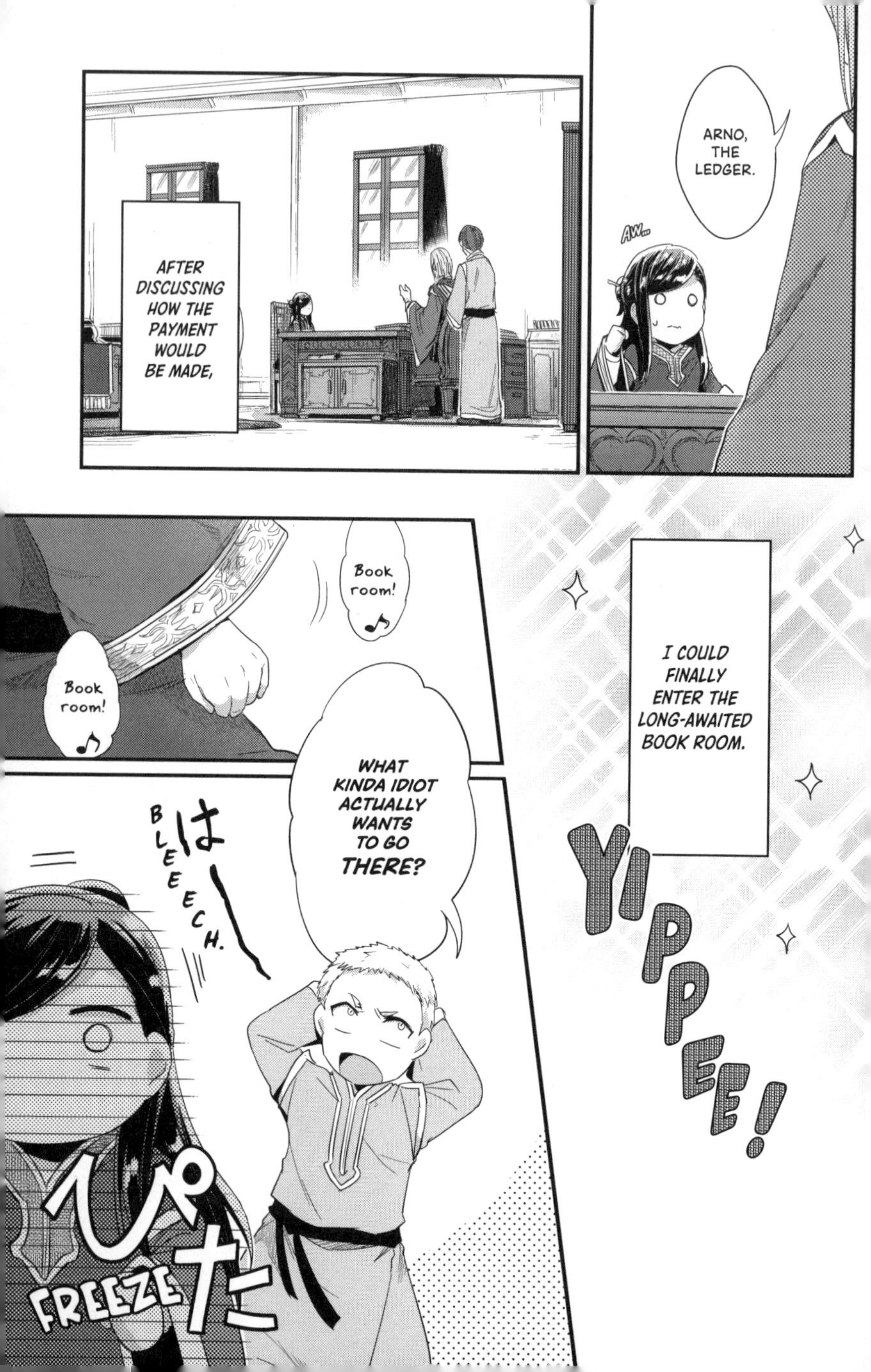
ARNO, THE LEDGER.
AW...
AFTER DISCUSSING HOW THE PAYMENT WOULD BE MADE,
I COULD FINALLY ENTER THE LONG-AWAITED BOOK ROOM.
YIPPEE!
Book room! ♪
Book room! ♪
WHAT KINDA IDIOT ACTUALLY WANTS TO GO THERE?
は
BLEEECH.
ぴた
FREEZE

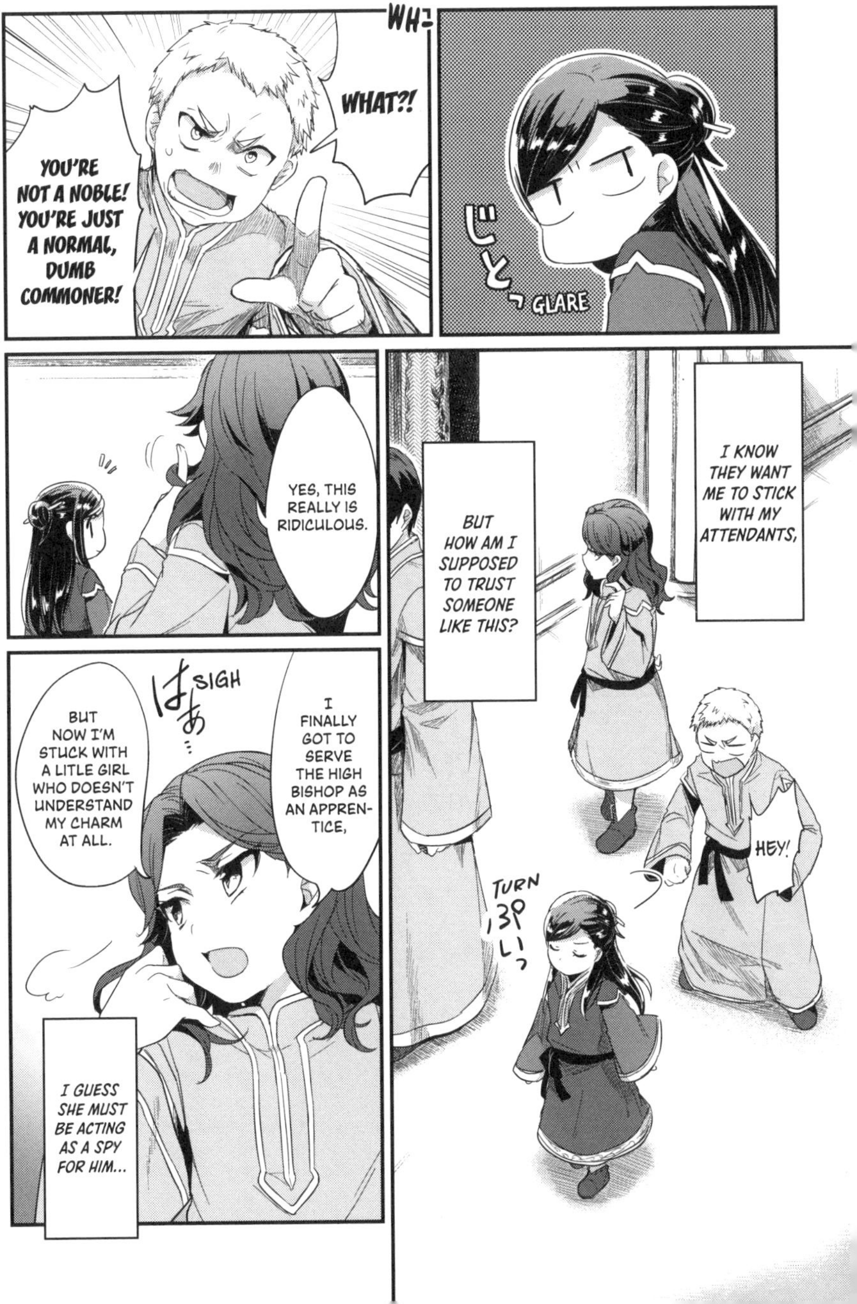
WH-
じとっ GLARE
WHAT?!
YOU'RE NOT A NOBLE! YOU'RE JUST A NORMAL, DUMB COMMONER!
I KNOW THEY WANT ME TO STICK WITH MY ATTENDANTS,
BUT HOW AM I SUPPOSED TO TRUST SOMEONE LIKE THIS?
HEY!
TURN ぷいっ
YES, THIS REALLY IS RIDICULOUS.
I FINALLY GOT TO SERVE THE HIGH BISHOP AS AN APPRENTICE,
BUT NOW I'M STUCK WITH A LITLE GIRL WHO DOESN'T UNDERSTAND MY CHARM AT ALL.
はぁ… SIGH
I GUESS SHE MUST BE ACTING AS A SPY FOR HIM…

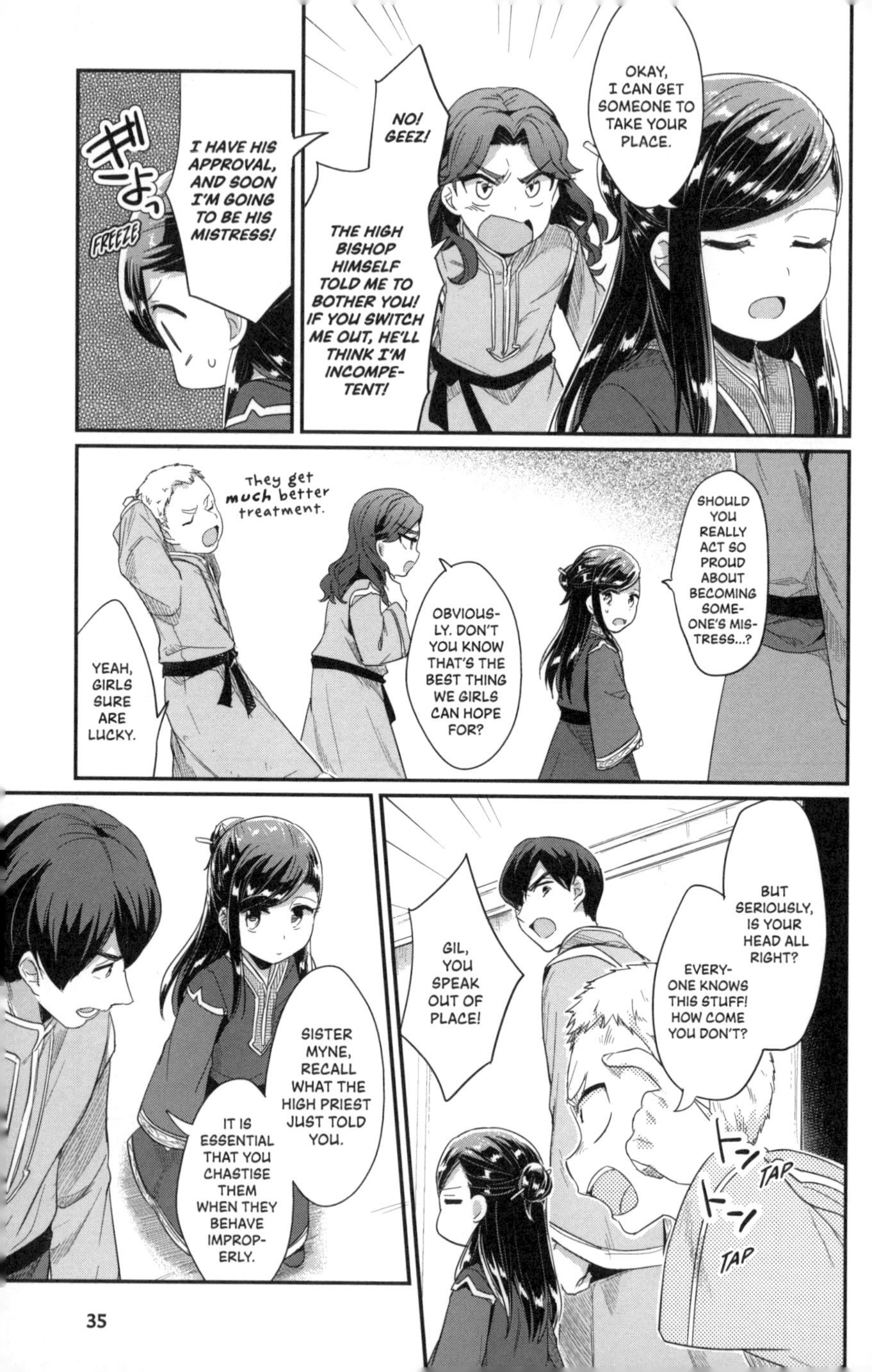
OKAY, I CAN GET SOMEONE TO TAKE YOUR PLACE.
NO! GEEZ!
THE HIGH BISHOP HIMSELF TOLD ME TO BOTHER YOU! IF YOU SWITCH ME OUT, HE'LL THINK I'M INCOMPETENT!
I HAVE HIS APPROVAL, AND SOON I'M GOING TO BE HIS MISTRESS!
ぎょっ
FREEZE
SHOULD YOU REALLY ACT SO PROUD ABOUT BECOMING SOMEONE'S MISTRESS...?
OBVIOUSLY. DON'T YOU KNOW THAT'S THE BEST THING WE GIRLS CAN HOPE FOR?
They get much better treatment.
YEAH, GIRLS SURE ARE LUCKY.
BUT SERIOUSLY, IS YOUR HEAD ALL RIGHT?
EVERYONE KNOWS THIS STUFF! HOW COME YOU DON'T?
GIL, YOU SPEAK OUT OF PLACE!
トン
TAP
トン
TAP
SISTER MYNE, RECALL WHAT THE HIGH PRIEST JUST TOLD YOU.
IT IS ESSENTIAL THAT YOU CHASTISE THEM WHEN THEY BEHAVE IMPROPERLY.

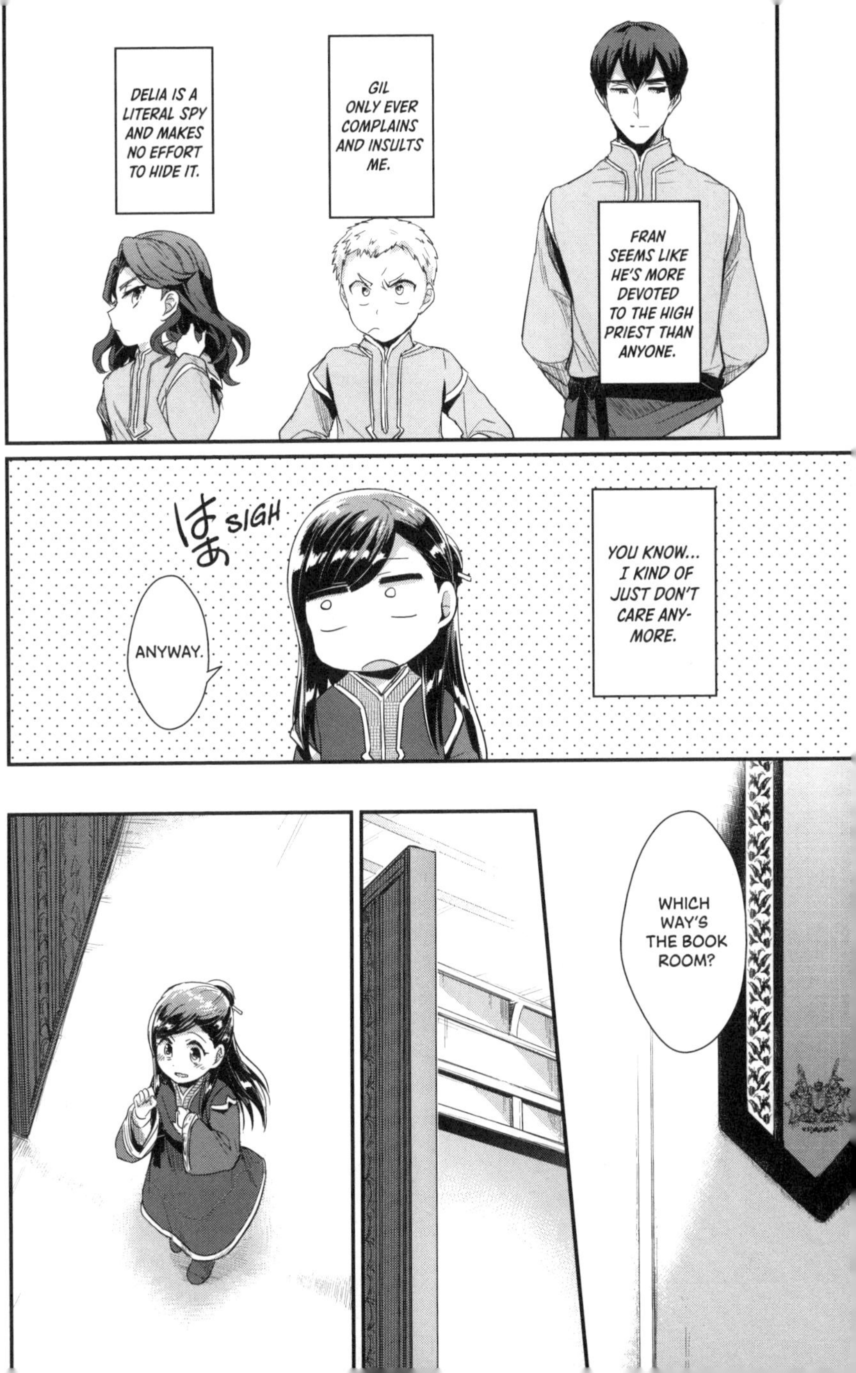
FRAN SEEMS LIKE HE'S MORE DEVOTED TO THE HIGH PRIEST THAN ANYONE.
GIL ONLY EVER COMPLAINS AND INSULTS ME.
DELIA IS A LITERAL SPY AND MAKES NO EFFORT TO HIDE IT.
YOU KNOW... I KIND OF JUST DON'T CARE ANY-MORE.
はあ SIGH
ANYWAY.
WHICH WAY'S THE BOOK ROOM?

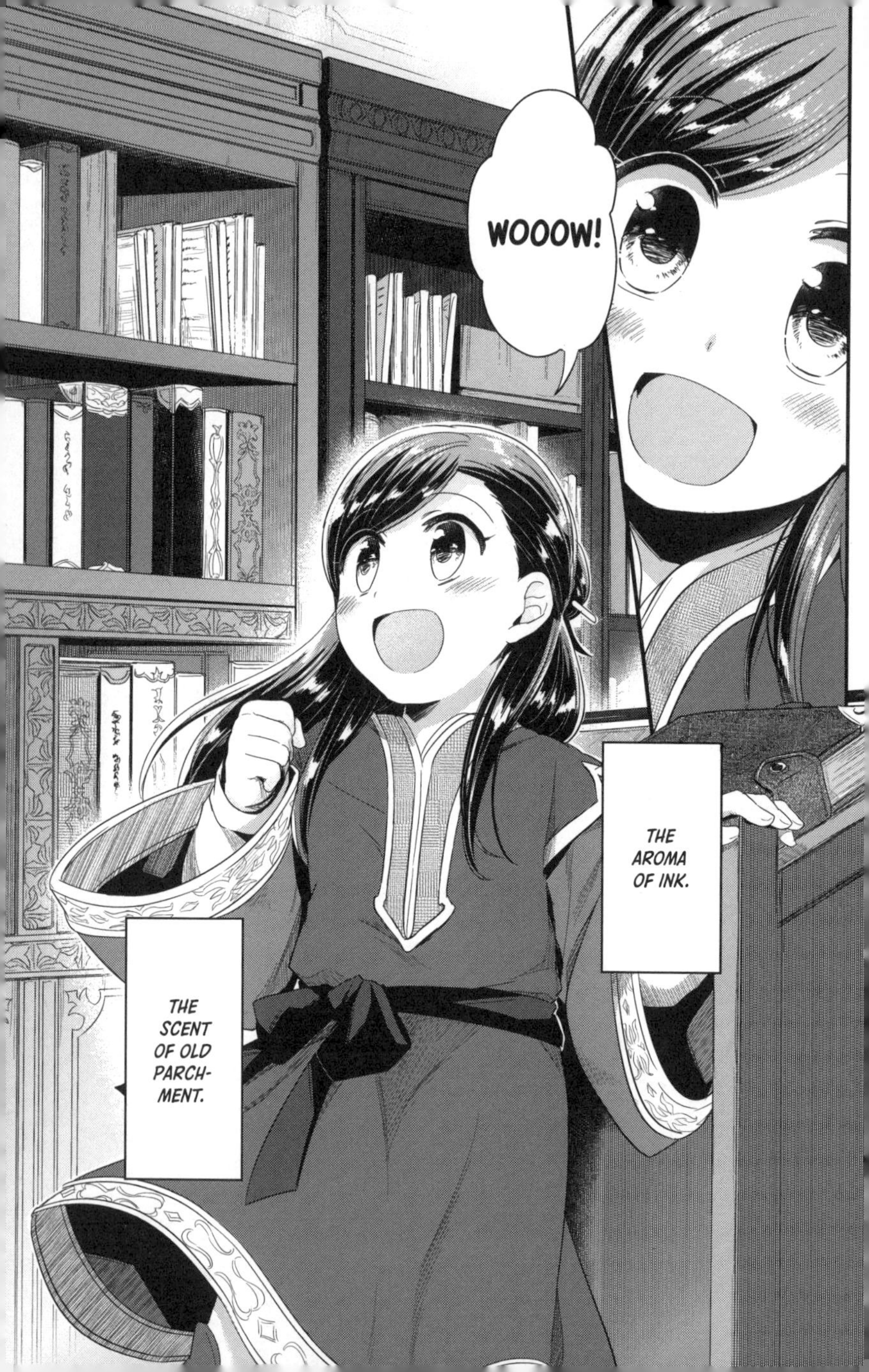
WOOOW!
THE AROMA OF INK.
THE SCENT OF OLD PARCHMENT.

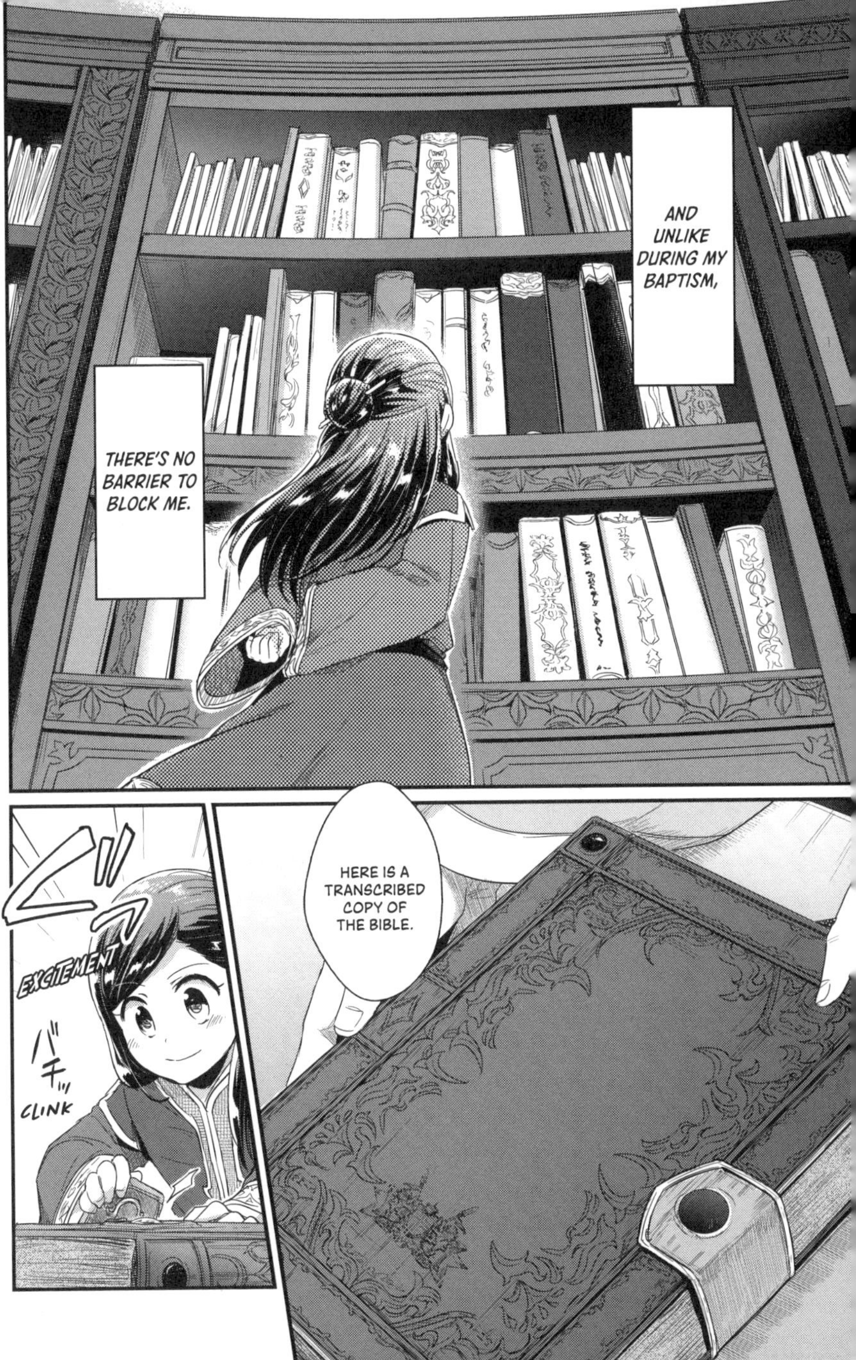
AND UNLIKE DURING MY BAPTISM,
THERE'S NO BARRIER TO BLOCK ME.
HERE IS A TRANSCRIBED COPY OF THE BIBLE.
EXCITEMENT
バチッ
CLINK

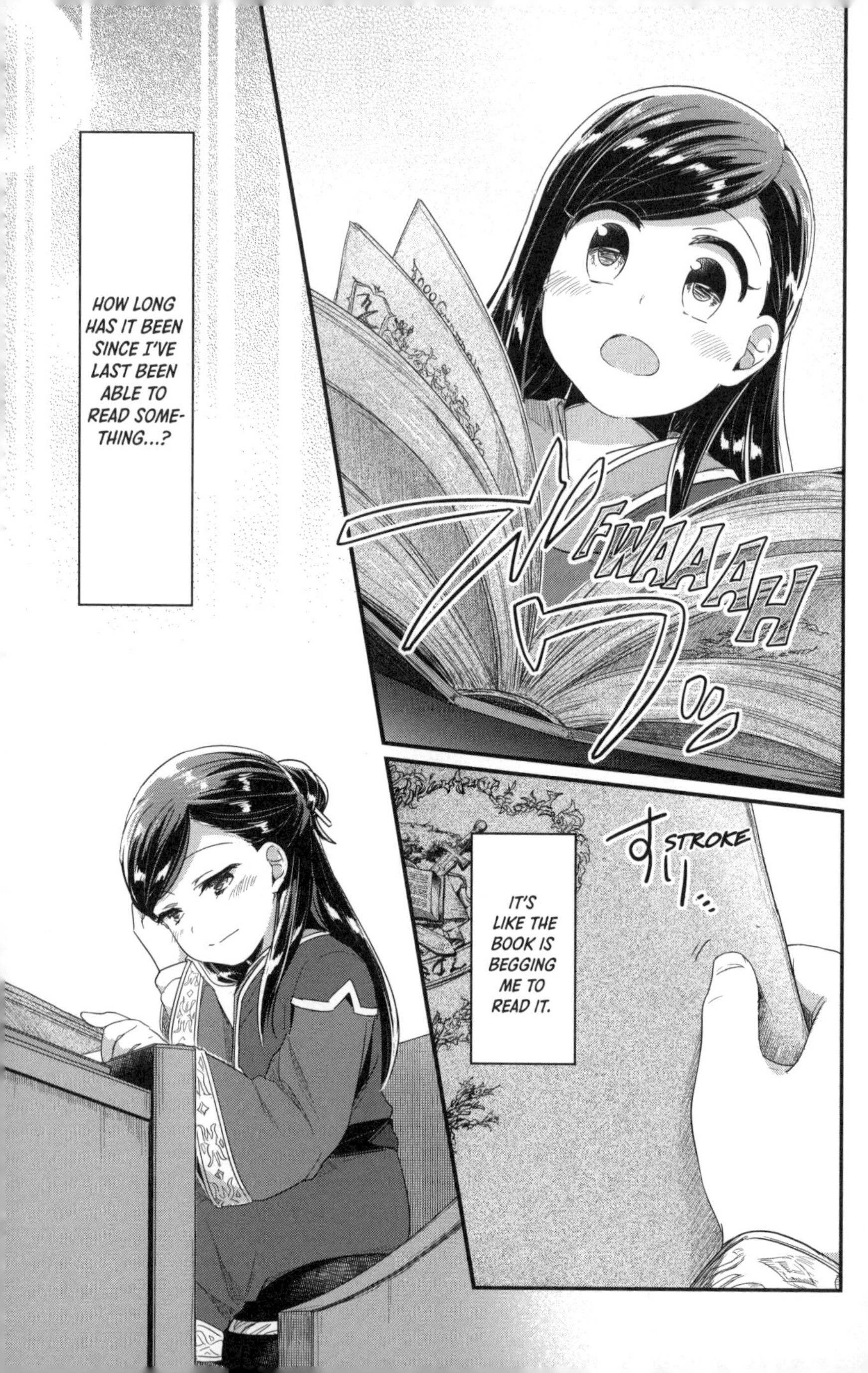
FWAAAH
HOW LONG HAS IT BEEN SINCE I'VE LAST BEEN ABLE TO READ SOME-THING...?
STROKE
IT'S LIKE THE BOOK IS BEGGING ME TO READ IT.

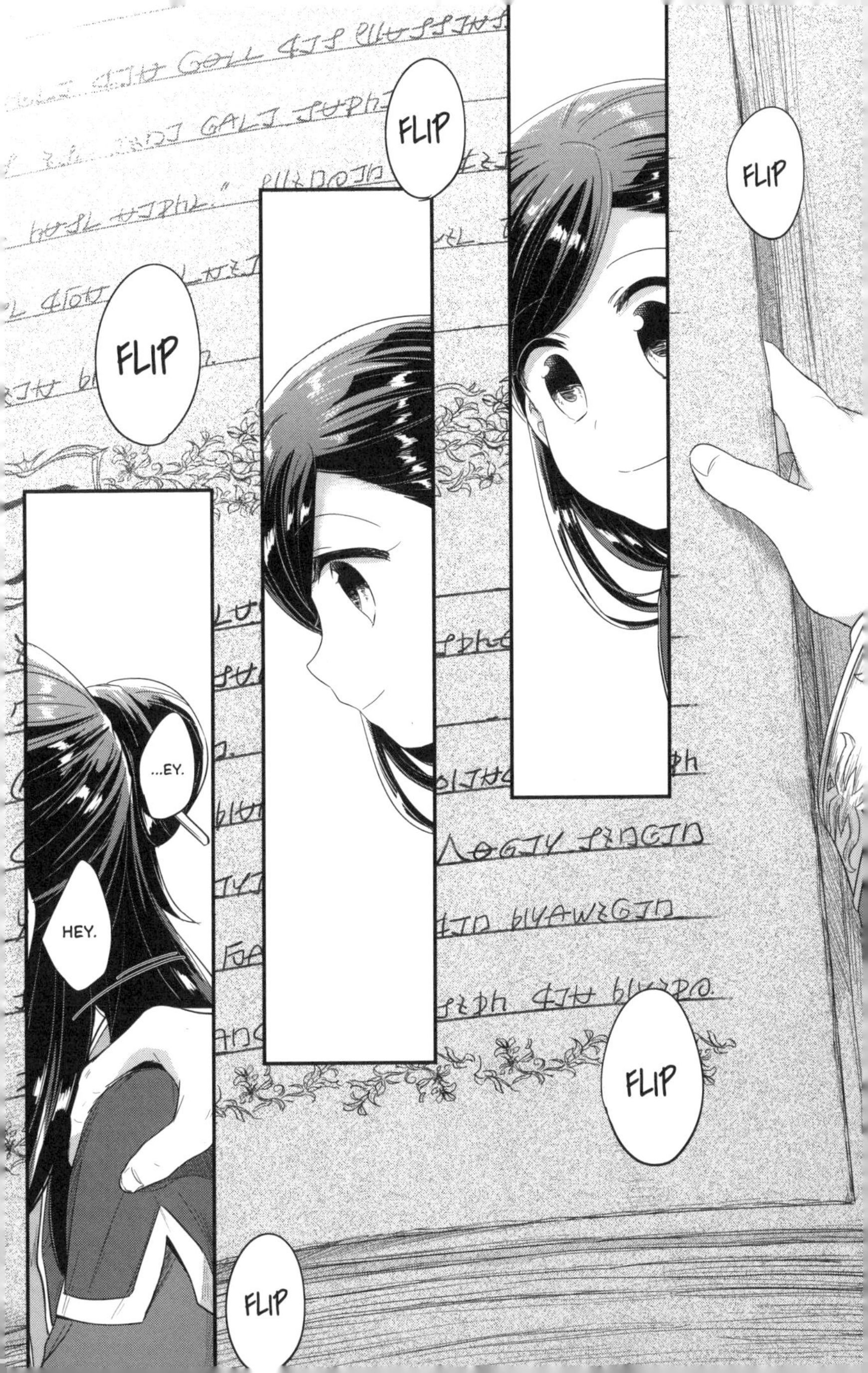
FLIP
FLIP
FLIP
FLIP
...EY.
HEY.
FLIP

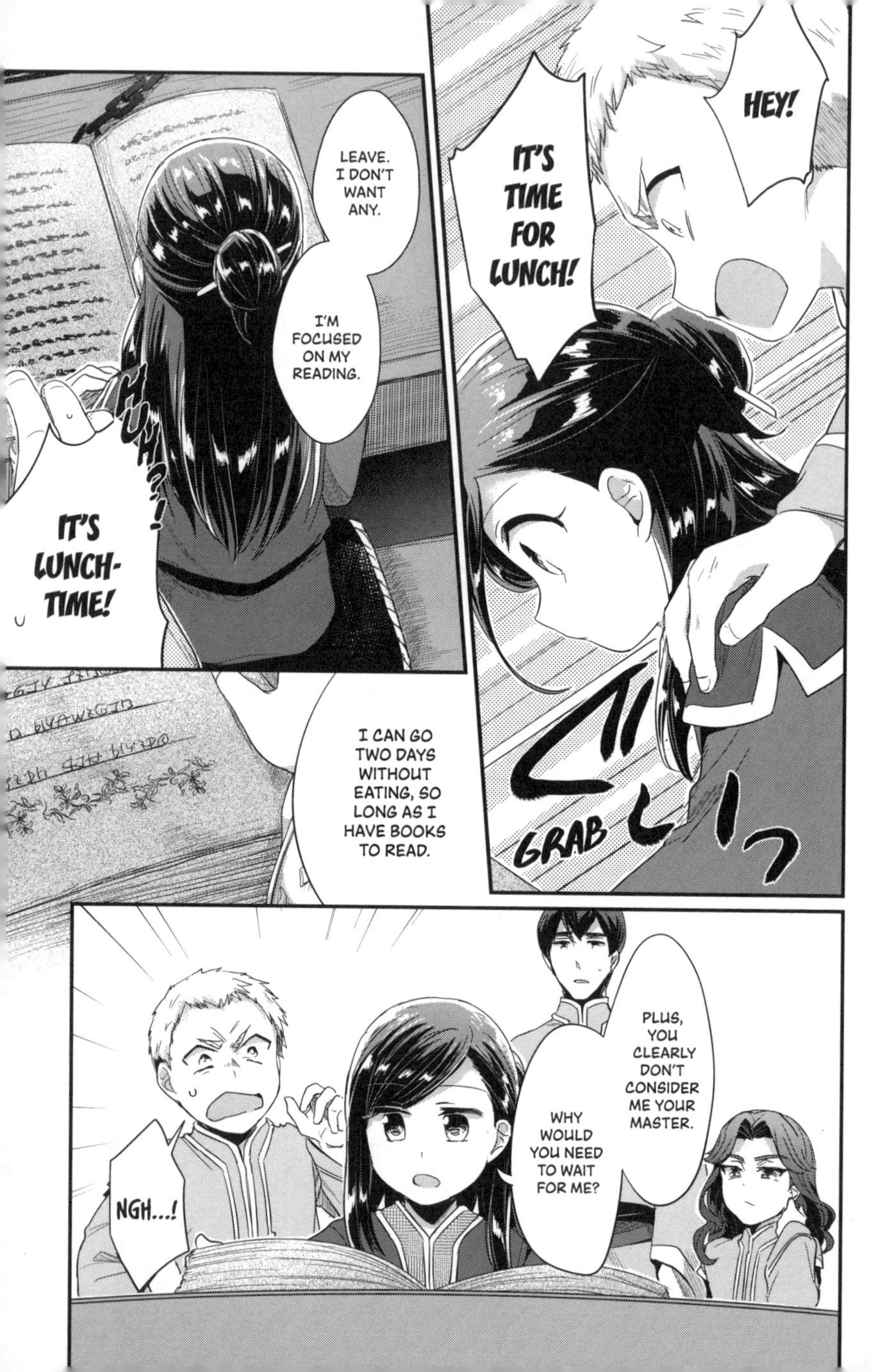
HEY!
IT'S TIME FOR LUNCH!
GRAB
LEAVE. I DON'T WANT ANY.
I'M FOCUSED ON MY READING.
HUH?!
IT'S LUNCH-TIME!
I CAN GO TWO DAYS WITHOUT EATING, SO LONG AS I HAVE BOOKS TO READ.
PLUS, YOU CLEARLY DON'T CONSIDER ME YOUR MASTER.
WHY WOULD YOU NEED TO WAIT FOR ME?
NGH...!

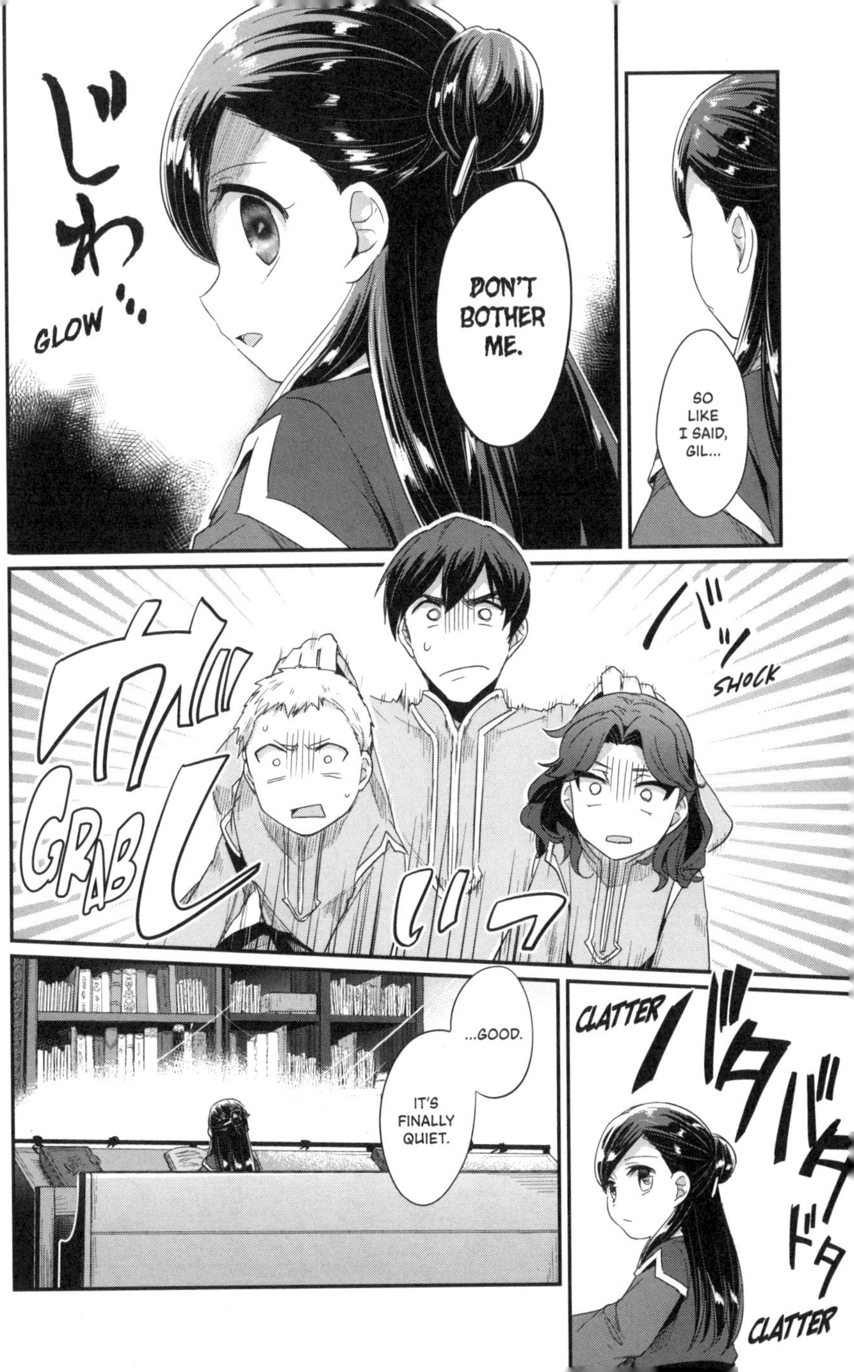
SO LIKE I SAID, GIL...
DON'T BOTHER ME.
じわ…
GLOW
バッ
SHOCK
ガシ
GRAB
CLATTER
バタバタドタ
CLATTER
...GOOD.
IT'S FINALLY QUIET.

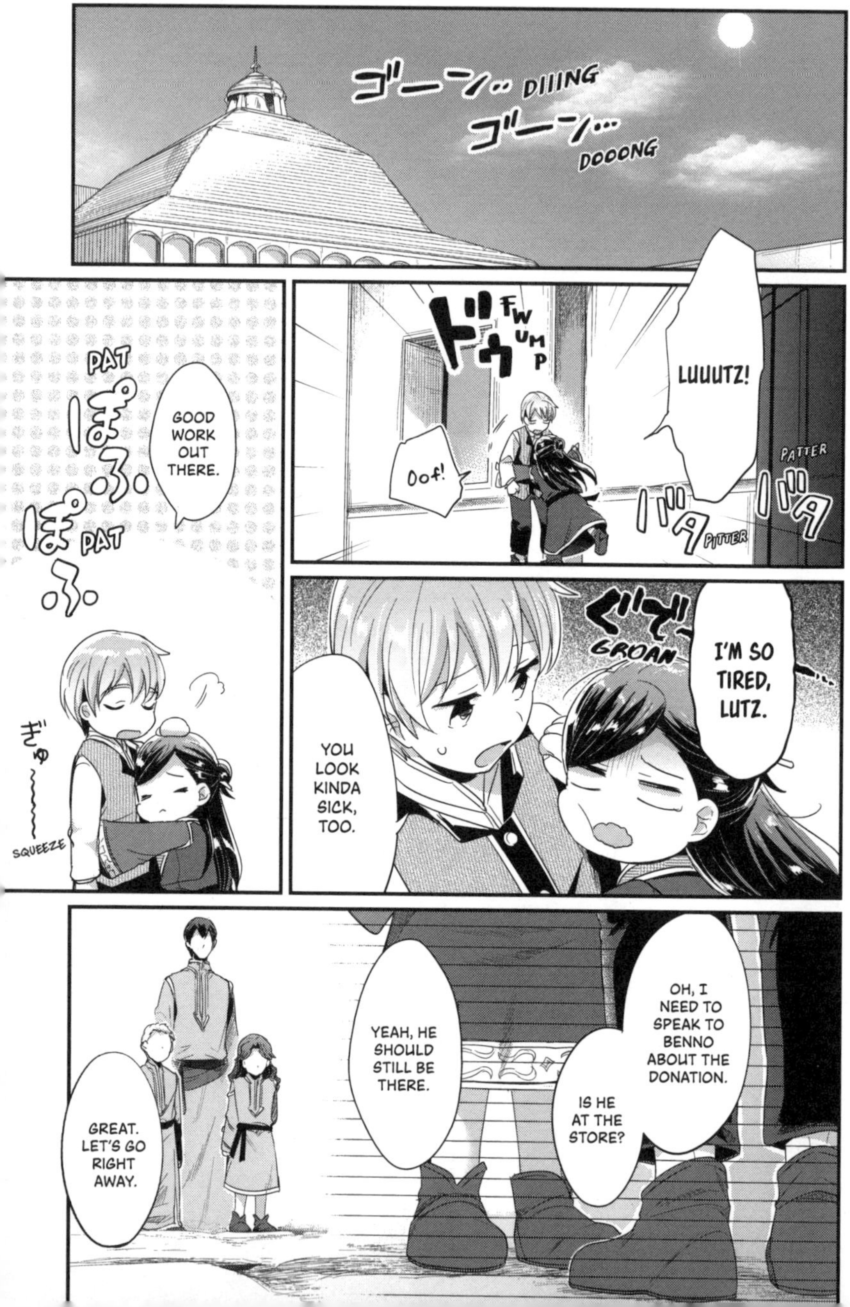
ゴーン… DIIING
ゴーン… DOOONG
LUUUTZ!
ドウ FWUMP
バタバタ PATTER PITTER
Oof!
I'M SO TIRED, LUTZ.
ぐでー GROAN
YOU LOOK KINDA SICK, TOO.
GOOD WORK OUT THERE.
ぽふぽふ PAT PAT
ぎゅ~ SQUEEZE
OH, I NEED TO SPEAK TO BENNO ABOUT THE DONATION.
IS HE AT THE STORE?
YEAH, HE SHOULD STILL BE THERE.
GREAT. LET'S GO RIGHT AWAY.

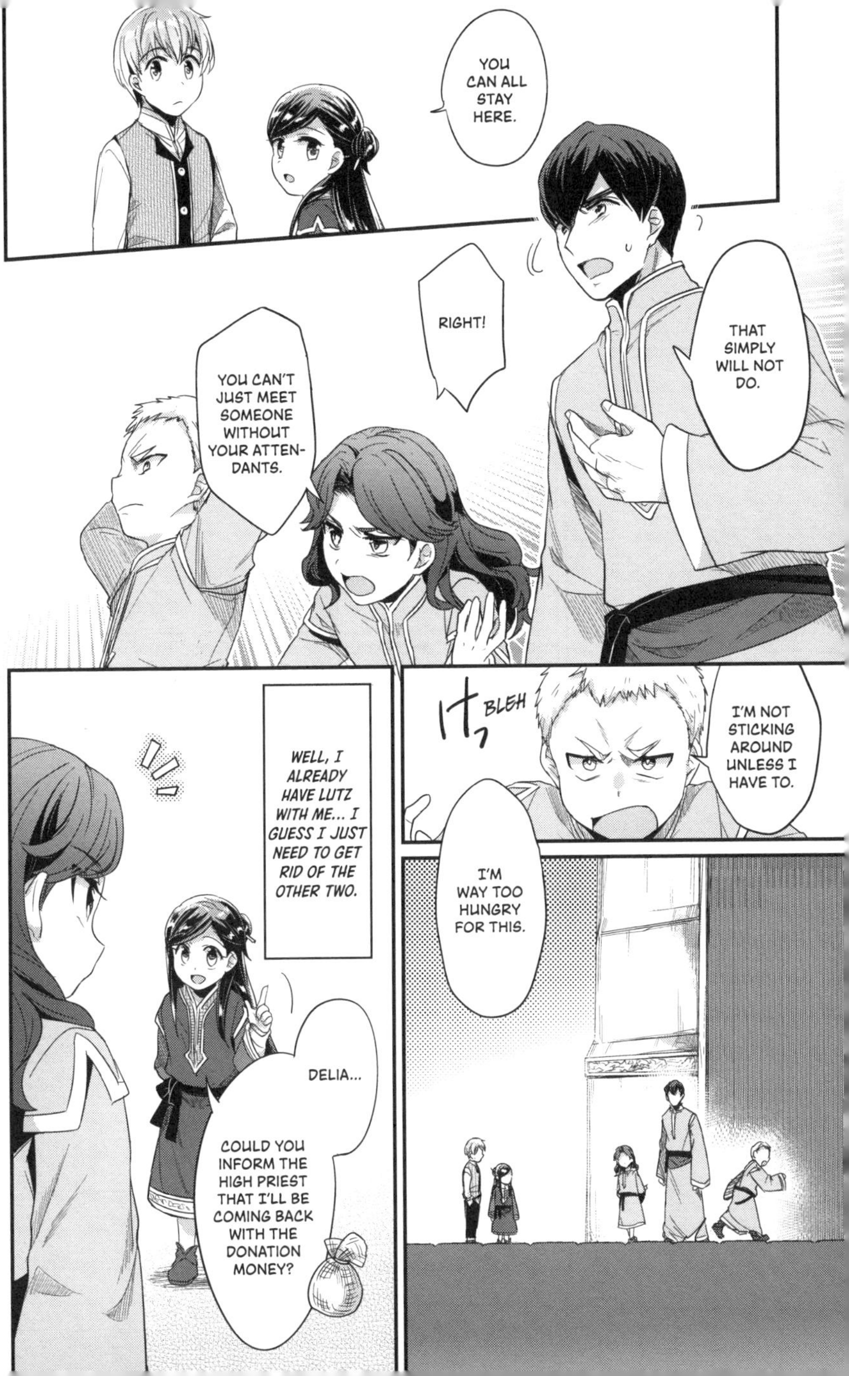
YOU CAN ALL STAY HERE.
THAT SIMPLY WILL NOT DO.
RIGHT!
YOU CAN'T JUST MEET SOMEONE WITHOUT YOUR ATTEN-DANTS.
BLEH
I'M NOT STICKING AROUND UNLESS I HAVE TO.
I'M WAY TOO HUNGRY FOR THIS.
WELL, I ALREADY HAVE LUTZ WITH ME... I GUESS I JUST NEED TO GET RID OF THE OTHER TWO.
DELIA...
COULD YOU INFORM THE HIGH PRIEST THAT I'LL BE COMING BACK WITH THE DONATION MONEY?

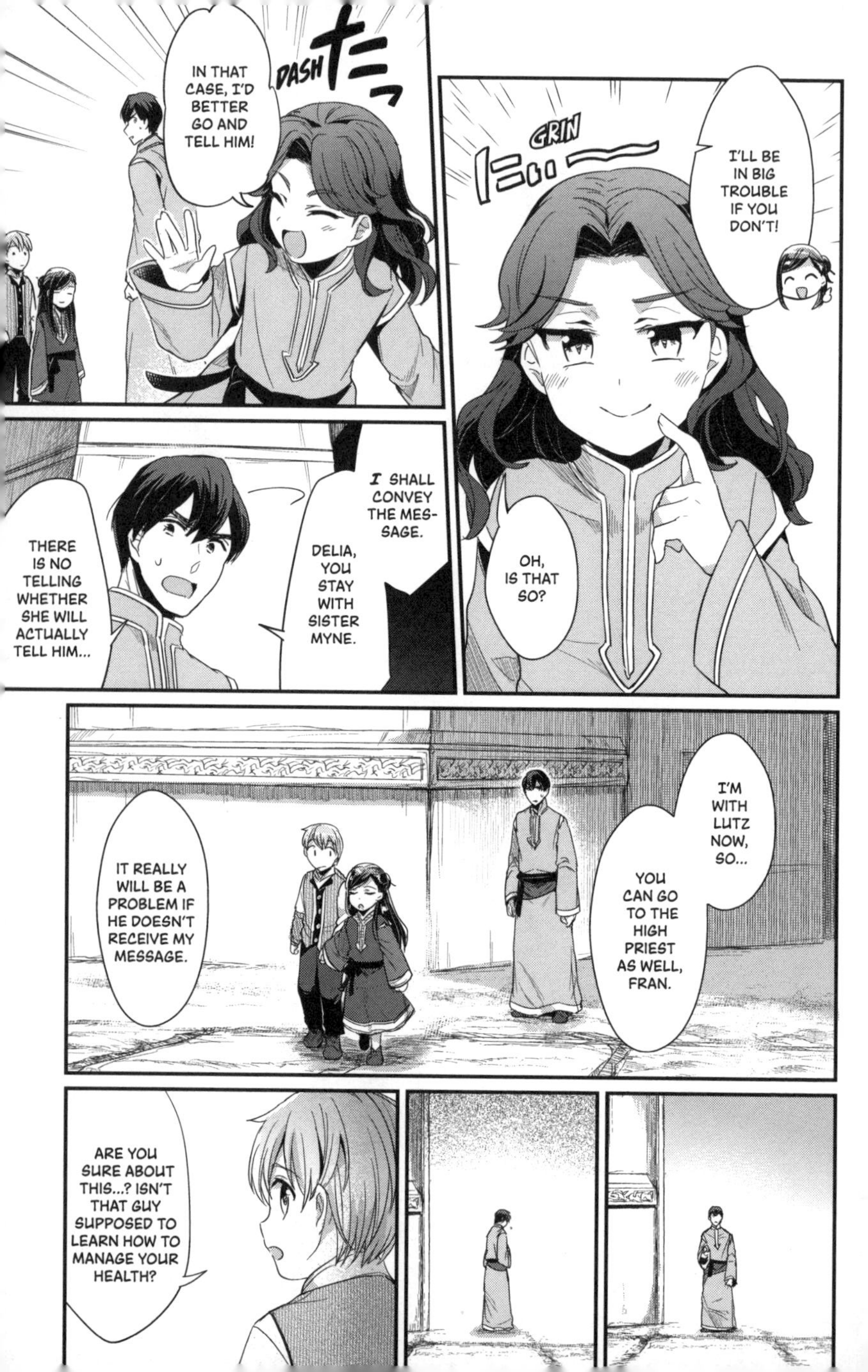
GRIN
I'LL BE IN BIG TROUBLE IF YOU DON'T!
OH, IS THAT SO?
IN THAT CASE, I'D BETTER GO AND TELL HIM!
DASH
I SHALL CONVEY THE MES-SAGE.
DELIA, YOU STAY WITH SISTER MYNE.
THERE IS NO TELLING WHETHER SHE WILL ACTUALLY TELL HIM...
I'M WITH LUTZ NOW, SO...
YOU CAN GO TO THE HIGH PRIEST AS WELL, FRAN.
IT REALLY WILL BE A PROBLEM IF HE DOESN'T RECEIVE MY MESSAGE.
ARE YOU SURE ABOUT THIS...? ISN'T THAT GUY SUPPOSED TO LEARN HOW TO MANAGE YOUR HEALTH?

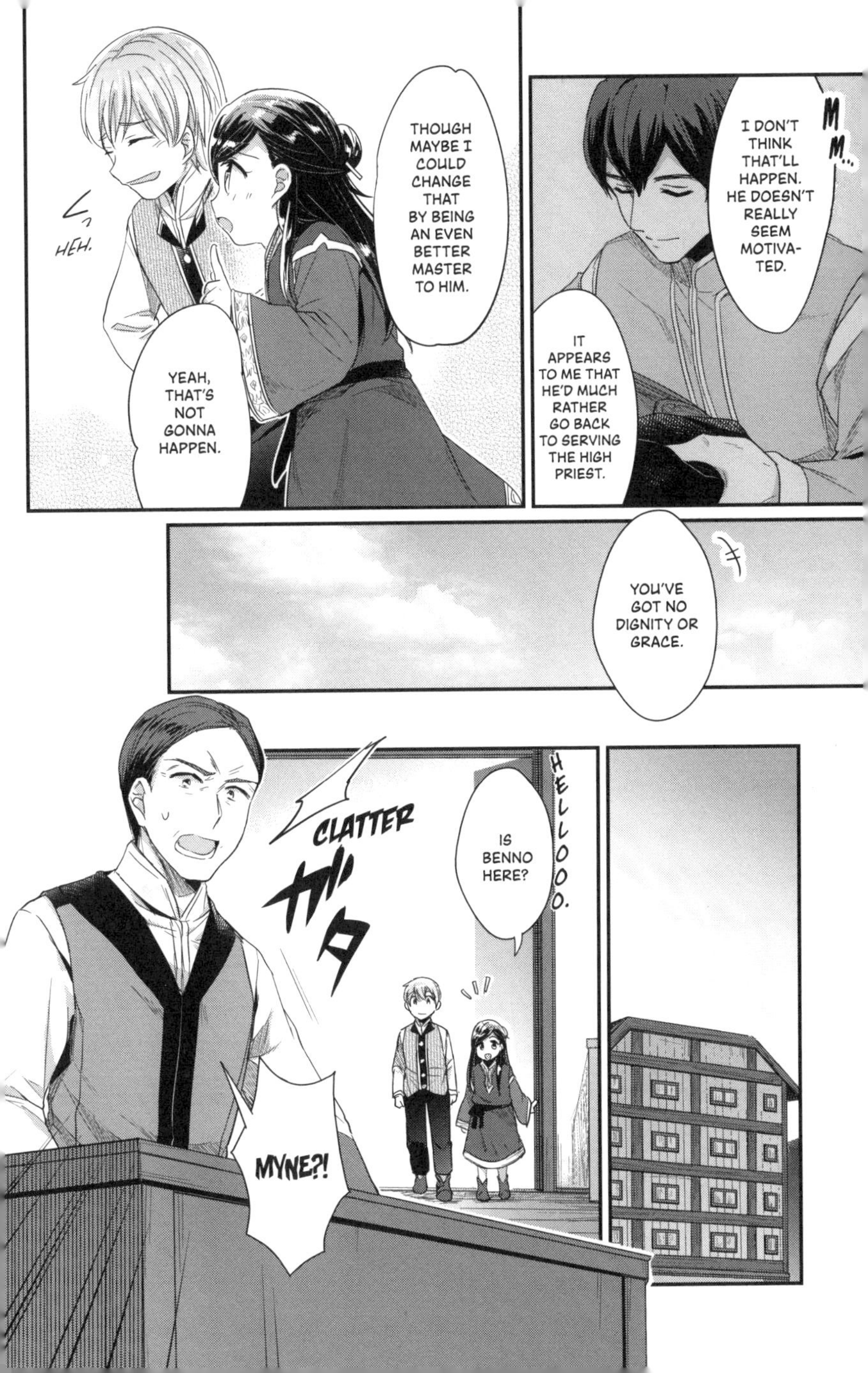
MM...
I DON'T THINK THAT'LL HAPPEN. HE DOESN'T REALLY SEEM MOTIVATED.
IT APPEARS TO ME THAT HE'D MUCH RATHER GO BACK TO SERVING THE HIGH PRIEST.
THOUGH MAYBE I COULD CHANGE THAT BY BEING AN EVEN BETTER MASTER TO HIM.
HEH.
YEAH, THAT'S NOT GONNA HAPPEN.
YOU'VE GOT NO DIGNITY OR GRACE.
HELLOOO.
IS BENNO HERE?
CLATTER
MYNE?!

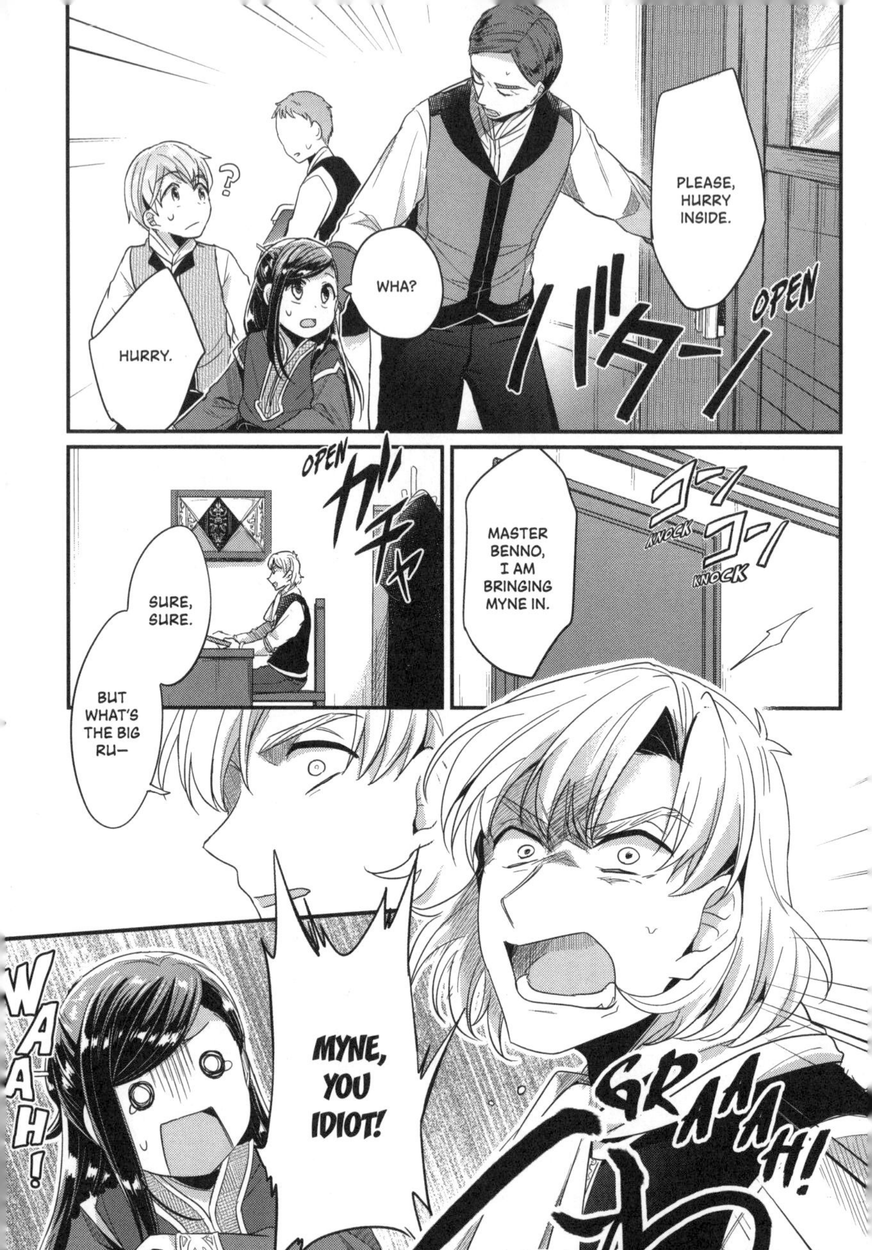
PLEASE, HURRY INSIDE.
OPEN
WHA?
HURRY.
KNOCK
KNOCK
MASTER BENNO, I AM BRINGING MYNE IN.
OPEN
SURE, SURE.
BUT WHAT'S THE BIG RU—
GRAAAH!
MYNE, YOU IDIOT!
WAAAH!

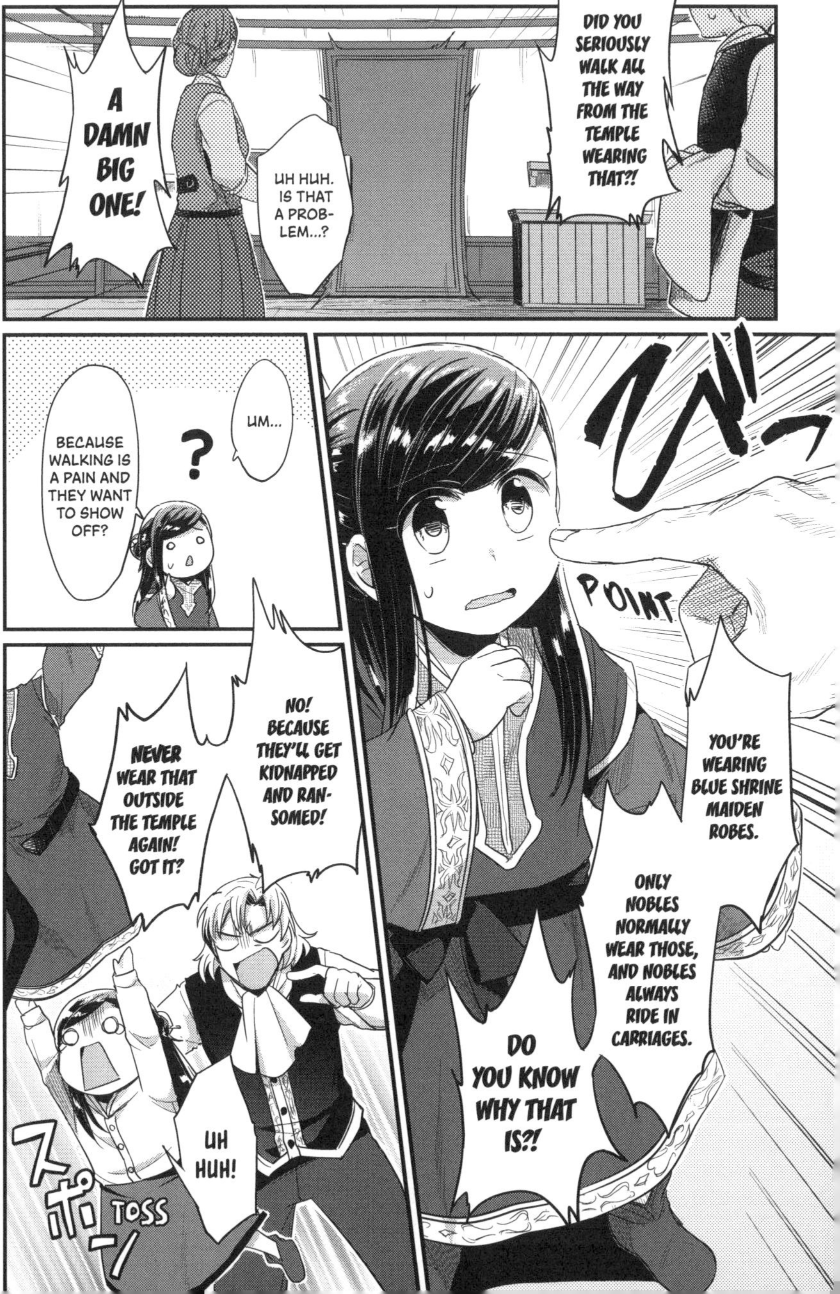
DID YOU SERIOUSLY WALK ALL THE WAY FROM THE TEMPLE WEARING THAT?!
UH HUH. IS THAT A PROB-LEM...?
A DAMN BIG ONE!
ズビッ
POINT
YOU'RE WEARING BLUE SHRINE MAIDEN ROBES.
ONLY NOBLES NORMALLY WEAR THOSE, AND NOBLES ALWAYS RIDE IN CARRIAGES.
DO YOU KNOW WHY THAT IS?!
UM...
?
BECAUSE WALKING IS A PAIN AND THEY WANT TO SHOW OFF?
NO! BECAUSE THEY'LL GET KIDNAPPED AND RAN-SOMED!
NEVER WEAR THAT OUTSIDE THE TEMPLE AGAIN! GOT IT?
UH HUH!
スポーン
TOSS

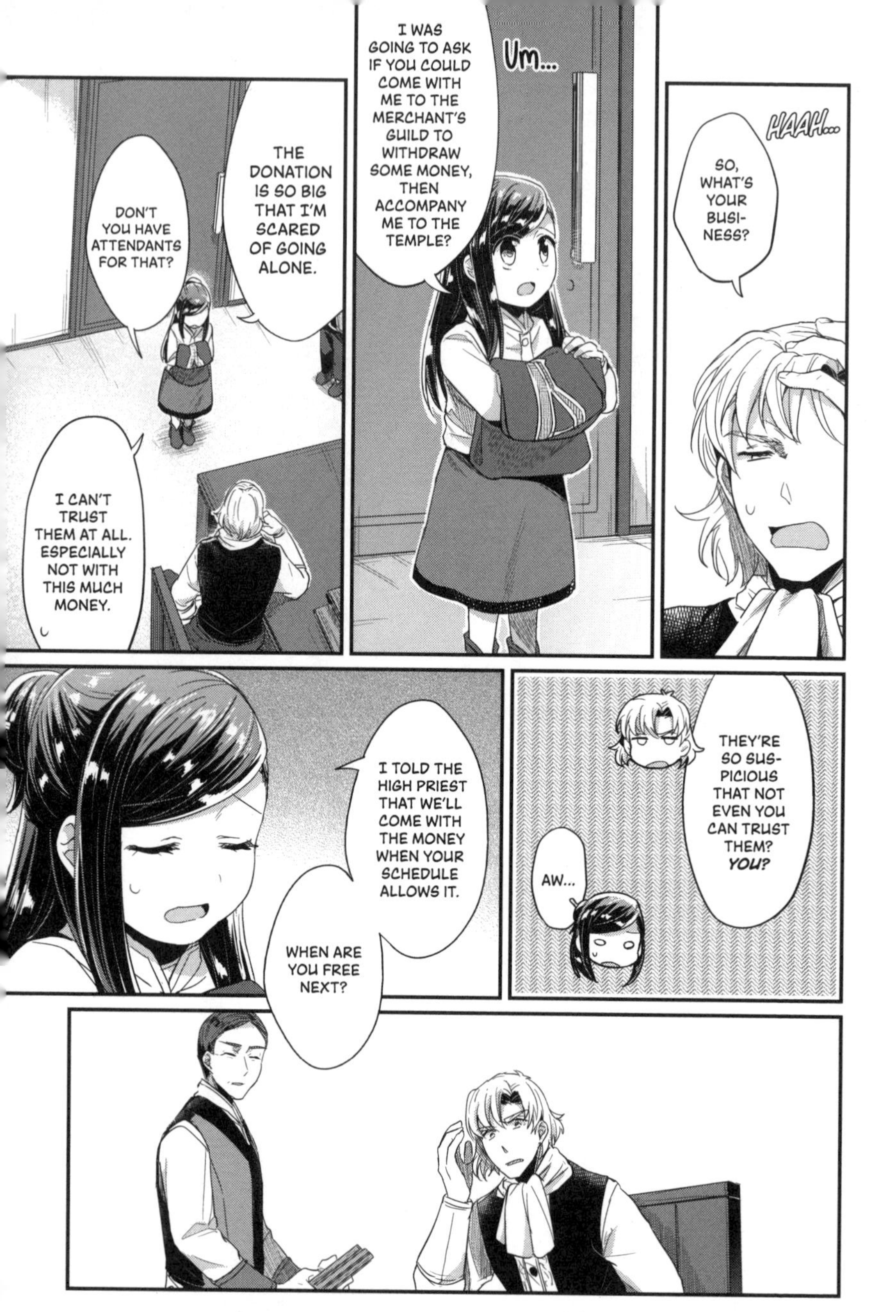
HAAH...
SO, WHAT'S YOUR BUSI-NESS?
Um...
I WAS GOING TO ASK IF YOU COULD COME WITH ME TO THE MERCHANT'S GUILD TO WITHDRAW SOME MONEY, THEN ACCOMPANY ME TO THE TEMPLE?
THE DONATION IS SO BIG THAT I'M SCARED OF GOING ALONE.
DON'T YOU HAVE ATTENDANTS FOR THAT?
I CAN'T TRUST THEM AT ALL. ESPECIALLY NOT WITH THIS MUCH MONEY.
THEY'RE SO SUS-PICIOUS THAT NOT EVEN YOU CAN TRUST THEM? *YOU?*
AW...
I TOLD THE HIGH PRIEST THAT WE'LL COME WITH THE MONEY WHEN YOUR SCHEDULE ALLOWS IT.
WHEN ARE YOU FREE NEXT?

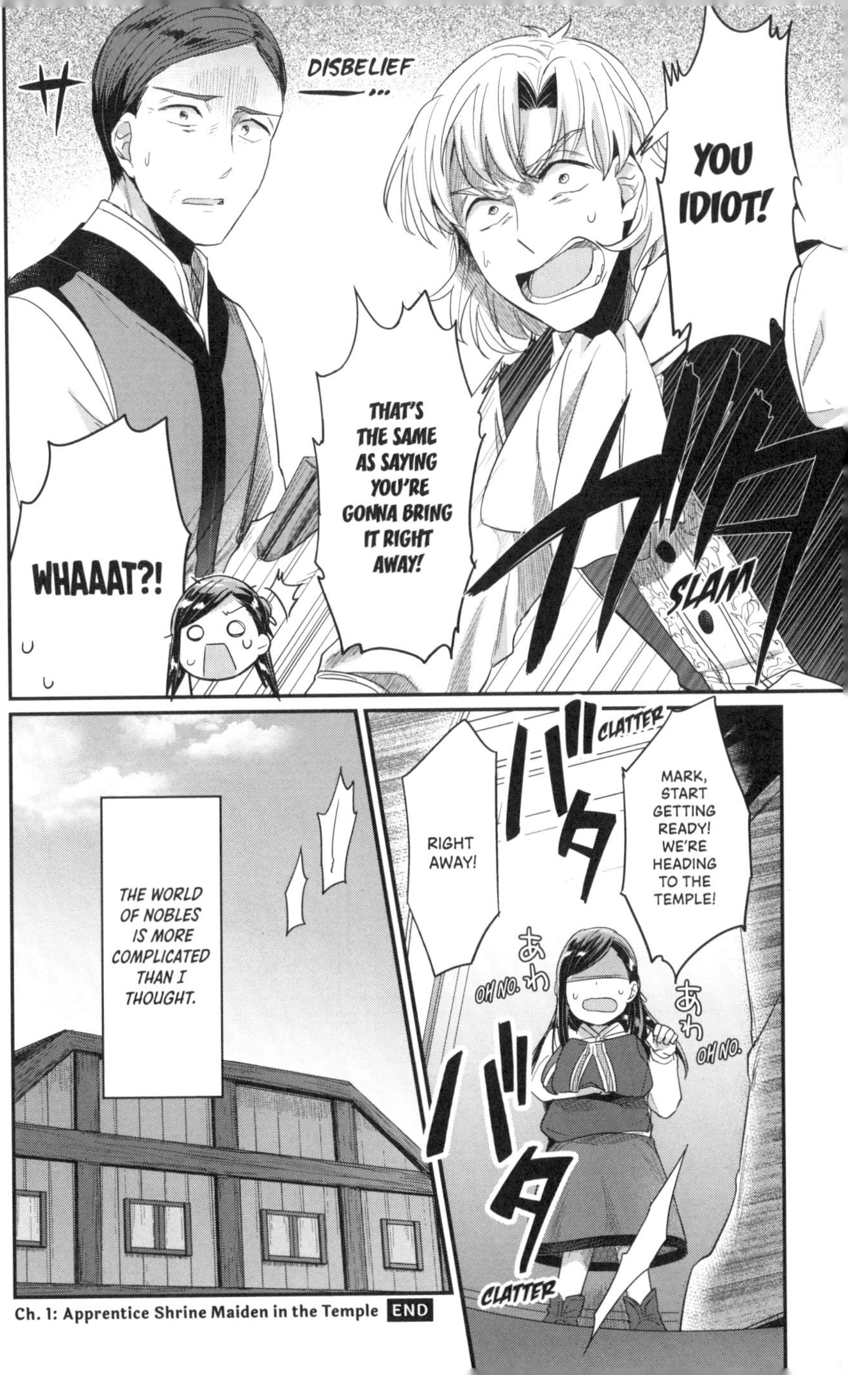
YOU IDIOT!
SLAM
THAT'S THE SAME AS SAYING YOU'RE GONNA BRING IT RIGHT AWAY!
DISBELIEF —...
WHAAAT?!
CLATTER
MARK, START GETTING READY! WE'RE HEADING TO THE TEMPLE!
RIGHT AWAY!
あわ
OH NO.
あわ
OH NO.
CLATTER
THE WORLD OF NOBLES IS MORE COMPLICATED THAN I THOUGHT.

Ch. 1: Apprentice Shrine Maiden in the Temple **END**

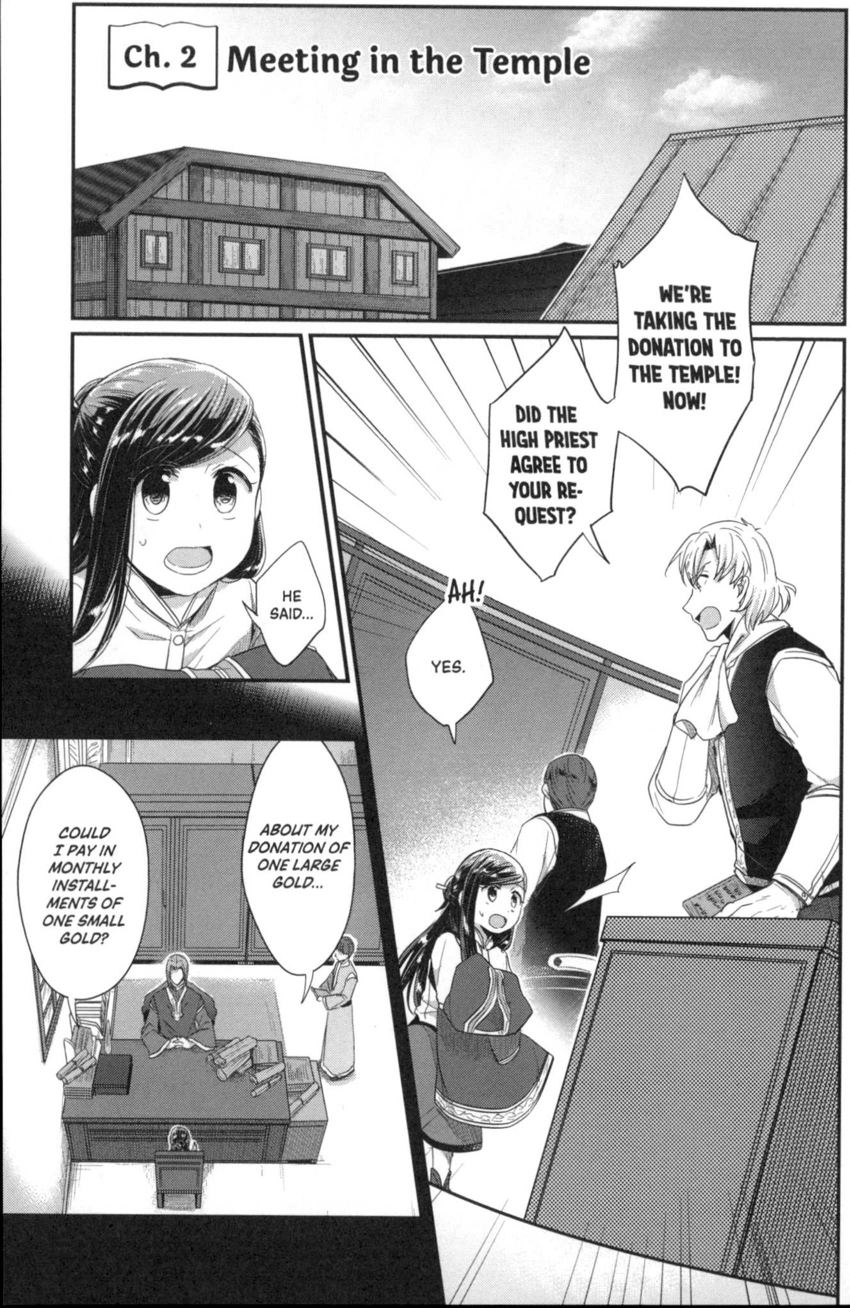
Ch. 2 Meeting in the Temple
WE'RE TAKING THE DONATION TO THE TEMPLE! NOW!
DID THE HIGH PRIEST AGREE TO YOUR RE-QUEST?
AH!
YES.
HE SAID...
ABOUT MY DONATION OF ONE LARGE GOLD...
COULD I PAY IN MONTHLY INSTALL-MENTS OF ONE SMALL GOLD?

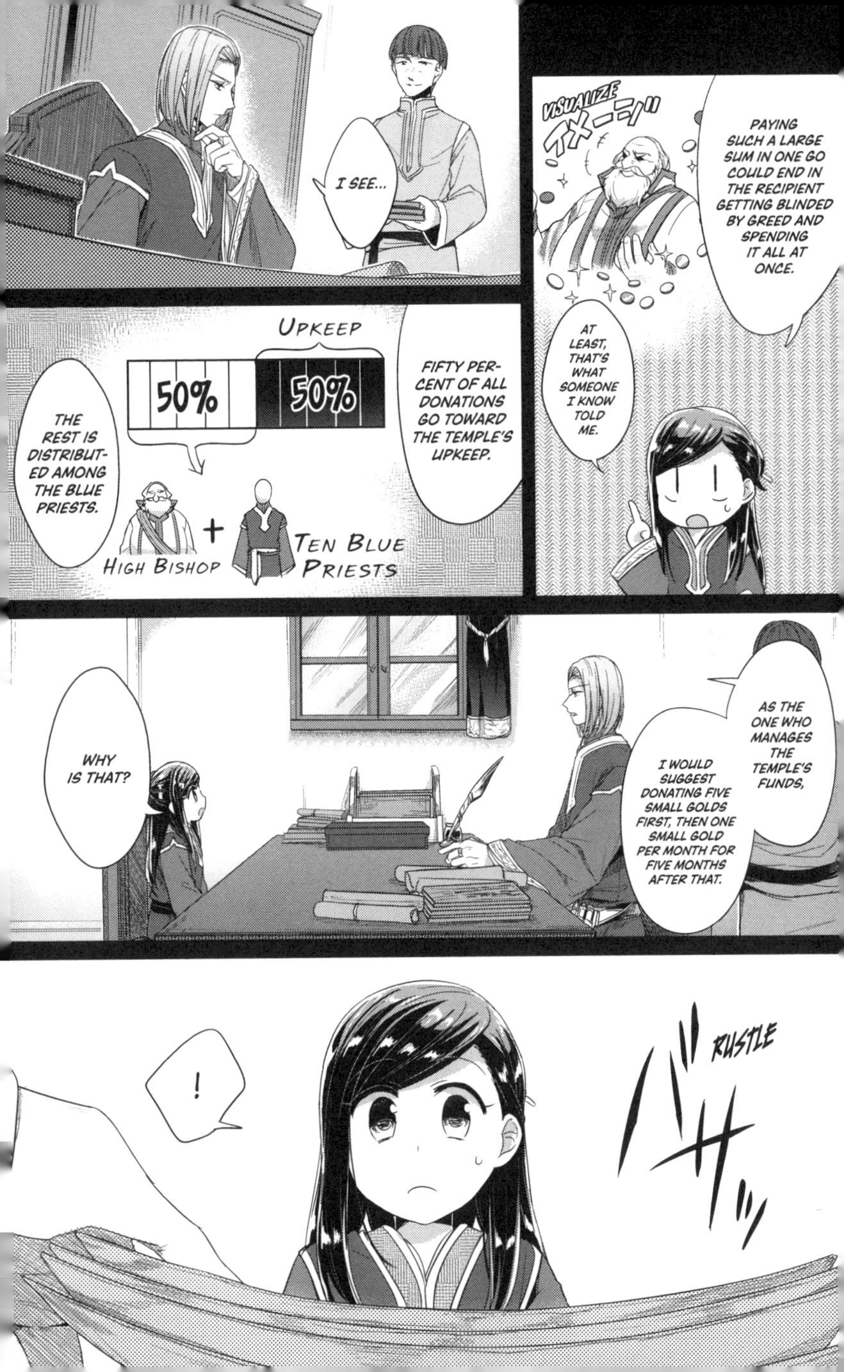
I SEE...
VISUALIZE
PAYING SUCH A LARGE SUM IN ONE GO COULD END IN THE RECIPIENT GETTING BLINDED BY GREED AND SPENDING IT ALL AT ONCE.
AT LEAST, THAT'S WHAT SOMEONE I KNOW TOLD ME.
UPKEEP
50%
50%
FIFTY PERCENT OF ALL DONATIONS GO TOWARD THE TEMPLE'S UPKEEP.
THE REST IS DISTRIBUTED AMONG THE BLUE PRIESTS.
HIGH BISHOP
+
TEN BLUE PRIESTS
AS THE ONE WHO MANAGES THE TEMPLE'S FUNDS,
I WOULD SUGGEST DONATING FIVE SMALL GOLDS FIRST, THEN ONE SMALL GOLD PER MONTH FOR FIVE MONTHS AFTER THAT.
WHY IS THAT?
RUSTLE
!

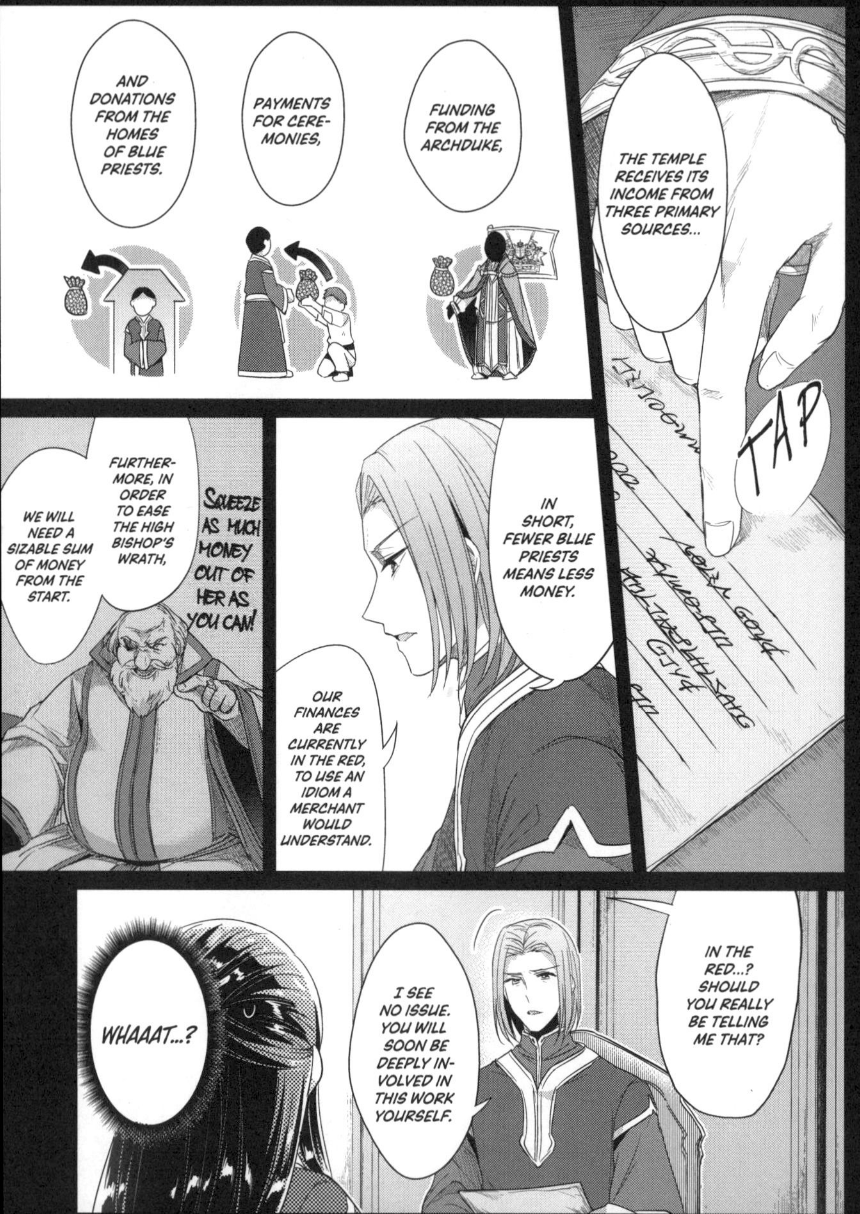
THE TEMPLE RECEIVES ITS INCOME FROM THREE PRIMARY SOURCES...
TAP
FUNDING FROM THE ARCHDUKE,
PAYMENTS FOR CERE-MONIES,
AND DONATIONS FROM THE HOMES OF BLUE PRIESTS.
IN SHORT, FEWER BLUE PRIESTS MEANS LESS MONEY.
OUR FINANCES ARE CURRENTLY IN THE RED, TO USE AN IDIOM A MERCHANT WOULD UNDERSTAND.
FURTHER-MORE, IN ORDER TO EASE THE HIGH BISHOP'S WRATH,
SQUEEZE AS MUCH MONEY OUT OF HER AS YOU CAN!
WE WILL NEED A SIZABLE SUM OF MONEY FROM THE START.
IN THE RED...? SHOULD YOU REALLY BE TELLING ME THAT?
I SEE NO ISSUE. YOU WILL SOON BE DEEPLY IN-VOLVED IN THIS WORK YOURSELF.
WHAAAT...?

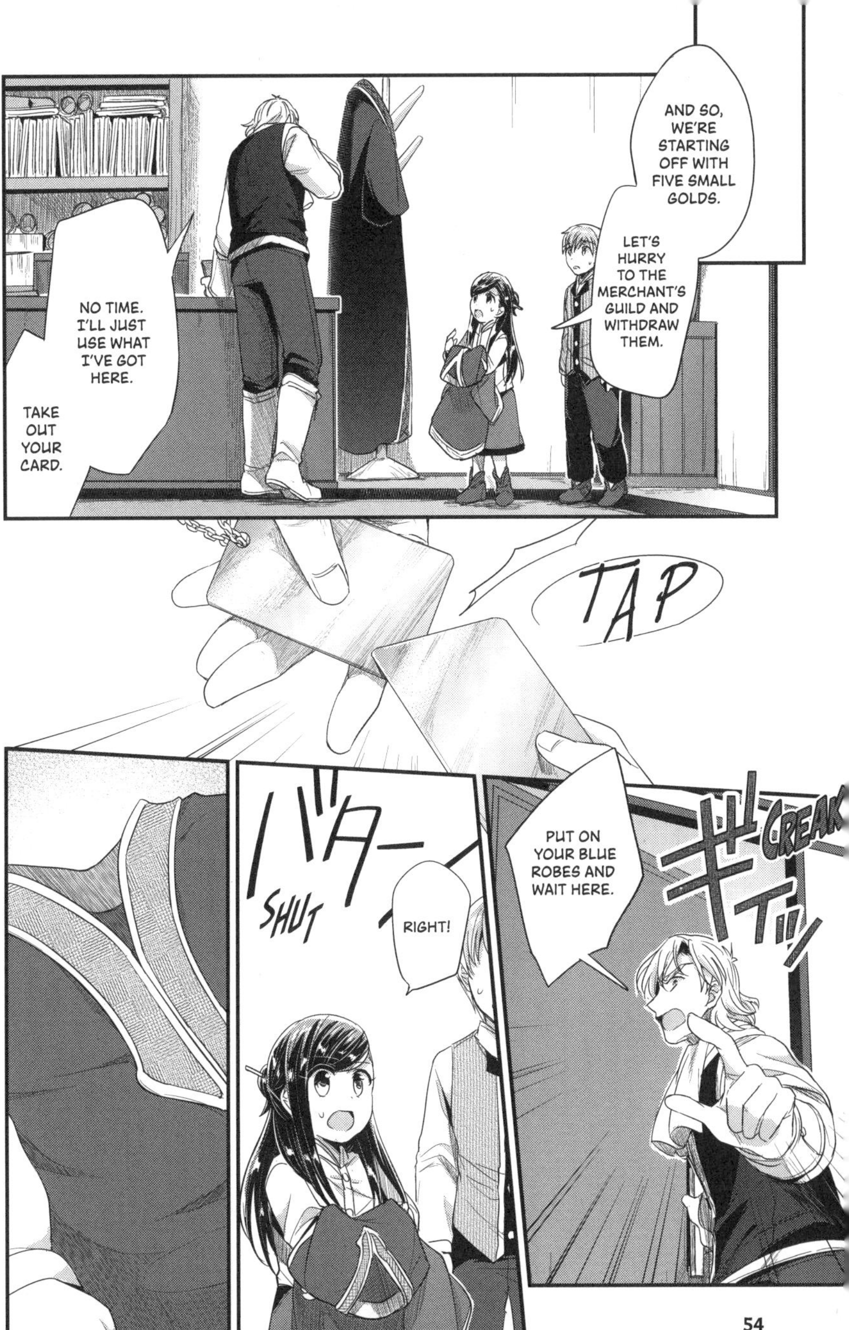
AND SO, WE'RE STARTING OFF WITH FIVE SMALL GOLDS.
LET'S HURRY TO THE MERCHANT'S GUILD AND WITHDRAW THEM.
NO TIME. I'LL JUST USE WHAT I'VE GOT HERE.
TAKE OUT YOUR CARD.
TAP
CREAK
PUT ON YOUR BLUE ROBES AND WAIT HERE.
RIGHT!
SHUT

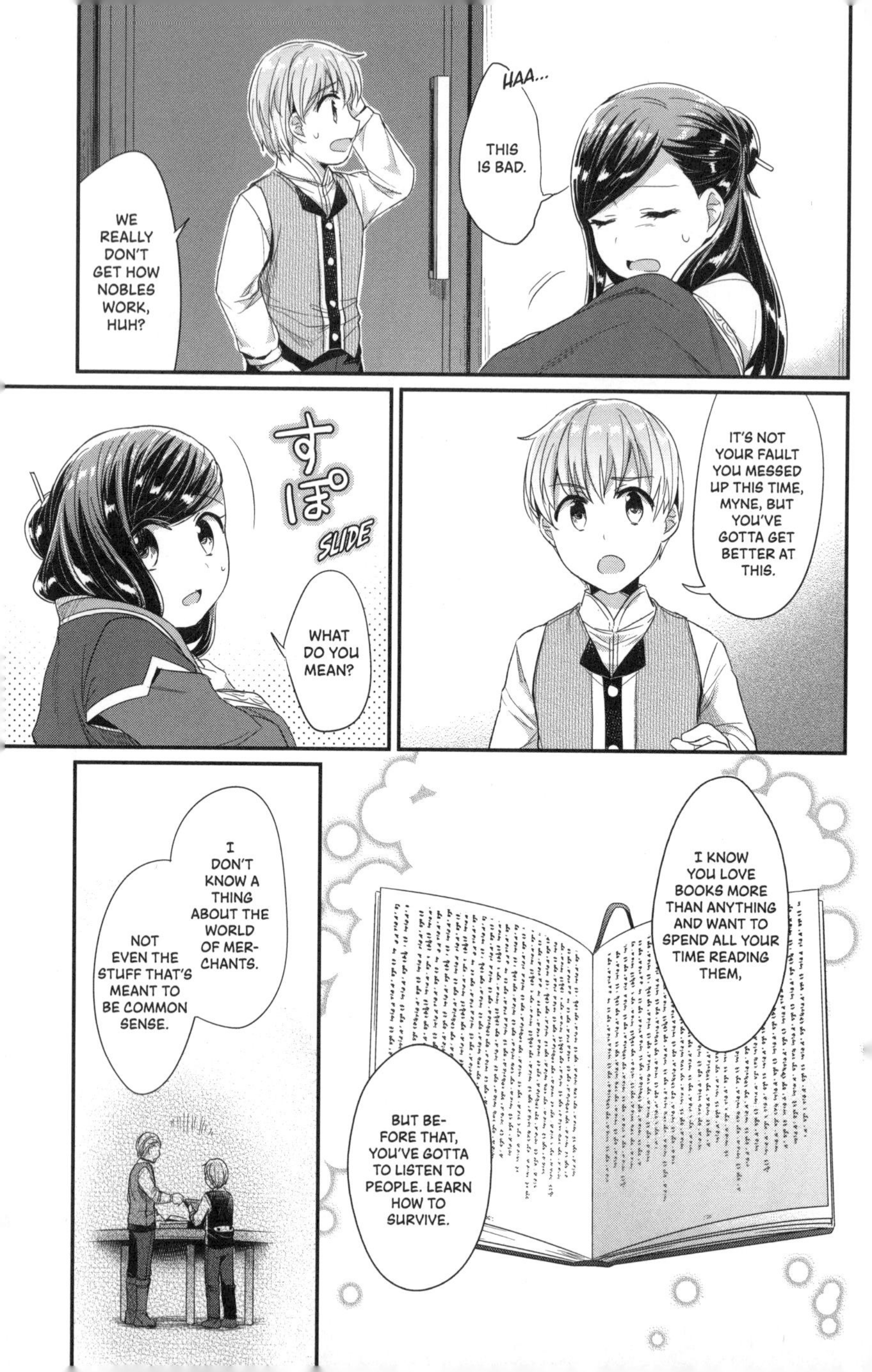
HAA...
THIS IS BAD.
WE REALLY DON'T GET HOW NOBLES WORK, HUH?
IT'S NOT YOUR FAULT YOU MESSED UP THIS TIME, MYNE, BUT YOU'VE GOTTA GET BETTER AT THIS.
すぽ
SLIDE
WHAT DO YOU MEAN?
I KNOW YOU LOVE BOOKS MORE THAN ANYTHING AND WANT TO SPEND ALL YOUR TIME READING THEM,
BUT BE-FORE THAT, YOU'VE GOTTA TO LISTEN TO PEOPLE. LEARN HOW TO SURVIVE.
I DON'T KNOW A THING ABOUT THE WORLD OF MER-CHANTS.
NOT EVEN THE STUFF THAT'S MEANT TO BE COMMON SENSE.

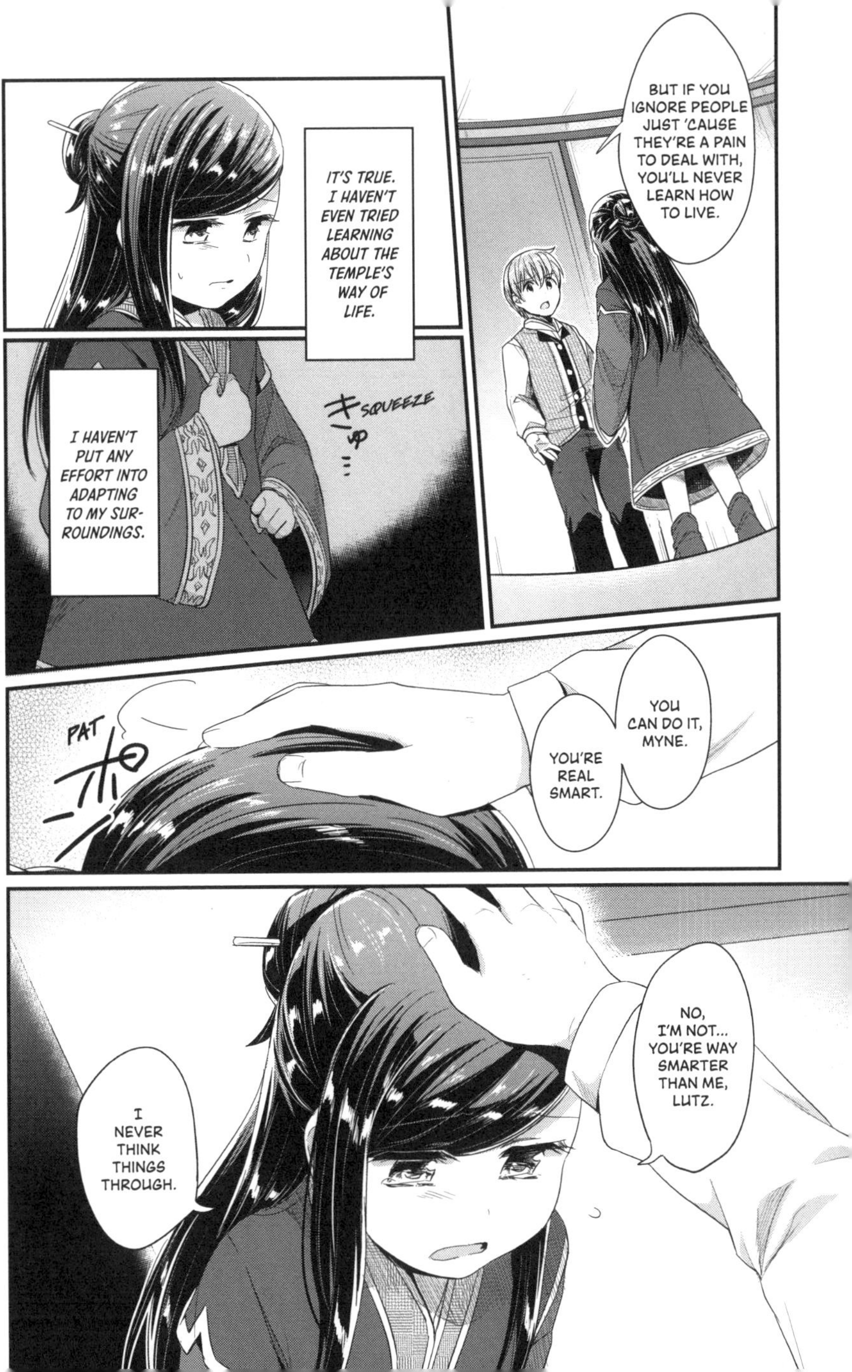
BUT IF YOU IGNORE PEOPLE JUST 'CAUSE THEY'RE A PAIN TO DEAL WITH, YOU'LL NEVER LEARN HOW TO LIVE.
IT'S TRUE. I HAVEN'T EVEN TRIED LEARNING ABOUT THE TEMPLE'S WAY OF LIFE.
SQUEEZE
I HAVEN'T PUT ANY EFFORT INTO ADAPTING TO MY SUR-ROUNDINGS.
YOU CAN DO IT, MYNE.
YOU'RE REAL SMART.
PAT
NO, I'M NOT... YOU'RE WAY SMARTER THAN ME, LUTZ.
I NEVER THINK THINGS THROUGH.

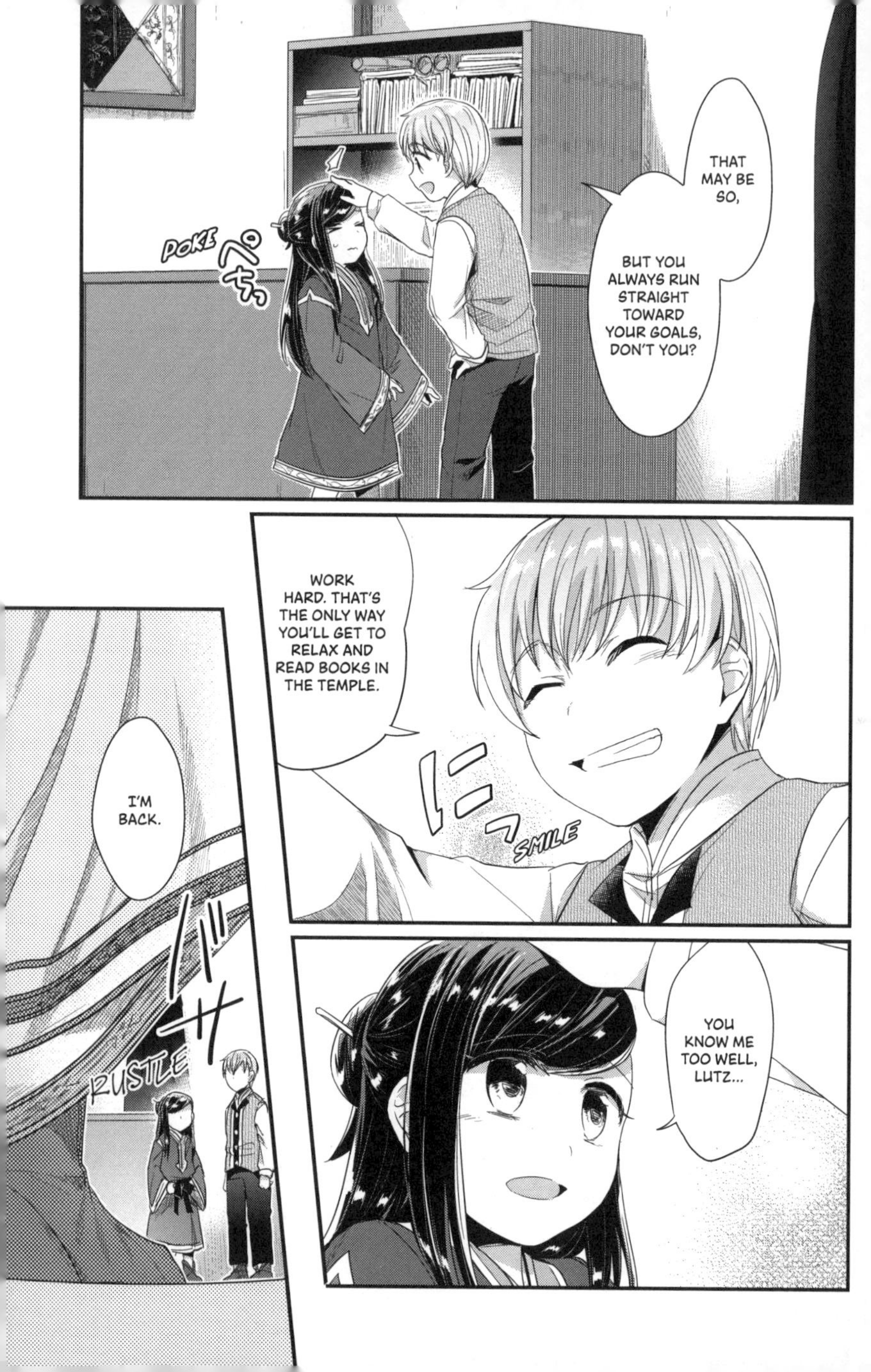
THAT MAY BE SO,
BUT YOU ALWAYS RUN STRAIGHT TOWARD YOUR GOALS, DON'T YOU?
POKE
WORK HARD. THAT'S THE ONLY WAY YOU'LL GET TO RELAX AND READ BOOKS IN THE TEMPLE.
SMILE
YOU KNOW ME TOO WELL, LUTZ...
I'M BACK.
RUSTLE

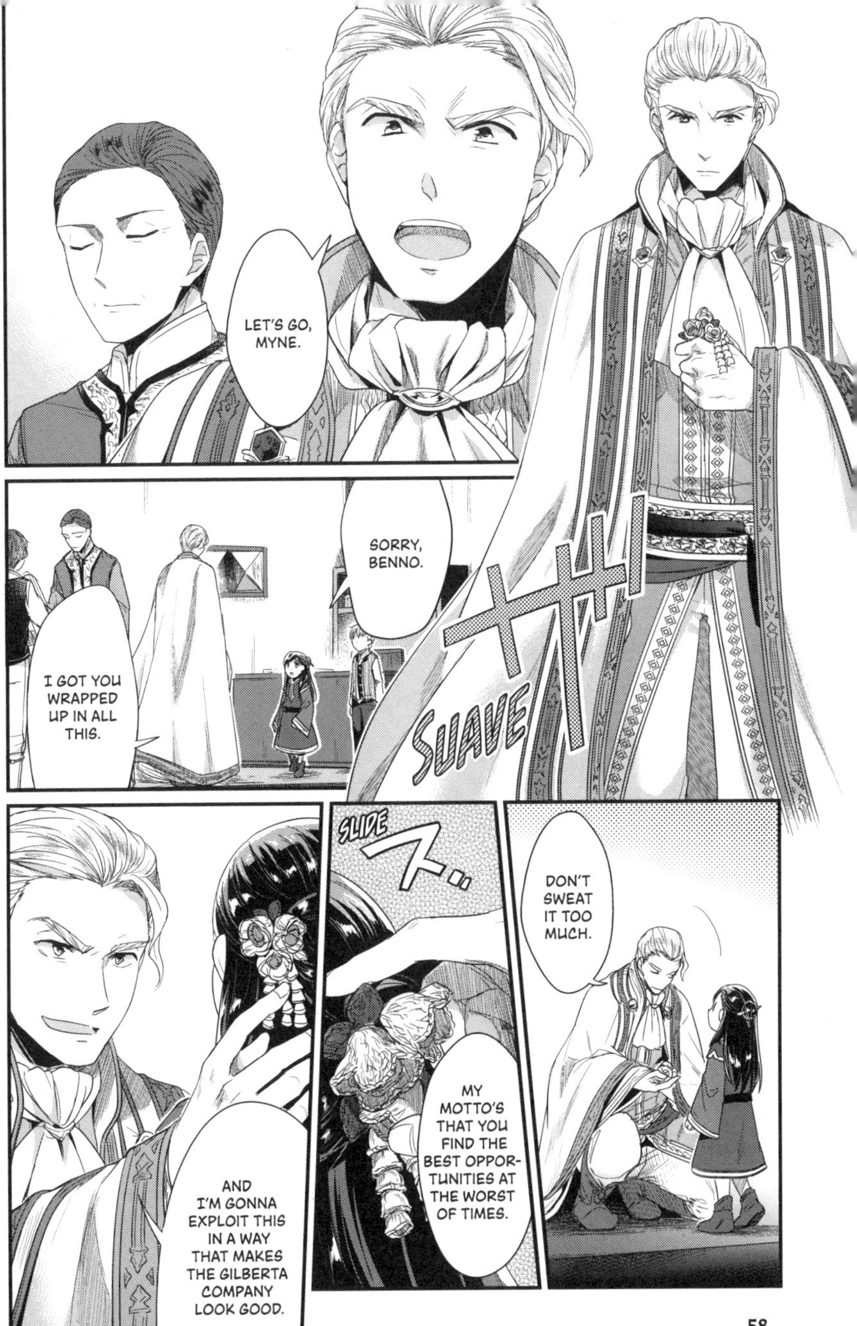
SUAVE
LET'S GO, MYNE.
SORRY, BENNO.
I GOT YOU WRAPPED UP IN ALL THIS.
DON'T SWEAT IT TOO MUCH.
SLIDE
MY MOTTO'S THAT YOU FIND THE BEST OPPOR-TUNITIES AT THE WORST OF TIMES.
AND I'M GONNA EXPLOIT THIS IN A WAY THAT MAKES THE GILBERTA COMPANY LOOK GOOD.

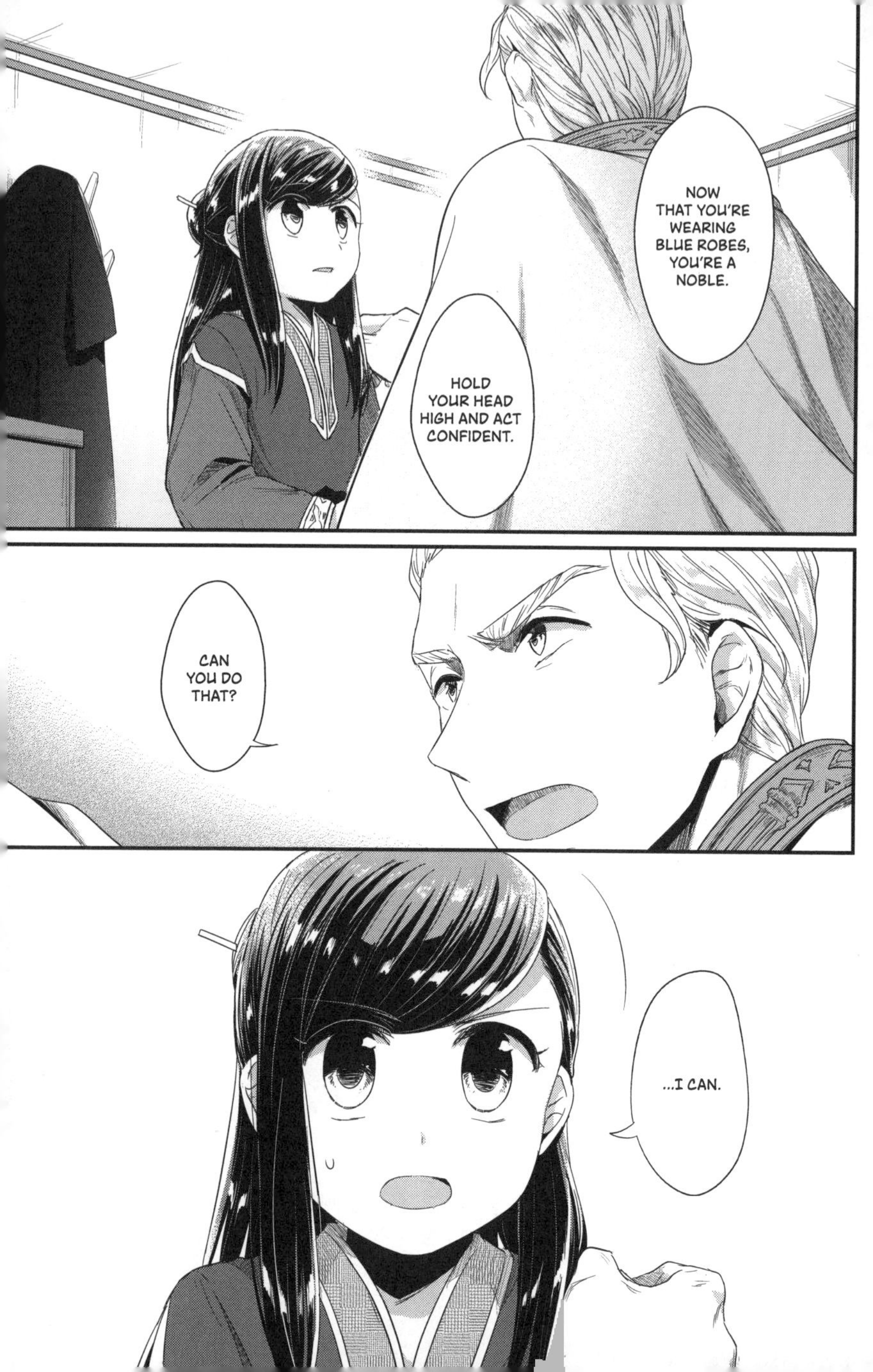
NOW THAT YOU'RE WEARING BLUE ROBES, YOU'RE A NOBLE.
HOLD YOUR HEAD HIGH AND ACT CONFIDENT.
CAN YOU DO THAT?
...I CAN.

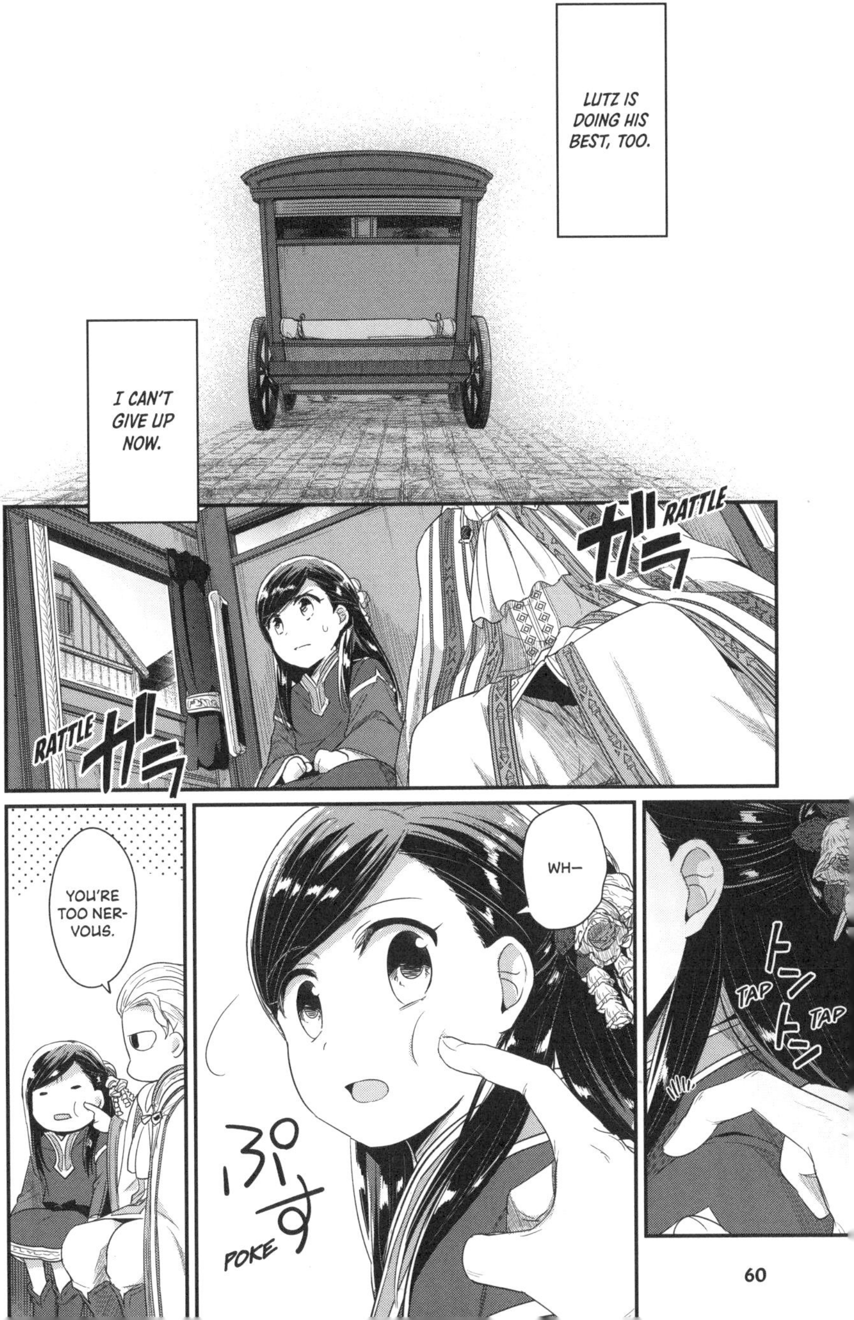
LUTZ IS DOING HIS BEST, TOO.
I CAN'T GIVE UP NOW.
ガラ RATTLE
ガラ RATTLE
トントン TAP TAP
WH—
ぷす POKE
YOU'RE TOO NER-VOUS.

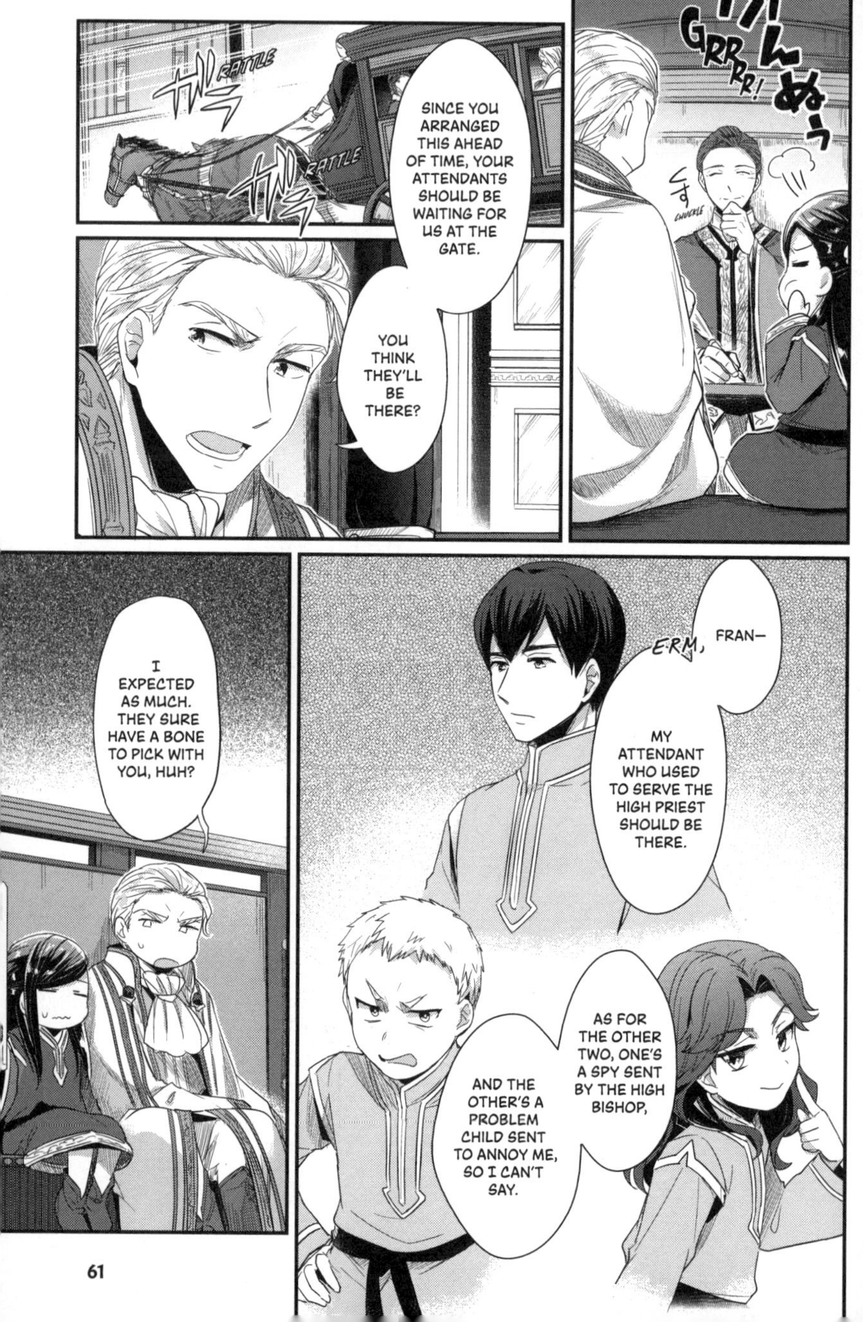
ふんぬぅ
GRRRR!
くす
CHUCKLE
ガラ RATTLE
ガラ RATTLE
SINCE YOU ARRANGED THIS AHEAD OF TIME, YOUR ATTENDANTS SHOULD BE WAITING FOR US AT THE GATE.
YOU THINK THEY'LL BE THERE?
ERM, FRAN—
MY ATTENDANT WHO USED TO SERVE THE HIGH PRIEST SHOULD BE THERE.
AS FOR THE OTHER TWO, ONE'S A SPY SENT BY THE HIGH BISHOP,
AND THE OTHER'S A PROBLEM CHILD SENT TO ANNOY ME, SO I CAN'T SAY.
I EXPECTED AS MUCH. THEY SURE HAVE A BONE TO PICK WITH YOU, HUH?

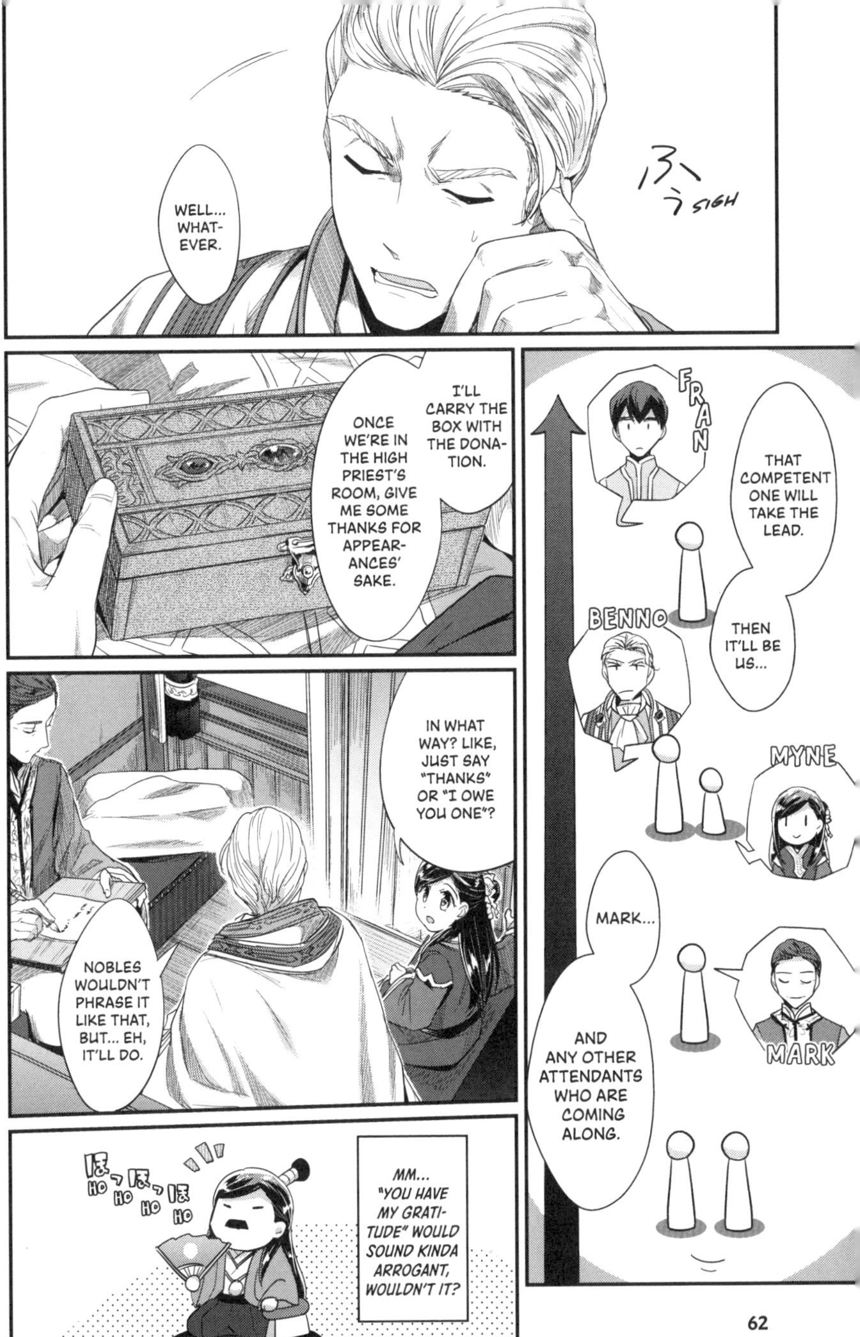
WELL... WHAT-EVER.
SIGH
FRAN
THAT COMPETENT ONE WILL TAKE THE LEAD.
BENNO
THEN IT'LL BE US...
MYNE
MARK...
MARK
AND ANY OTHER ATTENDANTS WHO ARE COMING ALONG.
I'LL CARRY THE BOX WITH THE DONA-TION.
ONCE WE'RE IN THE HIGH PRIEST'S ROOM, GIVE ME SOME THANKS FOR APPEAR-ANCES' SAKE.
IN WHAT WAY? LIKE, JUST SAY "THANKS" OR "I OWE YOU ONE"?
NOBLES WOULDN'T PHRASE IT LIKE THAT, BUT... EH, IT'LL DO.
MM... "YOU HAVE MY GRATI-TUDE" WOULD SOUND KINDA ARROGANT, WOULDN'T IT?
HO HO HO HO HO

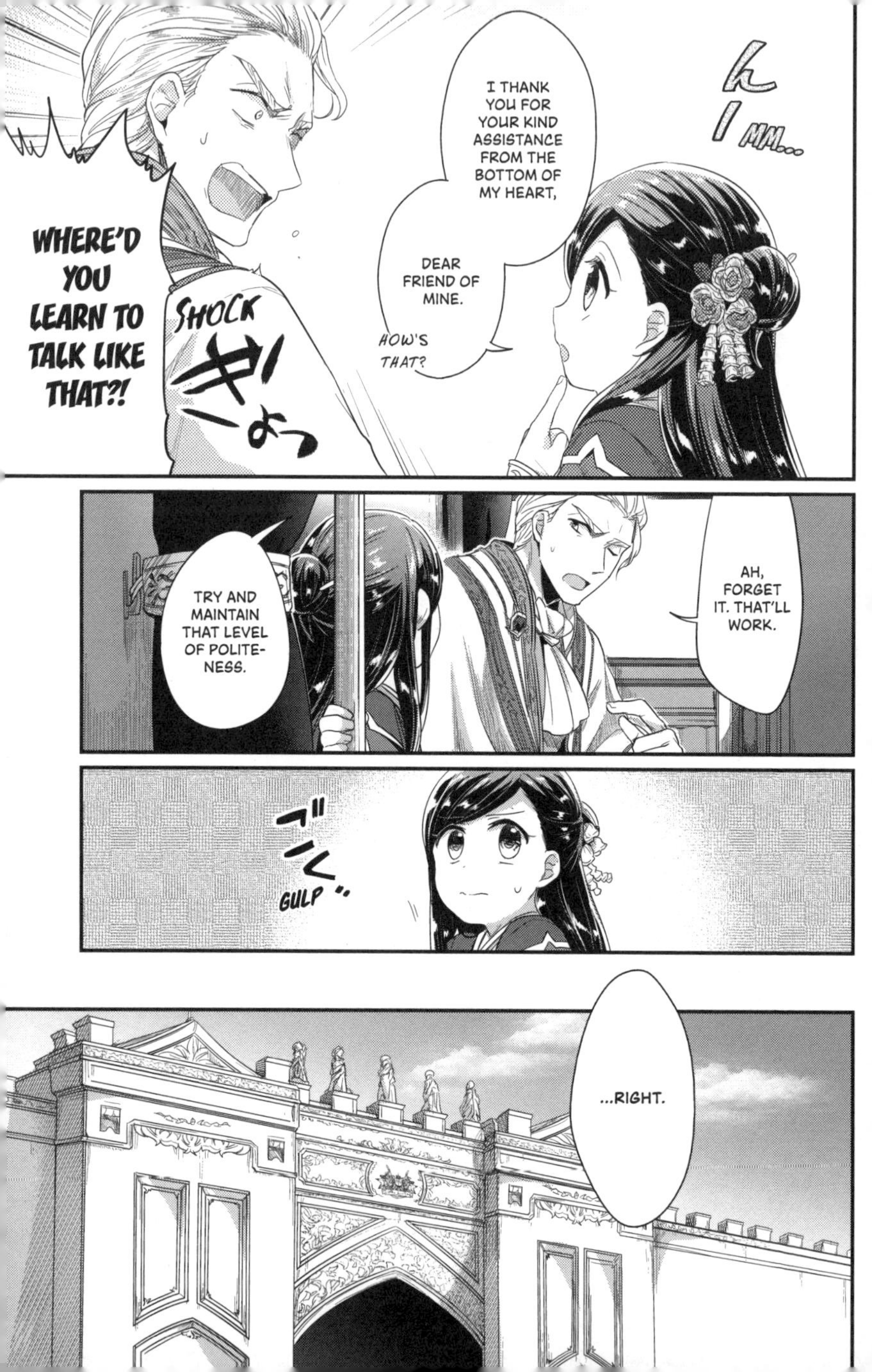
ん
MM...
I THANK YOU FOR YOUR KIND ASSISTANCE FROM THE BOTTOM OF MY HEART,
DEAR FRIEND OF MINE.
HOW'S THAT?
ぎょっ
SHOCK
WHERE'D YOU LEARN TO TALK LIKE THAT?!
AH, FORGET IT. THAT'LL WORK.
TRY AND MAINTAIN THAT LEVEL OF POLITE-NESS.
ゴくっ
GULP
...RIGHT.

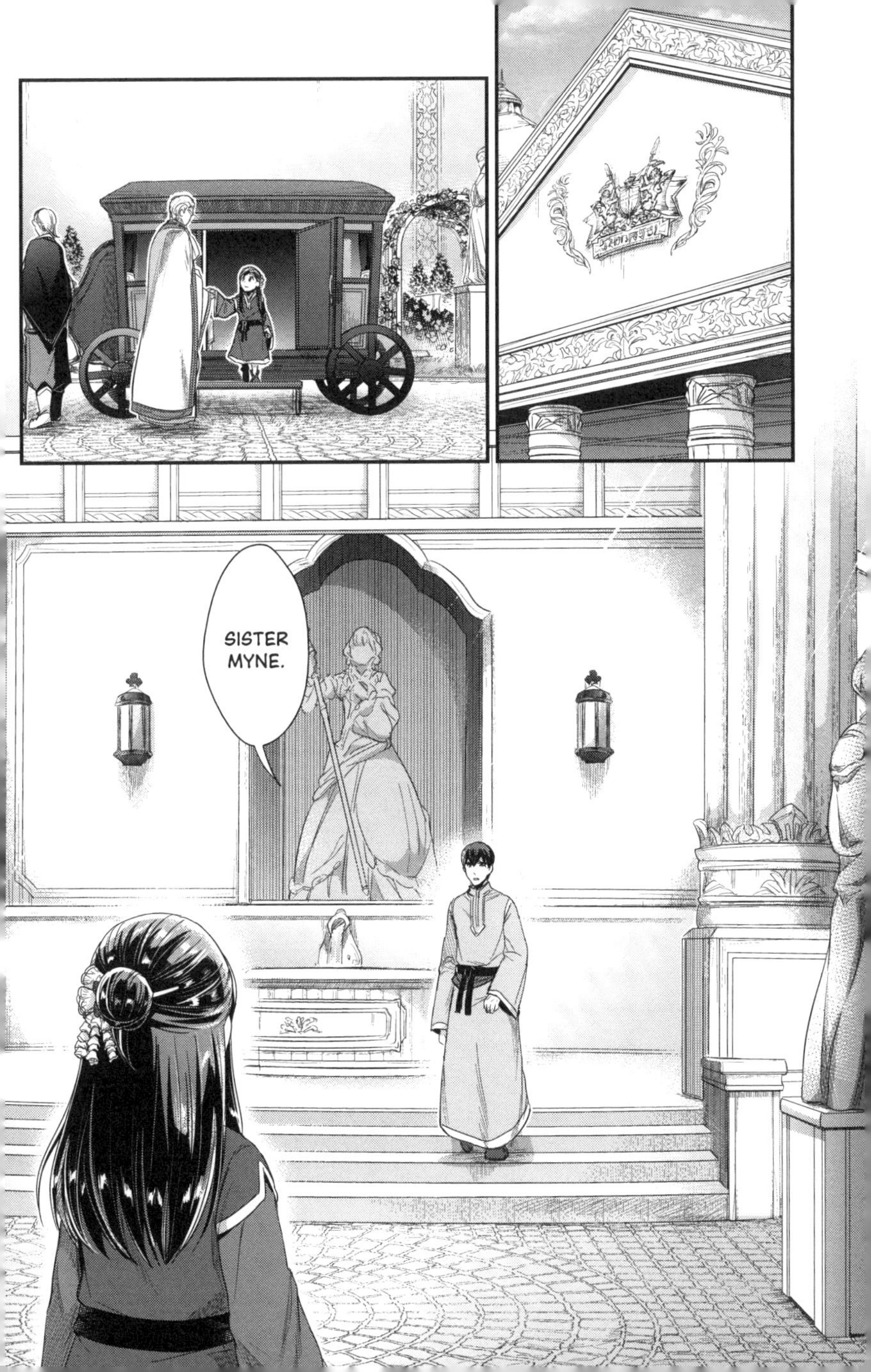
SISTER MYNE.

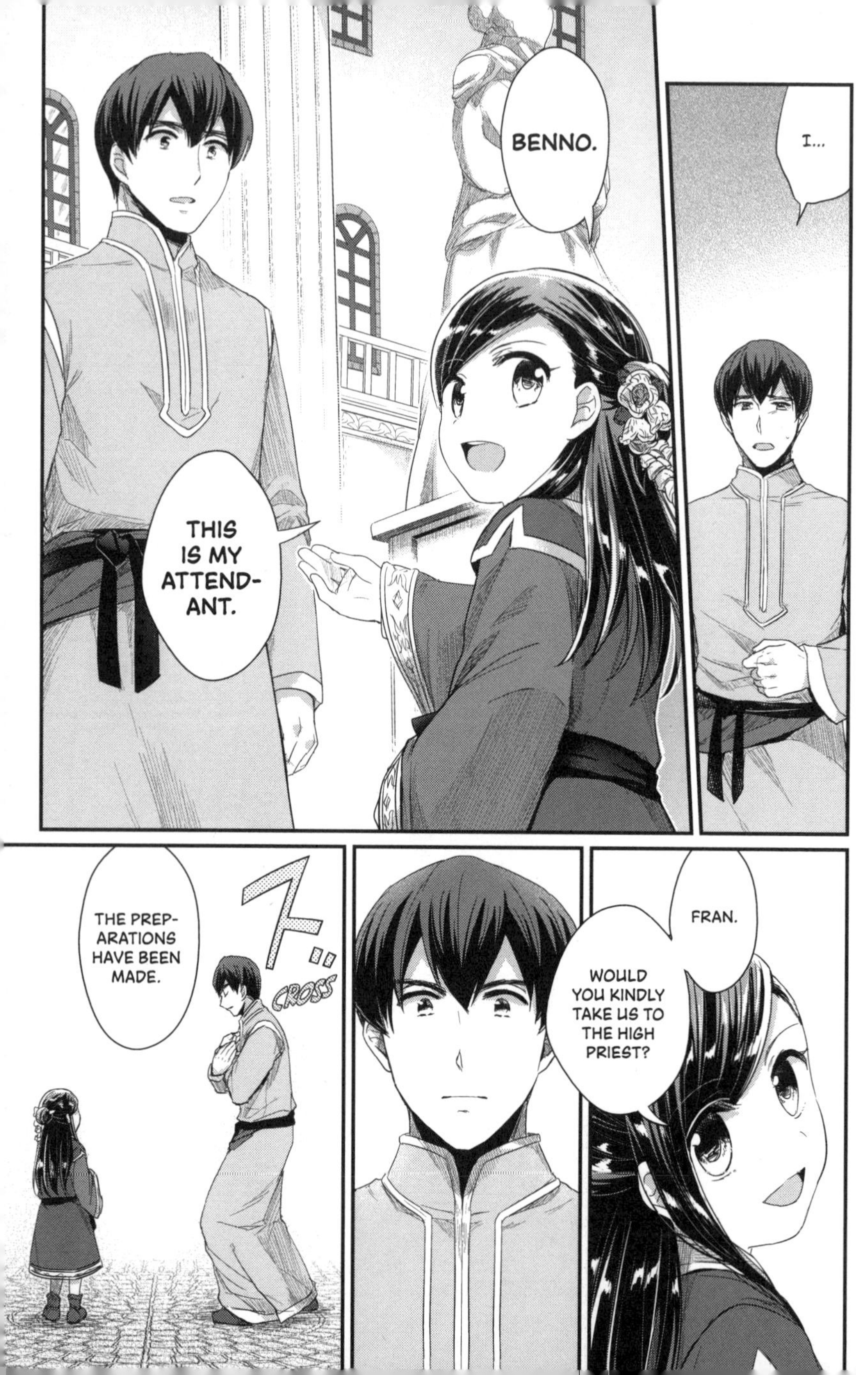
I...
BENNO.
THIS IS MY ATTEND-ANT.
FRAN.
WOULD YOU KINDLY TAKE US TO THE HIGH PRIEST?
THE PREP-ARATIONS HAVE BEEN MADE.
CROSS

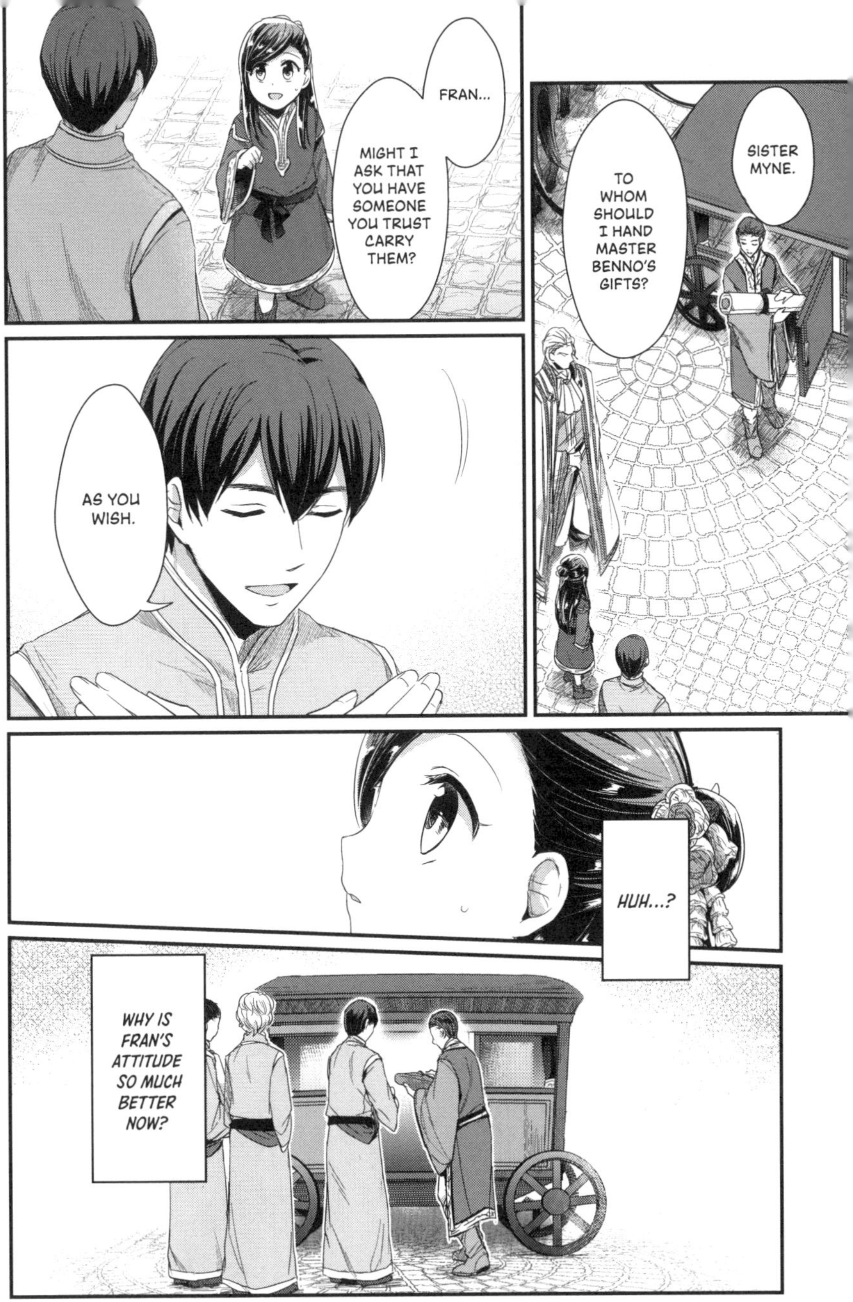
SISTER MYNE.
TO WHOM SHOULD I HAND MASTER BENNO'S GIFTS?
FRAN...
MIGHT I ASK THAT YOU HAVE SOMEONE YOU TRUST CARRY THEM?
AS YOU WISH.
HUH...?
WHY IS FRAN'S ATTITUDE SO MUCH BETTER NOW?

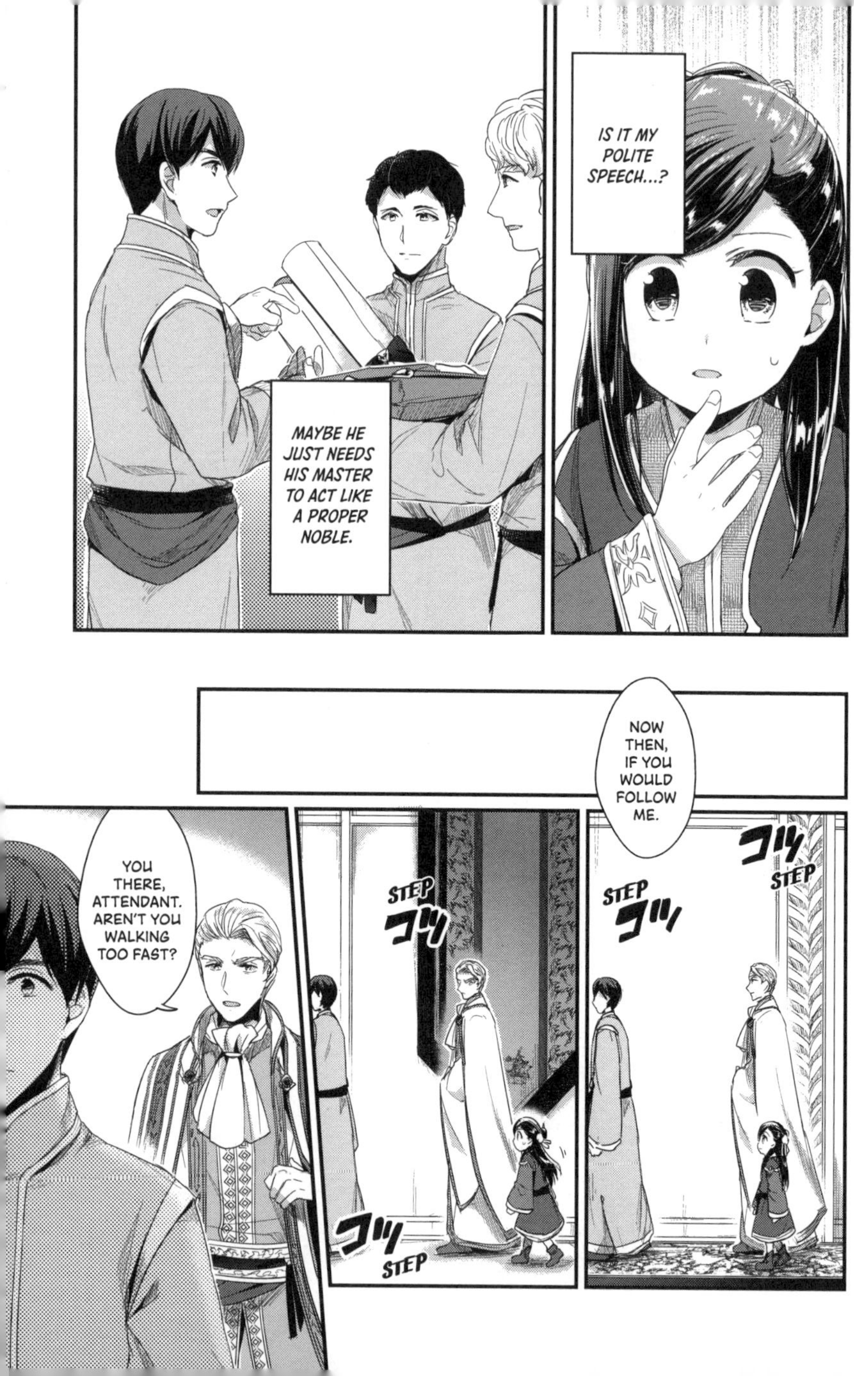
IS IT MY POLITE SPEECH...?
MAYBE HE JUST NEEDS HIS MASTER TO ACT LIKE A PROPER NOBLE.
NOW THEN, IF YOU WOULD FOLLOW ME.
コツ
STEP
STEP
コツ
STEP
コツ
コツ
STEP
YOU THERE, ATTENDANT. AREN'T YOU WALKING TOO FAST?

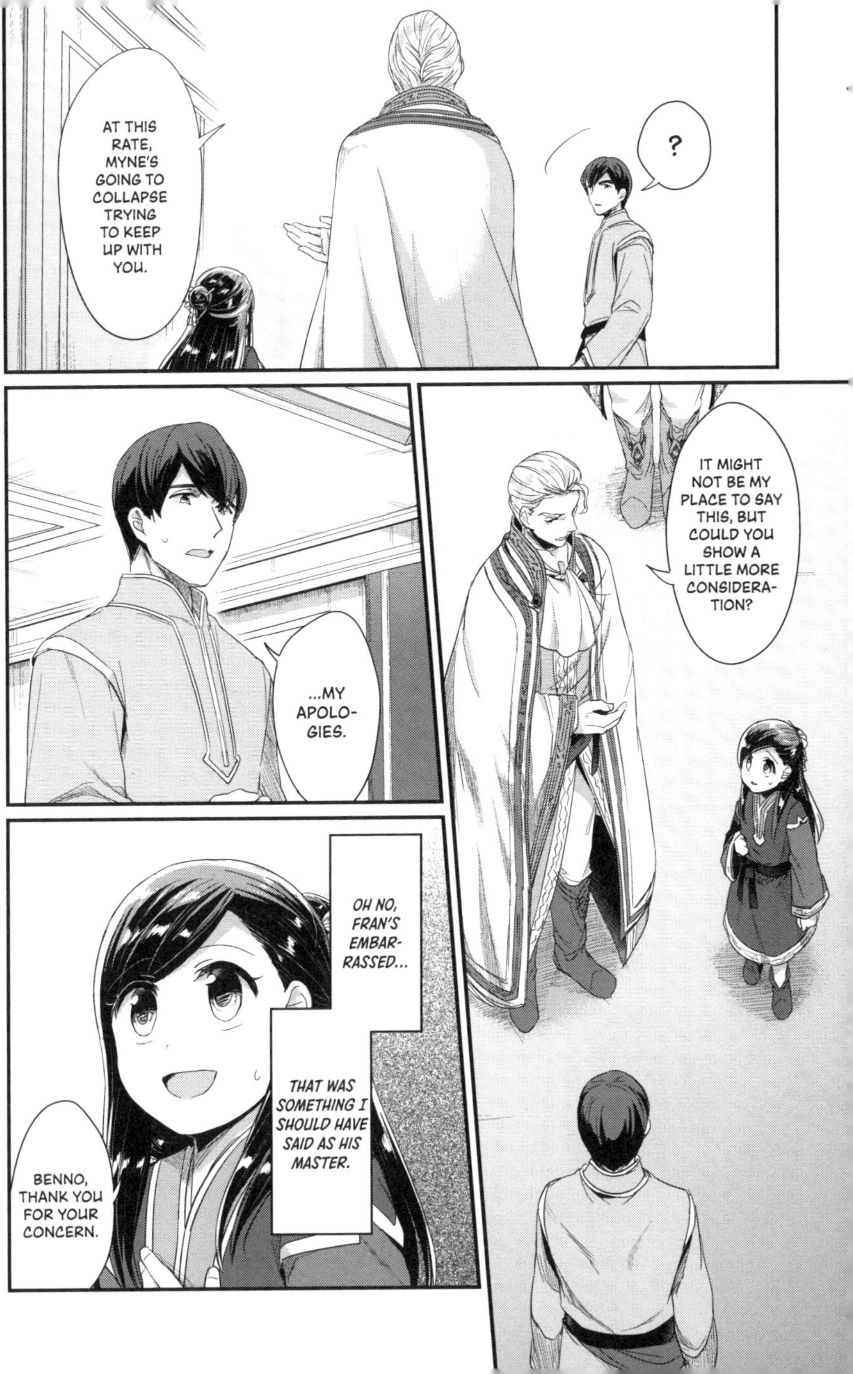
AT THIS RATE, MYNE'S GOING TO COLLAPSE TRYING TO KEEP UP WITH YOU.
?
IT MIGHT NOT BE MY PLACE TO SAY THIS, BUT COULD YOU SHOW A LITTLE MORE CONSIDERA-TION?
...MY APOLO-GIES.
OH NO, FRAN'S EMBAR-RASSED...
THAT WAS SOMETHING I SHOULD HAVE SAID AS HIS MASTER.
BENNO, THANK YOU FOR YOUR CONCERN.

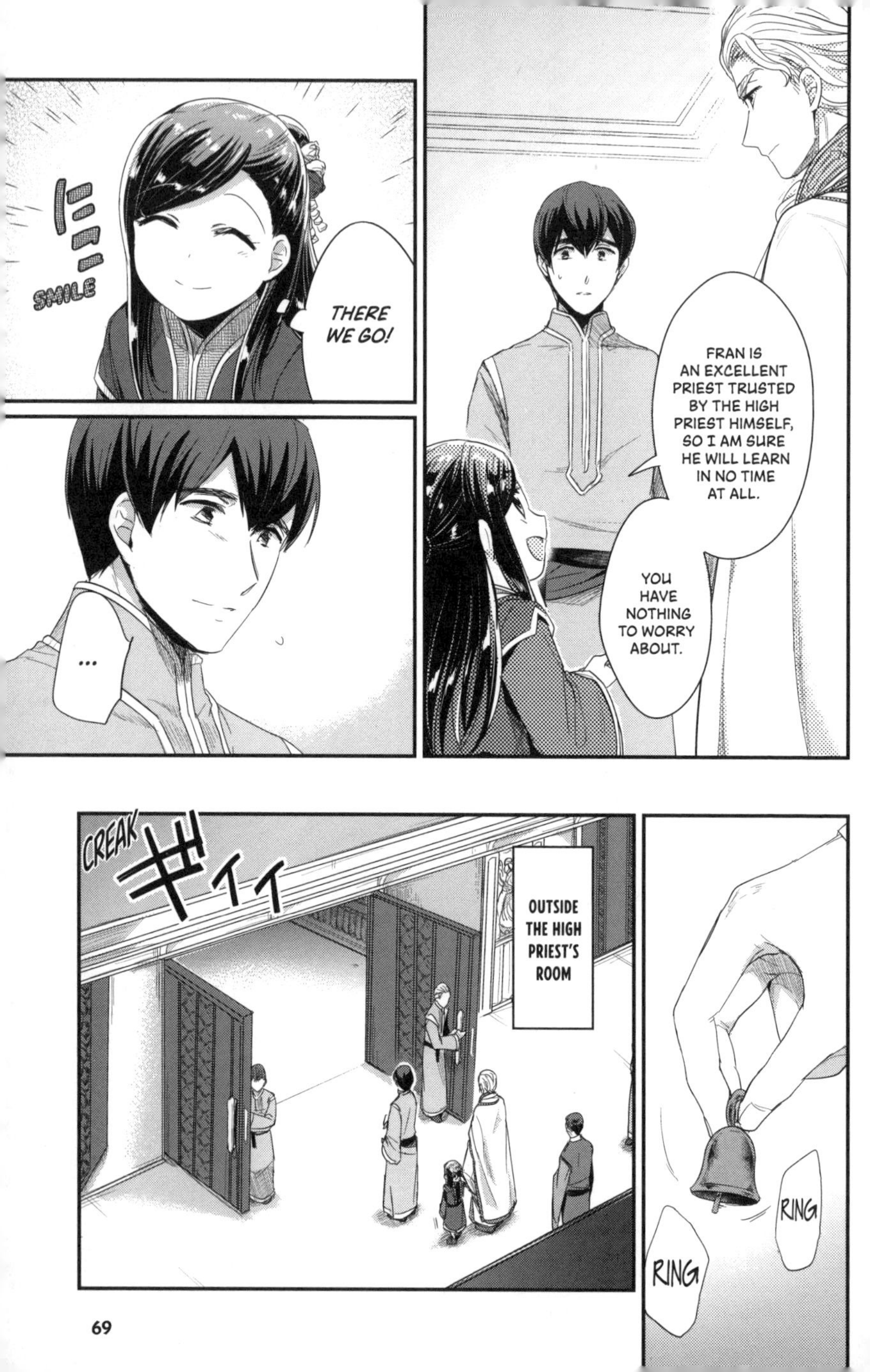
FRAN IS AN EXCELLENT PRIEST TRUSTED BY THE HIGH PRIEST HIMSELF, SO I AM SURE HE WILL LEARN IN NO TIME AT ALL.
YOU HAVE NOTHING TO WORRY ABOUT.
SMILE
THERE WE GO!
...
RING
RING
CREAK
OUTSIDE THE HIGH PRIEST'S ROOM

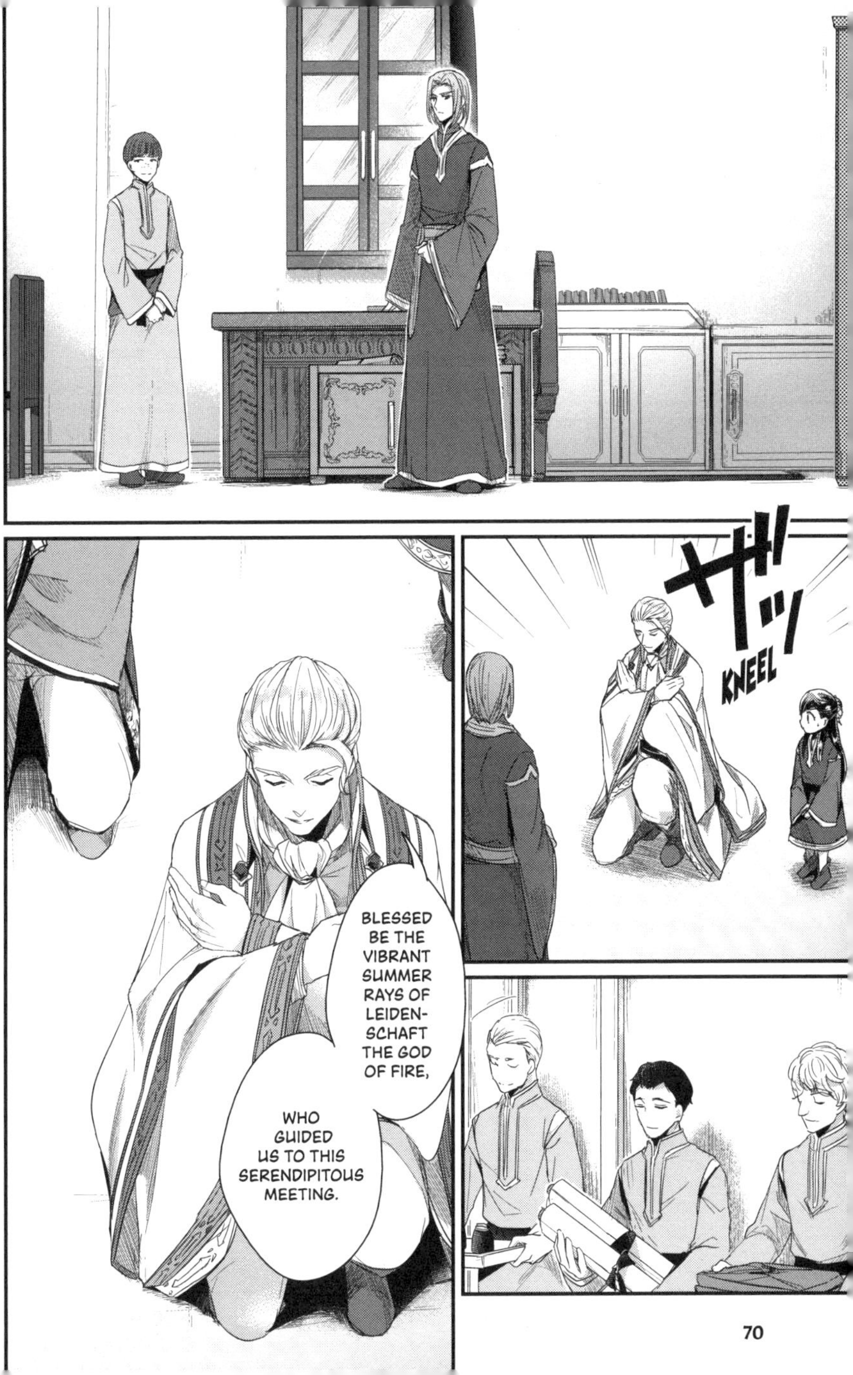

KNEEL
BLESSED BE THE VIBRANT SUMMER RAYS OF LEIDEN-SCHAFT THE GOD OF FIRE,
WHO GUIDED US TO THIS SERENDIPITOUS MEETING.

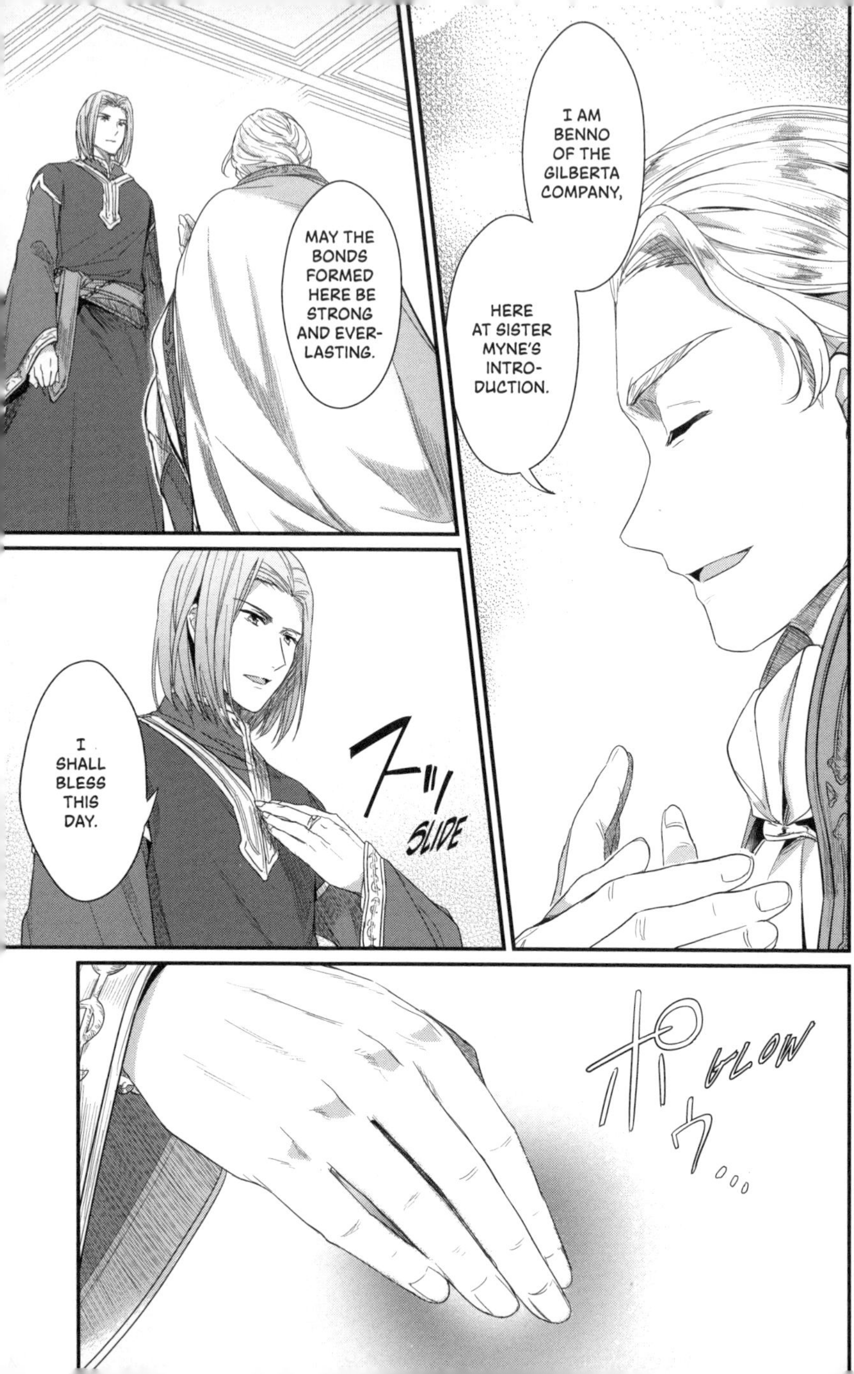
I AM BENNO OF THE GILBERTA COMPANY,
HERE AT SISTER MYNE'S INTRO-DUCTION.
MAY THE BONDS FORMED HERE BE STRONG AND EVER-LASTING.
I SHALL BLESS THIS DAY.
SLIDE
BLOW

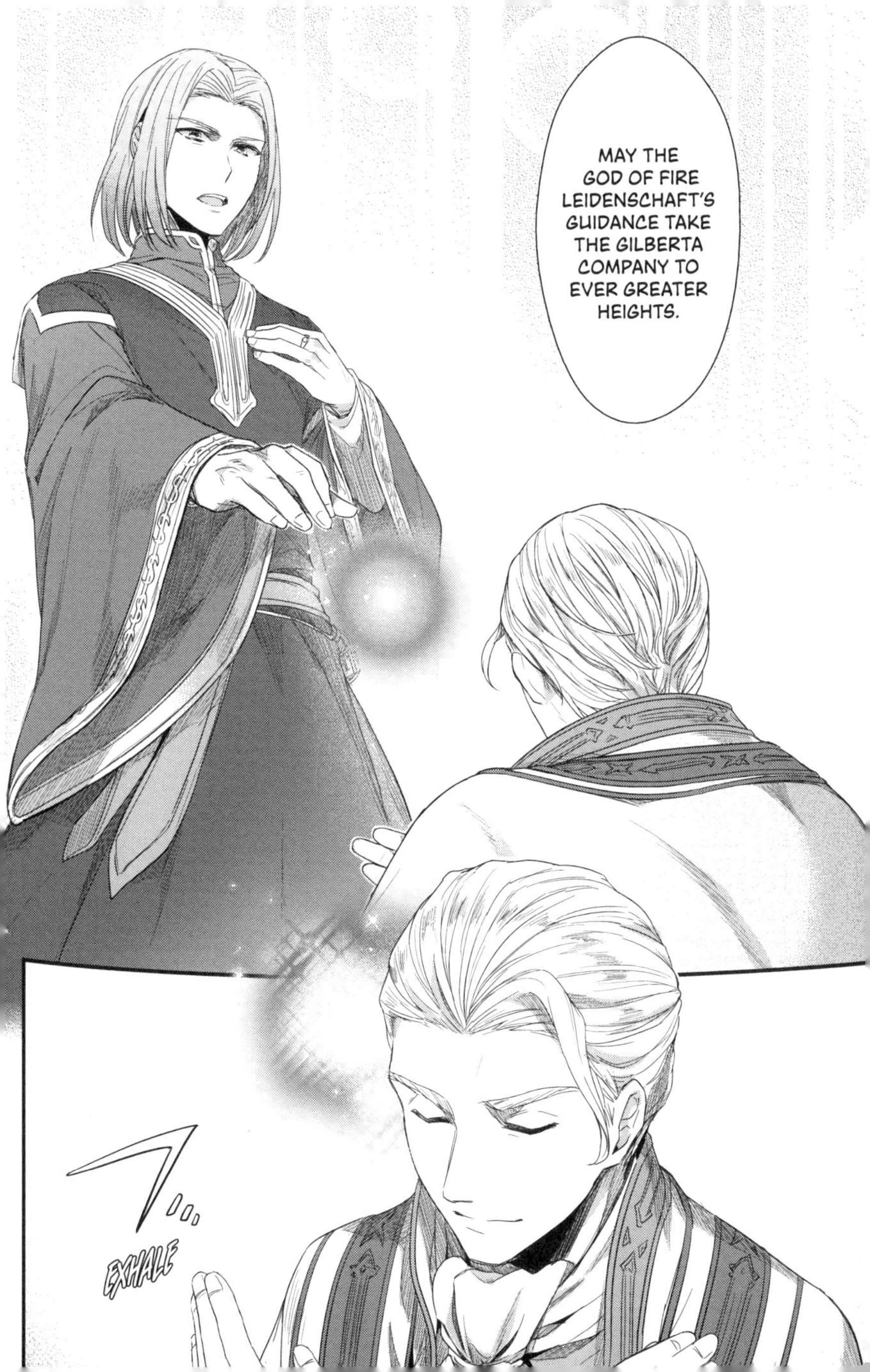
MAY THE GOD OF FIRE LEIDENSCHAFT'S GUIDANCE TAKE THE GILBERTA COMPANY TO EVER GREATER HEIGHTS.
EXHALE

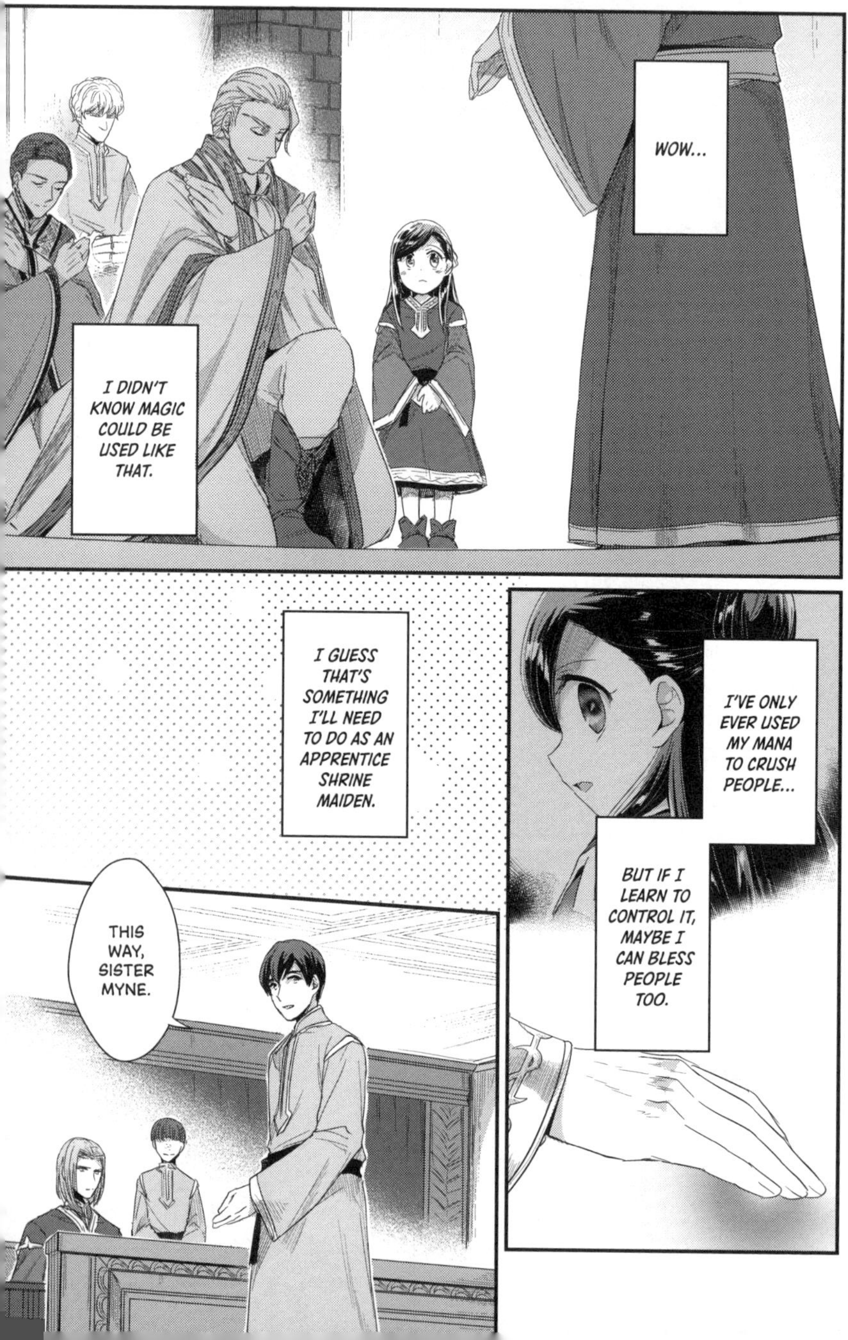
WOW...
I DIDN'T KNOW MAGIC COULD BE USED LIKE THAT.
I'VE ONLY EVER USED MY MANA TO CRUSH PEOPLE...
BUT IF I LEARN TO CONTROL IT, MAYBE I CAN BLESS PEOPLE TOO.
I GUESS THAT'S SOMETHING I'LL NEED TO DO AS AN APPRENTICE SHRINE MAIDEN.
THIS WAY, SISTER MYNE.

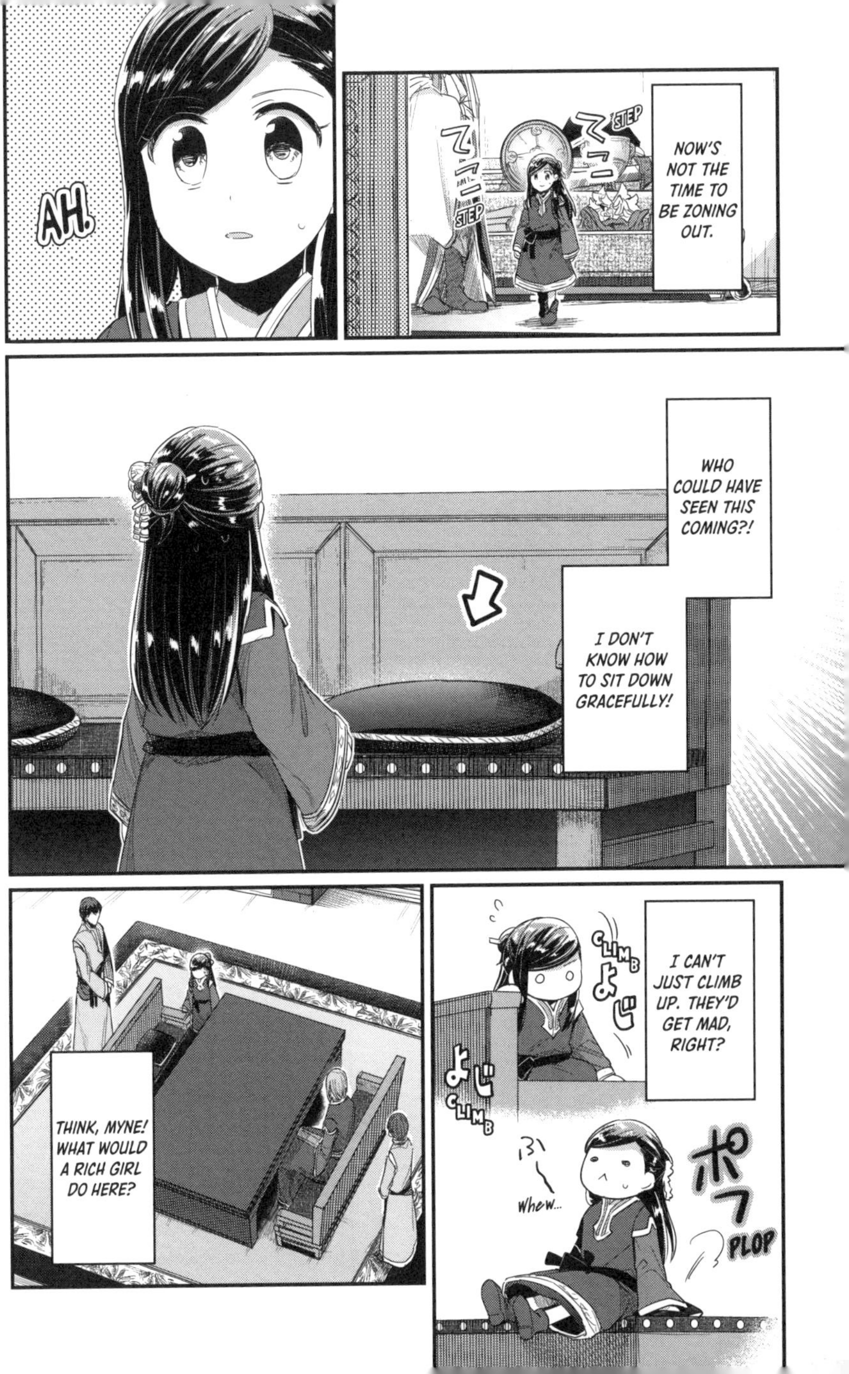
STEP
STEP
NOW'S NOT THE TIME TO BE ZONING OUT.
AH.
WHO COULD HAVE SEEN THIS COMING?!
I DON'T KNOW HOW TO SIT DOWN GRACEFULLY!
I CAN'T JUST CLIMB UP. THEY'D GET MAD, RIGHT?
よじ
CLIMB
よじ
CLIMB
Whew...
ポフ
PLOP
THINK, MYNE! WHAT WOULD A RICH GIRL DO HERE?

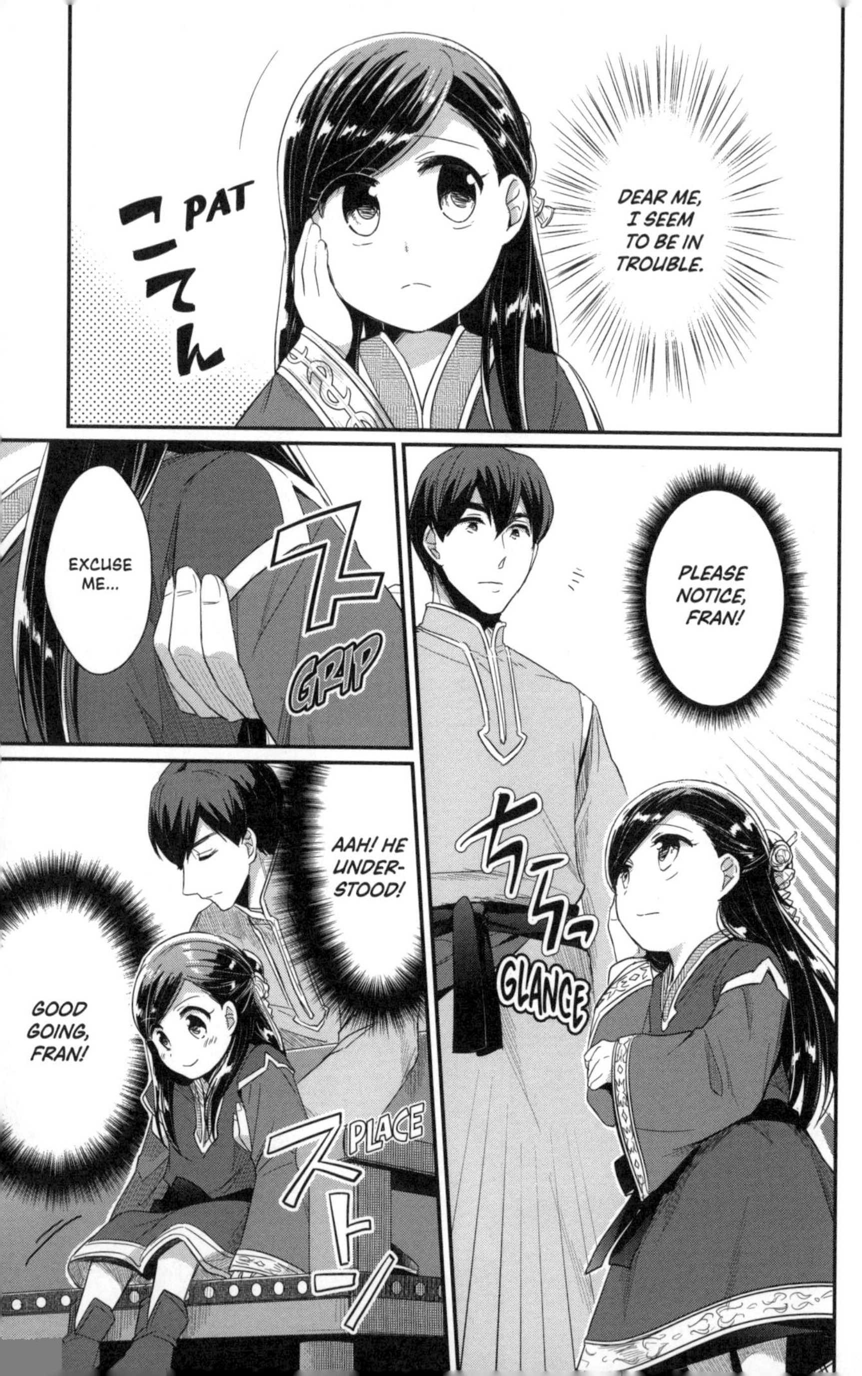
DEAR ME, I SEEM TO BE IN TROUBLE.
こてん
PAT
PLEASE NOTICE, FRAN!
ちらっ
GLANCE
EXCUSE ME...
ス
GRIP
AAH! HE UNDER-STOOD!
GOOD GOING, FRAN!
ストー
PLACE

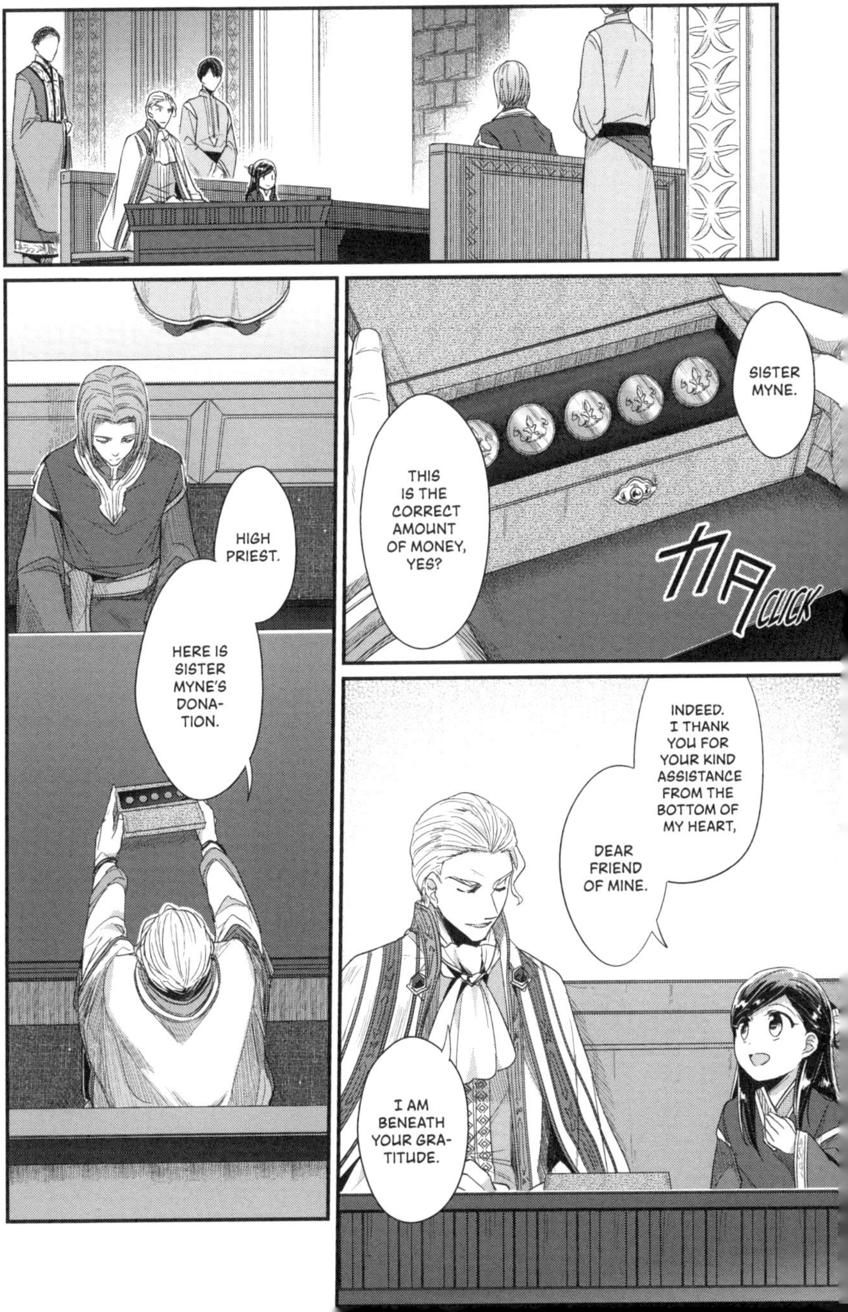
SISTER MYNE.
THIS IS THE CORRECT AMOUNT OF MONEY, YES?
カチ CLICK
INDEED. I THANK YOU FOR YOUR KIND ASSISTANCE FROM THE BOTTOM OF MY HEART,
DEAR FRIEND OF MINE.
I AM BENEATH YOUR GRATITUDE.
HIGH PRIEST.
HERE IS SISTER MYNE'S DONATION.

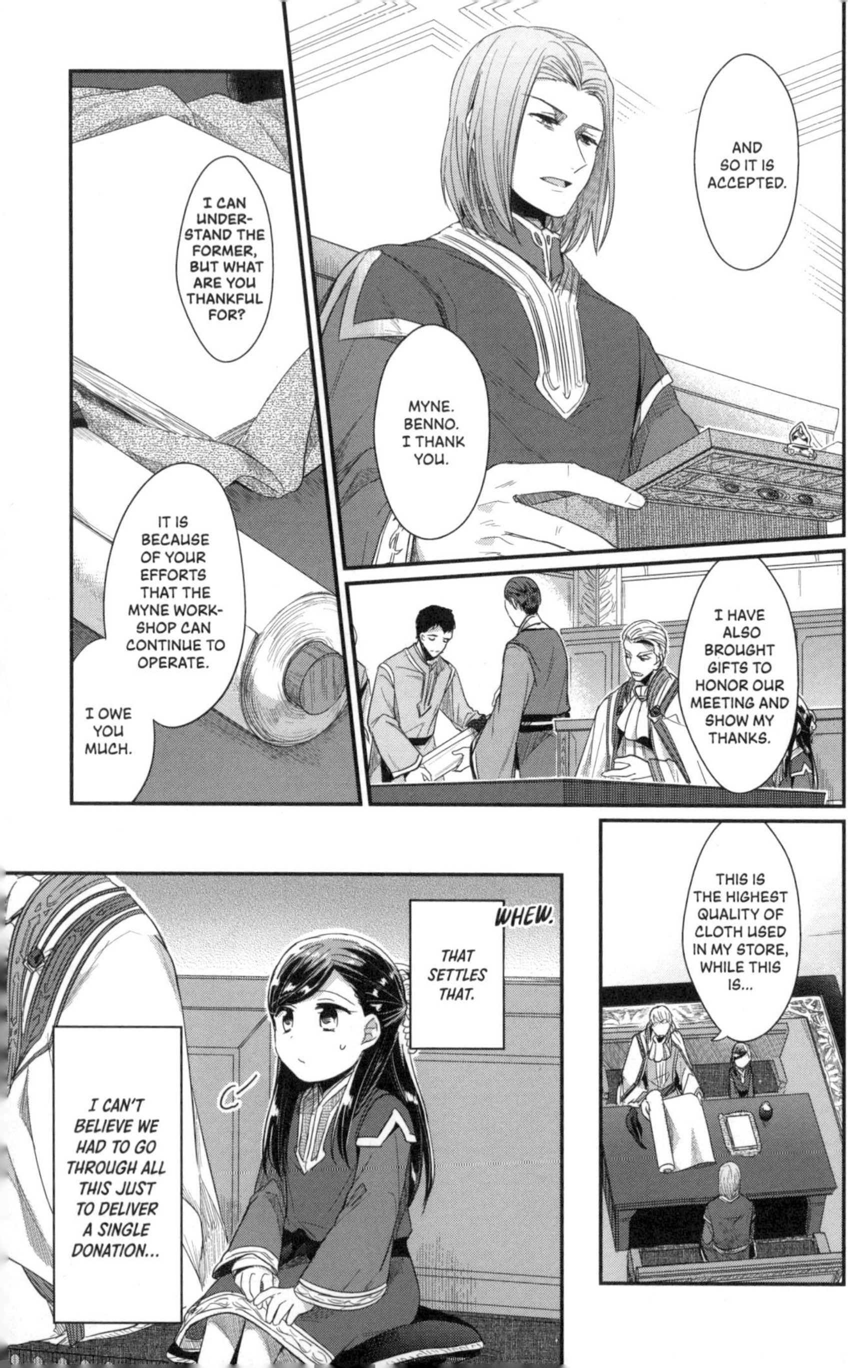
AND SO IT IS ACCEPTED.
MYNE. BENNO. I THANK YOU.
I HAVE ALSO BROUGHT GIFTS TO HONOR OUR MEETING AND SHOW MY THANKS.
I CAN UNDER-STAND THE FORMER, BUT WHAT ARE YOU THANKFUL FOR?
IT IS BECAUSE OF YOUR EFFORTS THAT THE MYNE WORK-SHOP CAN CONTINUE TO OPERATE.
I OWE YOU MUCH.
THIS IS THE HIGHEST QUALITY OF CLOTH USED IN MY STORE, WHILE THIS IS...
WHEW.
THAT SETTLES THAT.
I CAN'T BELIEVE WE HAD TO GO THROUGH ALL THIS JUST TO DELIVER A SINGLE DONATION...

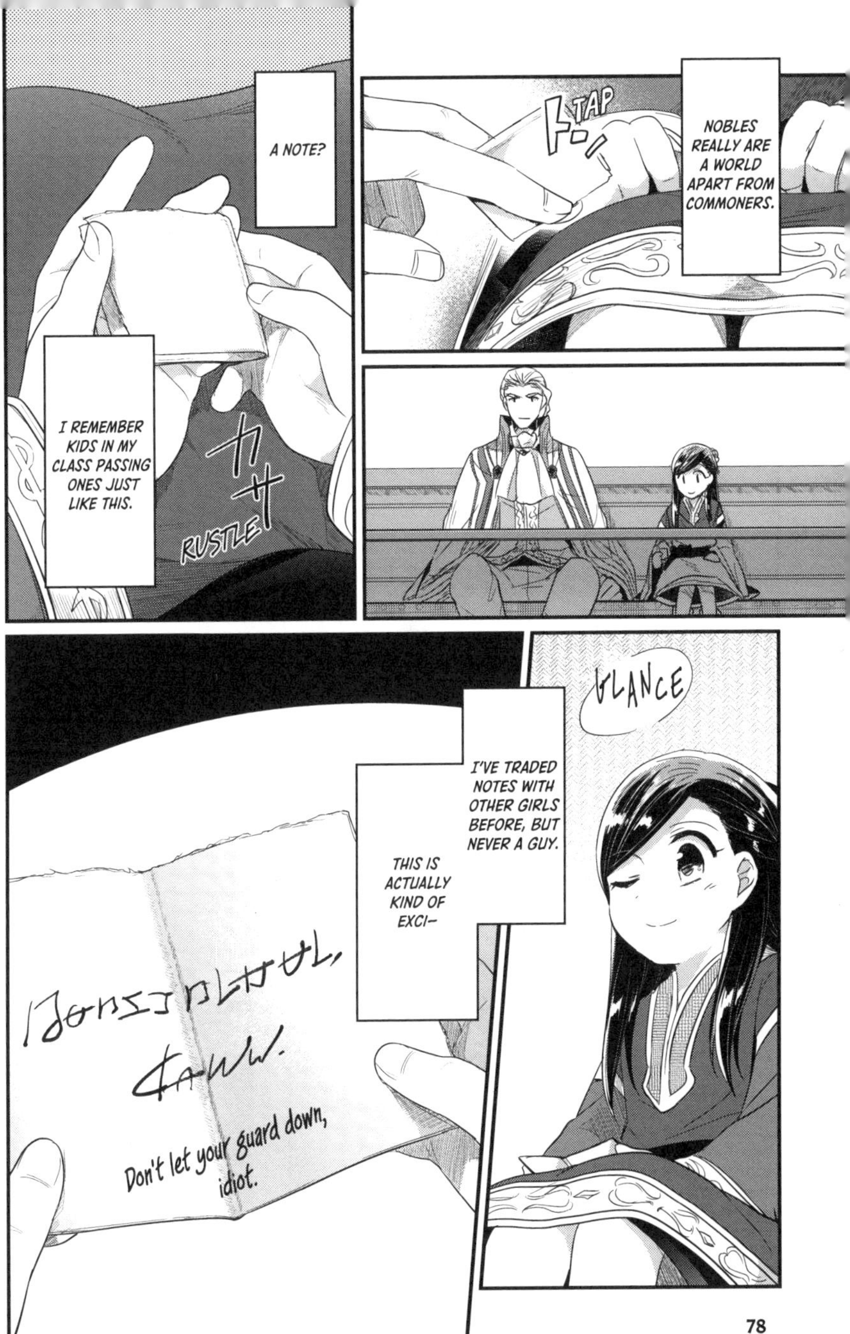
TAP
NOBLES REALLY ARE A WORLD APART FROM COMMONERS.
A NOTE?
I REMEMBER KIDS IN MY CLASS PASSING ONES JUST LIKE THIS.
RUSTLE
GLANCE
I'VE TRADED NOTES WITH OTHER GIRLS BEFORE, BUT NEVER A GUY.
THIS IS ACTUALLY KIND OF EXCI–
Don't let your guard down, idiot.

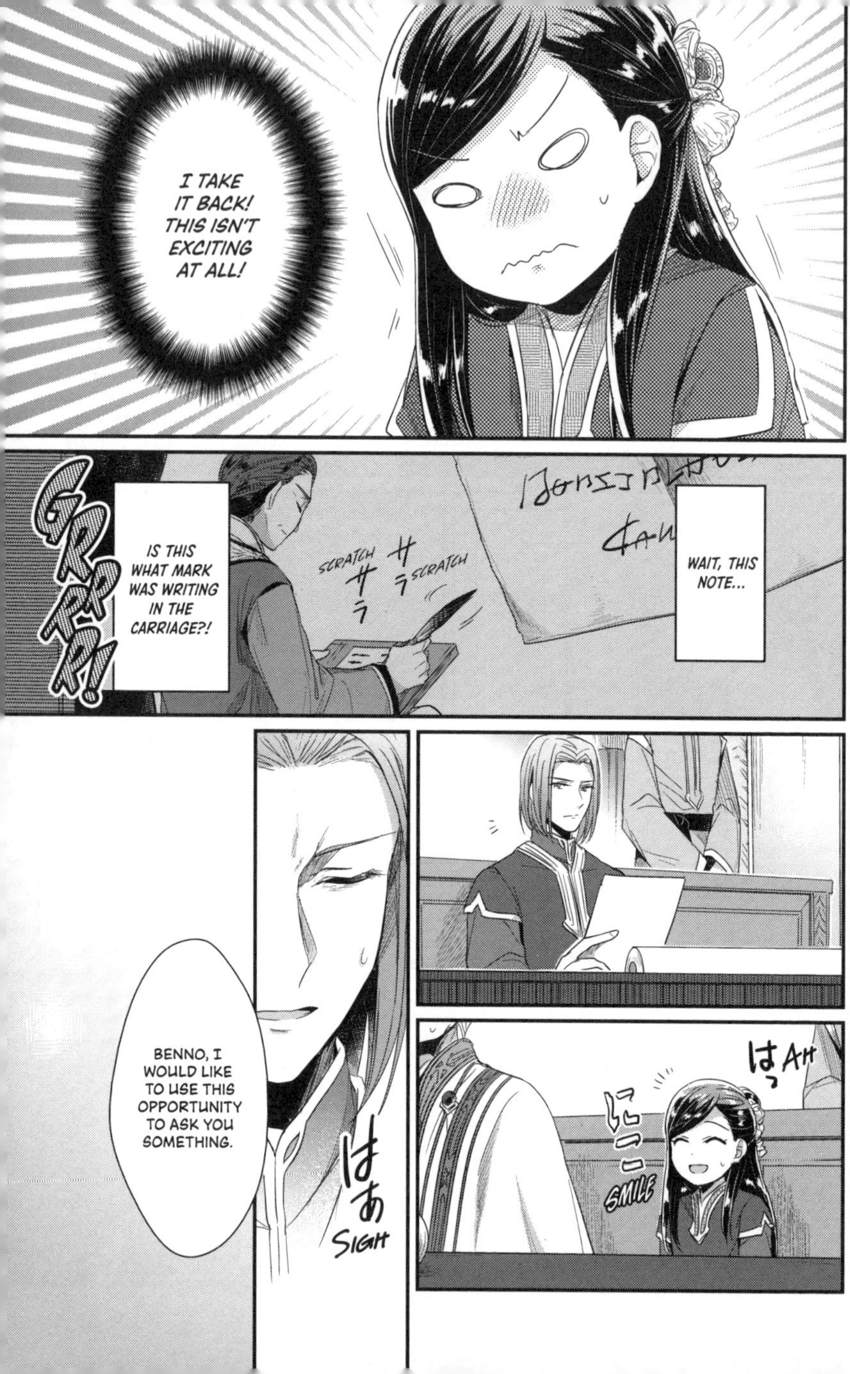
I TAKE IT BACK! THIS ISN'T EXCITING AT ALL!
WAIT, THIS NOTE...
サラ SCRATCH
サラ SCRATCH
IS THIS WHAT MARK WAS WRITING IN THE CARRIAGE?!
GRRRR!
はっ AH
にこー SMILE
はあ SIGH
BENNO, I WOULD LIKE TO USE THIS OPPORTUNITY TO ASK YOU SOMETHING.

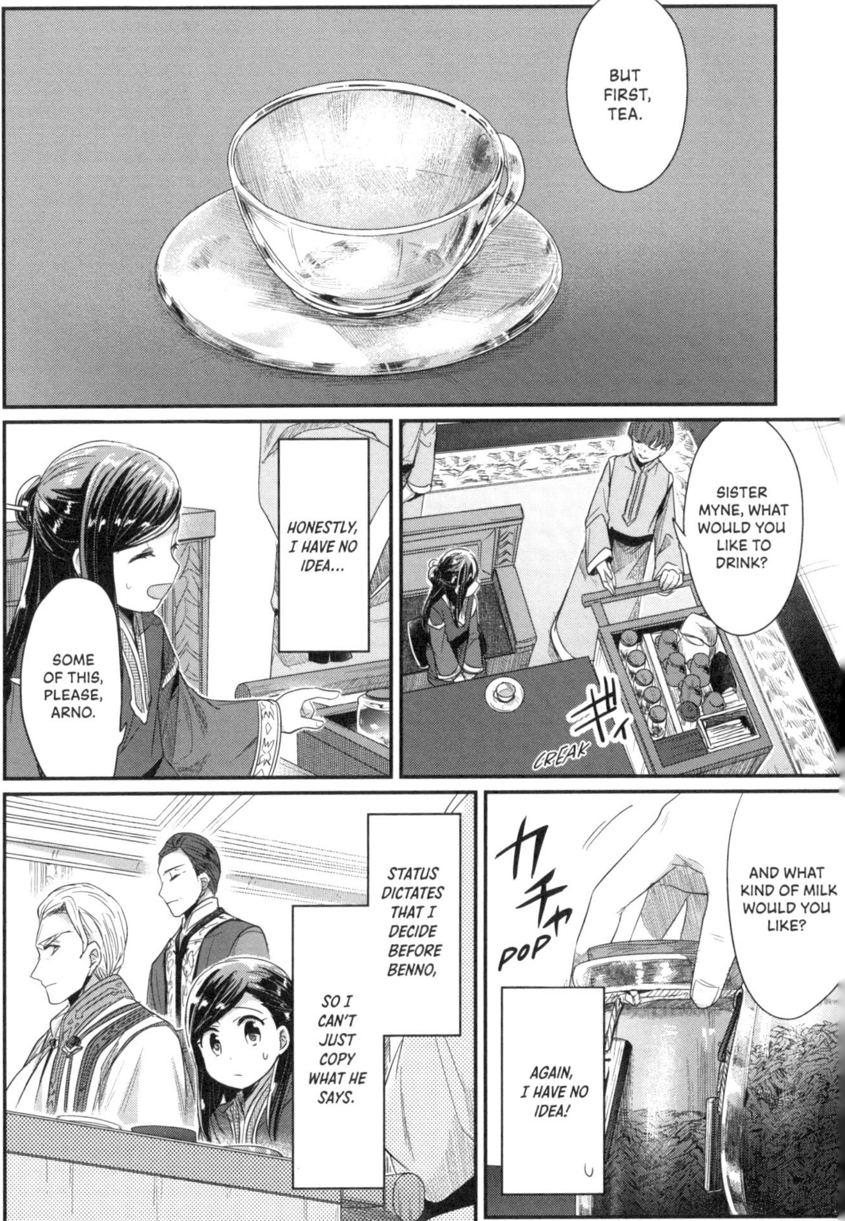
BUT FIRST, TEA.
SISTER MYNE, WHAT WOULD YOU LIKE TO DRINK?
ギィ
CREAK
HONESTLY, I HAVE NO IDEA...
SOME OF THIS, PLEASE, ARNO.
AND WHAT KIND OF MILK WOULD YOU LIKE?
カチャ
POP
AGAIN, I HAVE NO IDEA!
STATUS DICTATES THAT I DECIDE BEFORE BENNO,
SO I CAN'T JUST COPY WHAT HE SAYS.

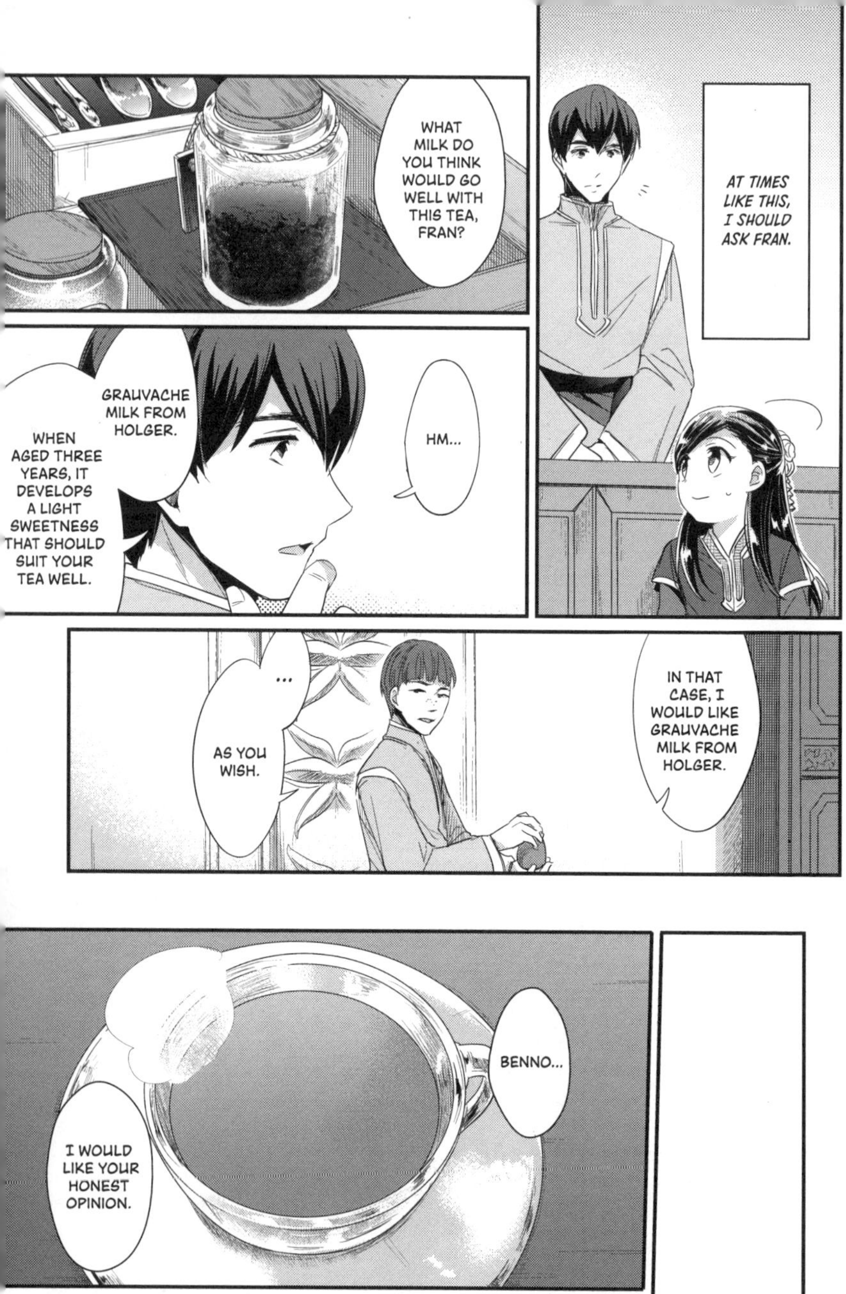
AT TIMES LIKE THIS, I SHOULD ASK FRAN.
WHAT MILK DO YOU THINK WOULD GO WELL WITH THIS TEA, FRAN?
HM...
GRAUVACHE MILK FROM HOLGER.
WHEN AGED THREE YEARS, IT DEVELOPS A LIGHT SWEETNESS THAT SHOULD SUIT YOUR TEA WELL.
IN THAT CASE, I WOULD LIKE GRAUVACHE MILK FROM HOLGER.
...
AS YOU WISH.
BENNO...
I WOULD LIKE YOUR HONEST OPINION.

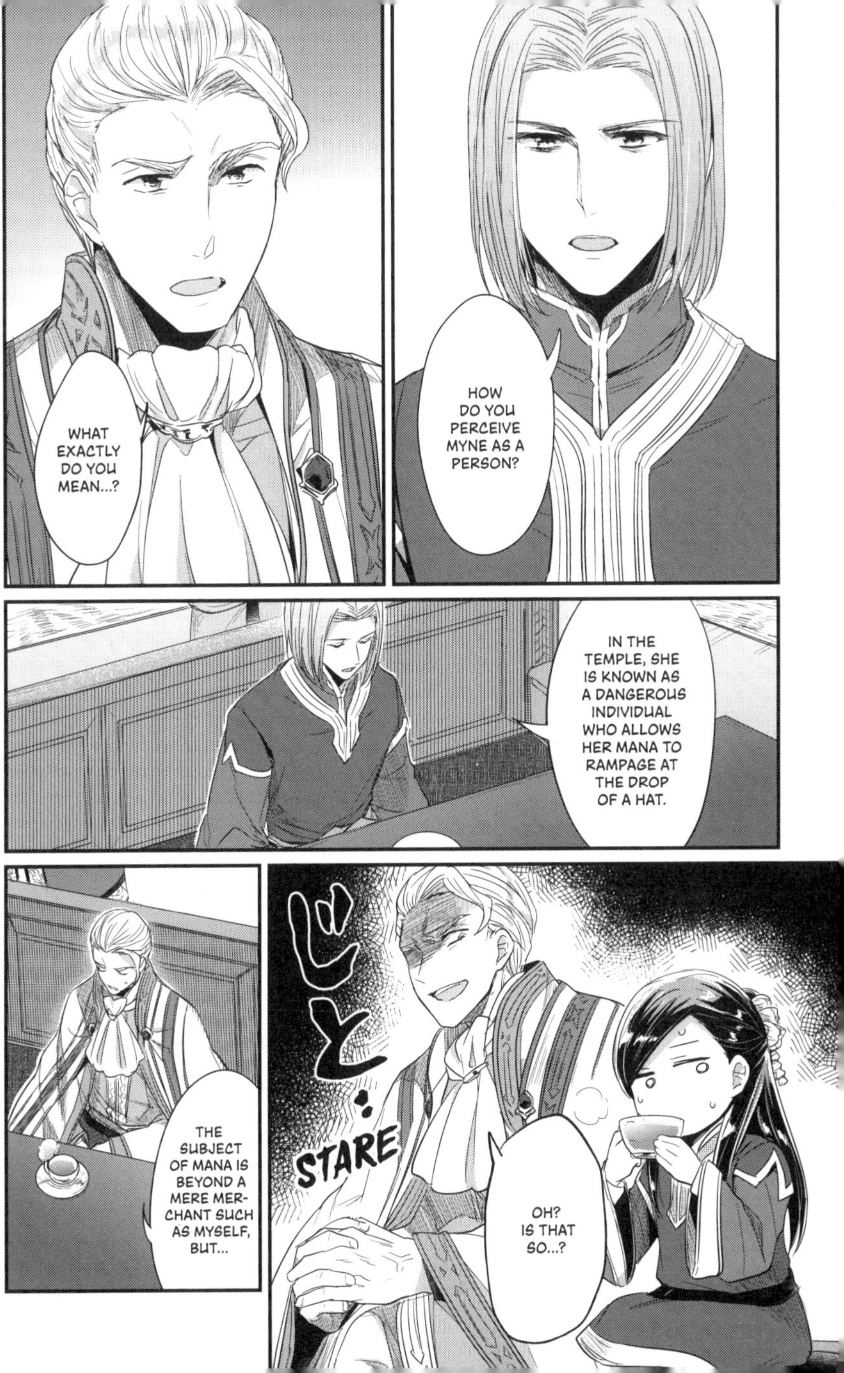
HOW DO YOU PERCEIVE MYNE AS A PERSON?
WHAT EXACTLY DO YOU MEAN...?
IN THE TEMPLE, SHE IS KNOWN AS A DANGEROUS INDIVIDUAL WHO ALLOWS HER MANA TO RAMPAGE AT THE DROP OF A HAT.
じと
STARE
OH? IS THAT SO...?
THE SUBJECT OF MANA IS BEYOND A MERE MER-CHANT SUCH AS MYSELF, BUT...

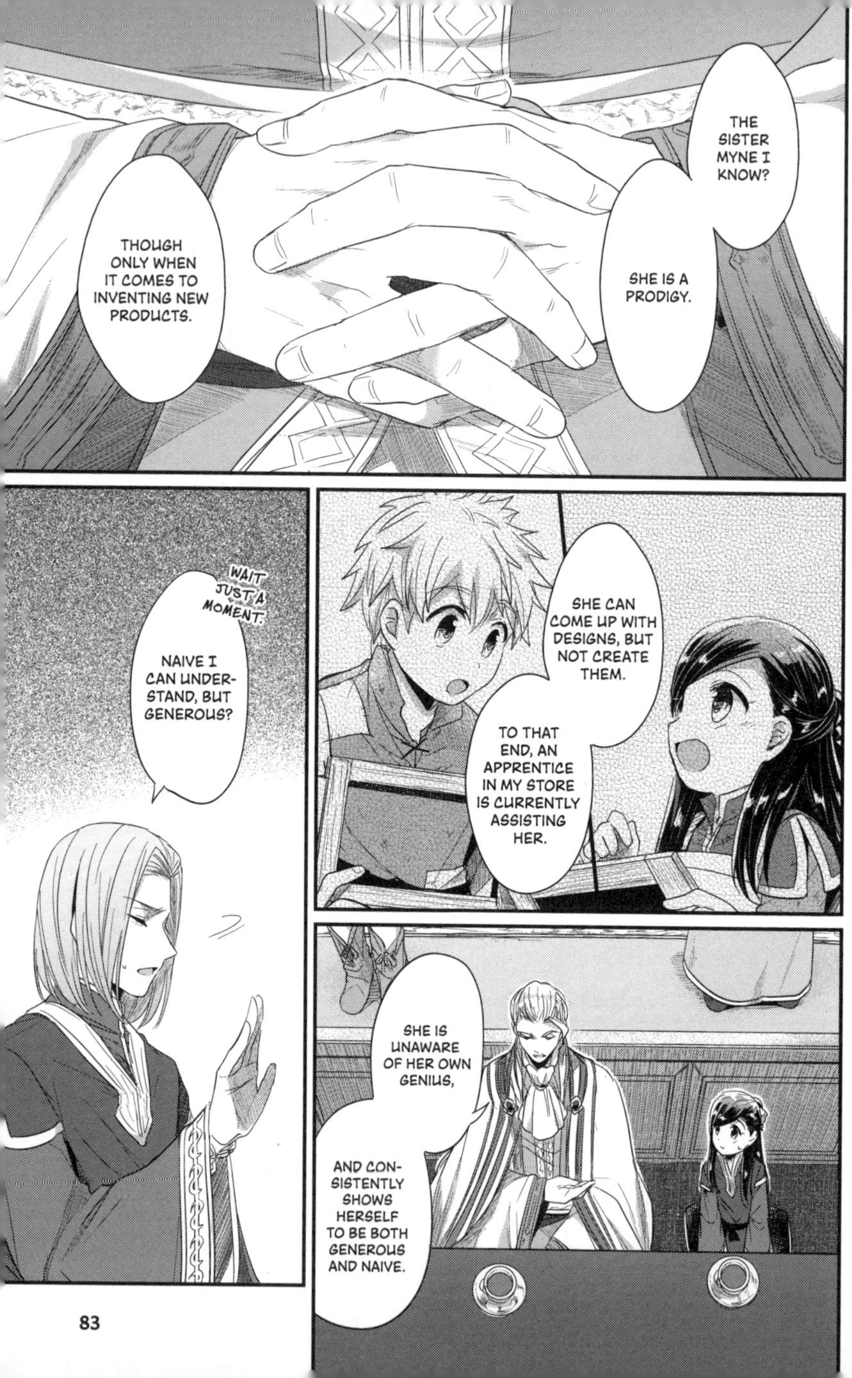
THE SISTER MYNE I KNOW?
SHE IS A PRODIGY.
THOUGH ONLY WHEN IT COMES TO INVENTING NEW PRODUCTS.
SHE CAN COME UP WITH DESIGNS, BUT NOT CREATE THEM.
TO THAT END, AN APPRENTICE IN MY STORE IS CURRENTLY ASSISTING HER.
SHE IS UNAWARE OF HER OWN GENIUS,
AND CON-SISTENTLY SHOWS HERSELF TO BE BOTH GENEROUS AND NAIVE.
WAIT JUST A MOMENT.
NAIVE I CAN UNDER-STAND, BUT GENEROUS?

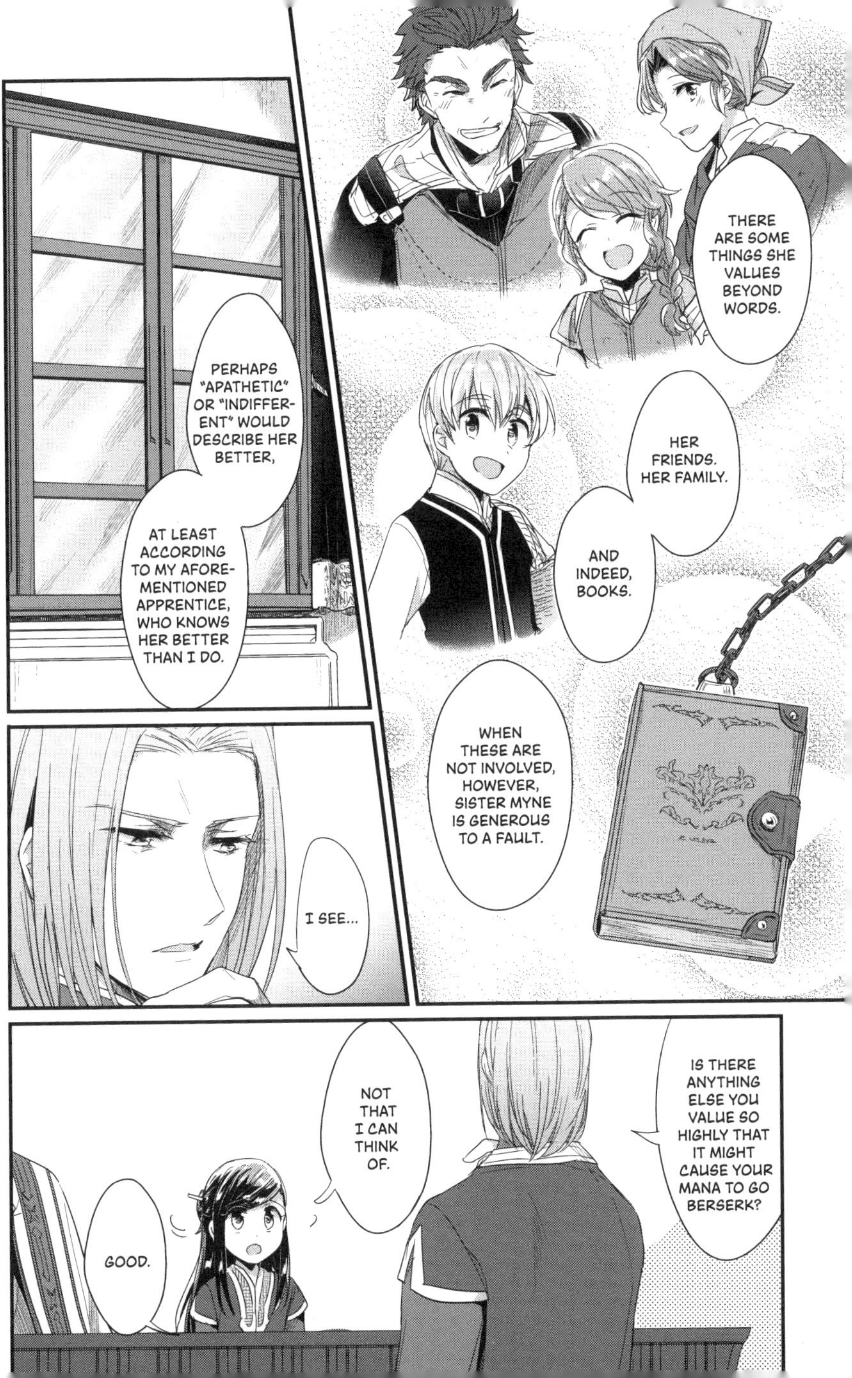
THERE ARE SOME THINGS SHE VALUES BEYOND WORDS.
HER FRIENDS. HER FAMILY.
AND INDEED, BOOKS.
WHEN THESE ARE NOT INVOLVED, HOWEVER, SISTER MYNE IS GENEROUS TO A FAULT.
PERHAPS "APATHETIC" OR "INDIFFER-ENT" WOULD DESCRIBE HER BETTER,
AT LEAST ACCORDING TO MY AFORE-MENTIONED APPRENTICE, WHO KNOWS HER BETTER THAN I DO.
I SEE...
IS THERE ANYTHING ELSE YOU VALUE SO HIGHLY THAT IT MIGHT CAUSE YOUR MANA TO GO BERSERK?
NOT THAT I CAN THINK OF.
GOOD.

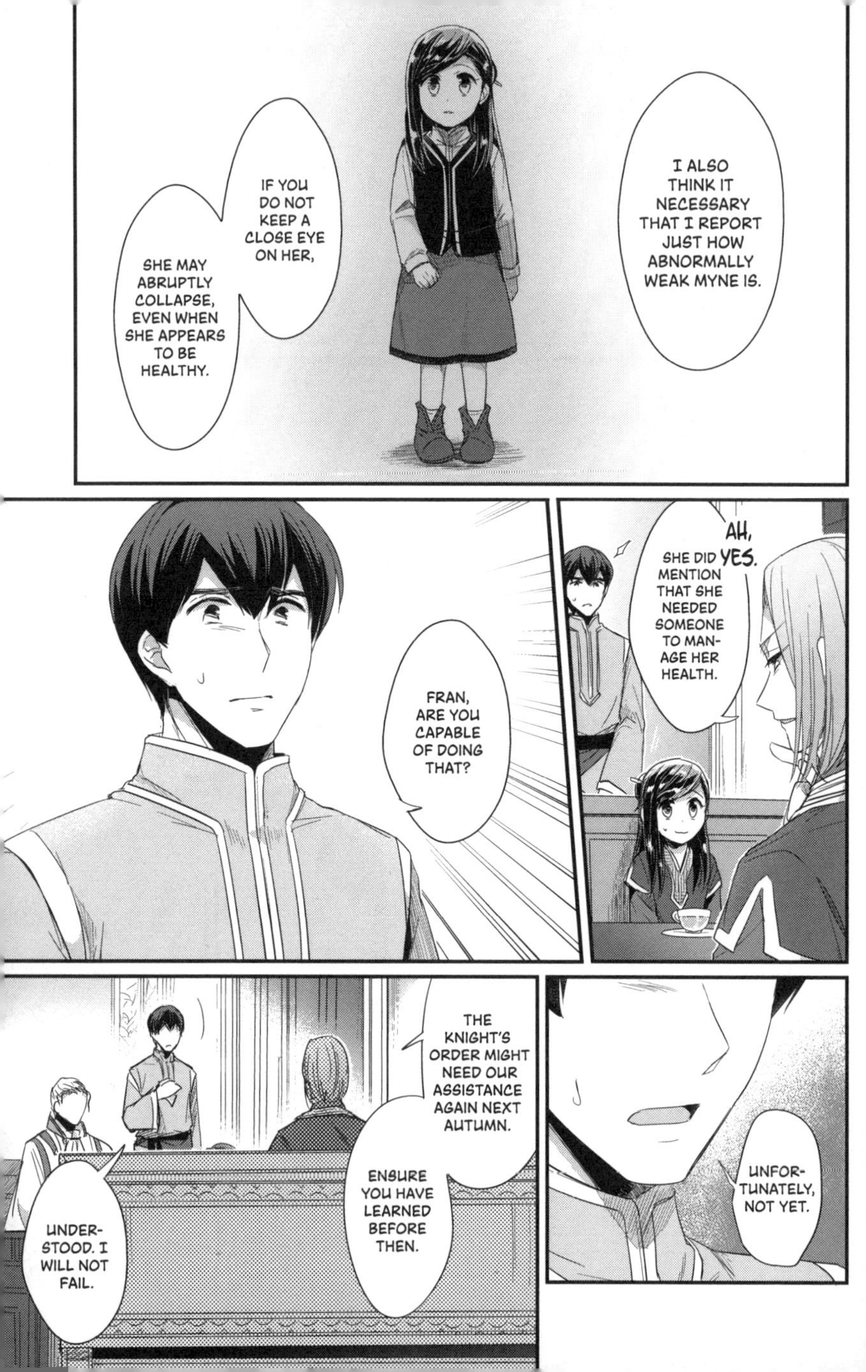
I ALSO THINK IT NECESSARY THAT I REPORT JUST HOW ABNORMALLY WEAK MYNE IS.
IF YOU DO NOT KEEP A CLOSE EYE ON HER,
SHE MAY ABRUPTLY COLLAPSE, EVEN WHEN SHE APPEARS TO BE HEALTHY.
AH, YES. SHE DID MENTION THAT SHE NEEDED SOMEONE TO MAN-AGE HER HEALTH.
FRAN, ARE YOU CAPABLE OF DOING THAT?
UNFOR-TUNATELY, NOT YET.
THE KNIGHT'S ORDER MIGHT NEED OUR ASSISTANCE AGAIN NEXT AUTUMN.
ENSURE YOU HAVE LEARNED BEFORE THEN.
UNDER-STOOD. I WILL NOT FAIL.

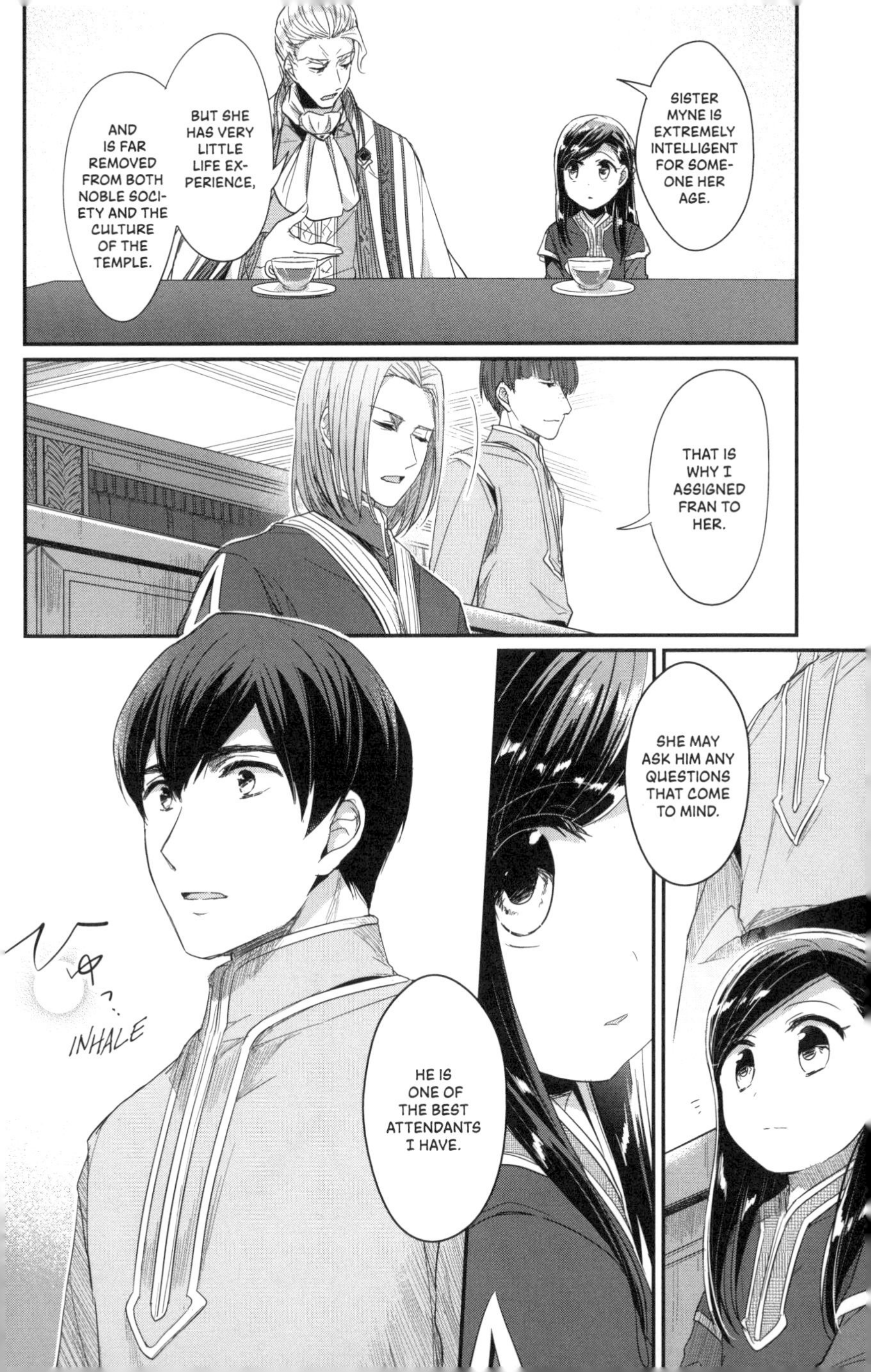
SISTER MYNE IS EXTREMELY INTELLIGENT FOR SOME-ONE HER AGE.
BUT SHE HAS VERY LITTLE LIFE EX-PERIENCE,
AND IS FAR REMOVED FROM BOTH NOBLE SOCI-ETY AND THE CULTURE OF THE TEMPLE.
THAT IS WHY I ASSIGNED FRAN TO HER.
SHE MAY ASK HIM ANY QUESTIONS THAT COME TO MIND.
HE IS ONE OF THE BEST ATTENDANTS I HAVE.
INHALE

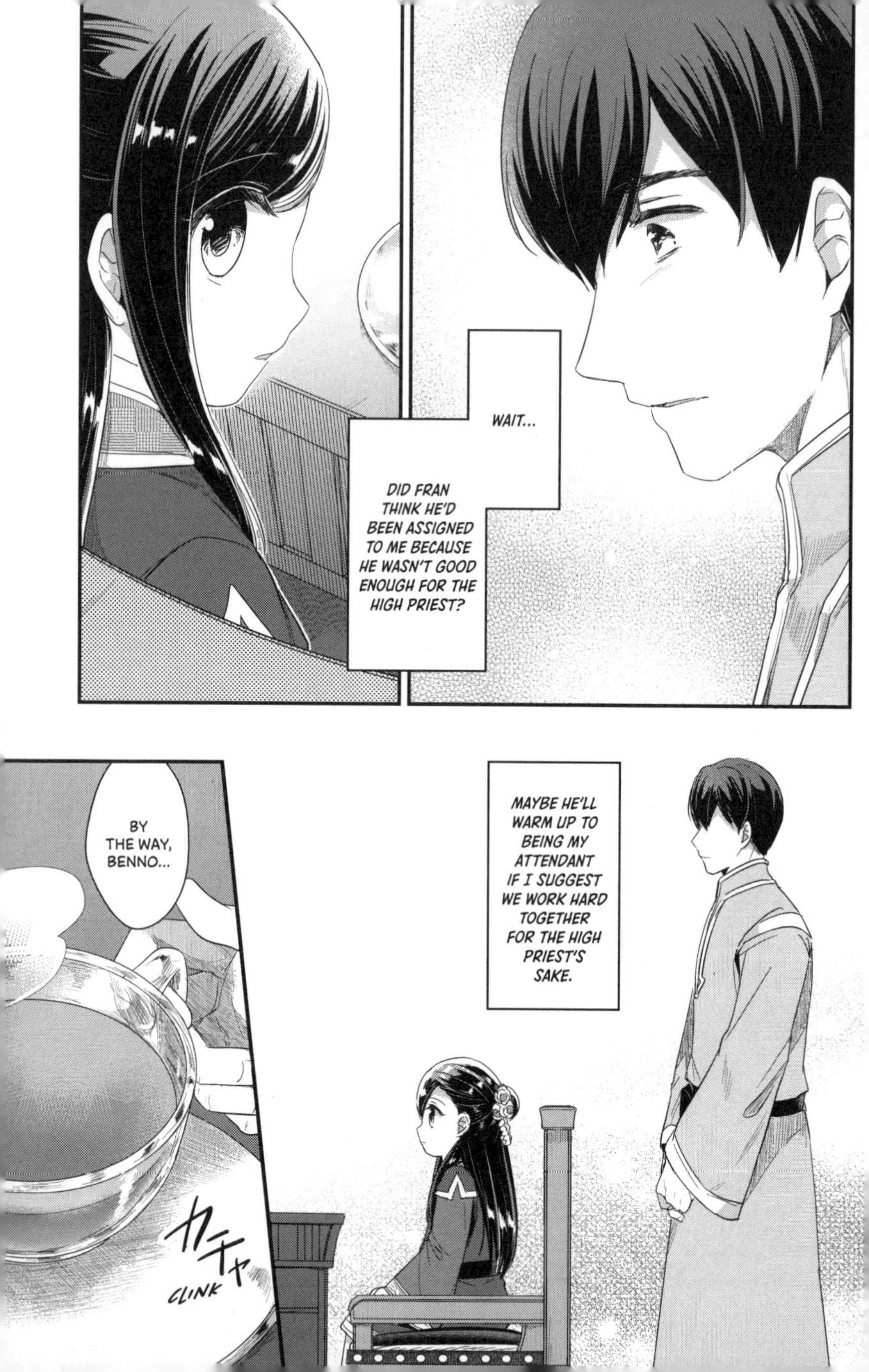
WAIT...
DID FRAN THINK HE'D BEEN ASSIGNED TO ME BECAUSE HE WASN'T GOOD ENOUGH FOR THE HIGH PRIEST?
MAYBE HE'LL WARM UP TO BEING MY ATTENDANT IF I SUGGEST WE WORK HARD TOGETHER FOR THE HIGH PRIEST'S SAKE.
BY THE WAY, BENNO...
カチャ
CLINK

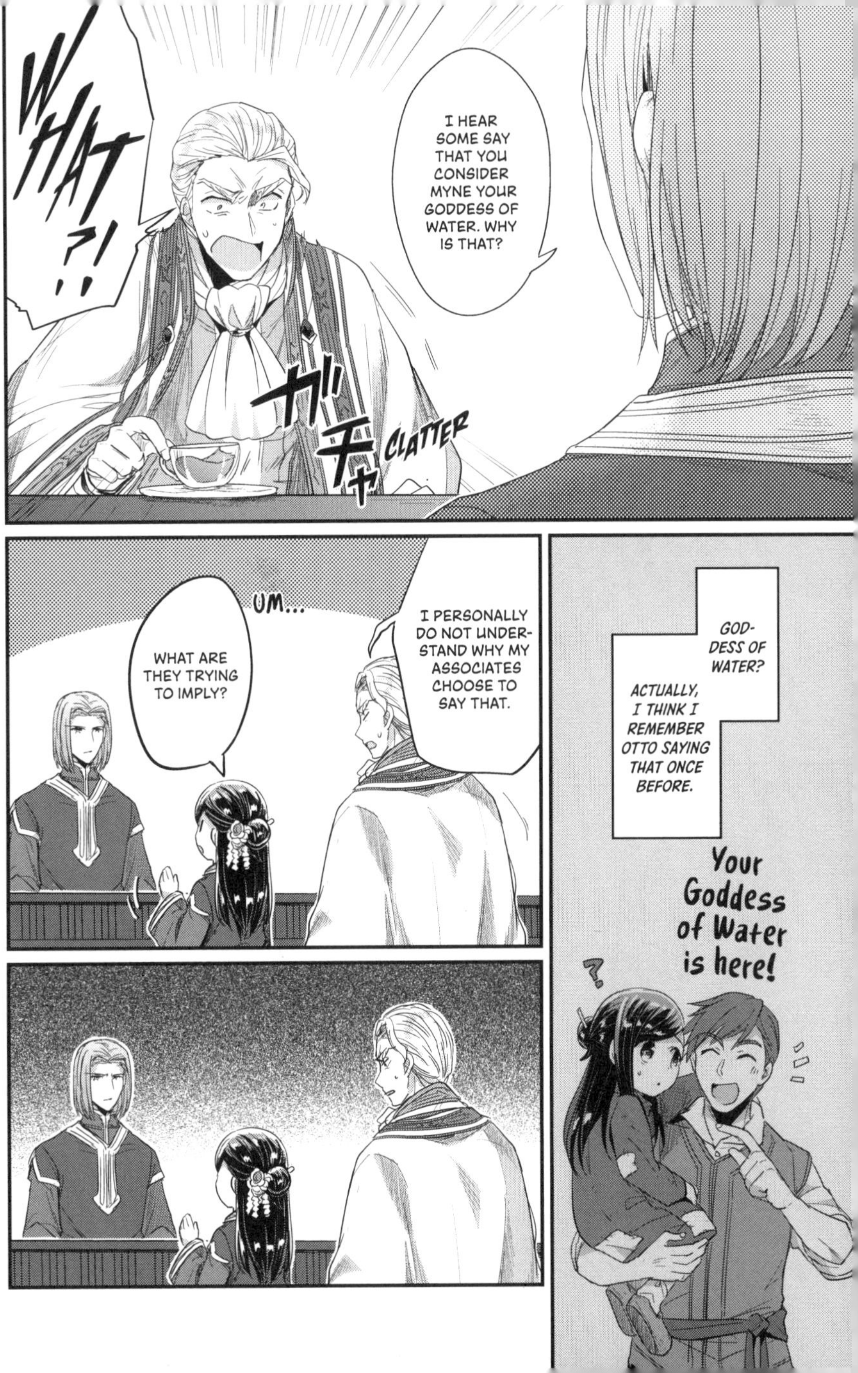
I HEAR SOME SAY THAT YOU CONSIDER MYNE YOUR GODDESS OF WATER. WHY IS THAT?
WHAT?!!
ガチャ
CLATTER
GOD-DESS OF WATER?
ACTUALLY, I THINK I REMEMBER OTTO SAYING THAT ONCE BEFORE.
Your Goddess of Water is here!
?
I PERSONALLY DO NOT UNDER-STAND WHY MY ASSOCIATES CHOOSE TO SAY THAT.
UM...
WHAT ARE THEY TRYING TO IMPLY?

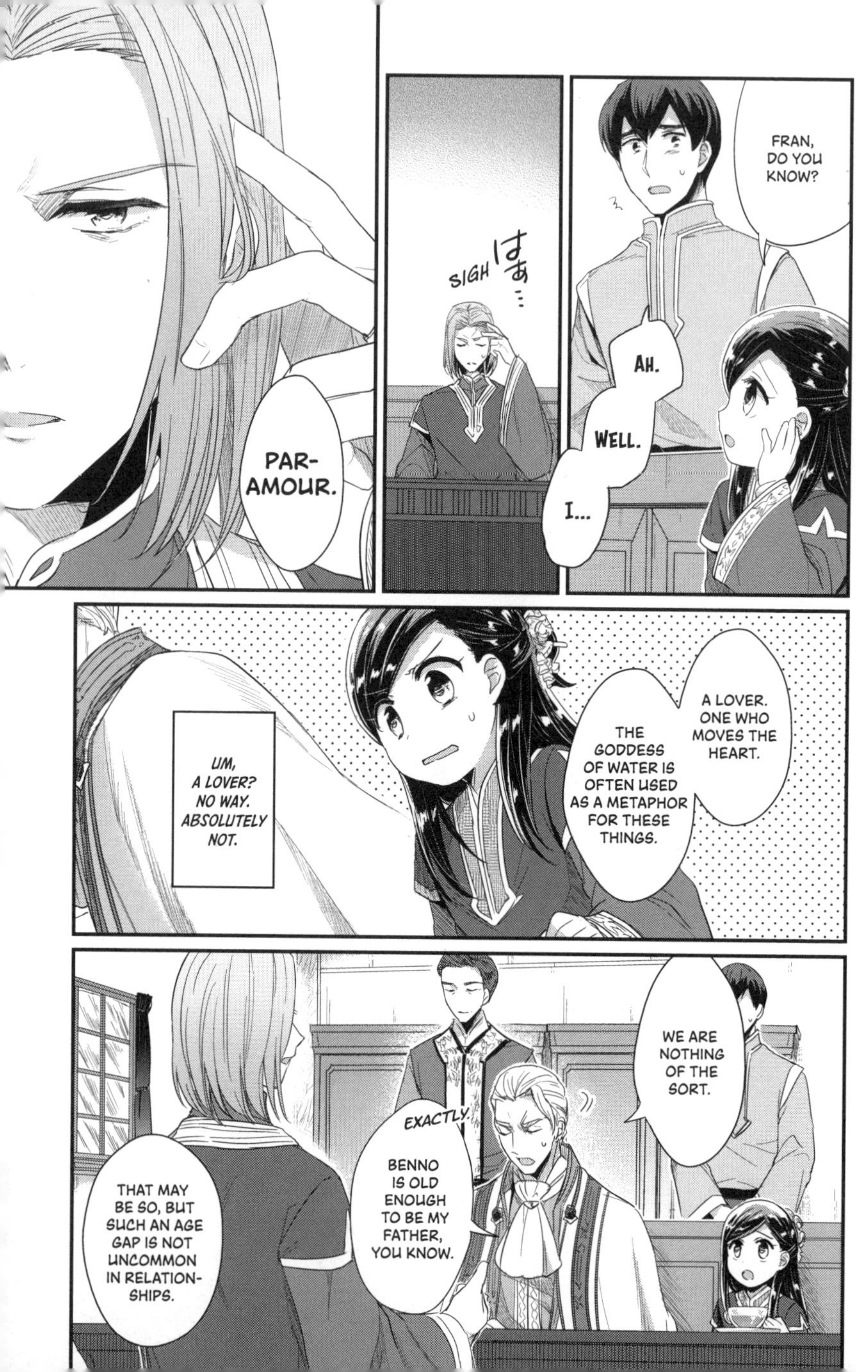
FRAN, DO YOU KNOW?
AH.
WELL.
I...
SIGH
はぁ
PAR-AMOUR.
A LOVER. ONE WHO MOVES THE HEART.
THE GODDESS OF WATER IS OFTEN USED AS A METAPHOR FOR THESE THINGS.
UM, A LOVER? NO WAY. ABSOLUTELY NOT.
WE ARE NOTHING OF THE SORT.
EXACTLY.
BENNO IS OLD ENOUGH TO BE MY FATHER, YOU KNOW.
THAT MAY BE SO, BUT SUCH AN AGE GAP IS NOT UNCOMMON IN RELATION-SHIPS.

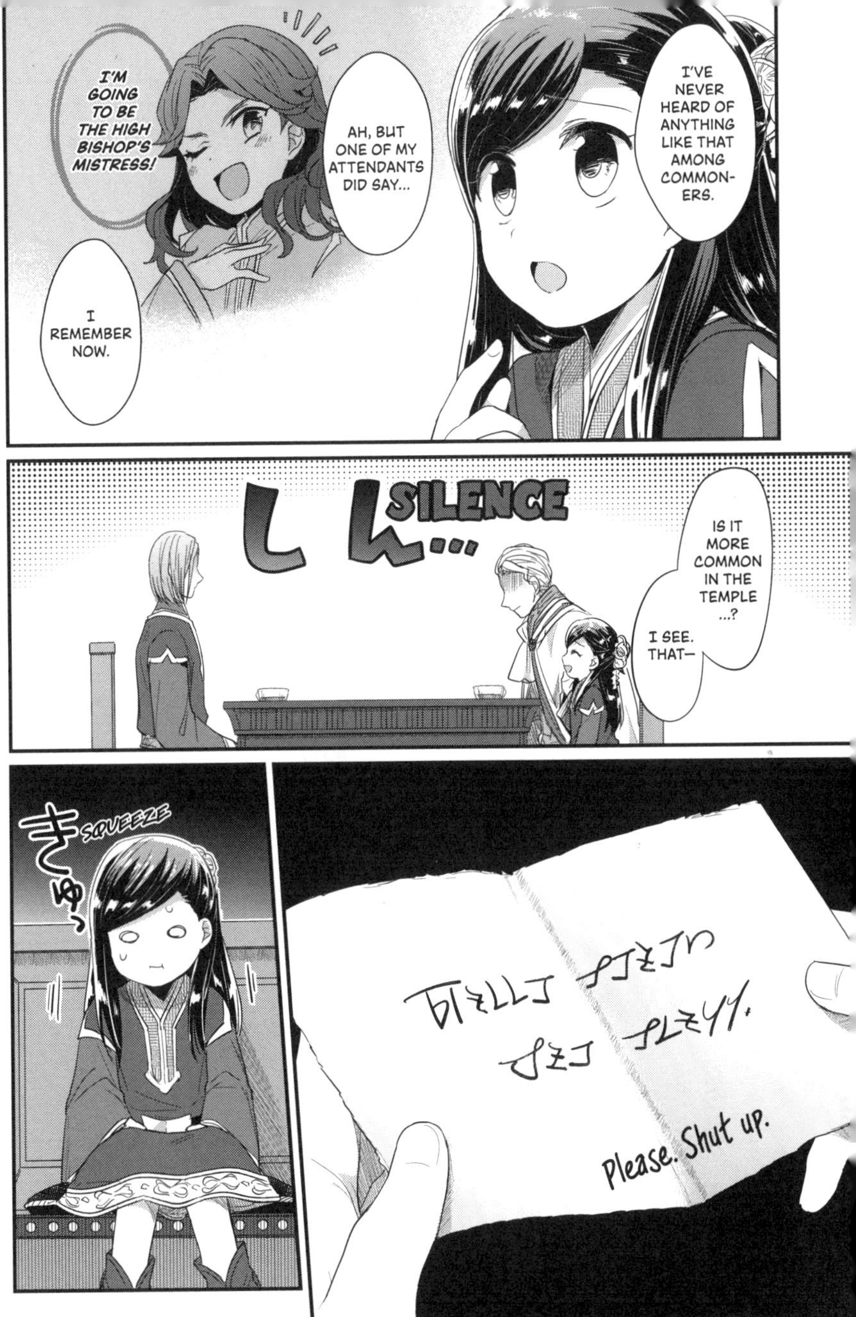
I'VE NEVER HEARD OF ANYTHING LIKE THAT AMONG COMMON-ERS.
AH, BUT ONE OF MY ATTENDANTS DID SAY...
I'M GOING TO BE THE HIGH BISHOP'S MISTRESS!
I REMEMBER NOW.
IS IT MORE COMMON IN THE TEMPLE ...?
I SEE. THAT—
しん... SILENCE
Please. Shut up.
きゅっ SQUEEZE

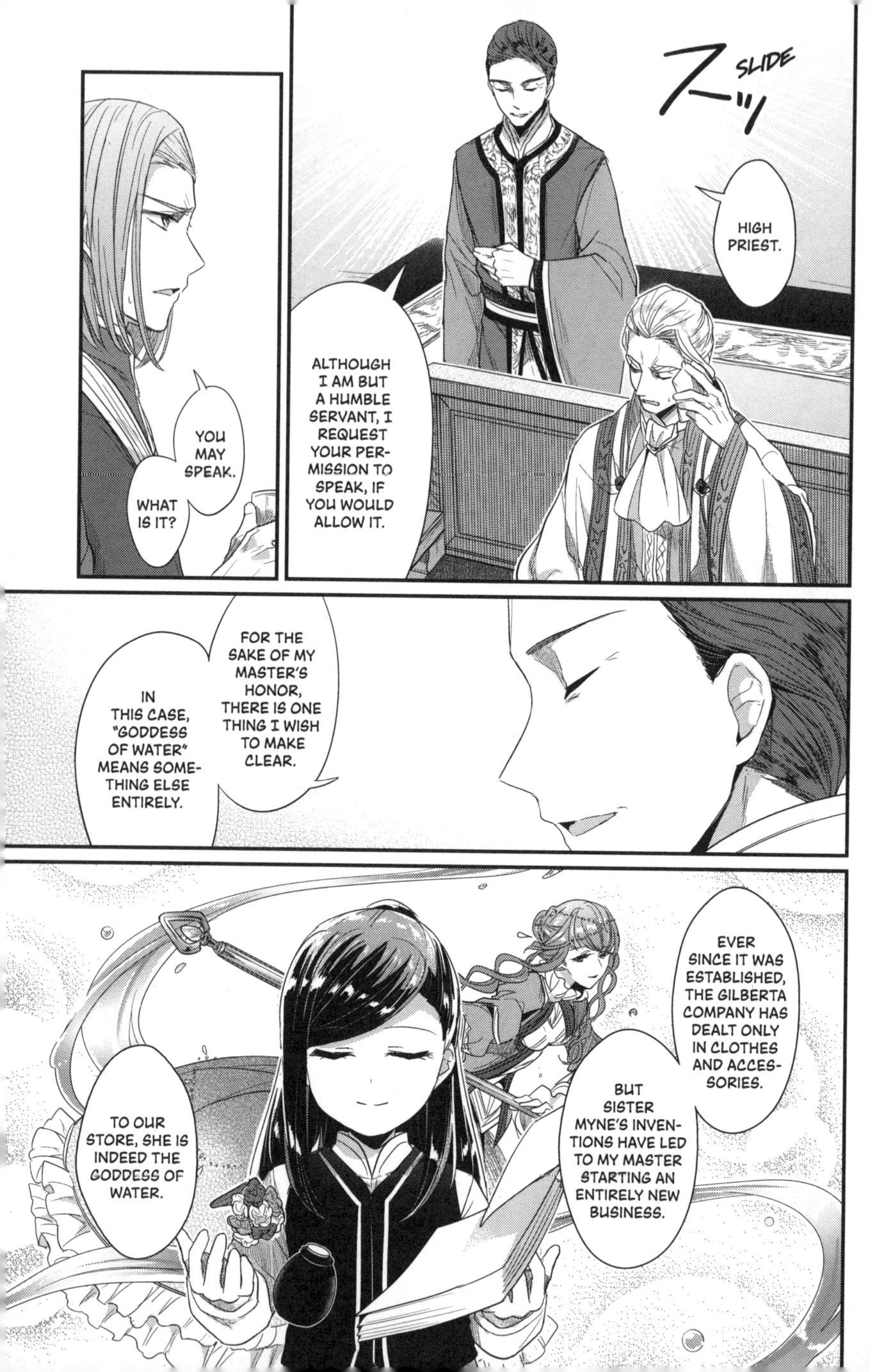
ズッ
SLIDE
HIGH PRIEST.
ALTHOUGH I AM BUT A HUMBLE SERVANT, I REQUEST YOUR PER-MISSION TO SPEAK, IF YOU WOULD ALLOW IT.
YOU MAY SPEAK.
WHAT IS IT?
FOR THE SAKE OF MY MASTER'S HONOR, THERE IS ONE THING I WISH TO MAKE CLEAR.
IN THIS CASE, "GODDESS OF WATER" MEANS SOME-THING ELSE ENTIRELY.
EVER SINCE IT WAS ESTABLISHED, THE GILBERTA COMPANY HAS DEALT ONLY IN CLOTHES AND ACCES-SORIES.
BUT SISTER MYNE'S INVEN-TIONS HAVE LED TO MY MASTER STARTING AN ENTIRELY NEW BUSINESS.
TO OUR STORE, SHE IS INDEED THE GODDESS OF WATER.

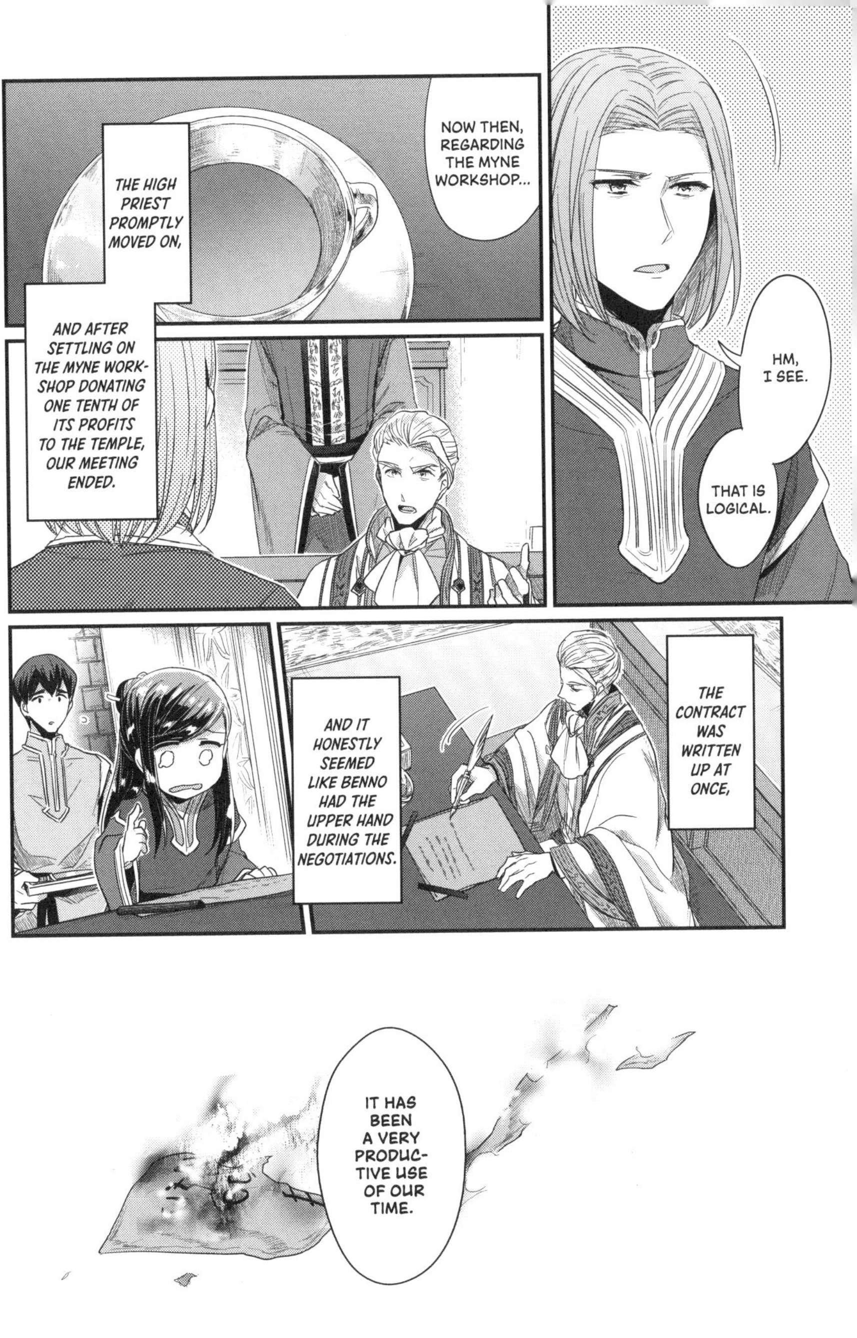
HM, I SEE.
THAT IS LOGICAL.
NOW THEN, REGARDING THE MYNE WORKSHOP...
THE HIGH PRIEST PROMPTLY MOVED ON,
AND AFTER SETTLING ON THE MYNE WORK-SHOP DONATING ONE TENTH OF ITS PROFITS TO THE TEMPLE, OUR MEETING ENDED.
THE CONTRACT WAS WRITTEN UP AT ONCE,
AND IT HONESTLY SEEMED LIKE BENNO HAD THE UPPER HAND DURING THE NEGOTIATIONS.
IT HAS BEEN A VERY PRODUC-TIVE USE OF OUR TIME.

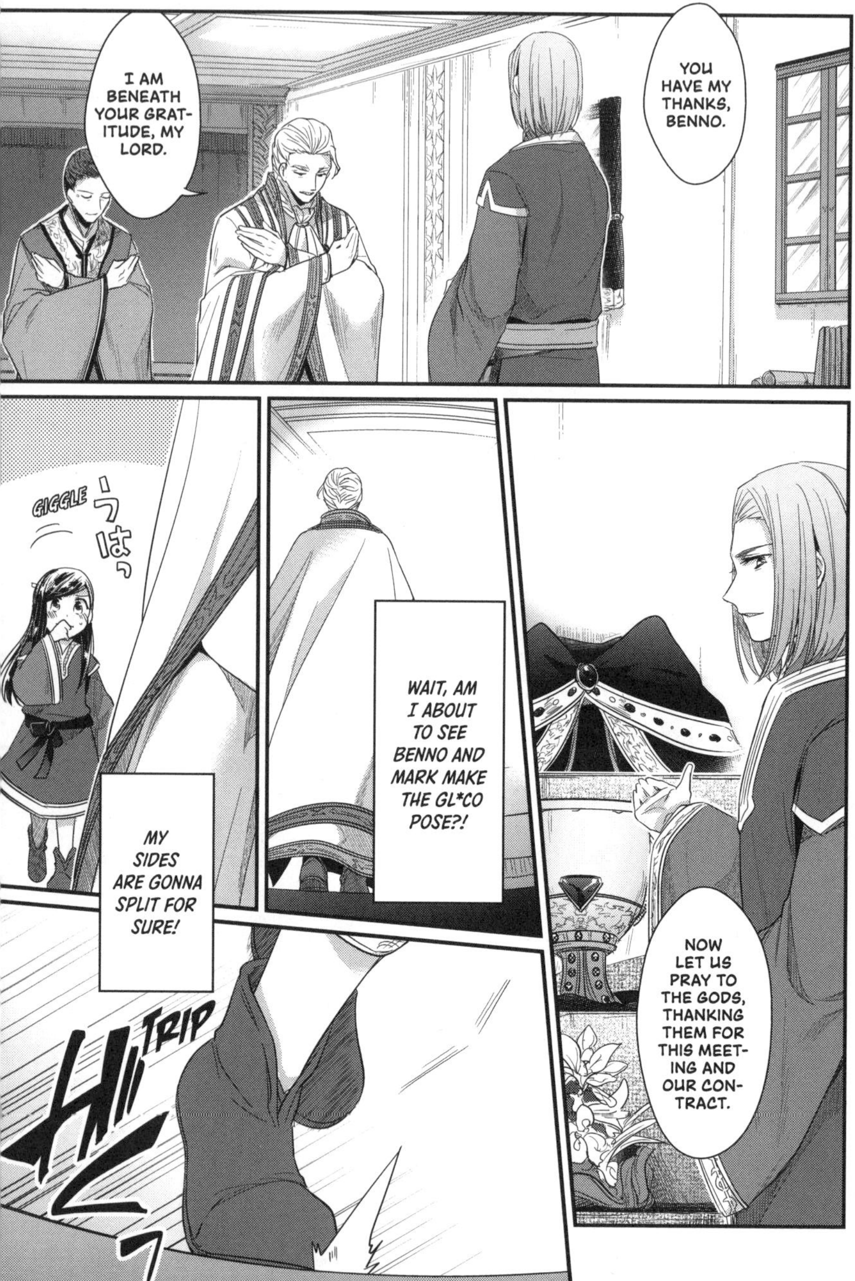
YOU HAVE MY THANKS, BENNO.
I AM BENEATH YOUR GRATITUDE, MY LORD.
NOW LET US PRAY TO THE GODS, THANKING THEM FOR THIS MEETING AND OUR CONTRACT.
WAIT, AM I ABOUT TO SEE BENNO AND MARK MAKE THE GL*CO POSE?!
GIGGLE
うはっ
MY SIDES ARE GONNA SPLIT FOR SURE!
TRIP

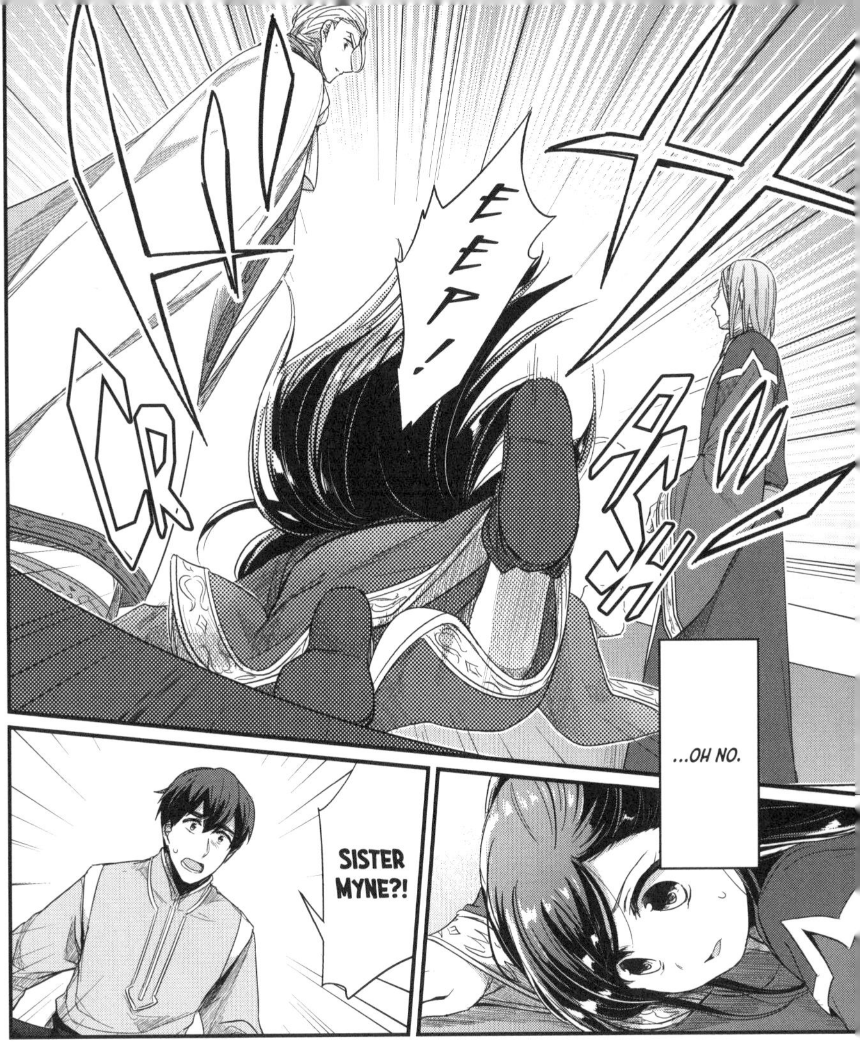
EEP!!
CR
ASH
...OH NO.
SISTER MYNE?!

NOW I WON'T GET TO SEE BENNO AND MARK MAKE THE GL*CO POSE...

Ch. 2: Meeting in the Temple **END**

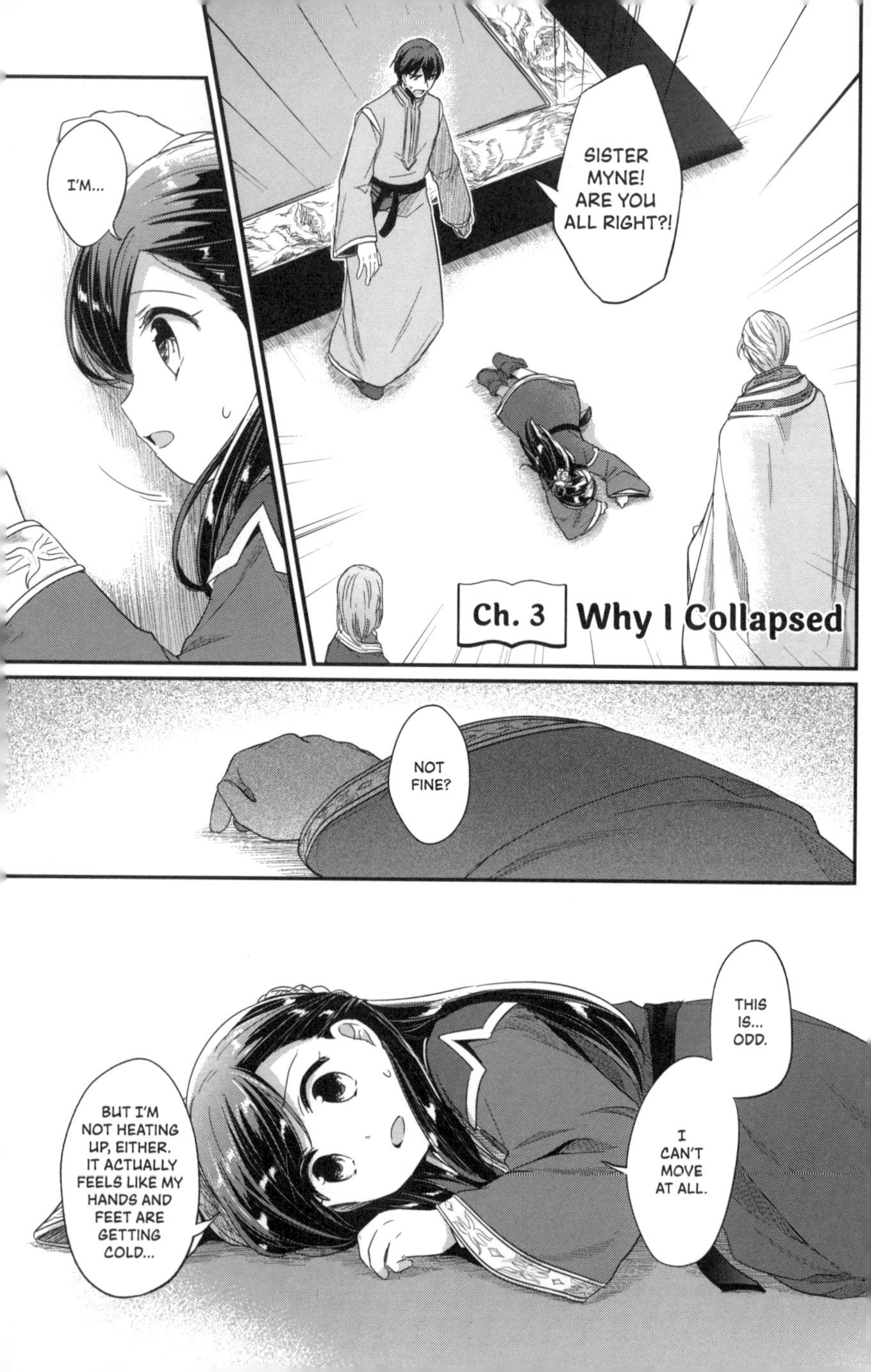
SISTER MYNE! ARE YOU ALL RIGHT?!
Ch. 3 Why I Collapsed
I'M...
NOT FINE?
THIS IS... ODD.
I CAN'T MOVE AT ALL.
BUT I'M NOT HEATING UP, EITHER. IT ACTUALLY FEELS LIKE MY HANDS AND FEET ARE GETTING COLD...

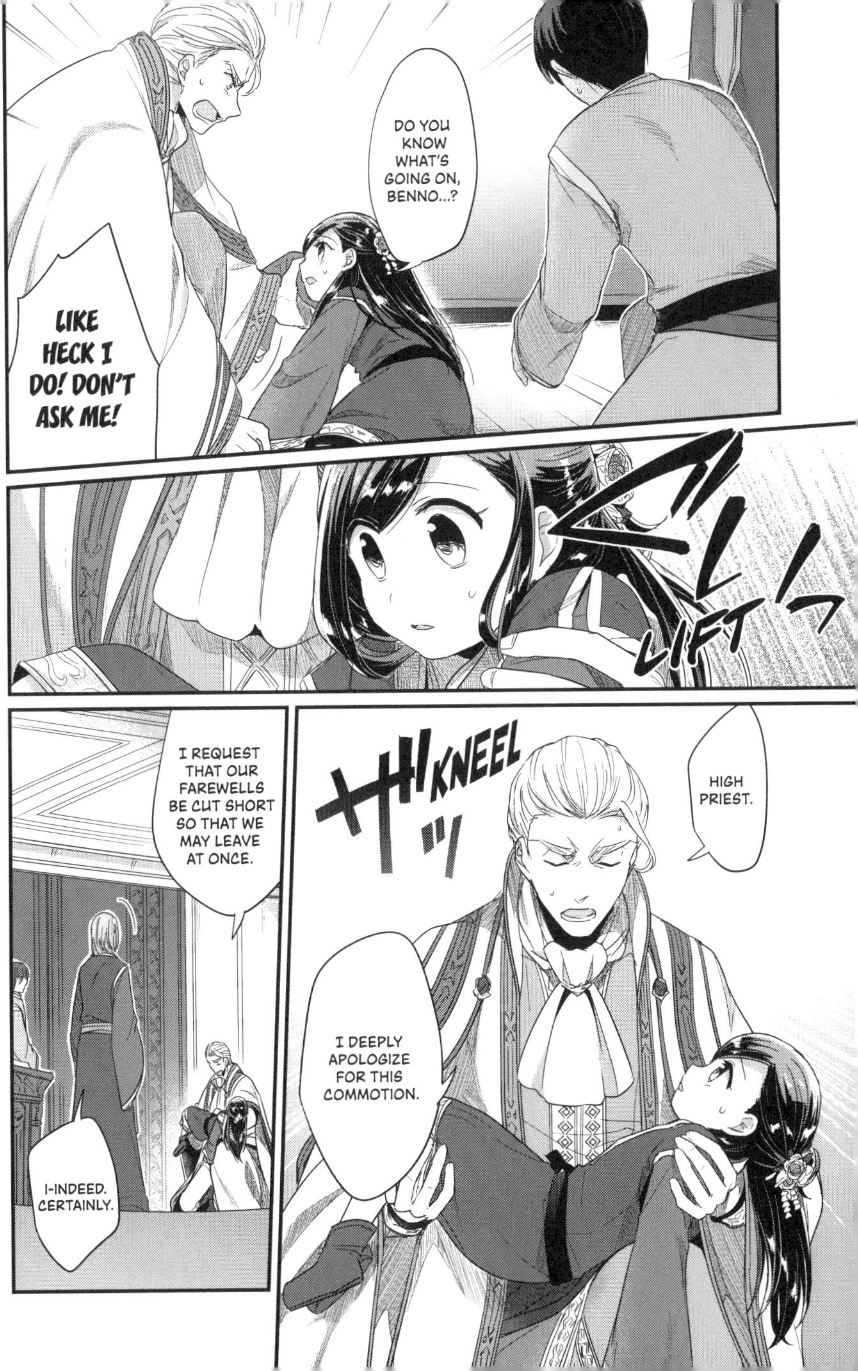
DO YOU KNOW WHAT'S GOING ON, BENNO...?
LIKE HECK I DO! DON'T ASK ME!
LIFT
HIGH PRIEST.
KNEEL
I DEEPLY APOLOGIZE FOR THIS COMMOTION.
I REQUEST THAT OUR FAREWELLS BE CUT SHORT SO THAT WE MAY LEAVE AT ONCE.
I-INDEED. CERTAINLY.

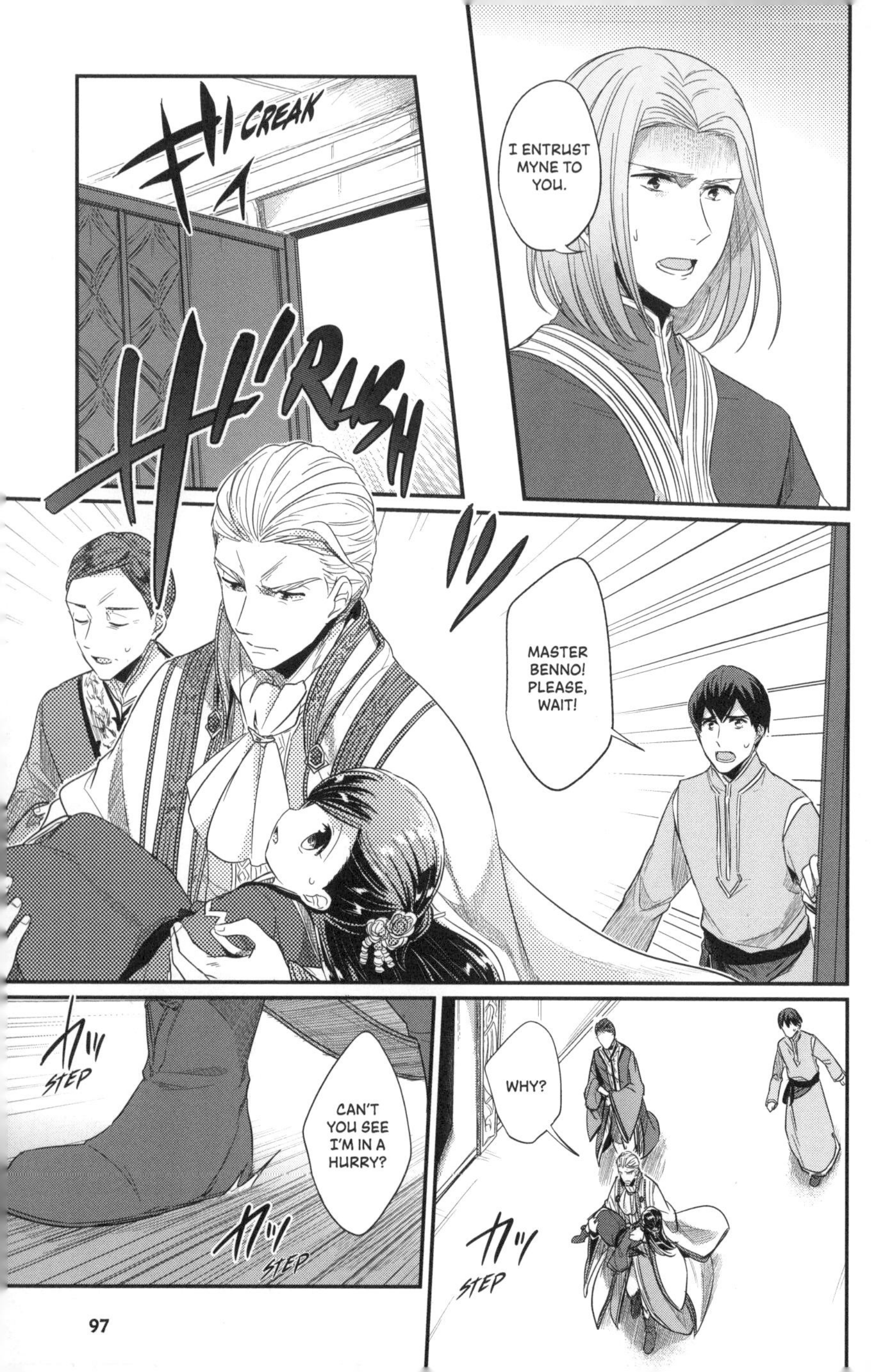
I ENTRUST MYNE TO YOU.
CREAK
RUSH
MASTER BENNO! PLEASE, WAIT!
WHY?
STEP
CAN'T YOU SEE I'M IN A HURRY?
STEP
STEP

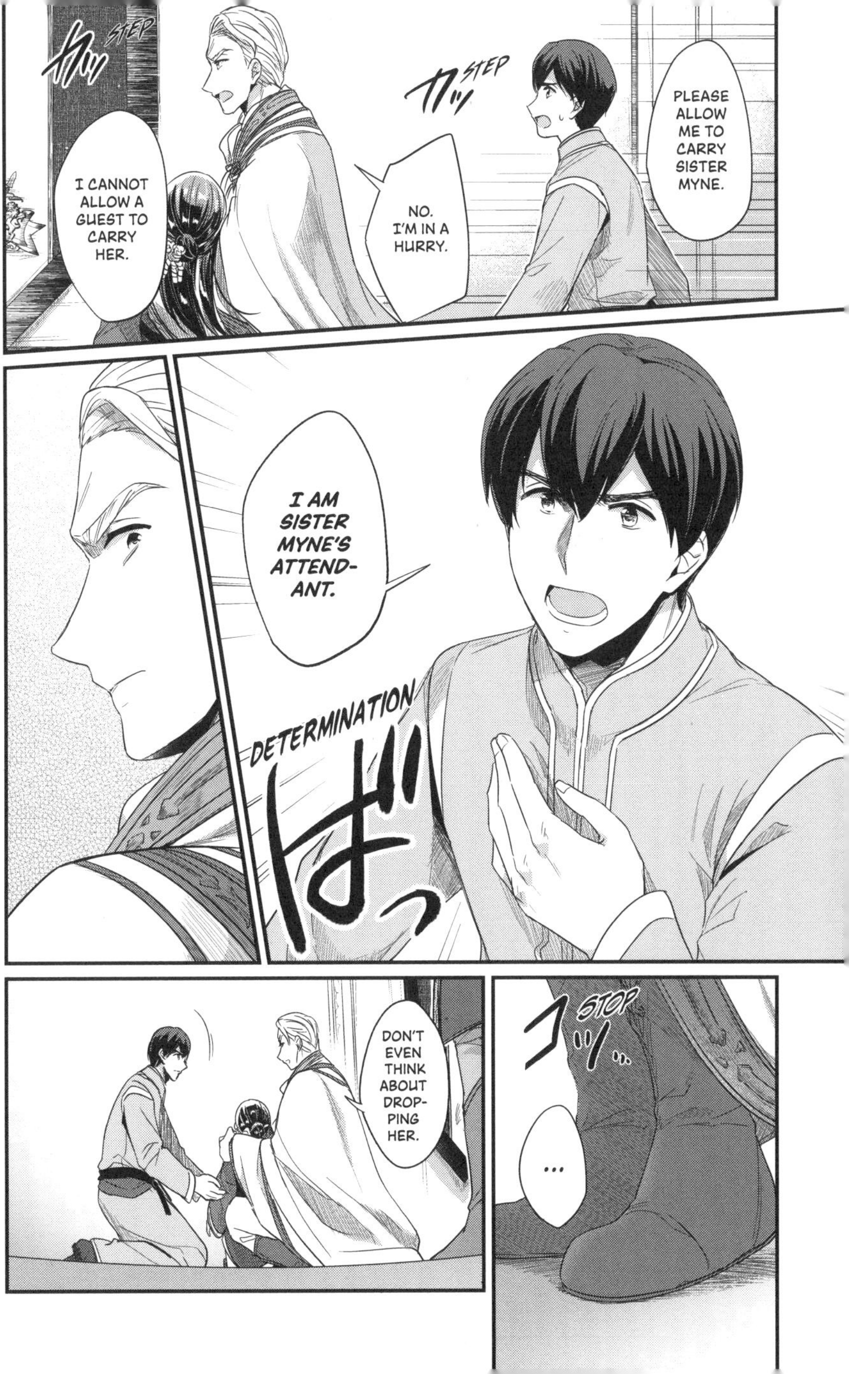
PLEASE ALLOW ME TO CARRY SISTER MYNE.
STEP
NO. I'M IN A HURRY.
I CANNOT ALLOW A GUEST TO CARRY HER.
STEP
I AM SISTER MYNE'S ATTEND-ANT.
DETERMINATION
STOP
...
DON'T EVEN THINK ABOUT DROP-PING HER.

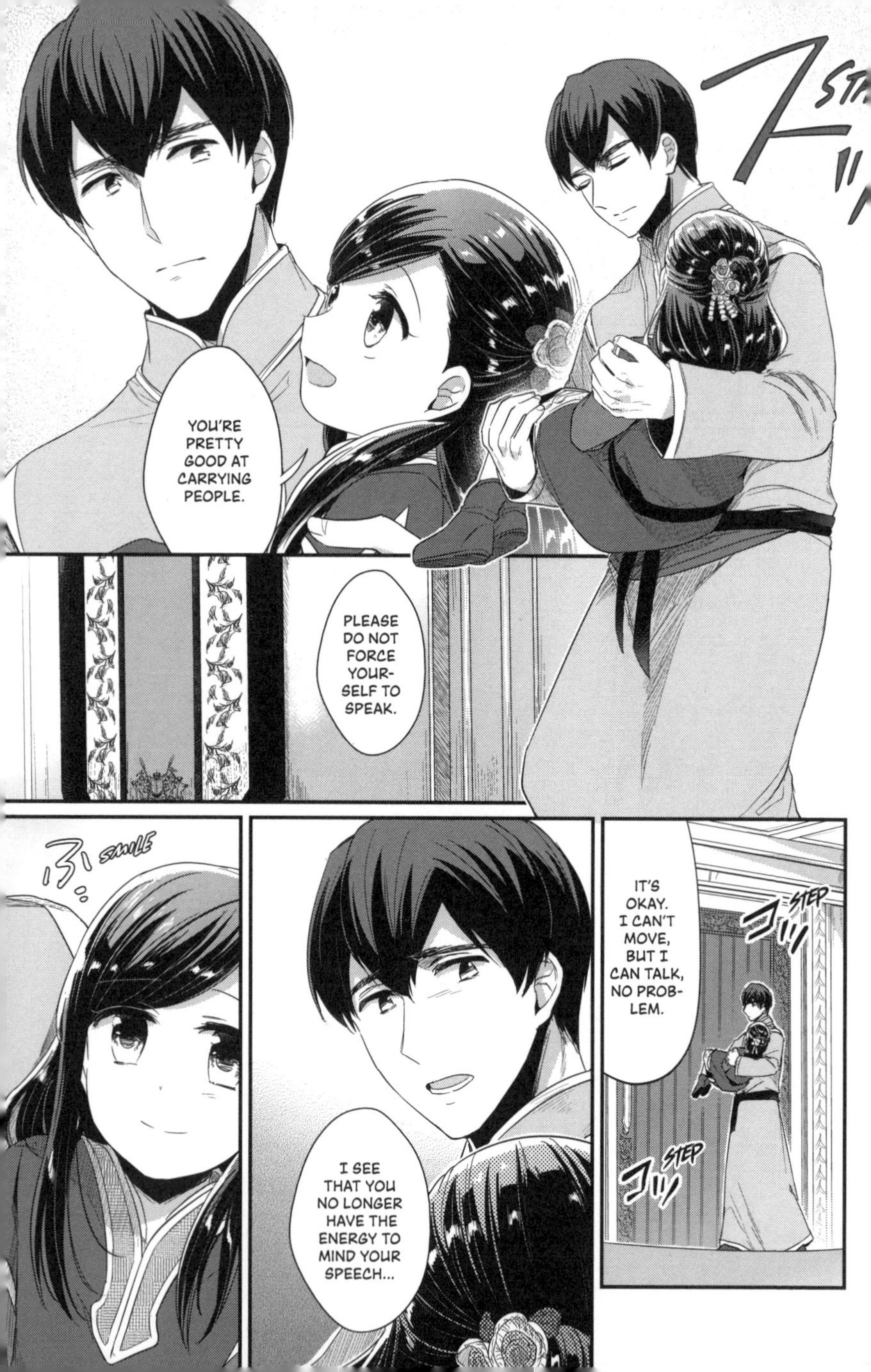

YOU'RE PRETTY GOOD AT CARRYING PEOPLE.
PLEASE DO NOT FORCE YOUR-SELF TO SPEAK.
STEP
IT'S OKAY. I CAN'T MOVE, BUT I CAN TALK, NO PROB-LEM.
STEP
I SEE THAT YOU NO LONGER HAVE THE ENERGY TO MIND YOUR SPEECH...
SMILE

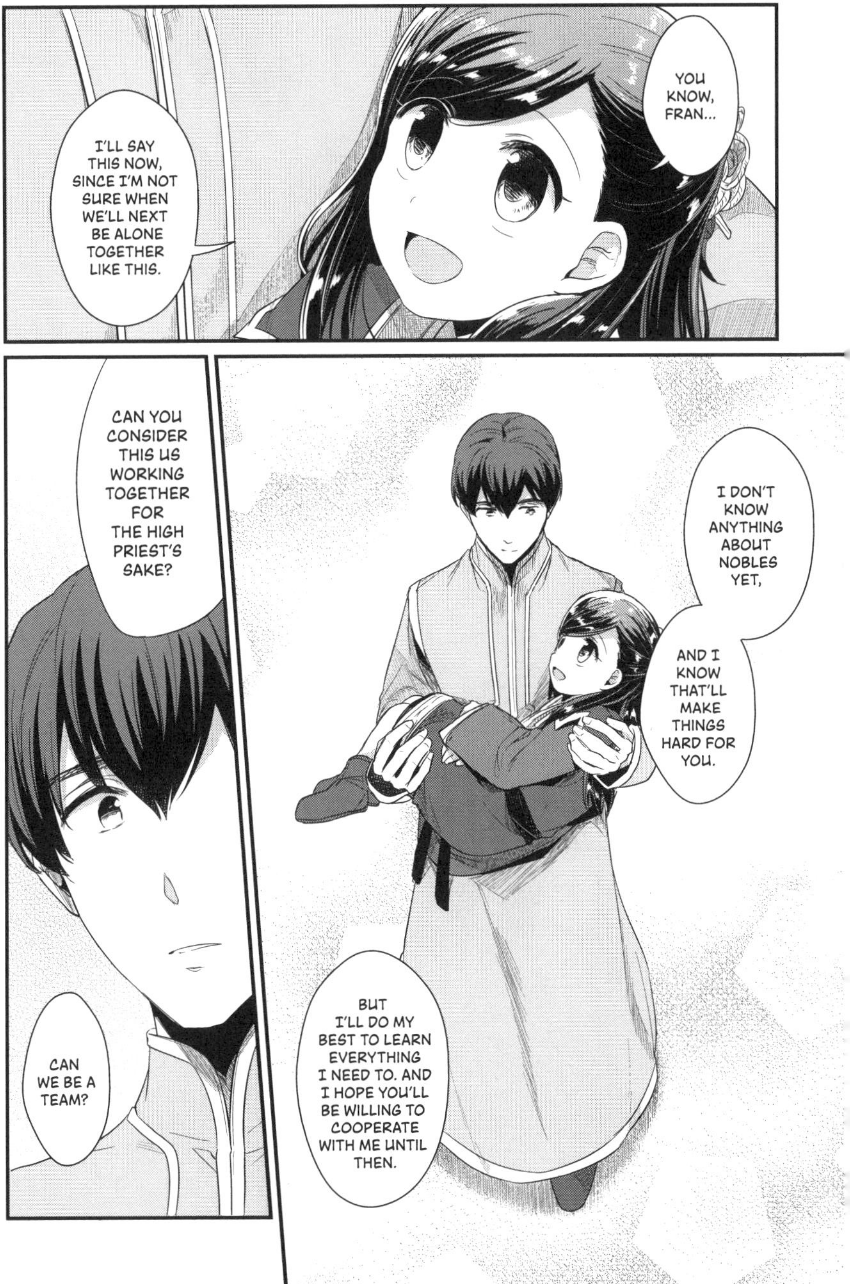
YOU KNOW, FRAN...
I'LL SAY THIS NOW, SINCE I'M NOT SURE WHEN WE'LL NEXT BE ALONE TOGETHER LIKE THIS.
I DON'T KNOW ANYTHING ABOUT NOBLES YET,
AND I KNOW THAT'LL MAKE THINGS HARD FOR YOU.
BUT I'LL DO MY BEST TO LEARN EVERYTHING I NEED TO. AND I HOPE YOU'LL BE WILLING TO COOPERATE WITH ME UNTIL THEN.
CAN YOU CONSIDER THIS US WORKING TOGETHER FOR THE HIGH PRIEST'S SAKE?
CAN WE BE A TEAM?

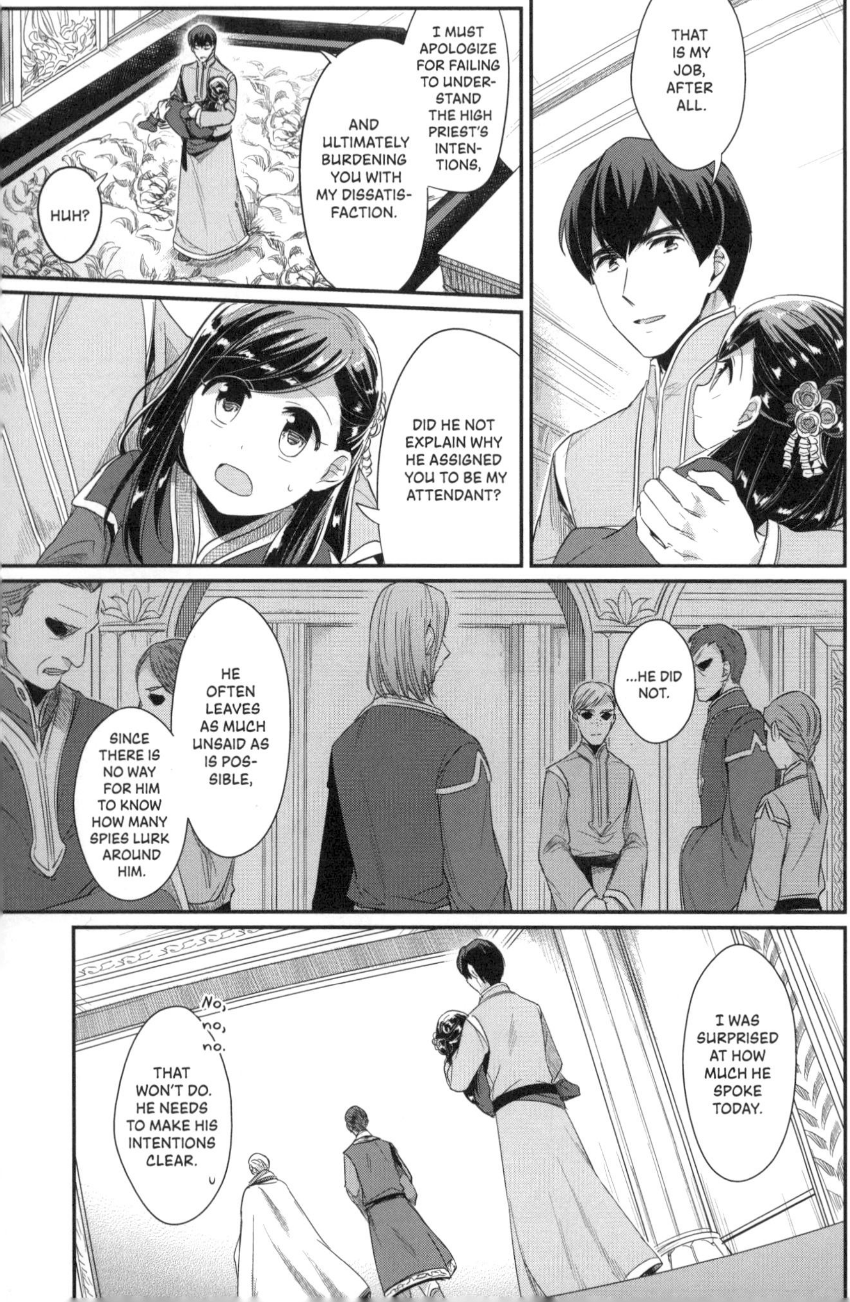
THAT IS MY JOB, AFTER ALL.
I MUST APOLOGIZE FOR FAILING TO UNDER-STAND THE HIGH PRIEST'S INTEN-TIONS,
AND ULTIMATELY BURDENING YOU WITH MY DISSATIS-FACTION.
HUH?
DID HE NOT EXPLAIN WHY HE ASSIGNED YOU TO BE MY ATTENDANT?
...HE DID NOT.
HE OFTEN LEAVES AS MUCH UNSAID AS IS POS-SIBLE,
SINCE THERE IS NO WAY FOR HIM TO KNOW HOW MANY SPIES LURK AROUND HIM.
I WAS SURPRISED AT HOW MUCH HE SPOKE TODAY.
No, no, no.
THAT WON'T DO. HE NEEDS TO MAKE HIS INTENTIONS CLEAR.

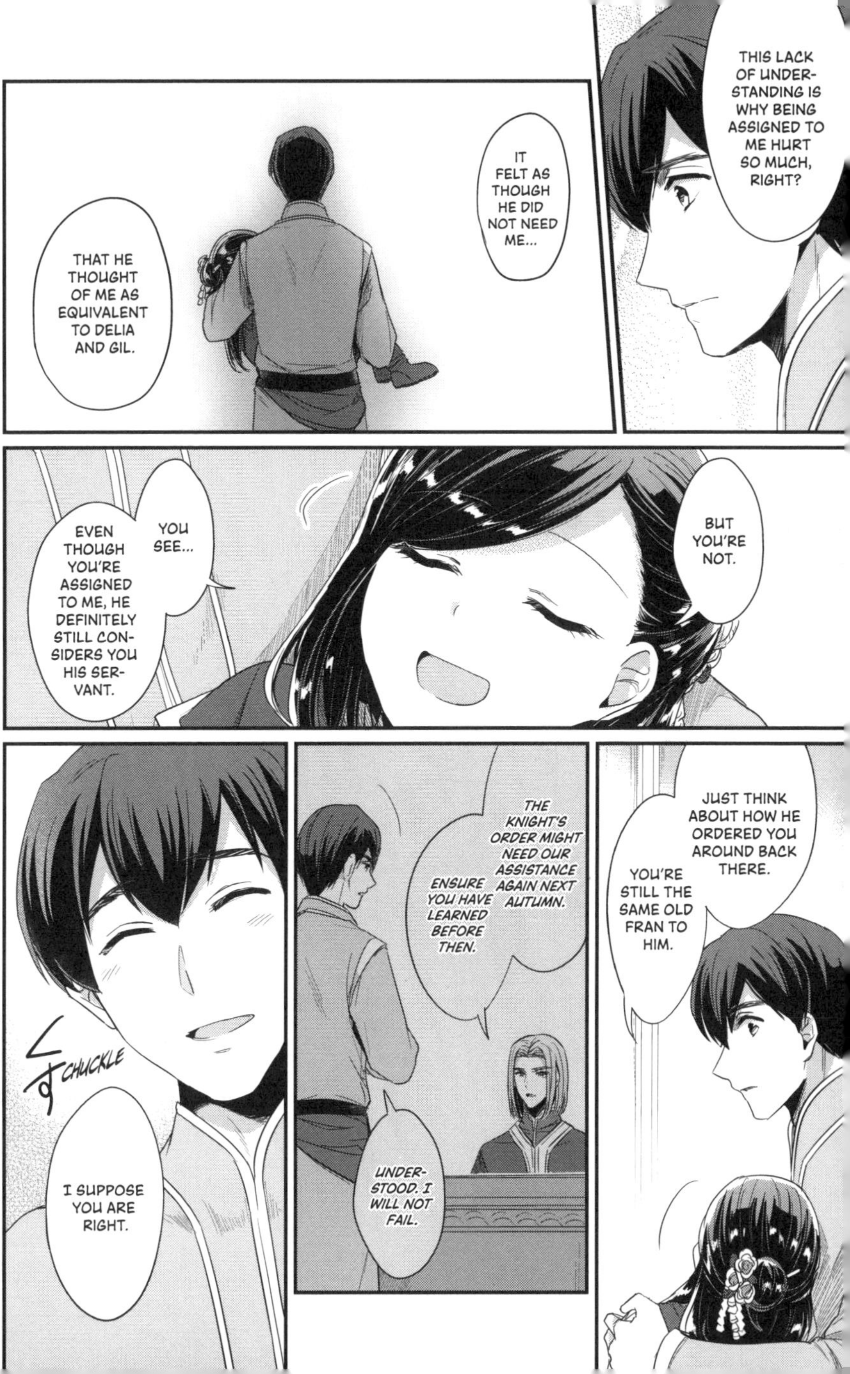
THIS LACK OF UNDERSTANDING IS WHY BEING ASSIGNED TO ME HURT SO MUCH, RIGHT?
IT FELT AS THOUGH HE DID NOT NEED ME...
THAT HE THOUGHT OF ME AS EQUIVALENT TO DELIA AND GIL.
BUT YOU'RE NOT.
YOU SEE...
EVEN THOUGH YOU'RE ASSIGNED TO ME, HE DEFINITELY STILL CONSIDERS YOU HIS SERVANT.
JUST THINK ABOUT HOW HE ORDERED YOU AROUND BACK THERE.
YOU'RE STILL THE SAME OLD FRAN TO HIM.
THE KNIGHT'S ORDER MIGHT NEED OUR ASSISTANCE AGAIN NEXT AUTUMN.
ENSURE YOU HAVE LEARNED BEFORE THEN.
UNDERSTOOD. I WILL NOT FAIL.
くす CHUCKLE
I SUPPOSE YOU ARE RIGHT.

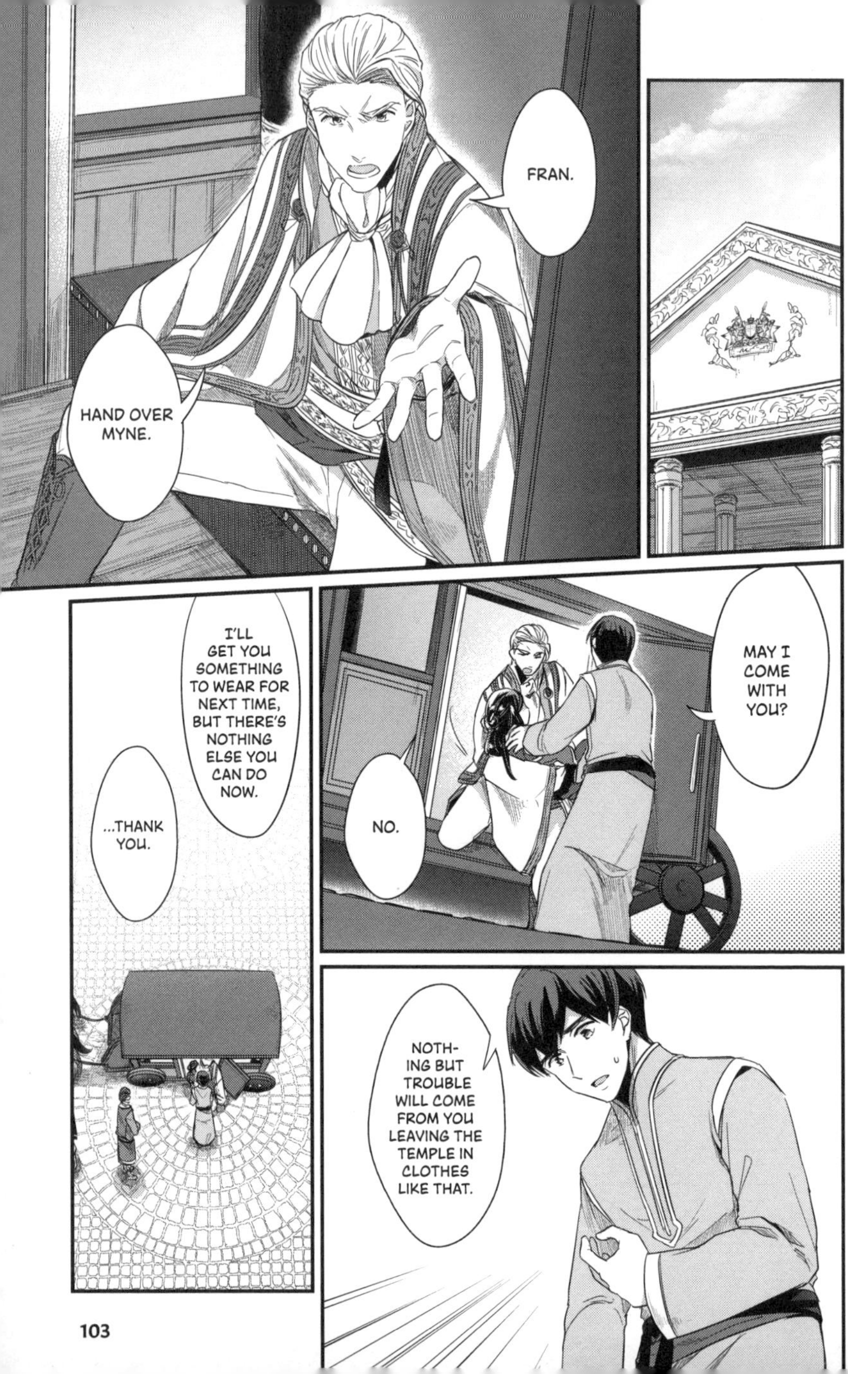
FRAN.
HAND OVER MYNE.
MAY I COME WITH YOU?
NO.
NOTHING BUT TROUBLE WILL COME FROM YOU LEAVING THE TEMPLE IN CLOTHES LIKE THAT.
I'LL GET YOU SOMETHING TO WEAR FOR NEXT TIME, BUT THERE'S NOTHING ELSE YOU CAN DO NOW.
...THANK YOU.

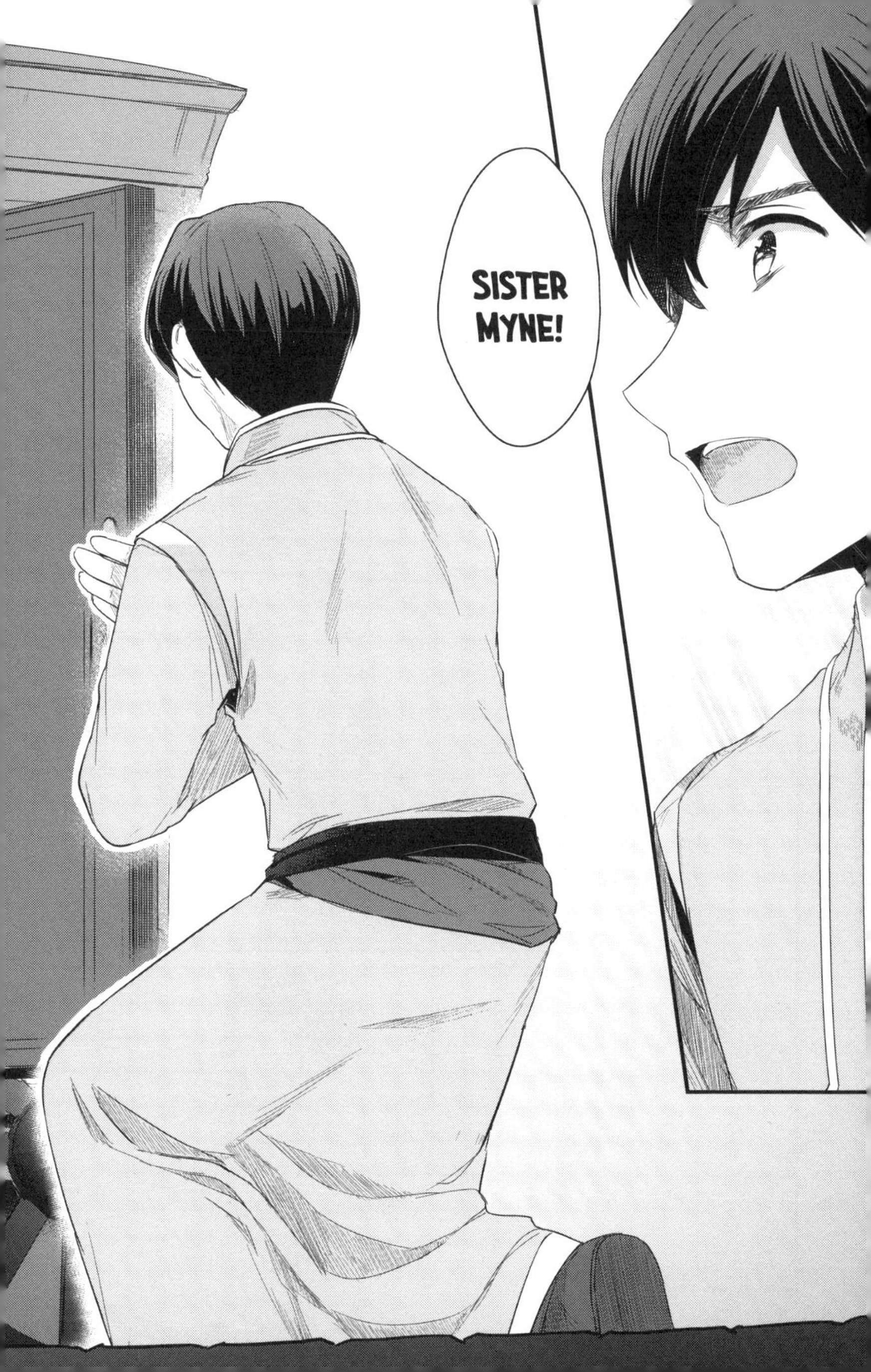
SISTER MYNE!

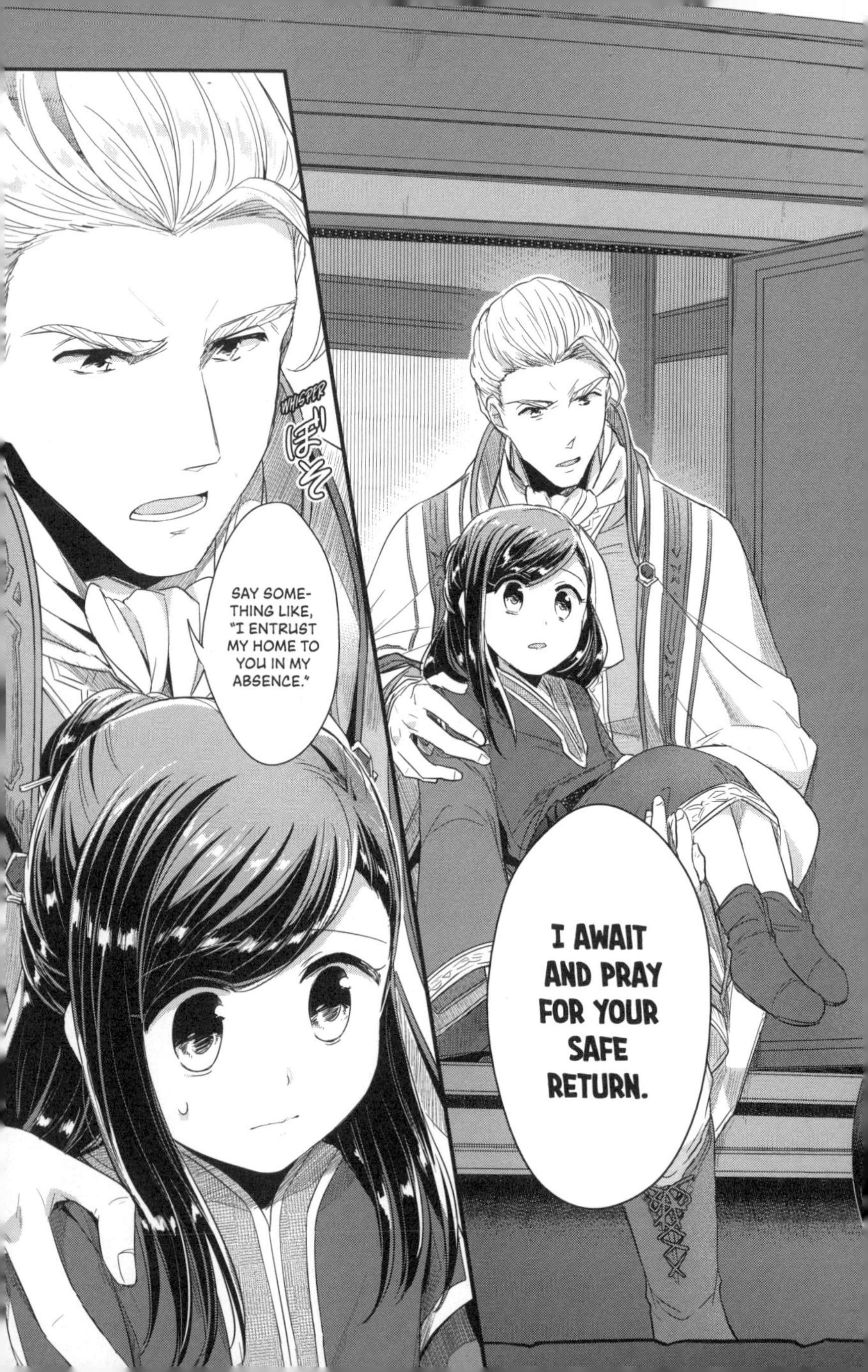
WHISPER
ぼそ
SAY SOMETHING LIKE, "I ENTRUST MY HOME TO YOU IN MY ABSENCE."
I AWAIT AND PRAY FOR YOUR SAFE RETURN.

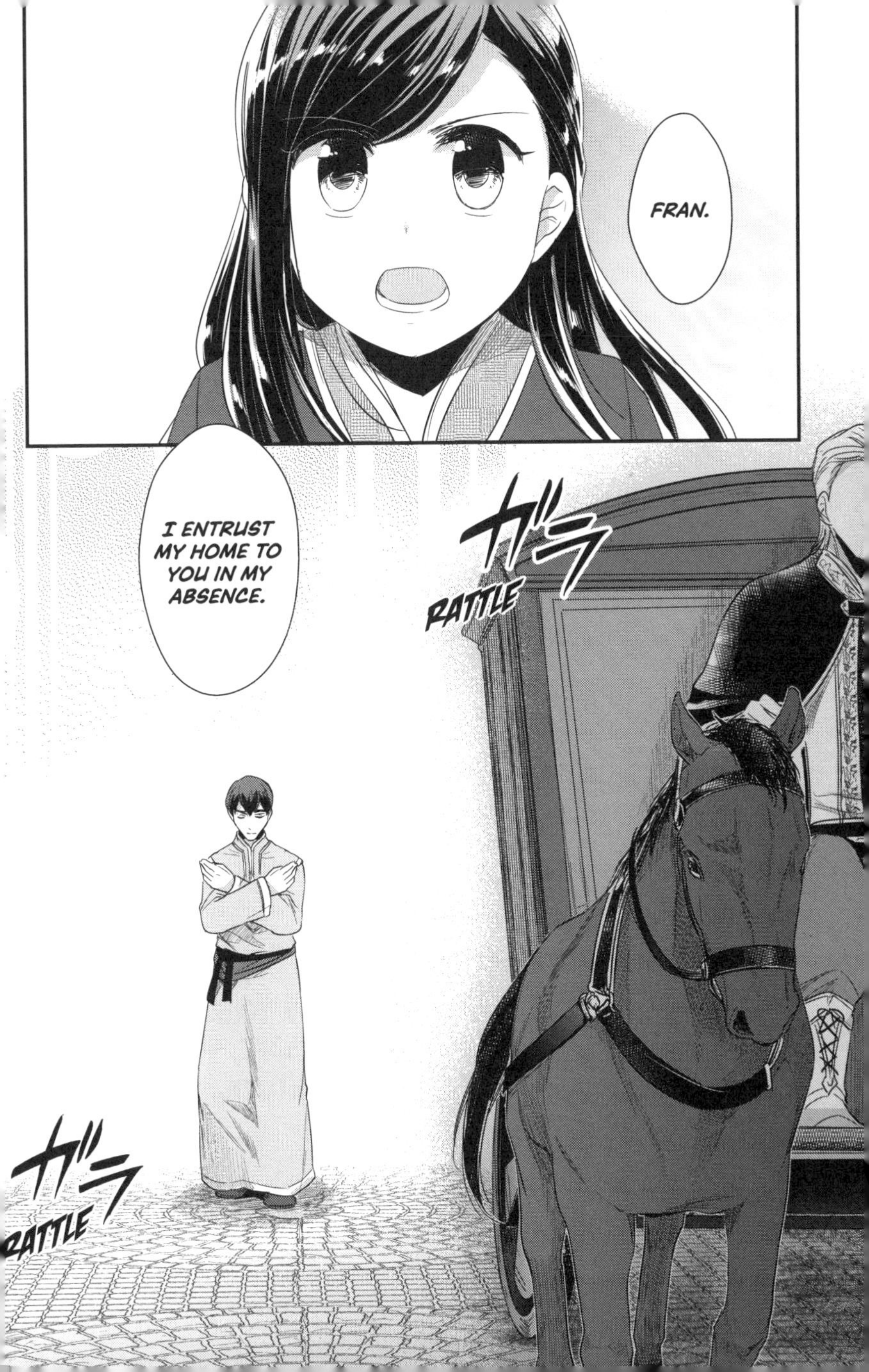
FRAN.
I ENTRUST MY HOME TO YOU IN MY ABSENCE.
ガラ
RATTLE
ガラ
RATTLE

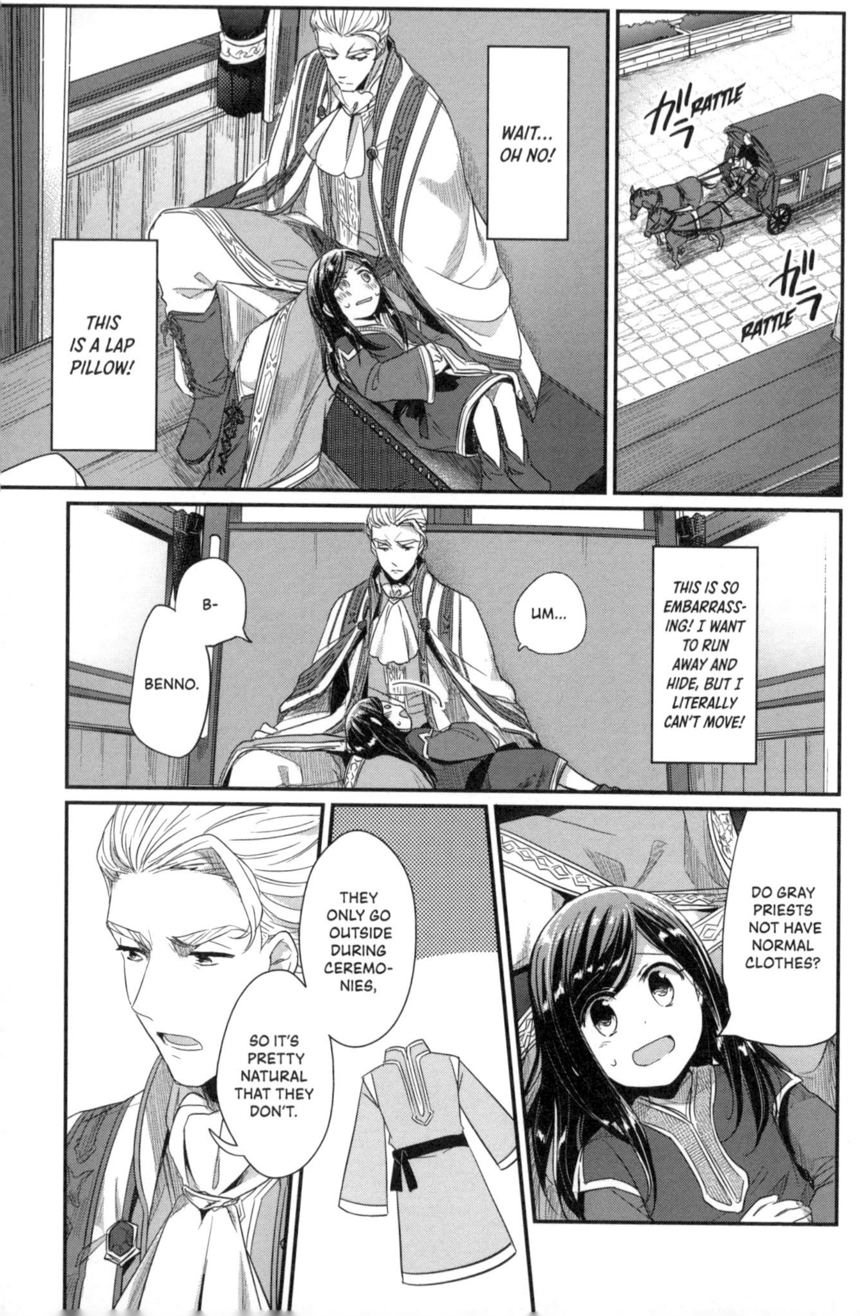
ガラ RATTLE
ガラ RATTLE
WAIT... OH NO!
THIS IS A LAP PILLOW!
THIS IS SO EMBARRASSING! I WANT TO RUN AWAY AND HIDE, BUT I LITERALLY CAN'T MOVE!
UM...
B- BENNO.
DO GRAY PRIESTS NOT HAVE NORMAL CLOTHES?
THEY ONLY GO OUTSIDE DURING CEREMONIES,
SO IT'S PRETTY NATURAL THAT THEY DON'T.

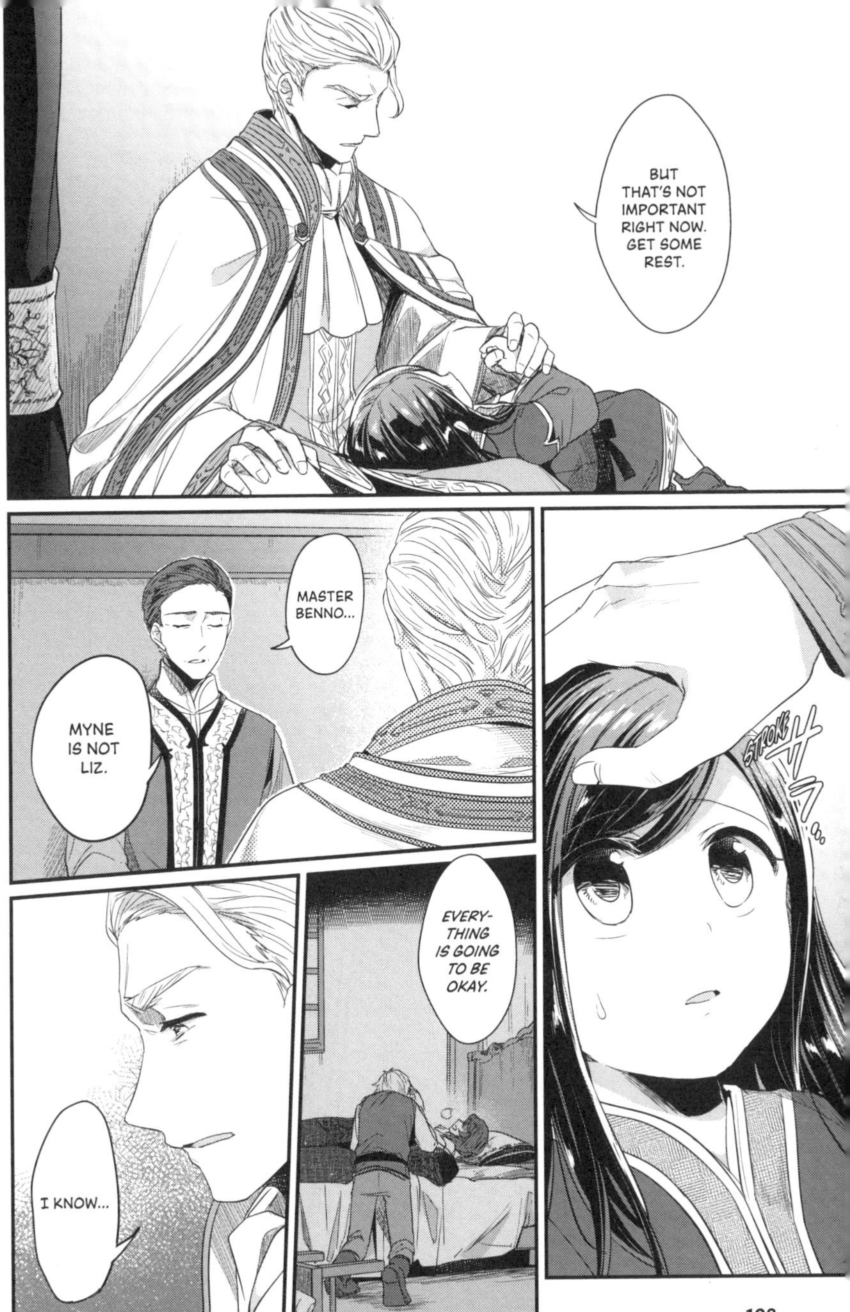
BUT THAT'S NOT IMPORTANT RIGHT NOW. GET SOME REST.
STROKE
MASTER BENNO...
MYNE IS NOT LIZ.
EVERY-THING IS GOING TO BE OKAY.
I KNOW...

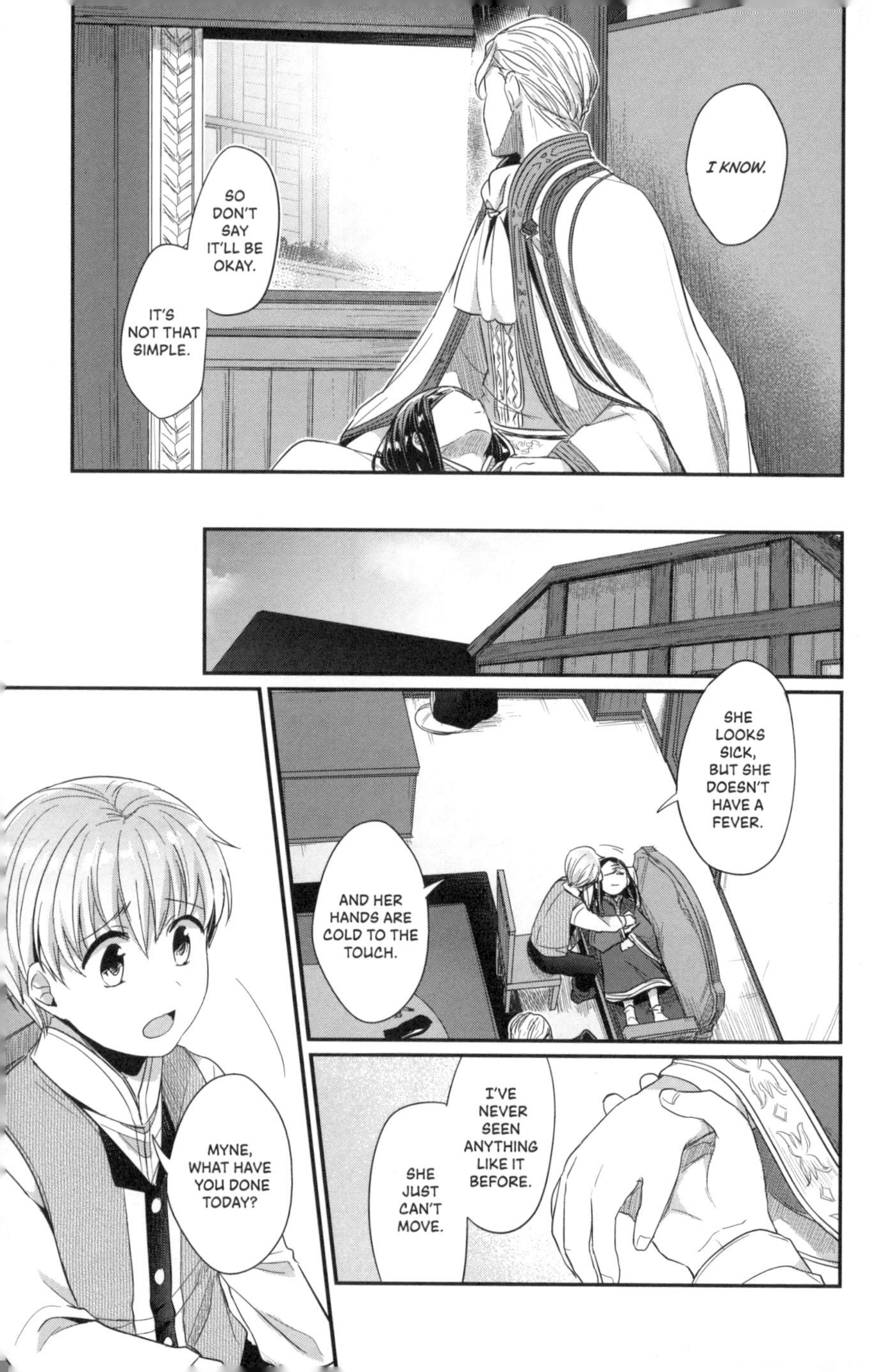
I KNOW.
SO DON'T SAY IT'LL BE OKAY.
IT'S NOT THAT SIMPLE.
SHE LOOKS SICK, BUT SHE DOESN'T HAVE A FEVER.
AND HER HANDS ARE COLD TO THE TOUCH.
I'VE NEVER SEEN ANYTHING LIKE IT BEFORE.
SHE JUST CAN'T MOVE.
MYNE, WHAT HAVE YOU DONE TODAY?

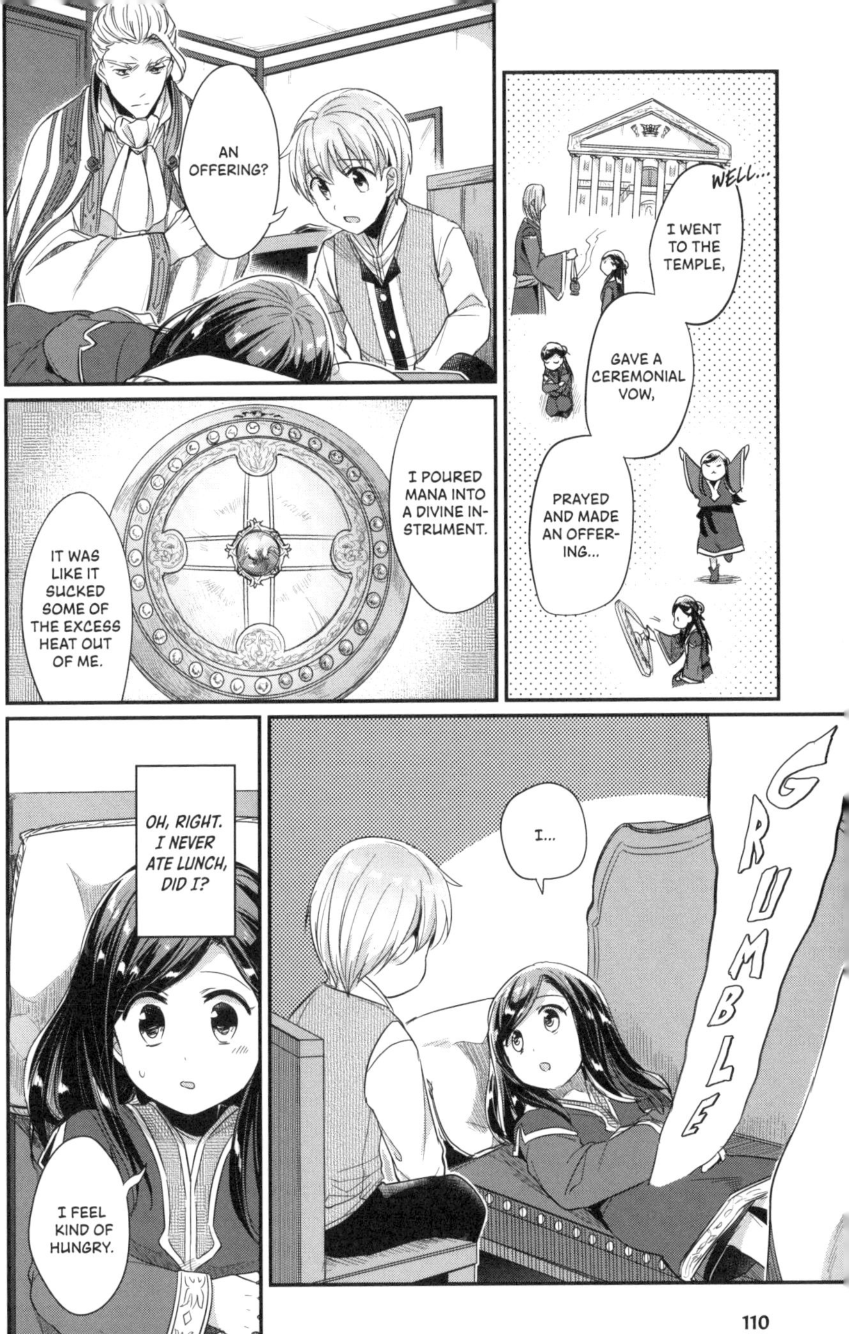
AN OFFERING?
WELL...
I WENT TO THE TEMPLE,
GAVE A CEREMONIAL VOW,
PRAYED AND MADE AN OFFERING...
I POURED MANA INTO A DIVINE INSTRUMENT.
IT WAS LIKE IT SUCKED SOME OF THE EXCESS HEAT OUT OF ME.
I...
GRUMBLE
OH, RIGHT. I NEVER ATE LUNCH, DID I?
I FEEL KIND OF HUNGRY.

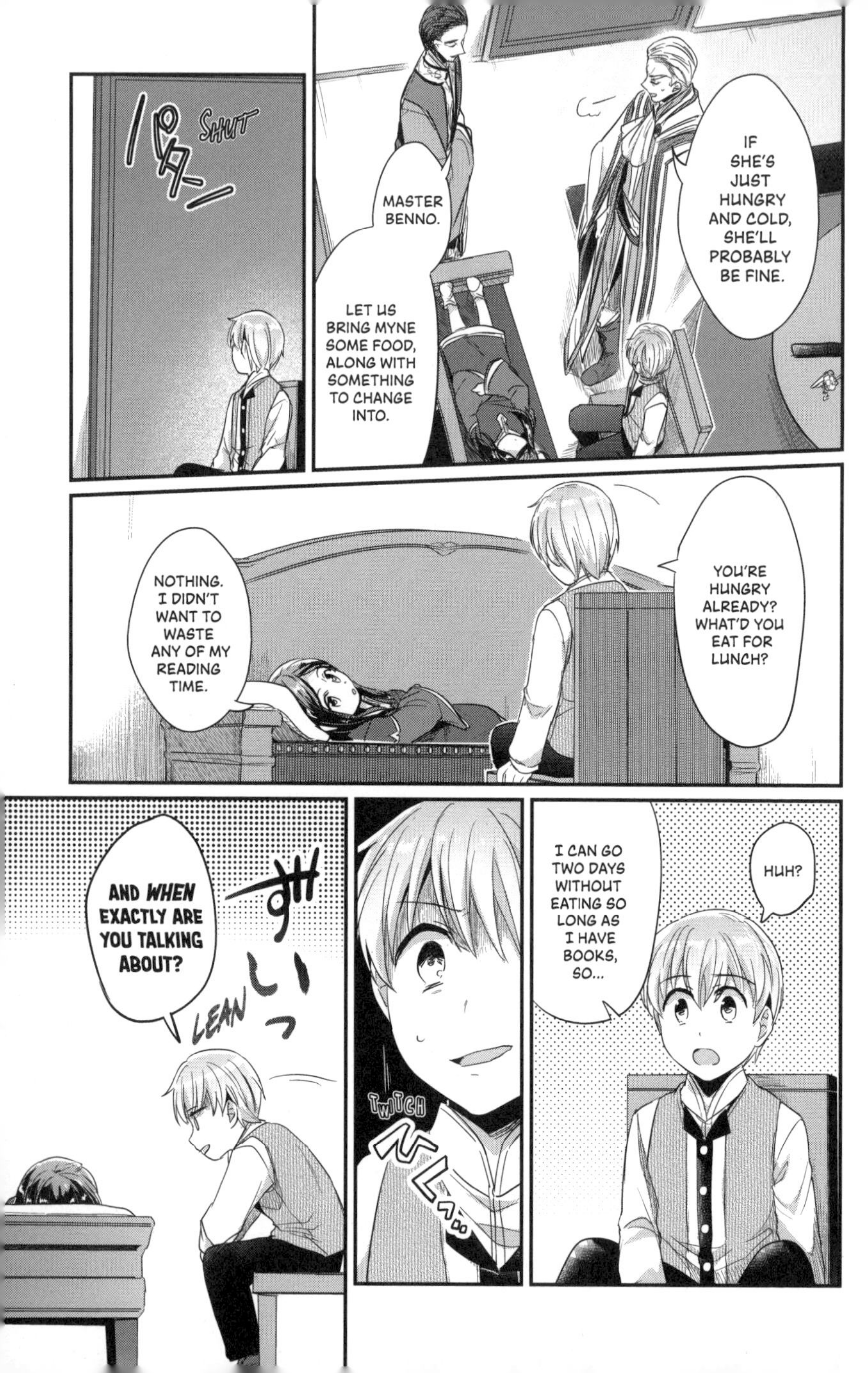
IF SHE'S JUST HUNGRY AND COLD, SHE'LL PROBABLY BE FINE.
MASTER BENNO.
LET US BRING MYNE SOME FOOD, ALONG WITH SOMETHING TO CHANGE INTO.
SHUT
YOU'RE HUNGRY ALREADY? WHAT'D YOU EAT FOR LUNCH?
NOTHING. I DIDN'T WANT TO WASTE ANY OF MY READING TIME.
HUH?
I CAN GO TWO DAYS WITHOUT EATING SO LONG AS I HAVE BOOKS, SO...
TWITCH
AND *WHEN* EXACTLY ARE YOU TALKING ABOUT?
LEAN

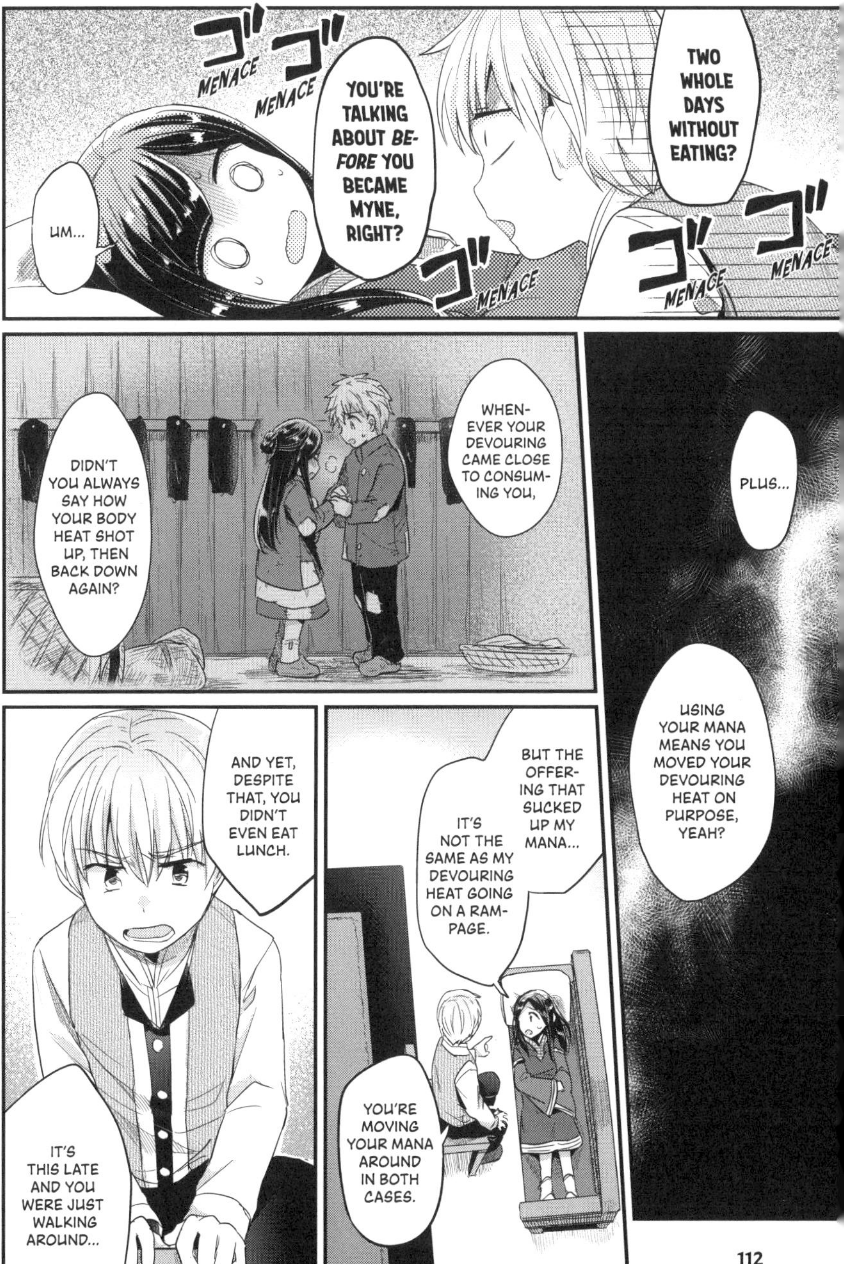
TWO WHOLE DAYS WITHOUT EATING?
ゴ MENACE
ゴ MENACE
ゴ MENACE
YOU'RE TALKING ABOUT BE-FORE YOU BECAME MYNE, RIGHT?
ゴ MENACE
ゴ MENACE
UM...
PLUS...
USING YOUR MANA MEANS YOU MOVED YOUR DEVOURING HEAT ON PURPOSE, YEAH?
WHEN-EVER YOUR DEVOURING CAME CLOSE TO CONSUM-ING YOU,
DIDN'T YOU ALWAYS SAY HOW YOUR BODY HEAT SHOT UP, THEN BACK DOWN AGAIN?
BUT THE OFFER-ING THAT SUCKED UP MY MANA...
IT'S NOT THE SAME AS MY DEVOURING HEAT GOING ON A RAM-PAGE.
YOU'RE MOVING YOUR MANA AROUND IN BOTH CASES.
AND YET, DESPITE THAT, YOU DIDN'T EVEN EAT LUNCH.
IT'S THIS LATE AND YOU WERE JUST WALKING AROUND...

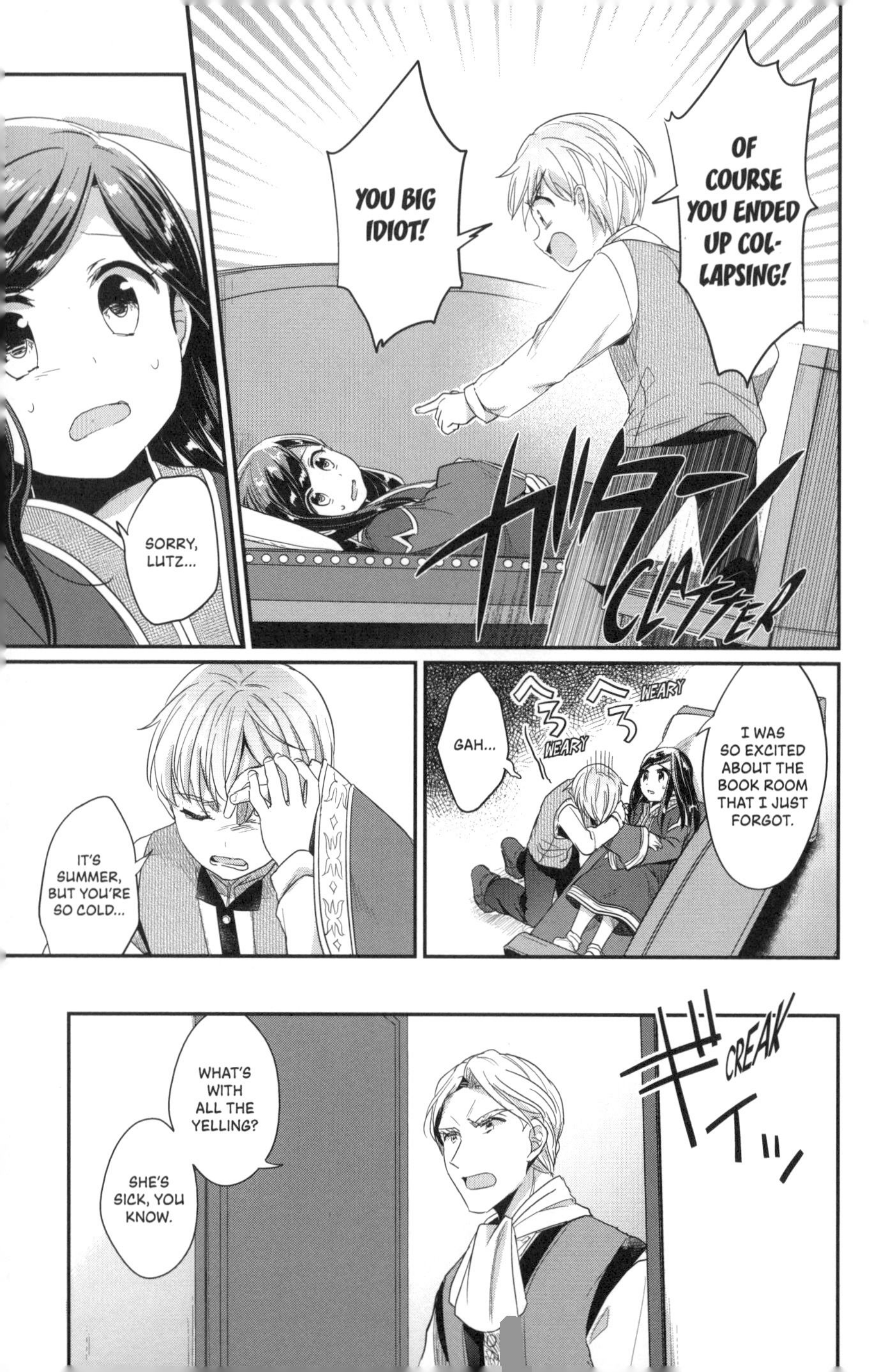
OF COURSE YOU ENDED UP COL-LAPSING!
YOU BIG IDIOT!
CLATTER
SORRY, LUTZ...
I WAS SO EXCITED ABOUT THE BOOK ROOM THAT I JUST FORGOT.
WEARY
WEARY
GAH...
IT'S SUMMER, BUT YOU'RE SO COLD...
CREAK
WHAT'S WITH ALL THE YELLING?
SHE'S SICK, YOU KNOW.

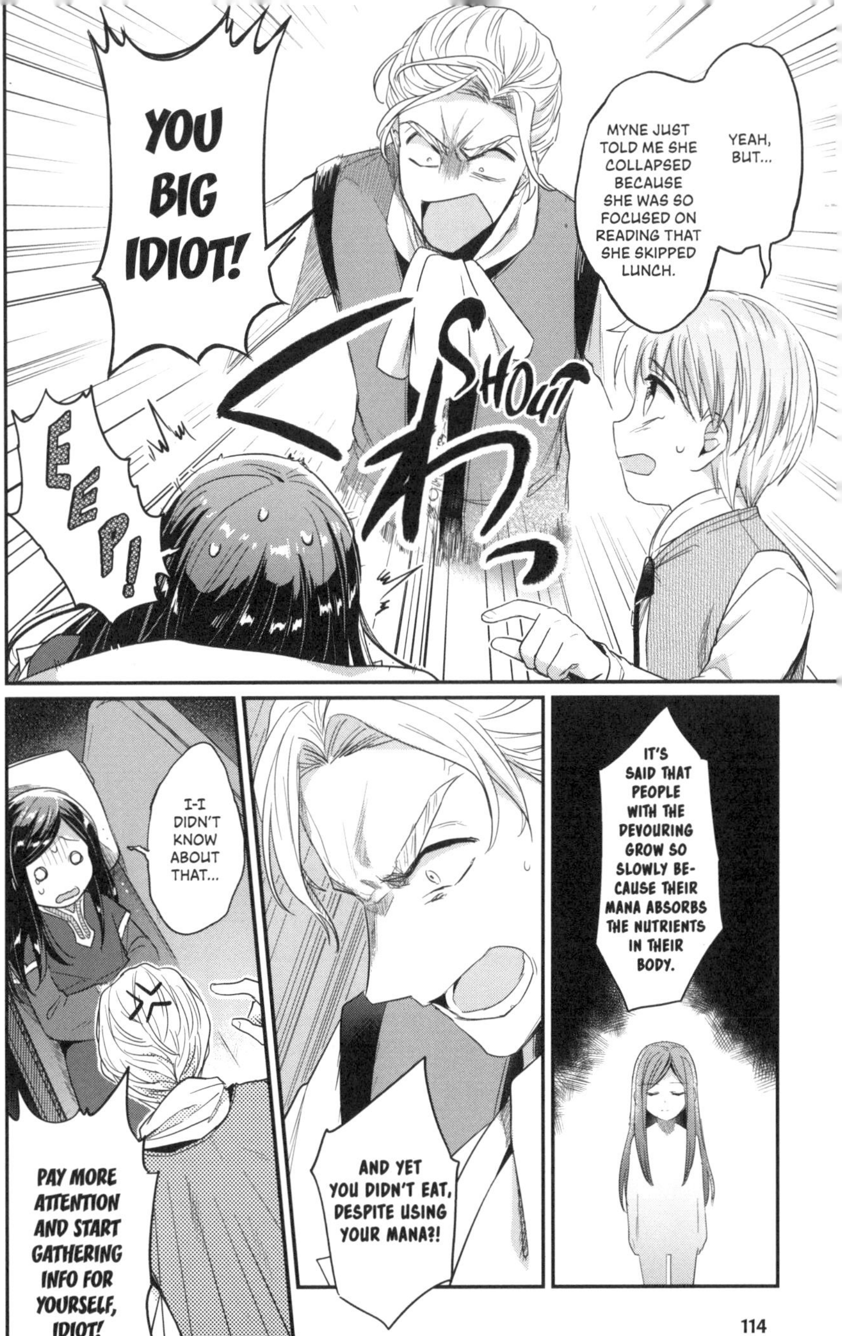
YEAH, BUT...
MYNE JUST TOLD ME SHE COLLAPSED BECAUSE SHE WAS SO FOCUSED ON READING THAT SHE SKIPPED LUNCH.
YOU BIG IDIOT!
SHOUT
EEP!
IT'S SAID THAT PEOPLE WITH THE DEVOURING GROW SO SLOWLY BE-CAUSE THEIR MANA ABSORBS THE NUTRIENTS IN THEIR BODY.
AND YET YOU DIDN'T EAT, DESPITE USING YOUR MANA?!
I-I DIDN'T KNOW ABOUT THAT...
PAY MORE ATTENTION AND START GATHERING INFO FOR YOURSELF, IDIOT!

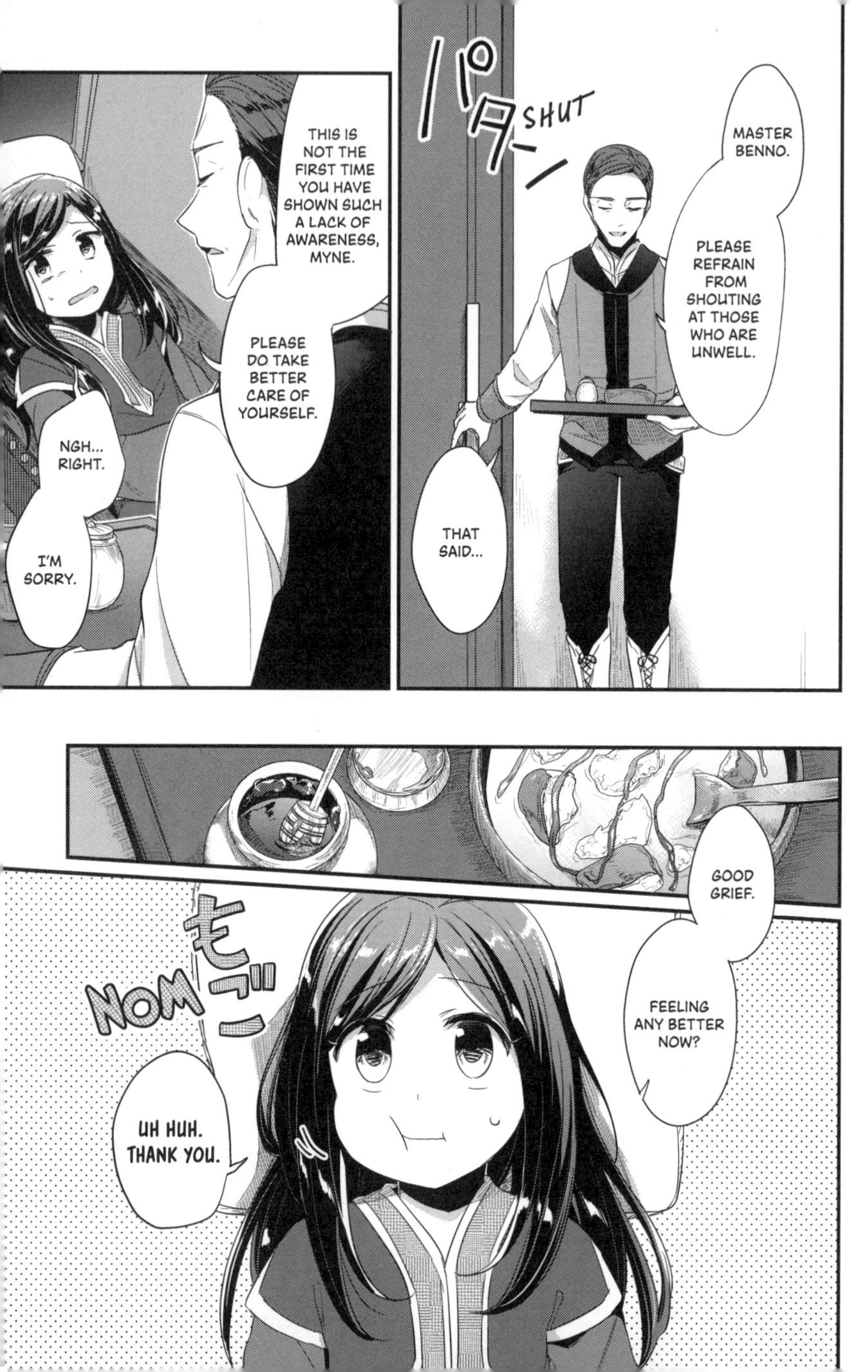
パタ
SHUT
MASTER BENNO.
PLEASE REFRAIN FROM SHOUTING AT THOSE WHO ARE UNWELL.
THAT SAID...
THIS IS NOT THE FIRST TIME YOU HAVE SHOWN SUCH A LACK OF AWARENESS, MYNE.
PLEASE DO TAKE BETTER CARE OF YOURSELF.
NGH... RIGHT.
I'M SORRY.
GOOD GRIEF.
FEELING ANY BETTER NOW?
もごー
NOM
UH HUH. THANK YOU.

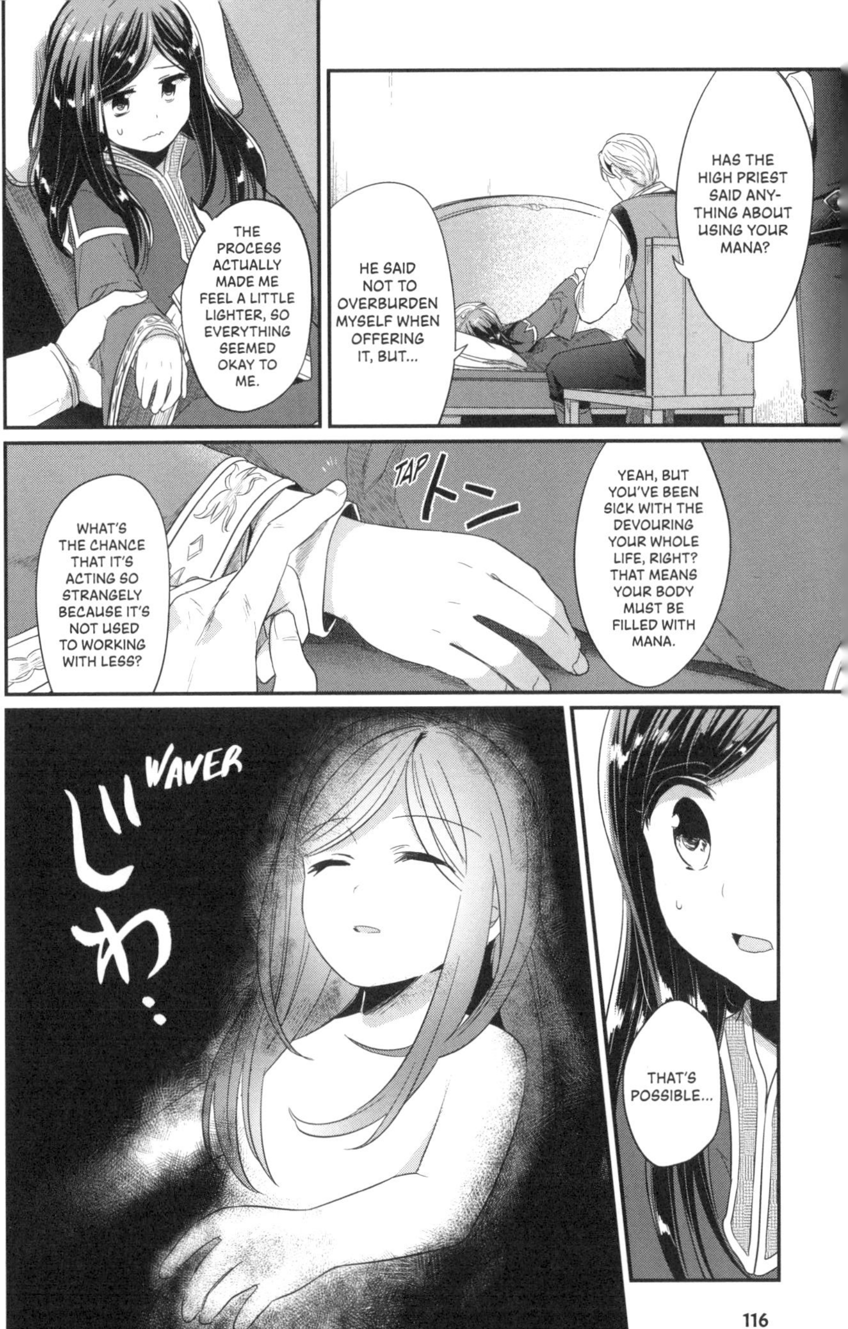
HAS THE HIGH PRIEST SAID ANYTHING ABOUT USING YOUR MANA?
HE SAID NOT TO OVERBURDEN MYSELF WHEN OFFERING IT, BUT...
THE PROCESS ACTUALLY MADE ME FEEL A LITTLE LIGHTER, SO EVERYTHING SEEMED OKAY TO ME.
YEAH, BUT YOU'VE BEEN SICK WITH THE DEVOURING YOUR WHOLE LIFE, RIGHT? THAT MEANS YOUR BODY MUST BE FILLED WITH MANA.
TAP トン
WHAT'S THE CHANCE THAT IT'S ACTING SO STRANGELY BECAUSE IT'S NOT USED TO WORKING WITH LESS?
THAT'S POSSIBLE...
WAVER じわ…

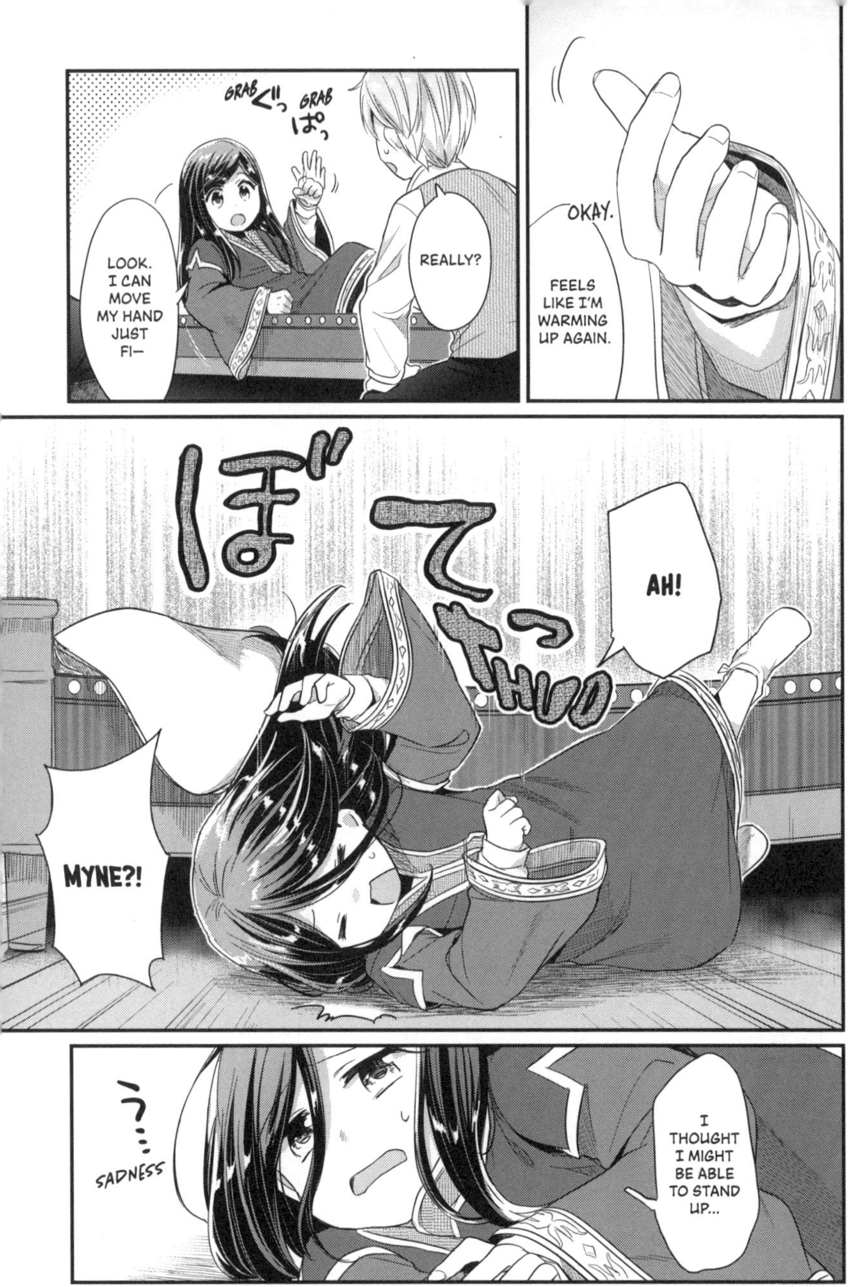
OKAY.
FEELS LIKE I'M WARMING UP AGAIN.
GRAB ぐっ
GRAB ぱっ
REALLY?
LOOK. I CAN MOVE MY HAND JUST FI—
ぼてっ
THUD
AH!
MYNE?!
I THOUGHT I MIGHT BE ABLE TO STAND UP...
う…
SADNESS

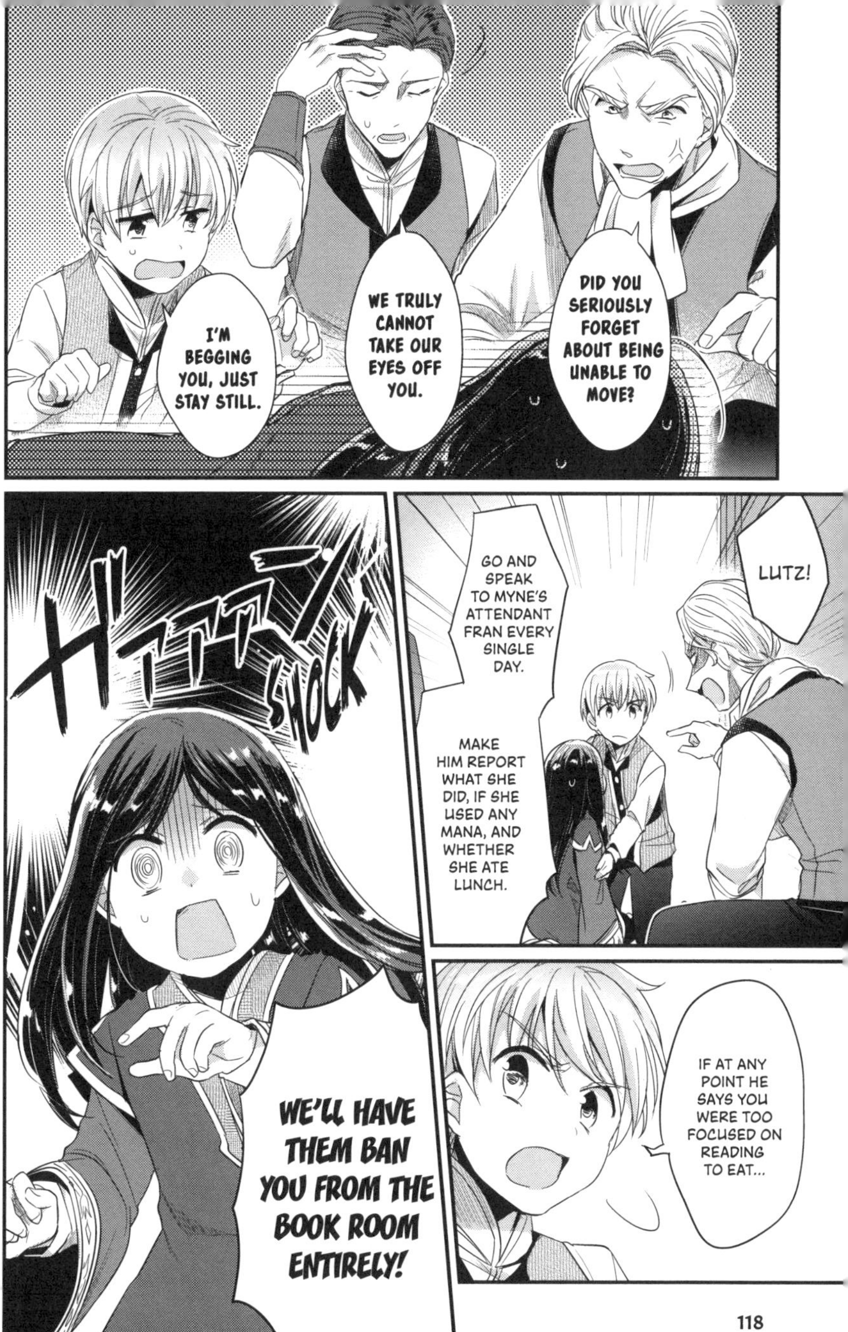
DID YOU SERIOUSLY FORGET ABOUT BEING UNABLE TO MOVE?
WE TRULY CANNOT TAKE OUR EYES OFF YOU.
I'M BEGGING YOU, JUST STAY STILL.
LUTZ!
GO AND SPEAK TO MYNE'S ATTENDANT FRAN EVERY SINGLE DAY.
MAKE HIM REPORT WHAT SHE DID, IF SHE USED ANY MANA, AND WHETHER SHE ATE LUNCH.
IF AT ANY POINT HE SAYS YOU WERE TOO FOCUSED ON READING TO EAT...
SHOCK
WE'LL HAVE THEM BAN YOU FROM THE BOOK ROOM ENTIRELY!

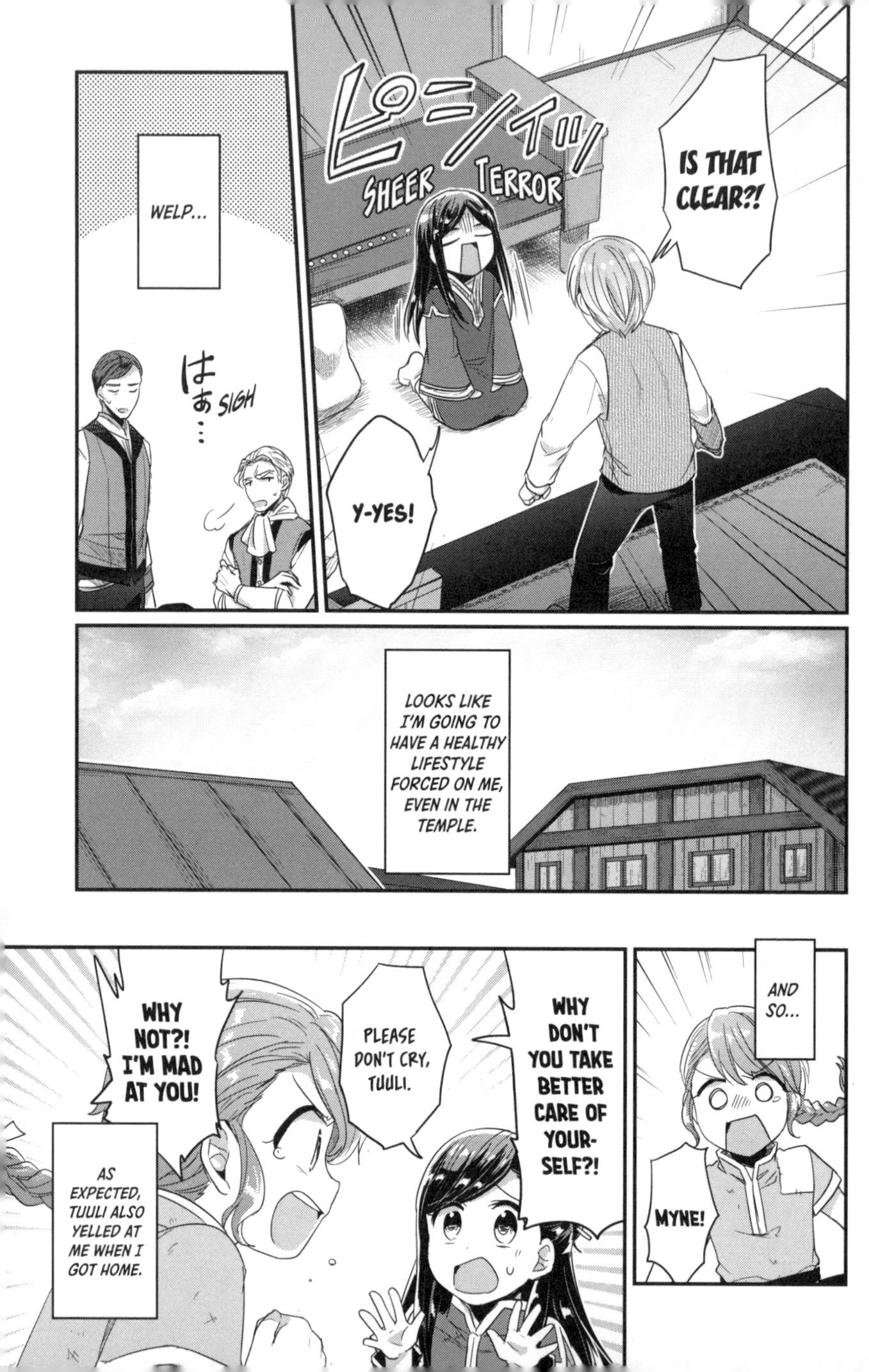
IS THAT CLEAR?!
SHEER TERROR
Y-YES!
WELP...
はぁ…
SIGH
LOOKS LIKE I'M GOING TO HAVE A HEALTHY LIFESTYLE FORCED ON ME, EVEN IN THE TEMPLE.
AND SO...
MYNE!
WHY DON'T YOU TAKE BETTER CARE OF YOURSELF?!
PLEASE DON'T CRY, TUULI.
WHY NOT?! I'M MAD AT YOU!
AS EXPECTED, TUULI ALSO YELLED AT ME WHEN I GOT HOME.

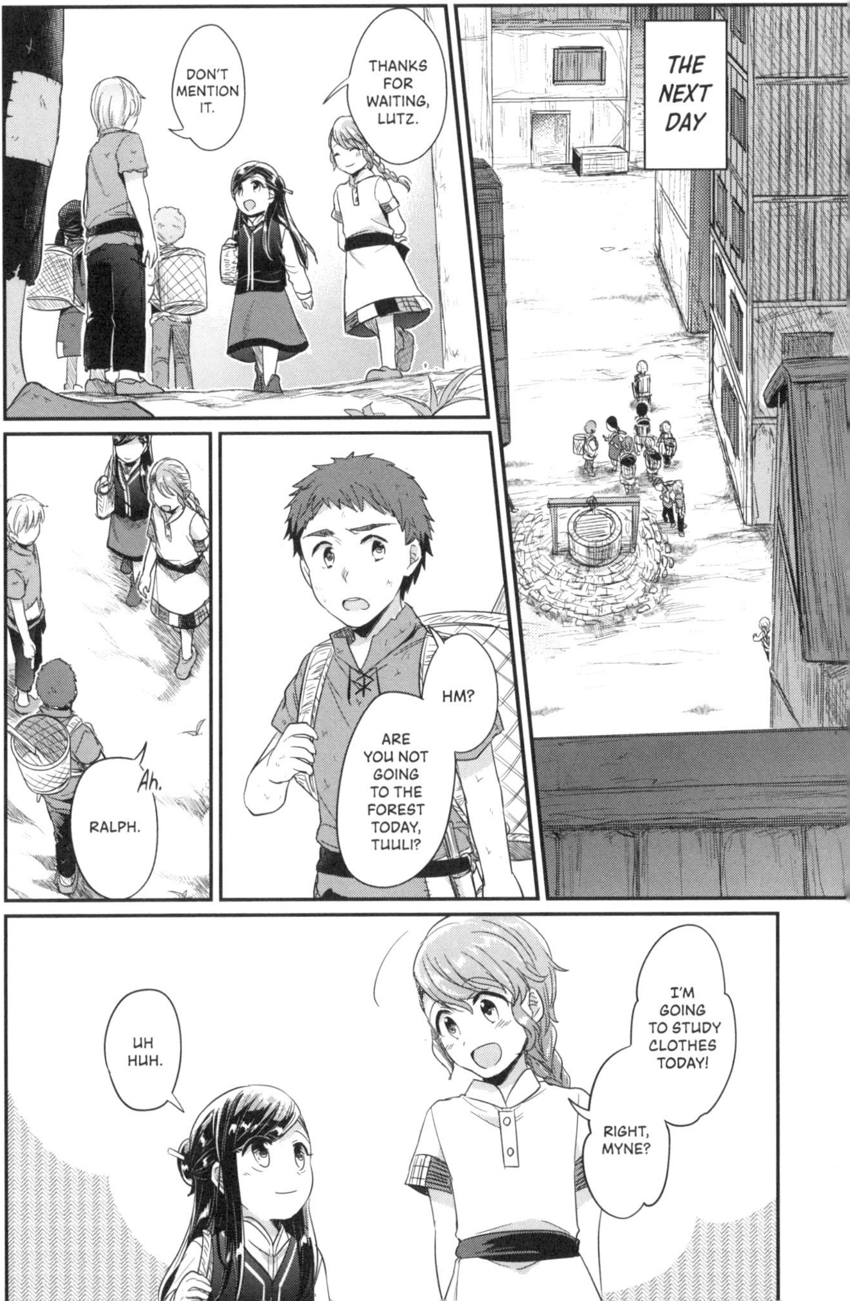
THE NEXT DAY
THANKS FOR WAITING, LUTZ.
DON'T MENTION IT.
HM?
ARE YOU NOT GOING TO THE FOREST TODAY, TUULI?
Ah.
RALPH.
I'M GOING TO STUDY CLOTHES TODAY!
RIGHT, MYNE?
UH HUH.

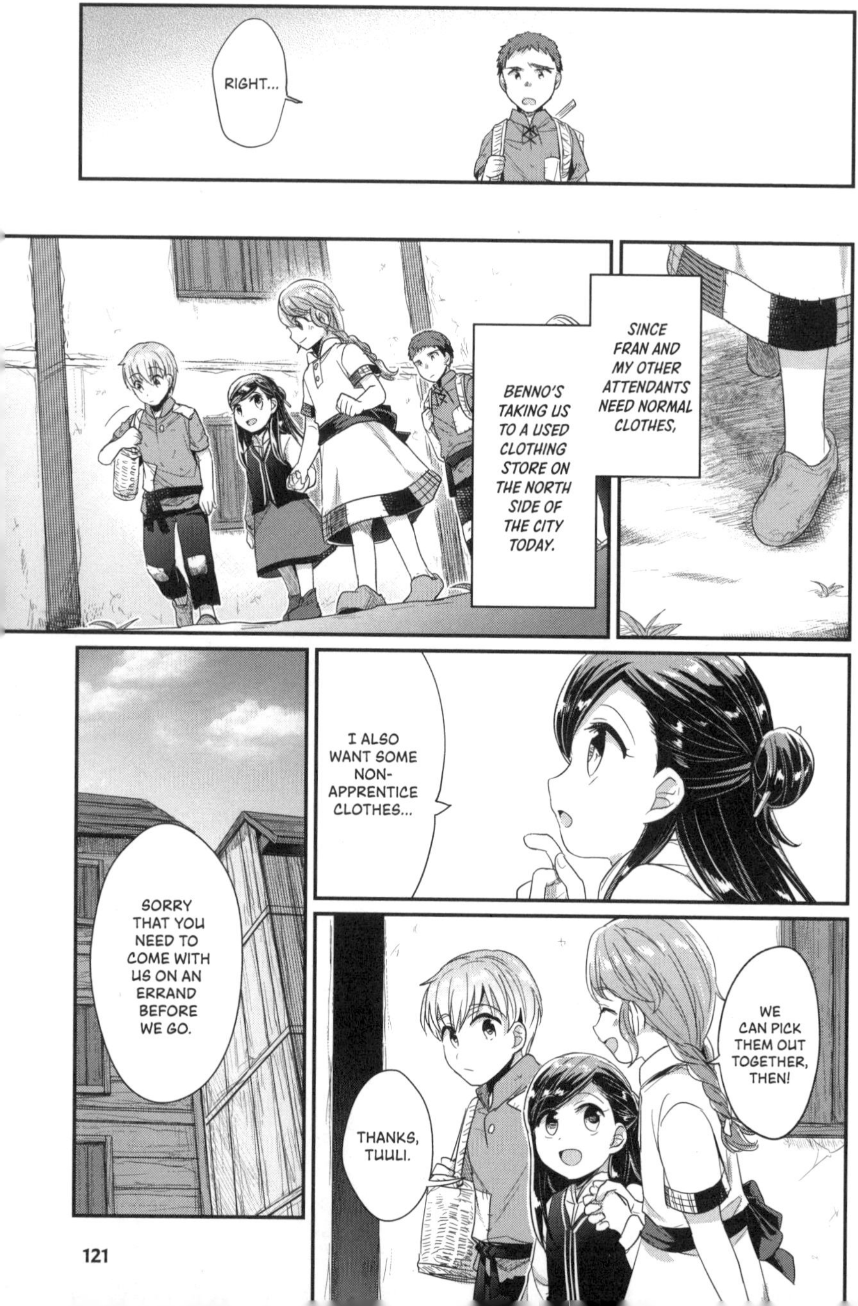
RIGHT...
SINCE FRAN AND MY OTHER ATTENDANTS NEED NORMAL CLOTHES,
BENNO'S TAKING US TO A USED CLOTHING STORE ON THE NORTH SIDE OF THE CITY TODAY.
I ALSO WANT SOME NON-APPRENTICE CLOTHES...
WE CAN PICK THEM OUT TOGETHER, THEN!
THANKS, TUULI.
SORRY THAT YOU NEED TO COME WITH US ON AN ERRAND BEFORE WE GO.

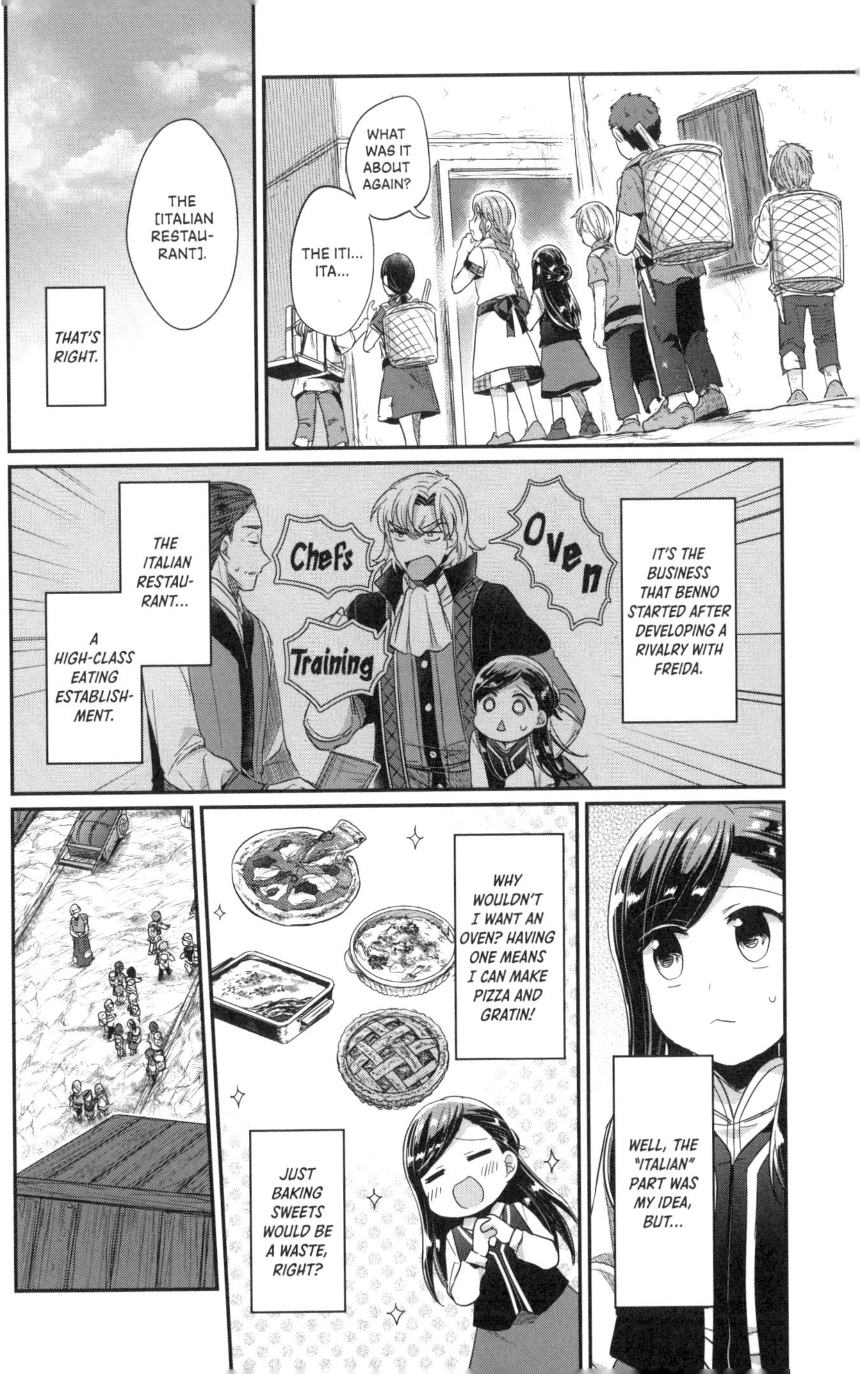
WHAT WAS IT ABOUT AGAIN?
THE ITI... ITA...
THE [ITALIAN RESTAURANT].
THAT'S RIGHT.
IT'S THE BUSINESS THAT BENNO STARTED AFTER DEVELOPING A RIVALRY WITH FREIDA.
Oven
Chefs
Training
THE ITALIAN RESTAURANT...
A HIGH-CLASS EATING ESTABLISHMENT.
WELL, THE "ITALIAN" PART WAS MY IDEA, BUT...
WHY WOULDN'T I WANT AN OVEN? HAVING ONE MEANS I CAN MAKE PIZZA AND GRATIN!
JUST BAKING SWEETS WOULD BE A WASTE, RIGHT?

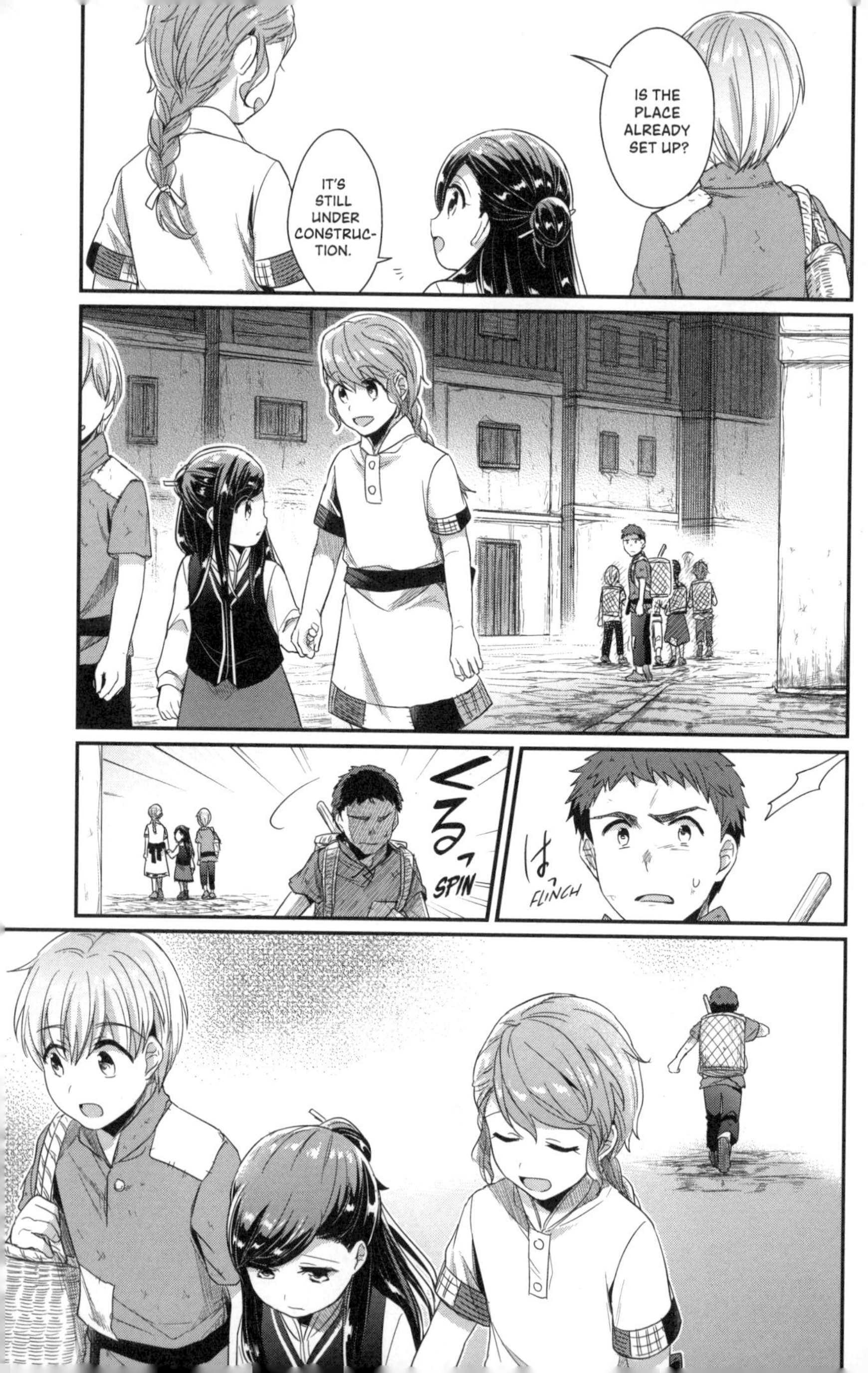
IS THE PLACE ALREADY SET UP?
IT'S STILL UNDER CONSTRUC-TION.
はっ
FLINCH
くるっ
SPIN

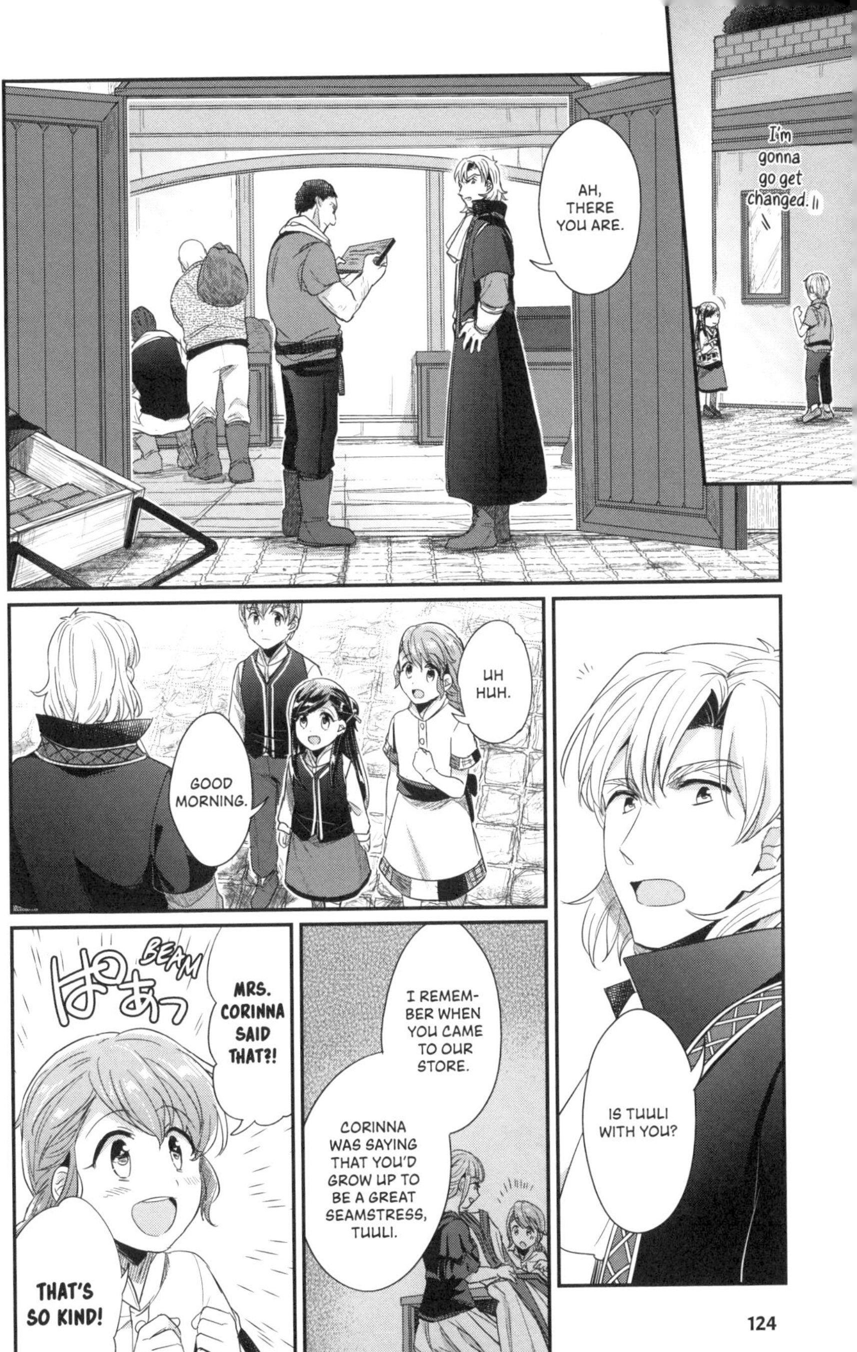
I'm gonna go get changed.
AH, THERE YOU ARE.
IS TUULI WITH YOU?
UH HUH.
GOOD MORNING.
I REMEM-BER WHEN YOU CAME TO OUR STORE.
CORINNA WAS SAYING THAT YOU'D GROW UP TO BE A GREAT SEAMSTRESS, TUULI.
BEAM
MRS. CORINNA SAID THAT?!
THAT'S SO KIND!

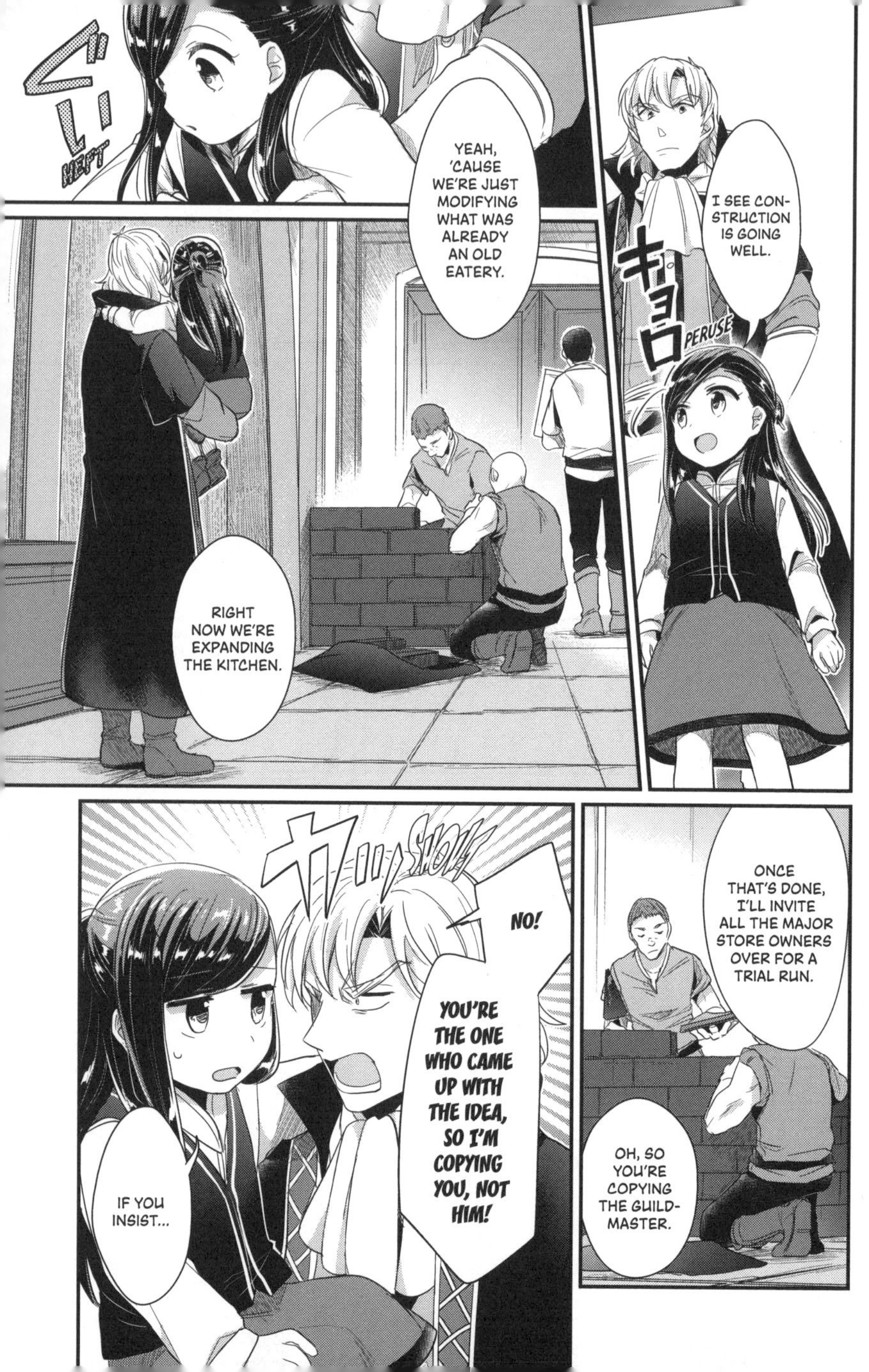
I SEE CON-STRUCTION IS GOING WELL.
キョロ
PERUSE
ぐい
HEFT
YEAH, 'CAUSE WE'RE JUST MODIFYING WHAT WAS ALREADY AN OLD EATERY.
RIGHT NOW WE'RE EXPANDING THE KITCHEN.
ONCE THAT'S DONE, I'LL INVITE ALL THE MAJOR STORE OWNERS OVER FOR A TRIAL RUN.
OH, SO YOU'RE COPYING THE GUILD-MASTER.
NO!
YOU'RE THE ONE WHO CAME UP WITH THE IDEA, SO I'M COPYING YOU, NOT HIM!
IF YOU INSIST...

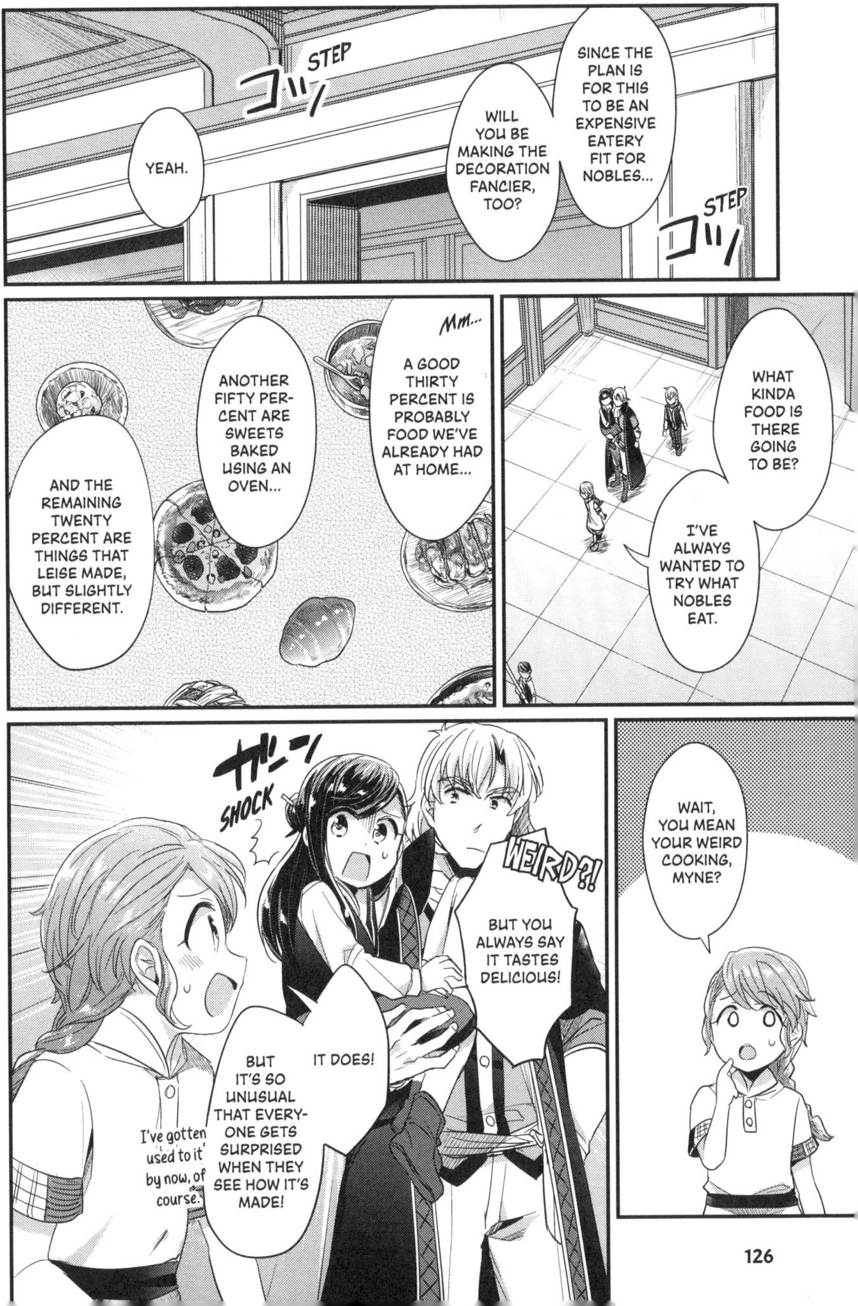
SINCE THE PLAN IS FOR THIS TO BE AN EXPENSIVE EATERY FIT FOR NOBLES...
WILL YOU BE MAKING THE DECORATION FANCIER, TOO?
STEP
STEP
YEAH.
WHAT KINDA FOOD IS THERE GOING TO BE?
I'VE ALWAYS WANTED TO TRY WHAT NOBLES EAT.
Mm...
A GOOD THIRTY PERCENT IS PROBABLY FOOD WE'VE ALREADY HAD AT HOME...
ANOTHER FIFTY PER-CENT ARE SWEETS BAKED USING AN OVEN...
AND THE REMAINING TWENTY PERCENT ARE THINGS THAT LEISE MADE, BUT SLIGHTLY DIFFERENT.
WAIT, YOU MEAN YOUR WEIRD COOKING, MYNE?
SHOCK
WEIRD?!
BUT YOU ALWAYS SAY IT TASTES DELICIOUS!
IT DOES!
BUT IT'S SO UNUSUAL THAT EVERY-ONE GETS SURPRISED WHEN THEY SEE HOW IT'S MADE!
I've gotten used to it by now, of course.

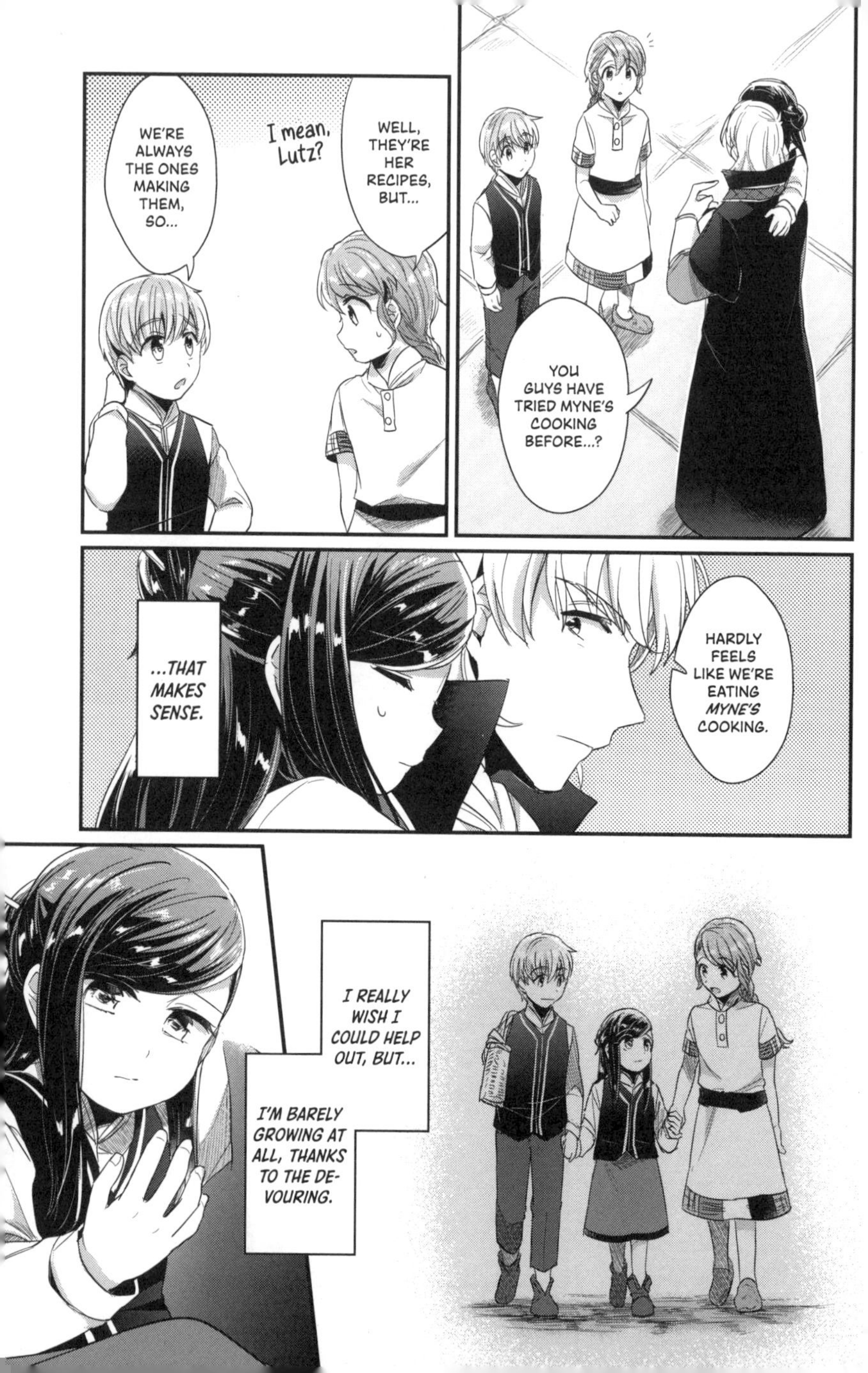
YOU GUYS HAVE TRIED MYNE'S COOKING BEFORE...?
WELL, THEY'RE HER RECIPES, BUT...
I mean, Lutz?
WE'RE ALWAYS THE ONES MAKING THEM, SO...
HARDLY FEELS LIKE WE'RE EATING *MYNE'S* COOKING.
...THAT MAKES SENSE.
I REALLY WISH I COULD HELP OUT, BUT...
I'M BARELY GROWING AT ALL, THANKS TO THE DE-VOURING.

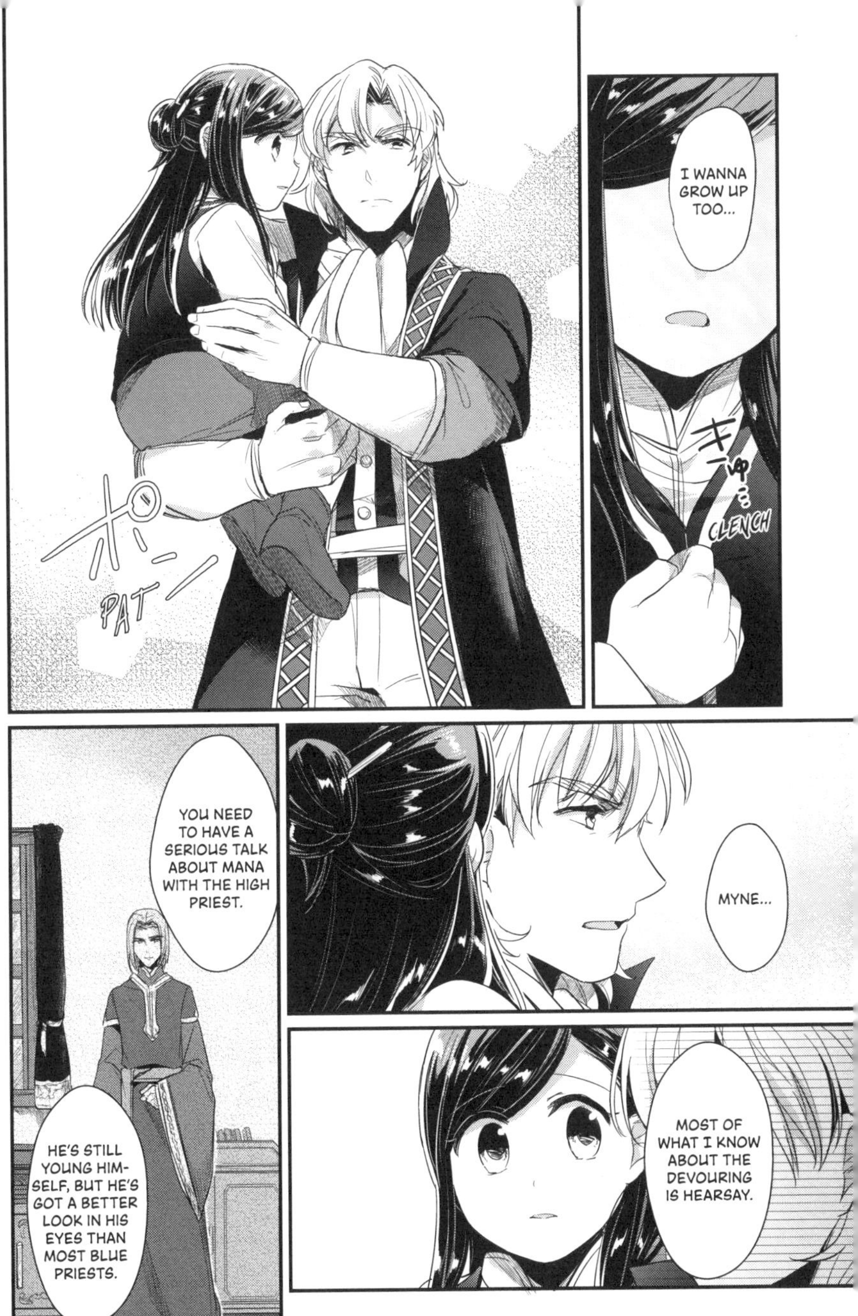
I WANNA GROW UP TOO...
CLENCH
PAT
MYNE...
MOST OF WHAT I KNOW ABOUT THE DEVOURING IS HEARSAY.
YOU NEED TO HAVE A SERIOUS TALK ABOUT MANA WITH THE HIGH PRIEST.
HE'S STILL YOUNG HIM-SELF, BUT HE'S GOT A BETTER LOOK IN HIS EYES THAN MOST BLUE PRIESTS.

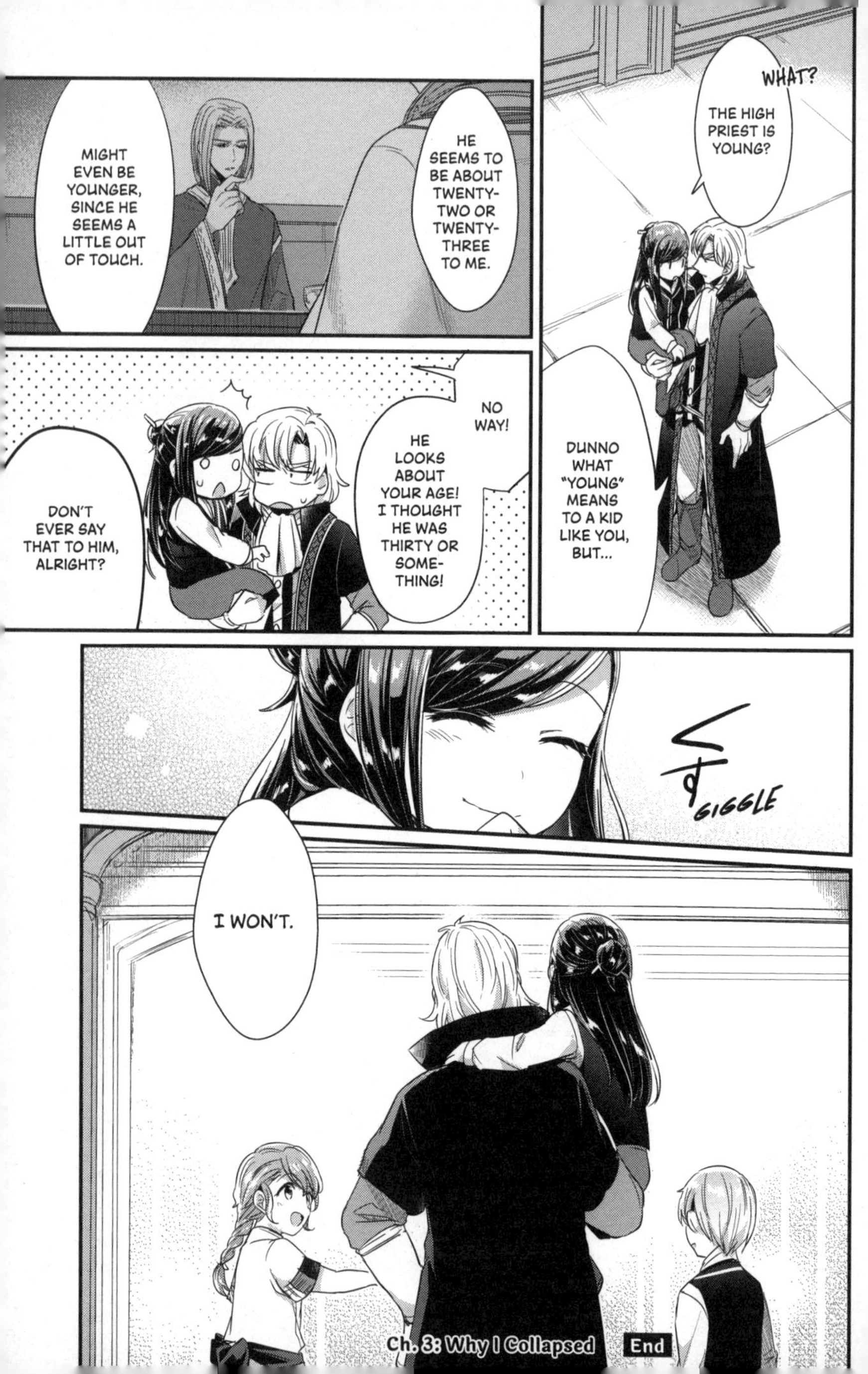
WHAT?
THE HIGH PRIEST IS YOUNG?
DUNNO WHAT "YOUNG" MEANS TO A KID LIKE YOU, BUT...
HE SEEMS TO BE ABOUT TWENTY-TWO OR TWENTY-THREE TO ME.
MIGHT EVEN BE YOUNGER, SINCE HE SEEMS A LITTLE OUT OF TOUCH.
NO WAY!
HE LOOKS ABOUT YOUR AGE! I THOUGHT HE WAS THIRTY OR SOME-THING!
DON'T EVER SAY THAT TO HIM, ALRIGHT?
くす
GIGGLE
I WON'T.
Ch. 3: Why I Collapsed End

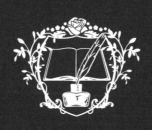

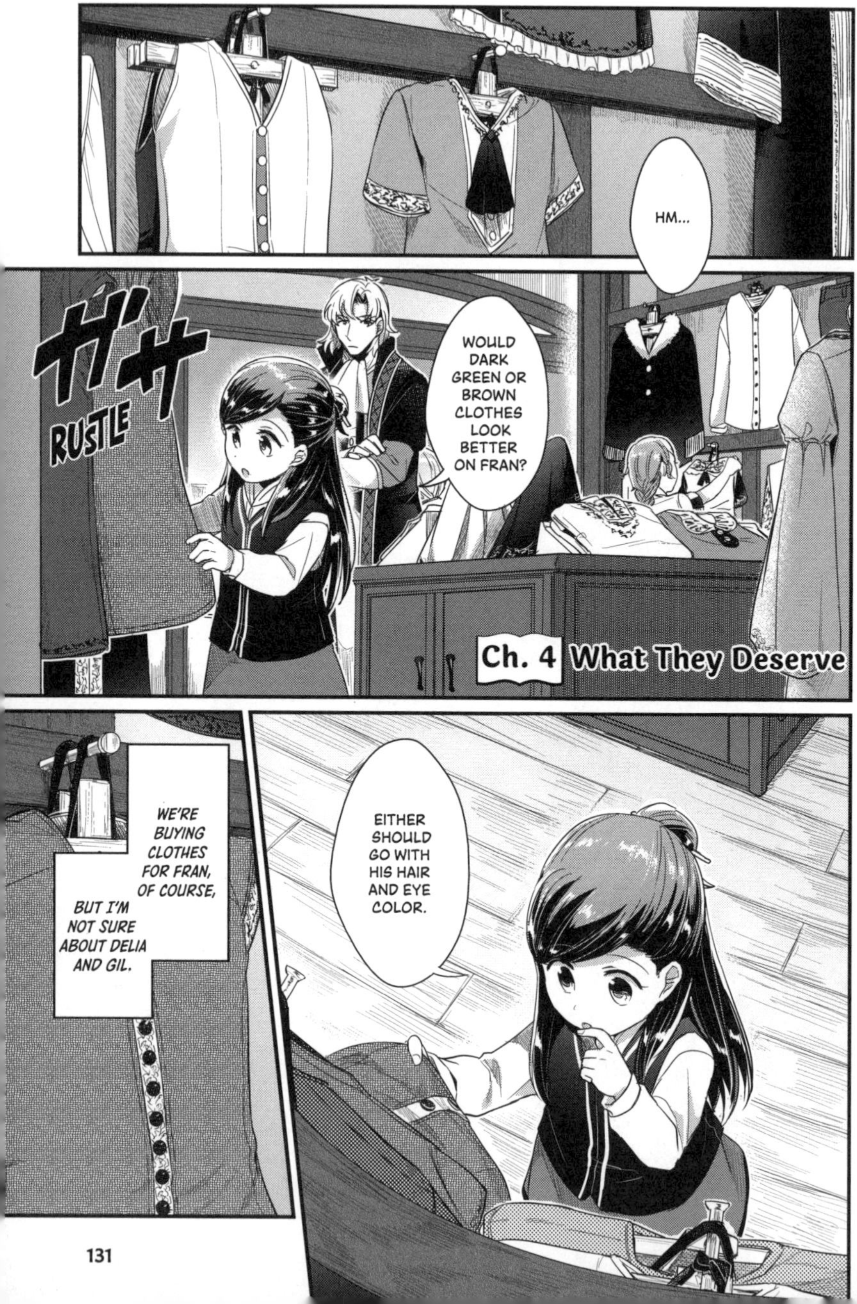
HM...
WOULD DARK GREEN OR BROWN CLOTHES LOOK BETTER ON FRAN?
RUSTLE
Ch. 4 What They Deserve
EITHER SHOULD GO WITH HIS HAIR AND EYE COLOR.
WE'RE BUYING CLOTHES FOR FRAN, OF COURSE,
BUT I'M NOT SURE ABOUT DELIA AND GIL.

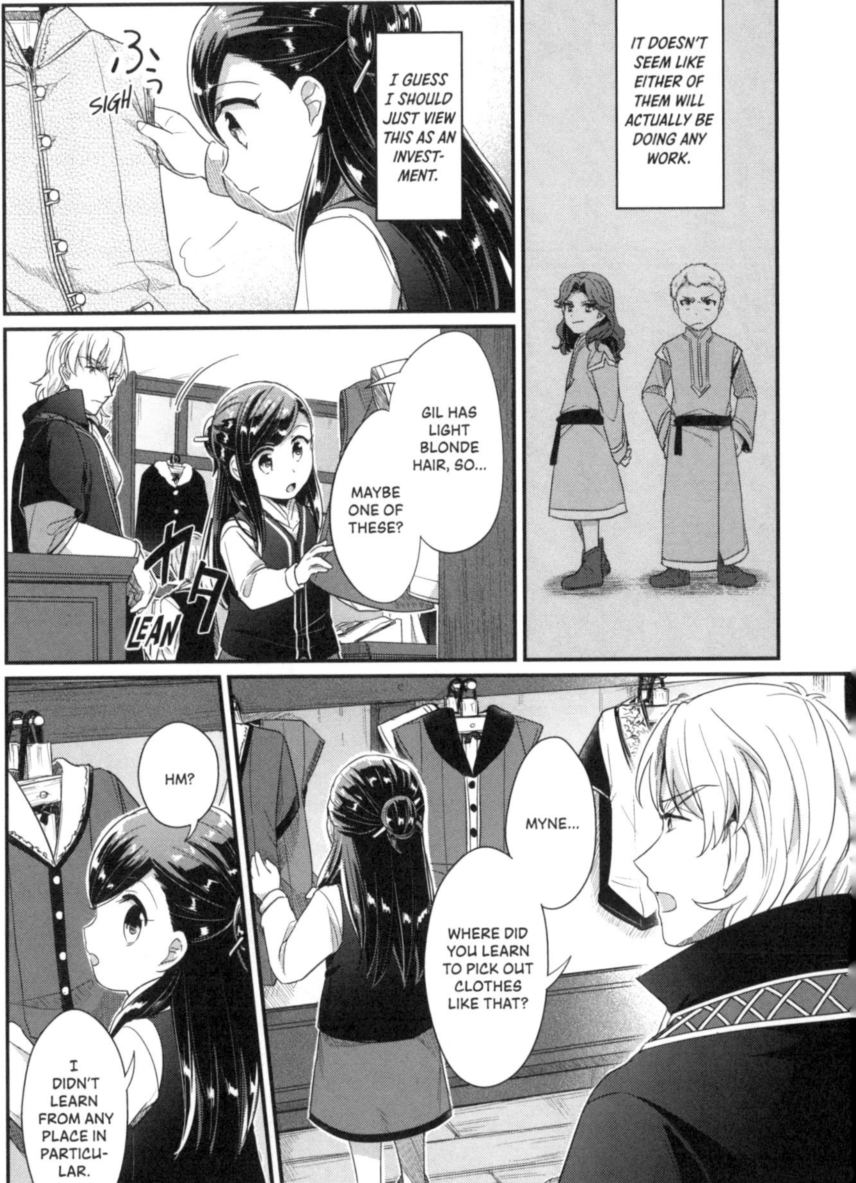
IT DOESN'T SEEM LIKE EITHER OF THEM WILL ACTUALLY BE DOING ANY WORK.
I GUESS I SHOULD JUST VIEW THIS AS AN INVEST-MENT.
SIGH
GIL HAS LIGHT BLONDE HAIR, SO...
MAYBE ONE OF THESE?
LEAN
MYNE...
WHERE DID YOU LEARN TO PICK OUT CLOTHES LIKE THAT?
HM?
I DIDN'T LEARN FROM ANY PLACE IN PARTICU-LAR.

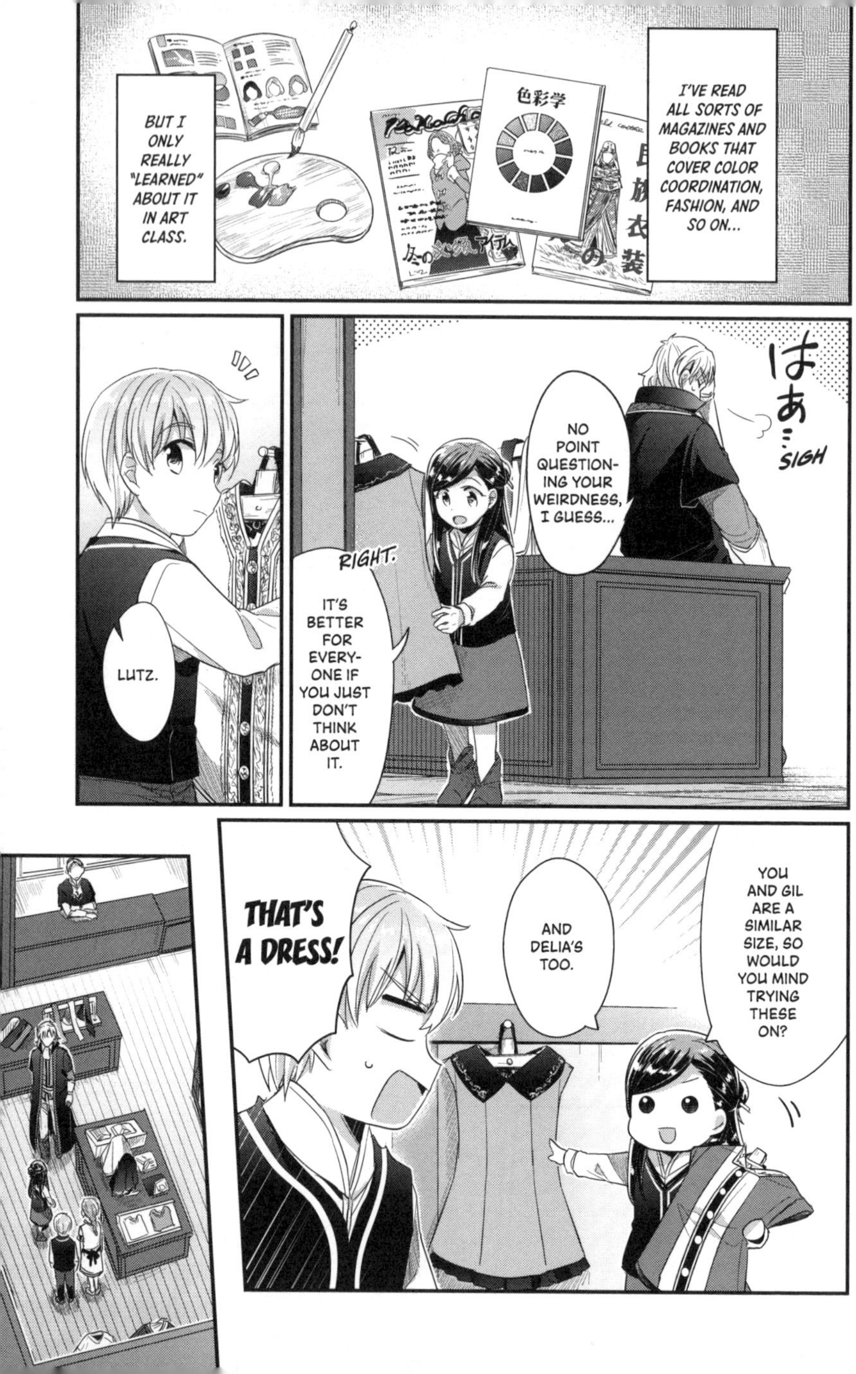

I'VE READ ALL SORTS OF MAGAZINES AND BOOKS THAT COVER COLOR COORDINATION, FASHION, AND SO ON...
色彩学
BUT I ONLY REALLY "LEARNED" ABOUT IT IN ART CLASS.
はぁ
SIGH
NO POINT QUESTIONING YOUR WEIRDNESS, I GUESS...
RIGHT.
IT'S BETTER FOR EVERYONE IF YOU JUST DON'T THINK ABOUT IT.
LUTZ.
YOU AND GIL ARE A SIMILAR SIZE, SO WOULD YOU MIND TRYING THESE ON?
AND DELIA'S TOO.
THAT'S A DRESS!

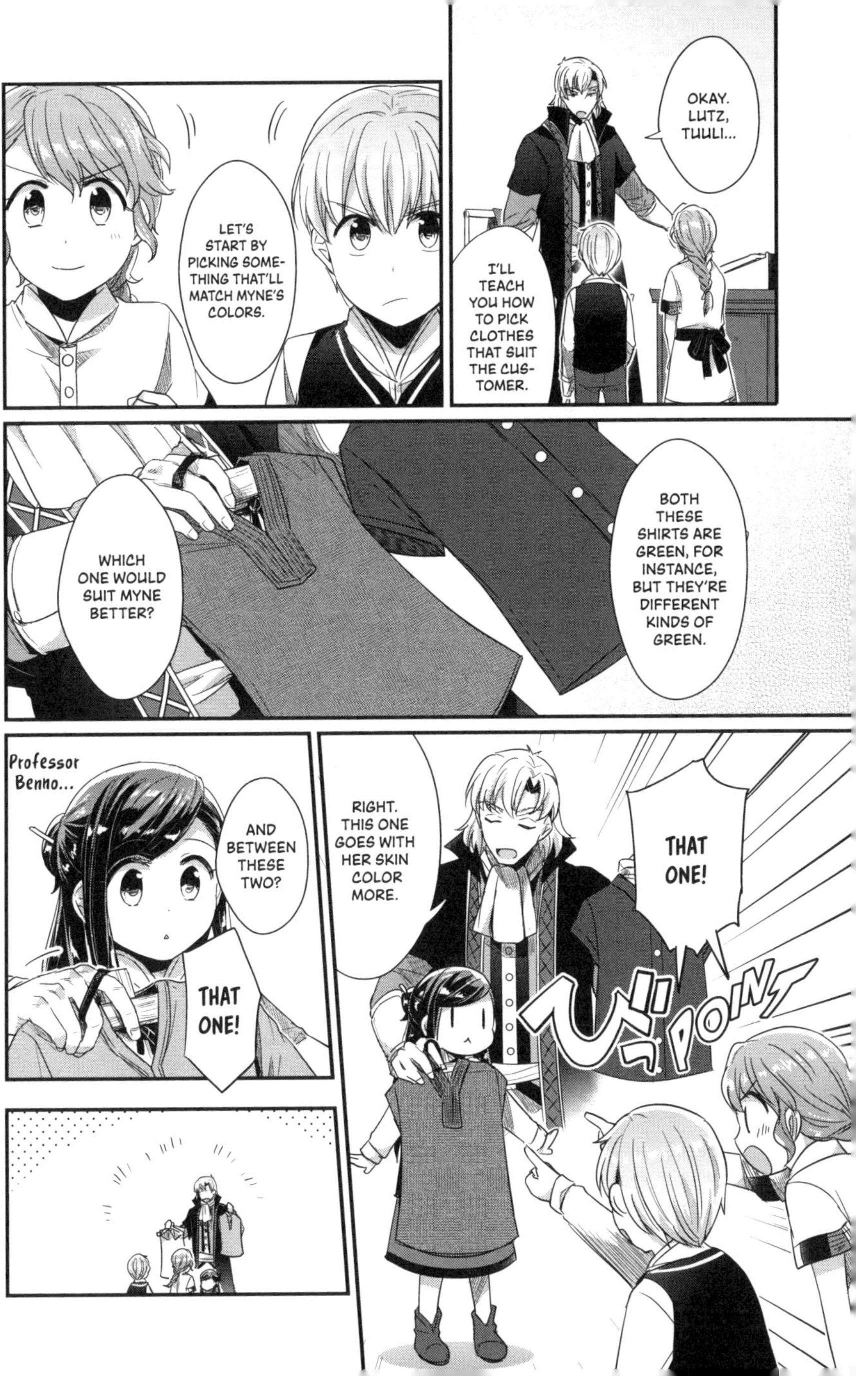
OKAY. LUTZ, TUULI...
I'LL TEACH YOU HOW TO PICK CLOTHES THAT SUIT THE CUSTOMER.
LET'S START BY PICKING SOMETHING THAT'LL MATCH MYNE'S COLORS.
BOTH THESE SHIRTS ARE GREEN, FOR INSTANCE, BUT THEY'RE DIFFERENT KINDS OF GREEN.
WHICH ONE WOULD SUIT MYNE BETTER?
THAT ONE!
RIGHT. THIS ONE GOES WITH HER SKIN COLOR MORE.
POINT
Professor Benno...
AND BETWEEN THESE TWO?
THAT ONE!

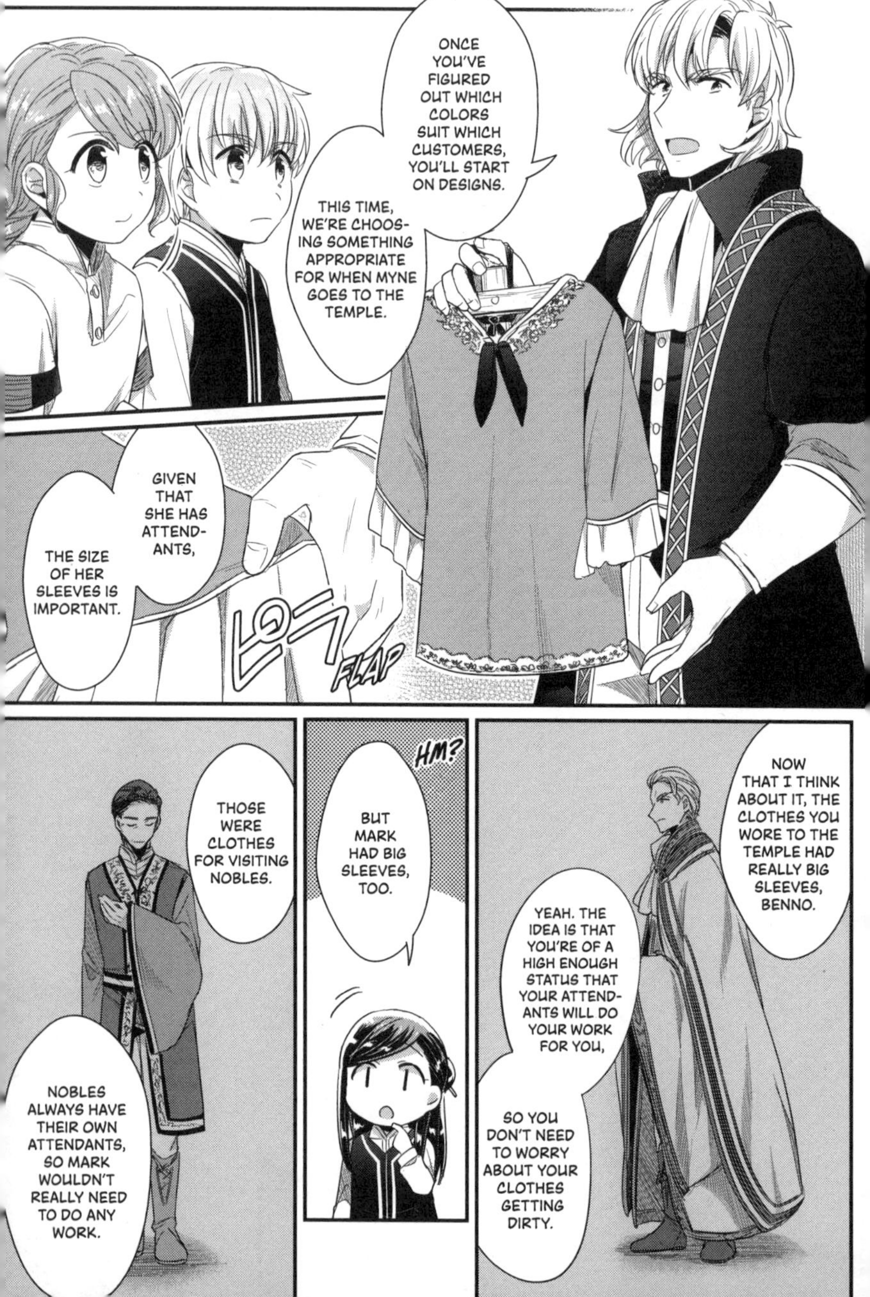
ONCE YOU'VE FIGURED OUT WHICH COLORS SUIT WHICH CUSTOMERS, YOU'LL START ON DESIGNS.
THIS TIME, WE'RE CHOOS-ING SOMETHING APPROPRIATE FOR WHEN MYNE GOES TO THE TEMPLE.
GIVEN THAT SHE HAS ATTEND-ANTS,
THE SIZE OF HER SLEEVES IS IMPORTANT.
FLAP
NOW THAT I THINK ABOUT IT, THE CLOTHES YOU WORE TO THE TEMPLE HAD REALLY BIG SLEEVES, BENNO.
YEAH. THE IDEA IS THAT YOU'RE OF A HIGH ENOUGH STATUS THAT YOUR ATTEND-ANTS WILL DO YOUR WORK FOR YOU,
SO YOU DON'T NEED TO WORRY ABOUT YOUR CLOTHES GETTING DIRTY.
HM?
BUT MARK HAD BIG SLEEVES, TOO.
THOSE WERE CLOTHES FOR VISITING NOBLES.
NOBLES ALWAYS HAVE THEIR OWN ATTENDANTS, SO MARK WOULDN'T REALLY NEED TO DO ANY WORK.

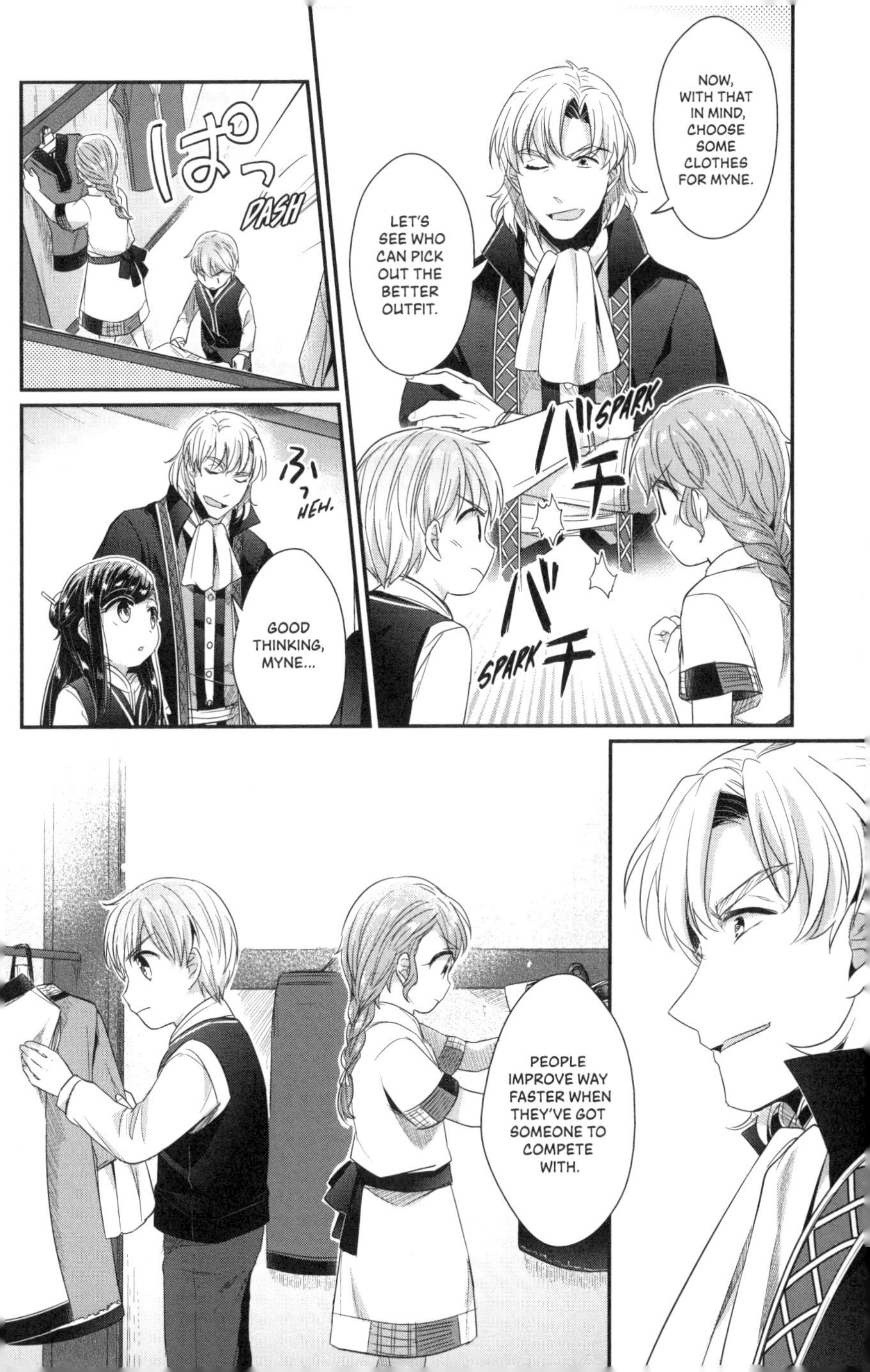
NOW, WITH THAT IN MIND, CHOOSE SOME CLOTHES FOR MYNE.
LET'S SEE WHO CAN PICK OUT THE BETTER OUTFIT.
バチ
SPARK
バチ
SPARK
ぱっ
DASH
ふっ
HEH.
GOOD THINKING, MYNE...
PEOPLE IMPROVE WAY FASTER WHEN THEY'VE GOT SOMEONE TO COMPETE WITH.

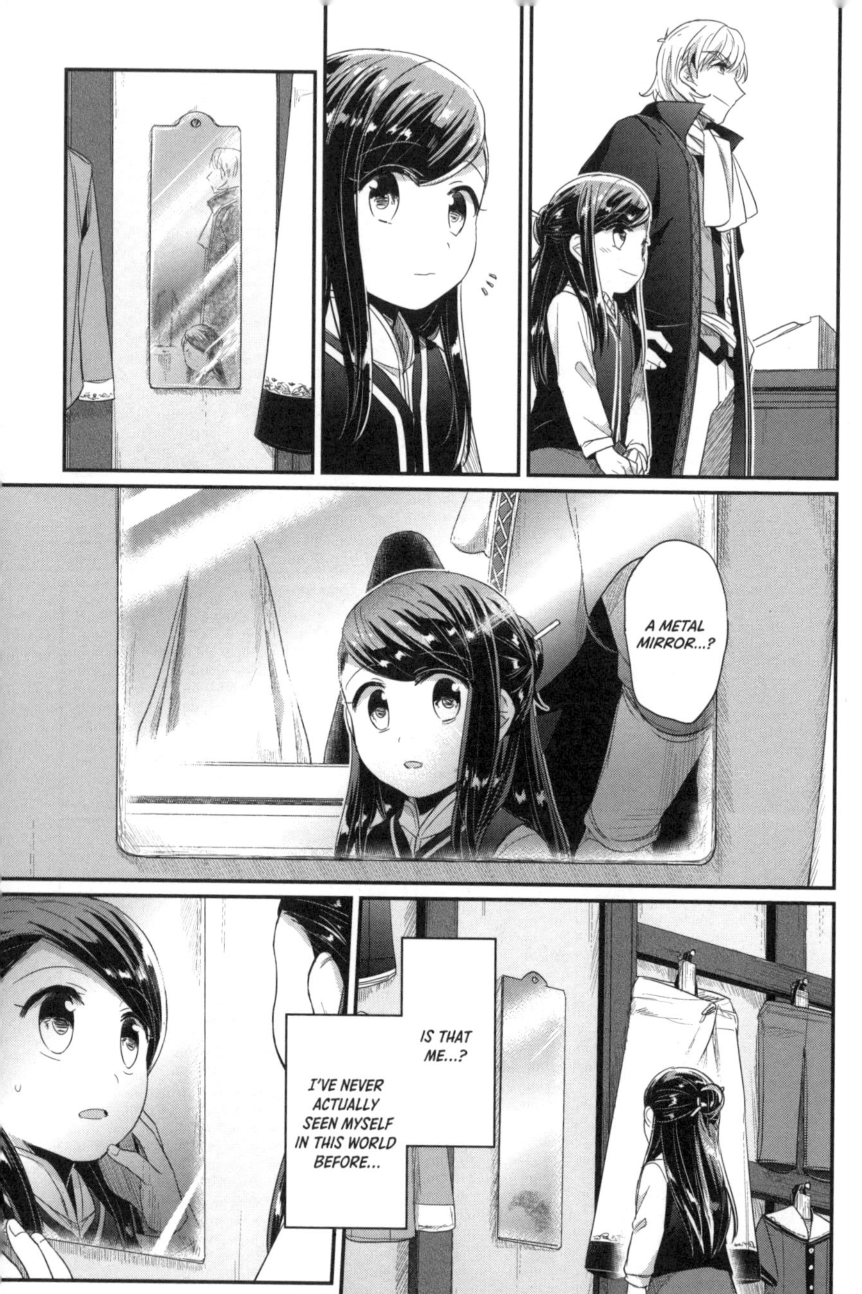

A METAL MIRROR...?
IS THAT ME...?
I'VE NEVER ACTUALLY SEEN MYSELF IN THIS WORLD BEFORE...

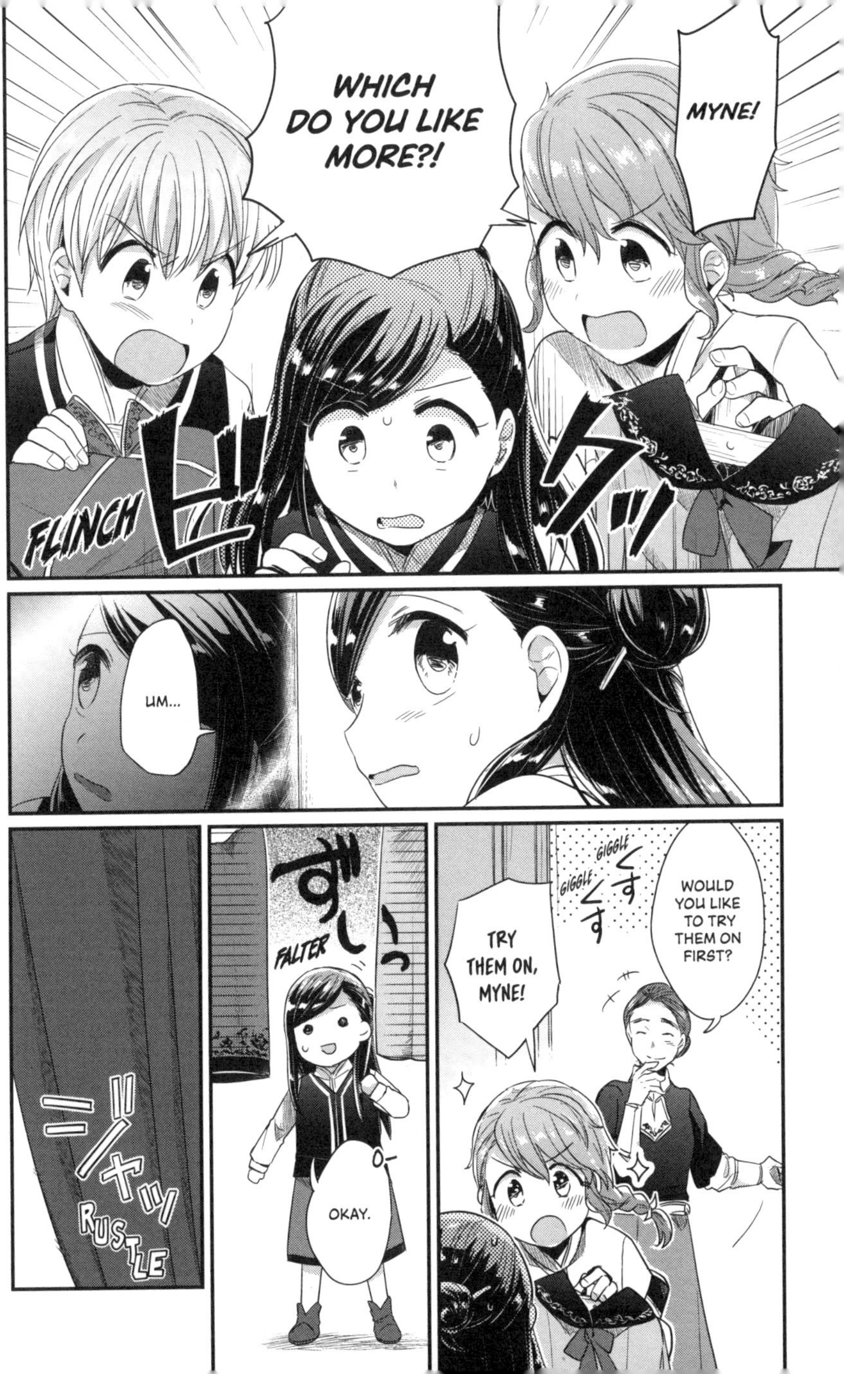
MYNE!
WHICH DO YOU LIKE MORE?!
グッ
ビッ
FLINCH
UM...
WOULD YOU LIKE TO TRY THEM ON FIRST?
くすくす
GIGGLE GIGGLE
TRY THEM ON, MYNE!
ずしっ
FALTER
O-OKAY.
RUSTLE

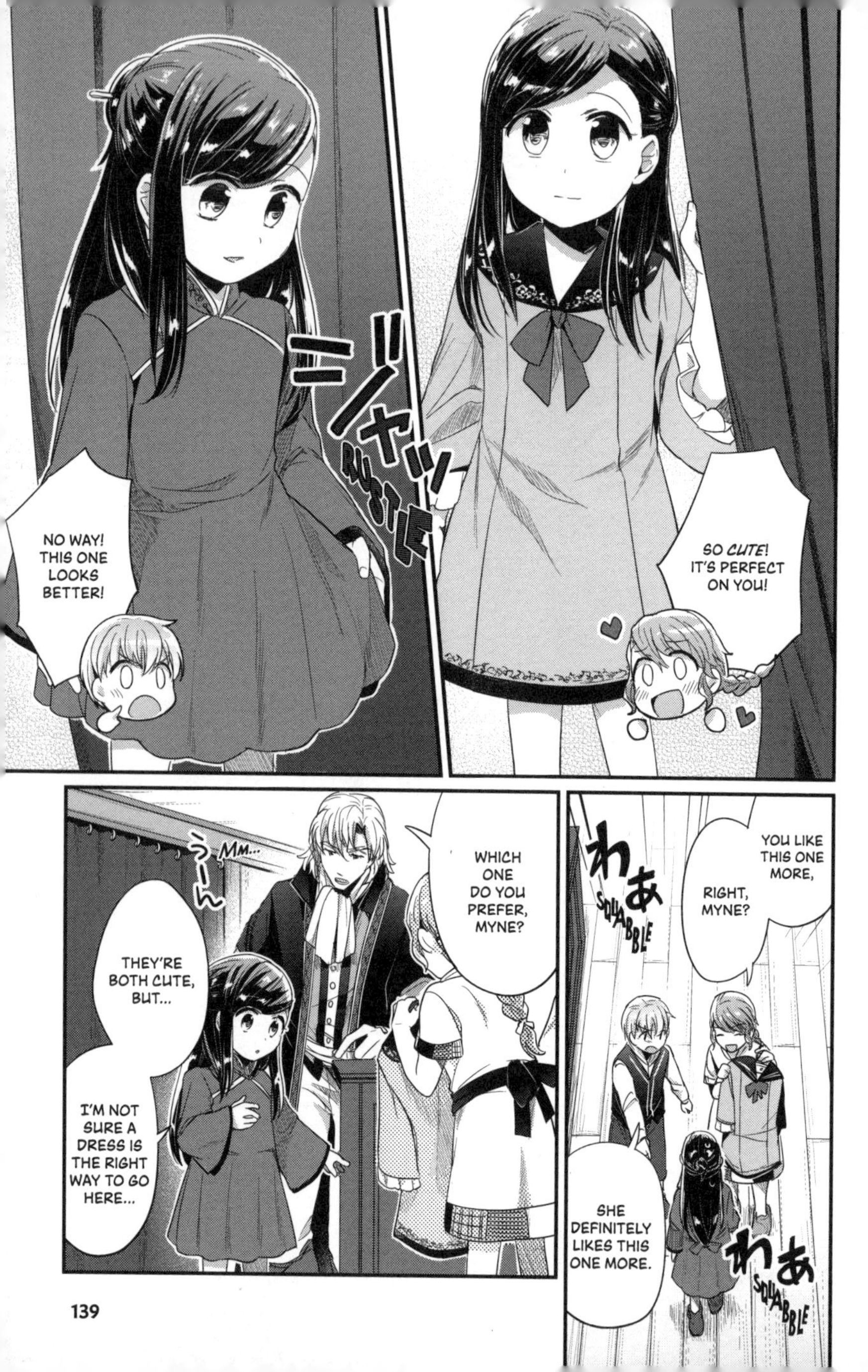
SO CUTE! IT'S PERFECT ON YOU!
RUSTLE
NO WAY! THIS ONE LOOKS BETTER!
YOU LIKE THIS ONE MORE,
RIGHT, MYNE?
わあ
SQUABBLE
SHE DEFINITELY LIKES THIS ONE MORE.
わあ
SQUABBLE
WHICH ONE DO YOU PREFER, MYNE?
うーん
MM...
THEY'RE BOTH CUTE, BUT...
I'M NOT SURE A DRESS IS THE RIGHT WAY TO GO HERE...

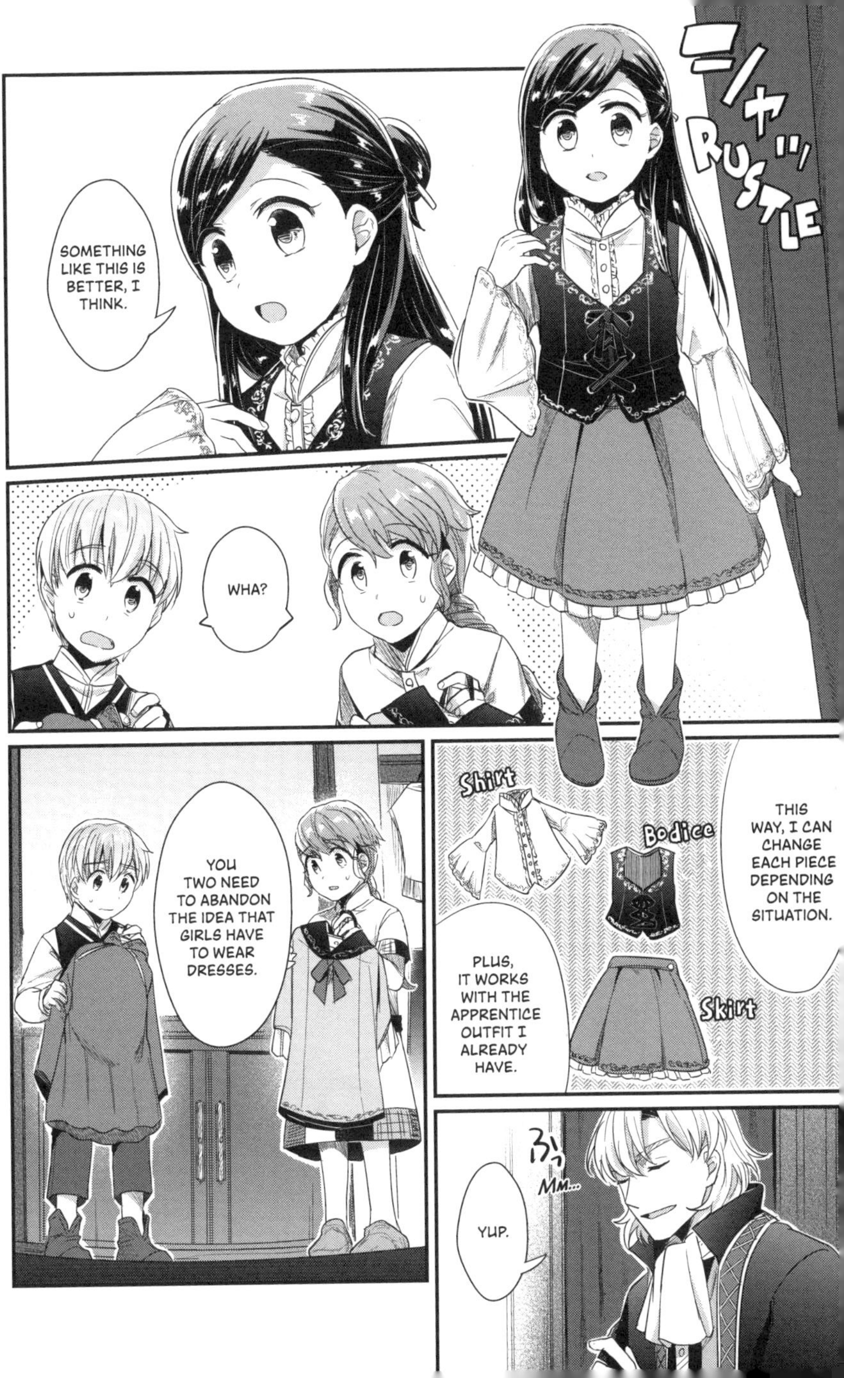
RUSTLE
SOMETHING LIKE THIS IS BETTER, I THINK.
WHA?
THIS WAY, I CAN CHANGE EACH PIECE DEPENDING ON THE SITUATION.
Shirt
Bodice
PLUS, IT WORKS WITH THE APPRENTICE OUTFIT I ALREADY HAVE.
Skirt
ふっ
MM...
YUP.
YOU TWO NEED TO ABANDON THE IDEA THAT GIRLS HAVE TO WEAR DRESSES.

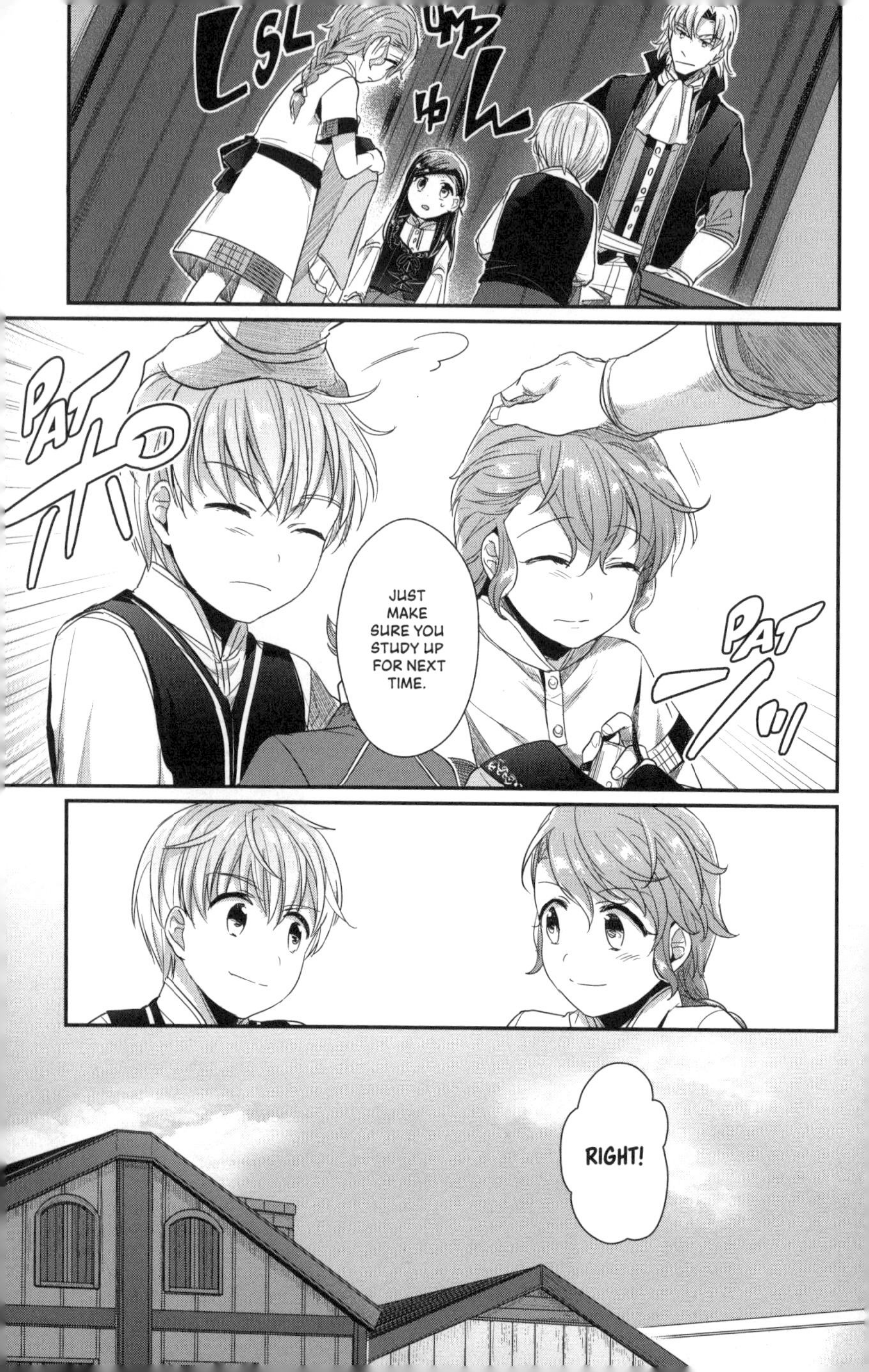
SLUMP
PAT
JUST MAKE SURE YOU STUDY UP FOR NEXT TIME.
PAT
RIGHT!

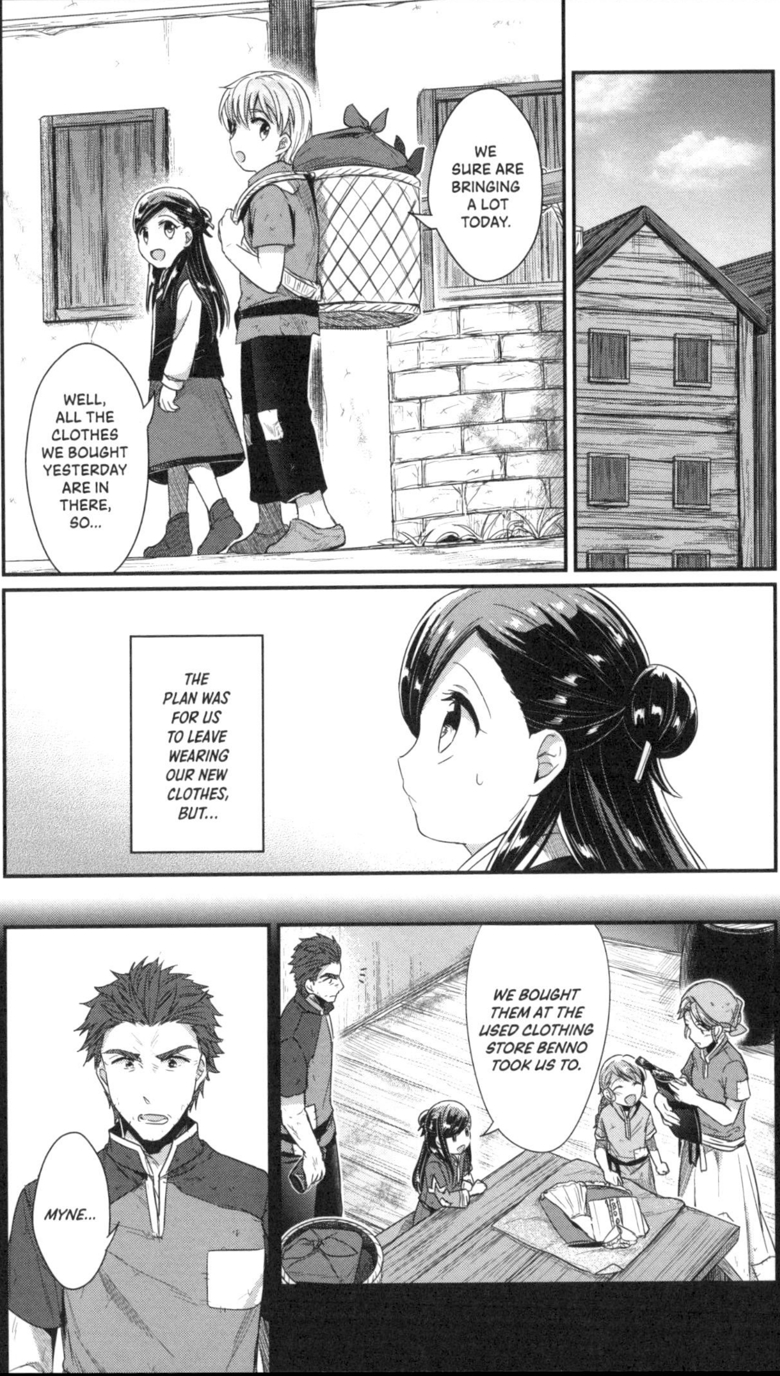
WE SURE ARE BRINGING A LOT TODAY.
WELL, ALL THE CLOTHES WE BOUGHT YESTERDAY ARE IN THERE, SO...
THE PLAN WAS FOR US TO LEAVE WEARING OUR NEW CLOTHES, BUT...
WE BOUGHT THEM AT THE USED CLOTHING STORE BENNO TOOK US TO.
MYNE...

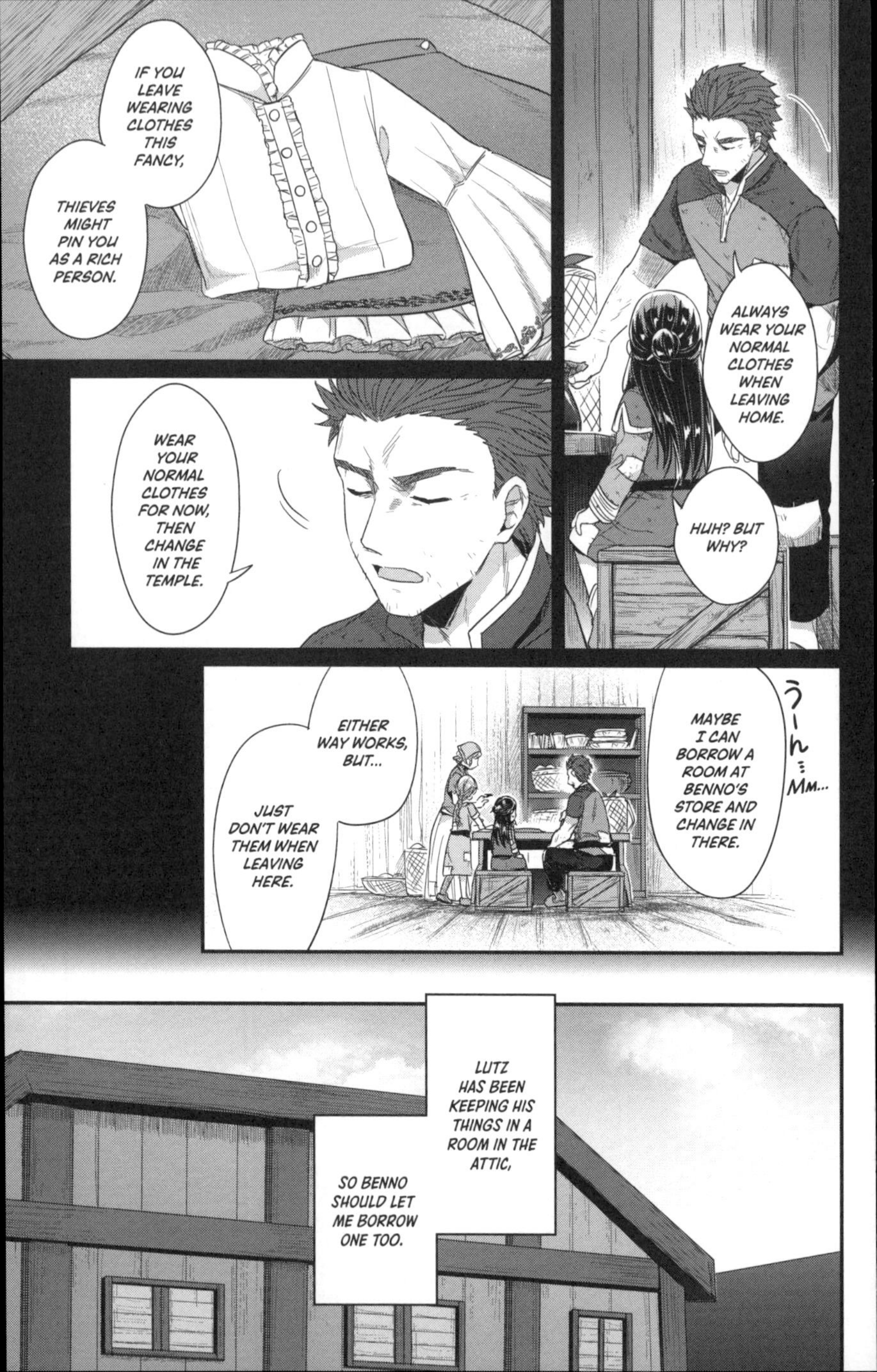
ALWAYS WEAR YOUR NORMAL CLOTHES WHEN LEAVING HOME.
HUH? BUT WHY?
IF YOU LEAVE WEARING CLOTHES THIS FANCY,
THIEVES MIGHT PIN YOU AS A RICH PERSON.
WEAR YOUR NORMAL CLOTHES FOR NOW, THEN CHANGE IN THE TEMPLE.
うーん… MM...
MAYBE I CAN BORROW A ROOM AT BENNO'S STORE AND CHANGE IN THERE.
EITHER WAY WORKS, BUT...
JUST DON'T WEAR THEM WHEN LEAVING HERE.
LUTZ HAS BEEN KEEPING HIS THINGS IN A ROOM IN THE ATTIC,
SO BENNO SHOULD LET ME BORROW ONE TOO.

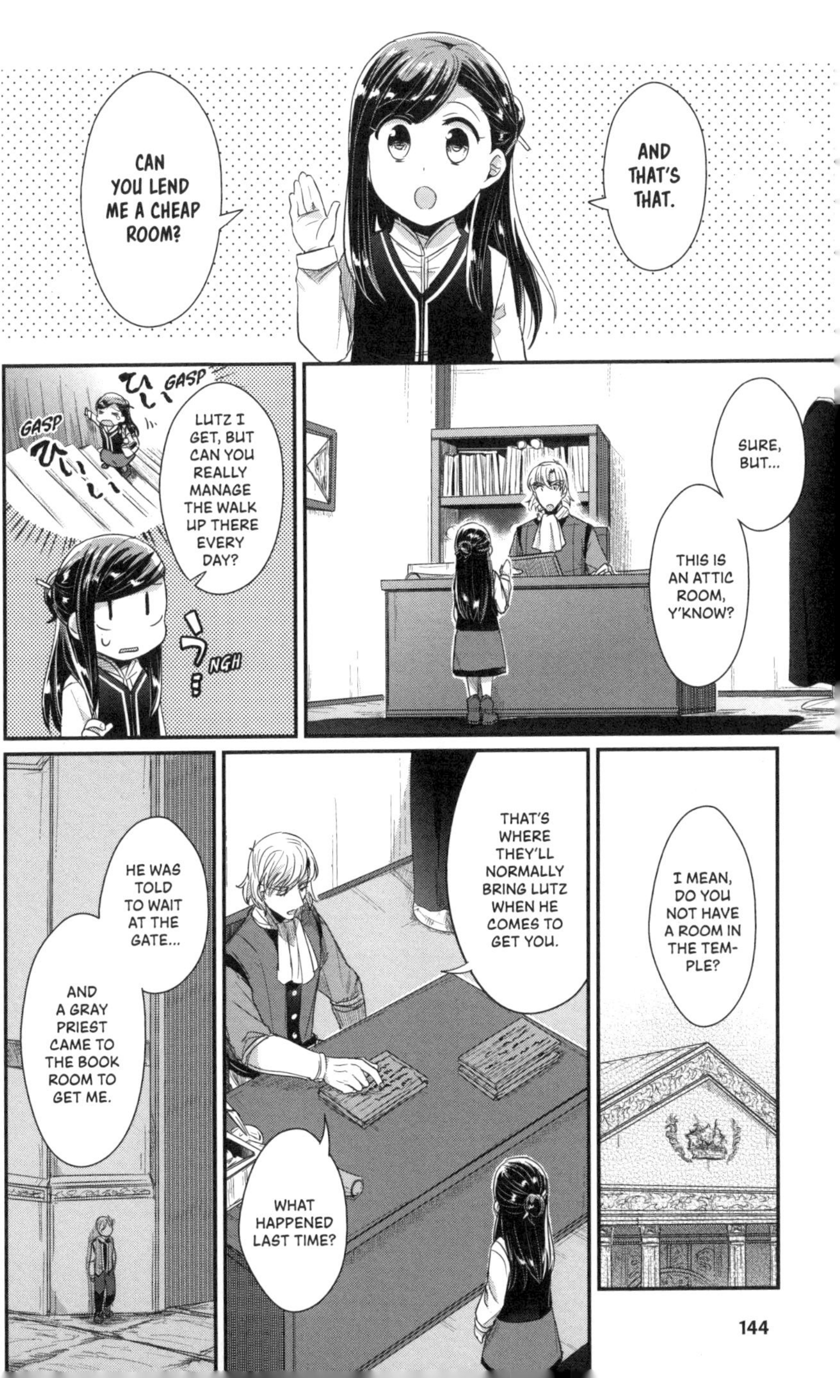
AND THAT'S THAT.
CAN YOU LEND ME A CHEAP ROOM?
SURE, BUT...
THIS IS AN ATTIC ROOM, Y'KNOW?
GASP
GASP
LUTZ I GET, BUT CAN YOU REALLY MANAGE THE WALK UP THERE EVERY DAY?
NGH
I MEAN, DO YOU NOT HAVE A ROOM IN THE TEM-PLE?
THAT'S WHERE THEY'LL NORMALLY BRING LUTZ WHEN HE COMES TO GET YOU.
WHAT HAPPENED LAST TIME?
HE WAS TOLD TO WAIT AT THE GATE...
AND A GRAY PRIEST CAME TO THE BOOK ROOM TO GET ME.

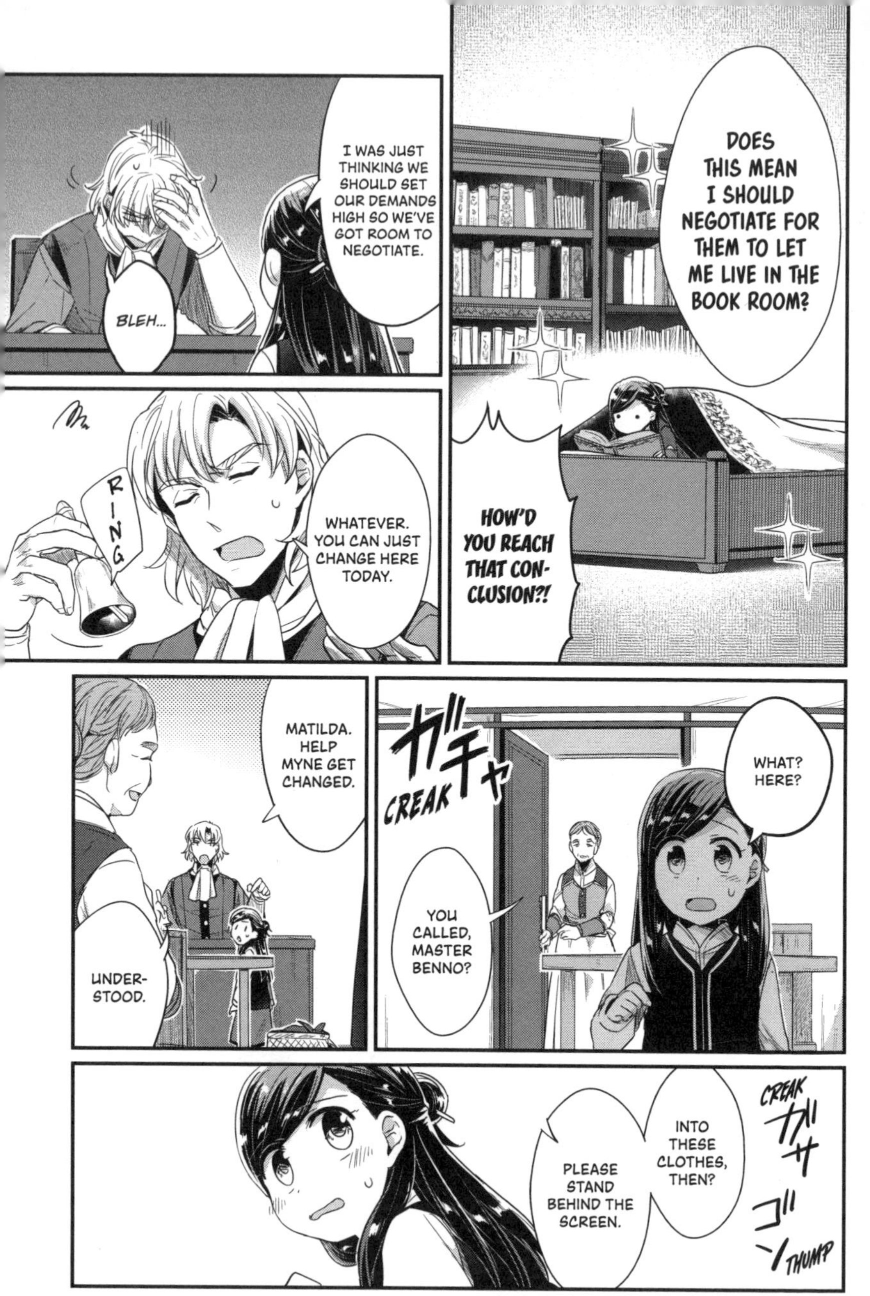

DOES THIS MEAN I SHOULD NEGOTIATE FOR THEM TO LET ME LIVE IN THE BOOK ROOM?
HOW'D YOU REACH THAT CON-CLUSION?!
I WAS JUST THINKING WE SHOULD SET OUR DEMANDS HIGH SO WE'VE GOT ROOM TO NEGOTIATE.
BLEH...
WHATEVER. YOU CAN JUST CHANGE HERE TODAY.
RING
ガチャ
CREAK
WHAT? HERE?
YOU CALLED, MASTER BENNO?
MATILDA. HELP MYNE GET CHANGED.
UNDER-STOOD.
CREAK
THUMP
INTO THESE CLOTHES, THEN?
PLEASE STAND BEHIND THE SCREEN.

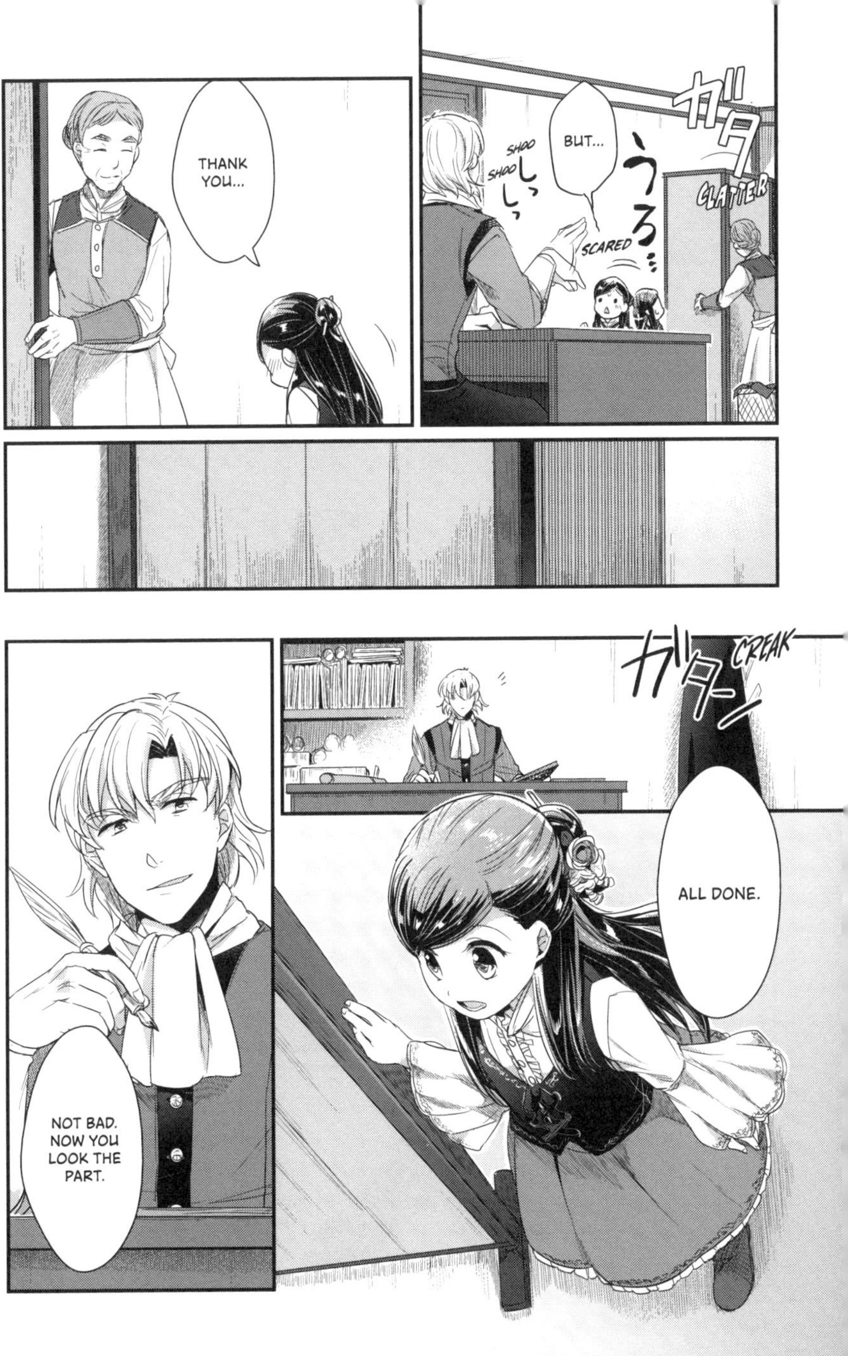
ガタ
CLATTER
BUT...
しっしっ
SHOO SHOO
うろ
SCARED
THANK YOU...
ガターン
CREAK
ALL DONE.
NOT BAD. NOW YOU LOOK THE PART.

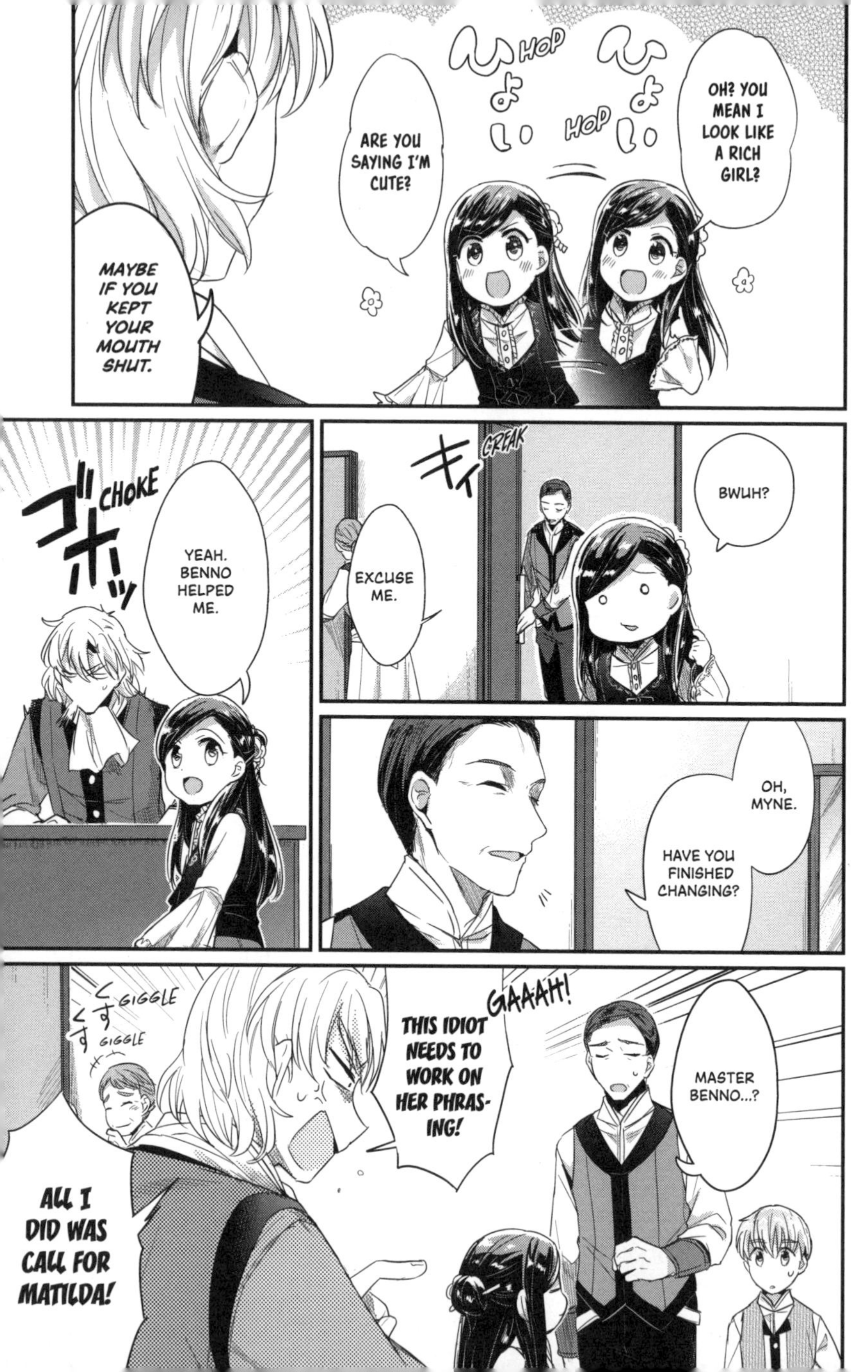
HOP
OH? YOU MEAN I LOOK LIKE A RICH GIRL?
HOP
ARE YOU SAYING I'M CUTE?
MAYBE IF YOU KEPT YOUR MOUTH SHUT.
BWUH?
キィ CREAK
EXCUSE ME.
OH, MYNE.
HAVE YOU FINISHED CHANGING?
ゴホッ CHOKE
YEAH. BENNO HELPED ME.
MASTER BENNO...?
GAAAH!
THIS IDIOT NEEDS TO WORK ON HER PHRAS-ING!
くす GIGGLE
くす GIGGLE
ALL I DID WAS CALL FOR MATILDA!

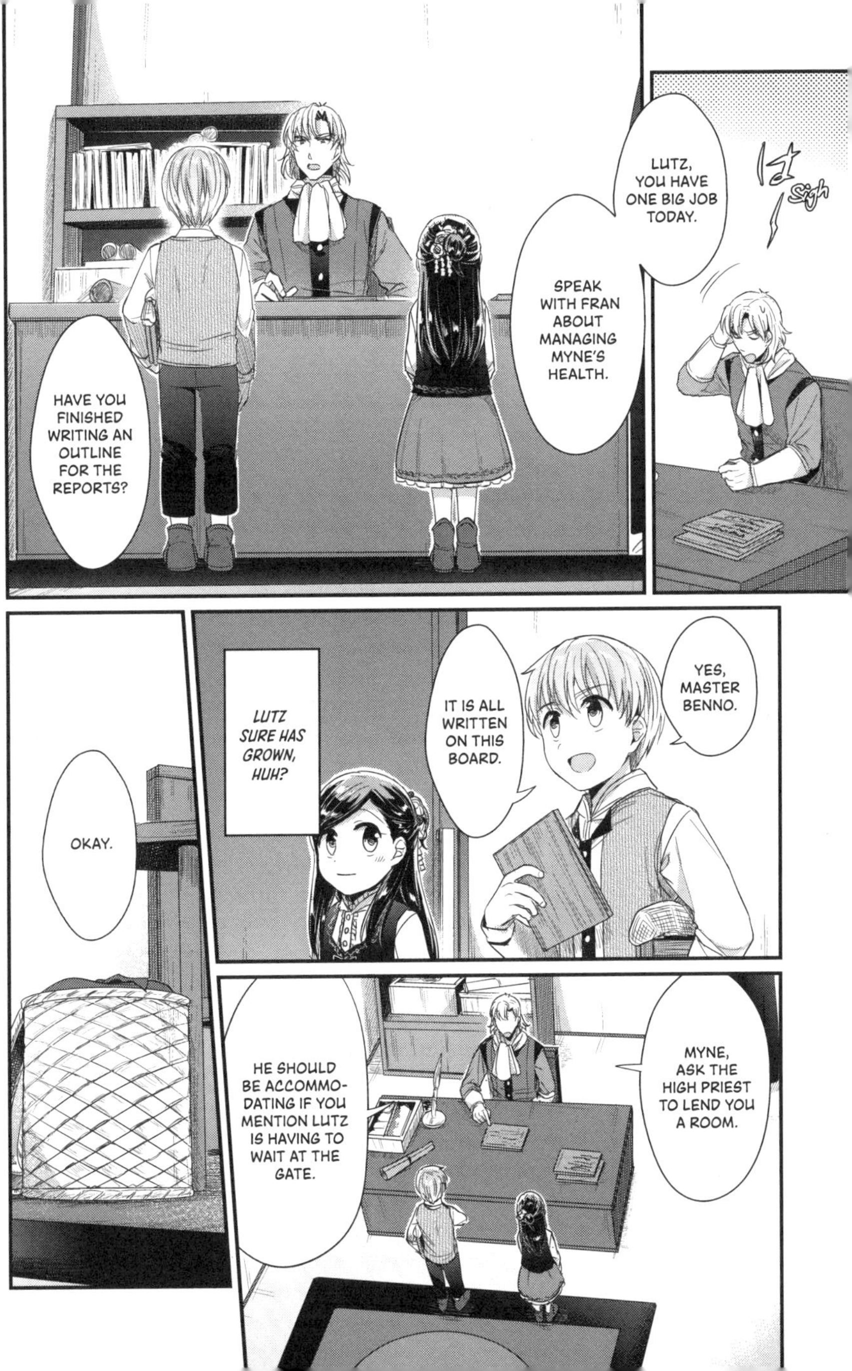
は
Sigh
LUTZ, YOU HAVE ONE BIG JOB TODAY.
SPEAK WITH FRAN ABOUT MANAGING MYNE'S HEALTH.
HAVE YOU FINISHED WRITING AN OUTLINE FOR THE REPORTS?
YES, MASTER BENNO.
IT IS ALL WRITTEN ON THIS BOARD.
LUTZ SURE HAS GROWN, HUH?
MYNE, ASK THE HIGH PRIEST TO LEND YOU A ROOM.
HE SHOULD BE ACCOMMODATING IF YOU MENTION LUTZ IS HAVING TO WAIT AT THE GATE.
OKAY.

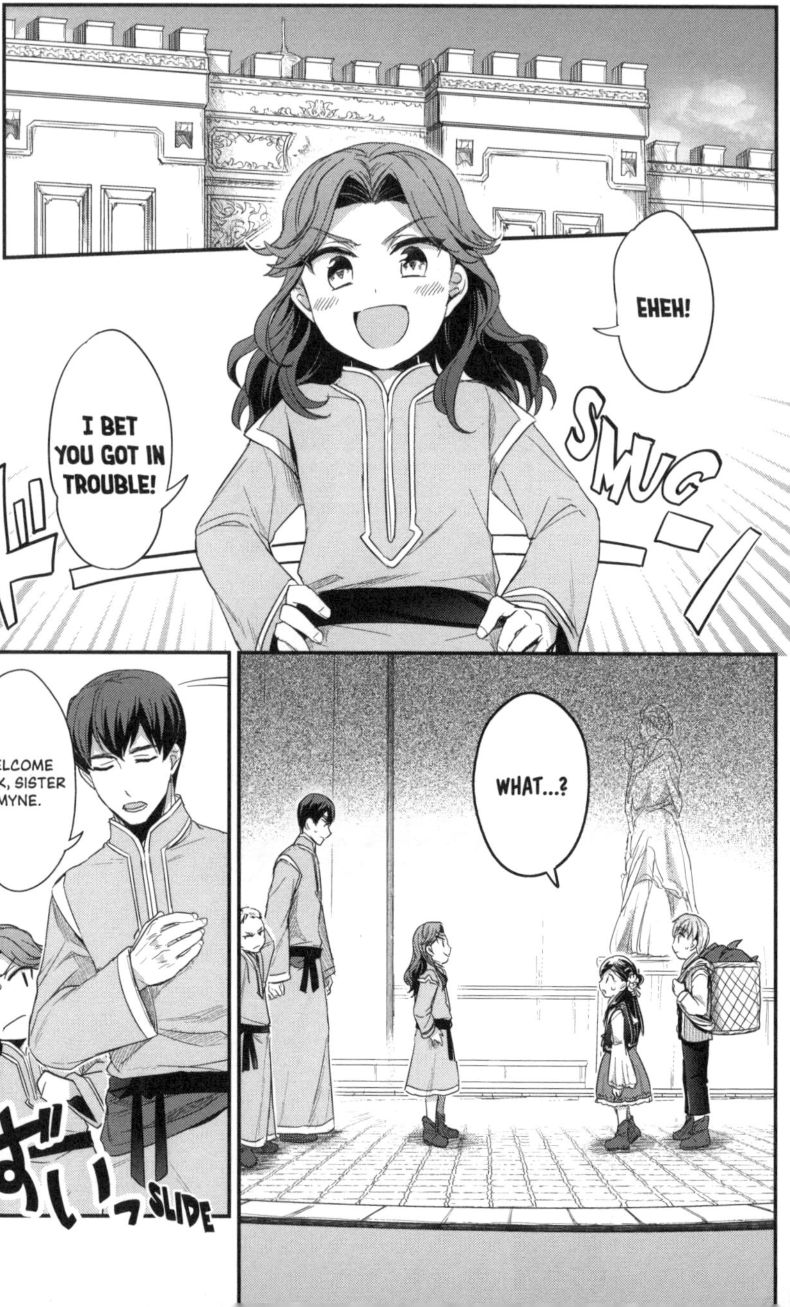
EHEH!
SMUG
I BET YOU GOT IN TROUBLE!
WHAT...?
WELCOME BACK, SISTER MYNE.
ずいっ
SLIDE

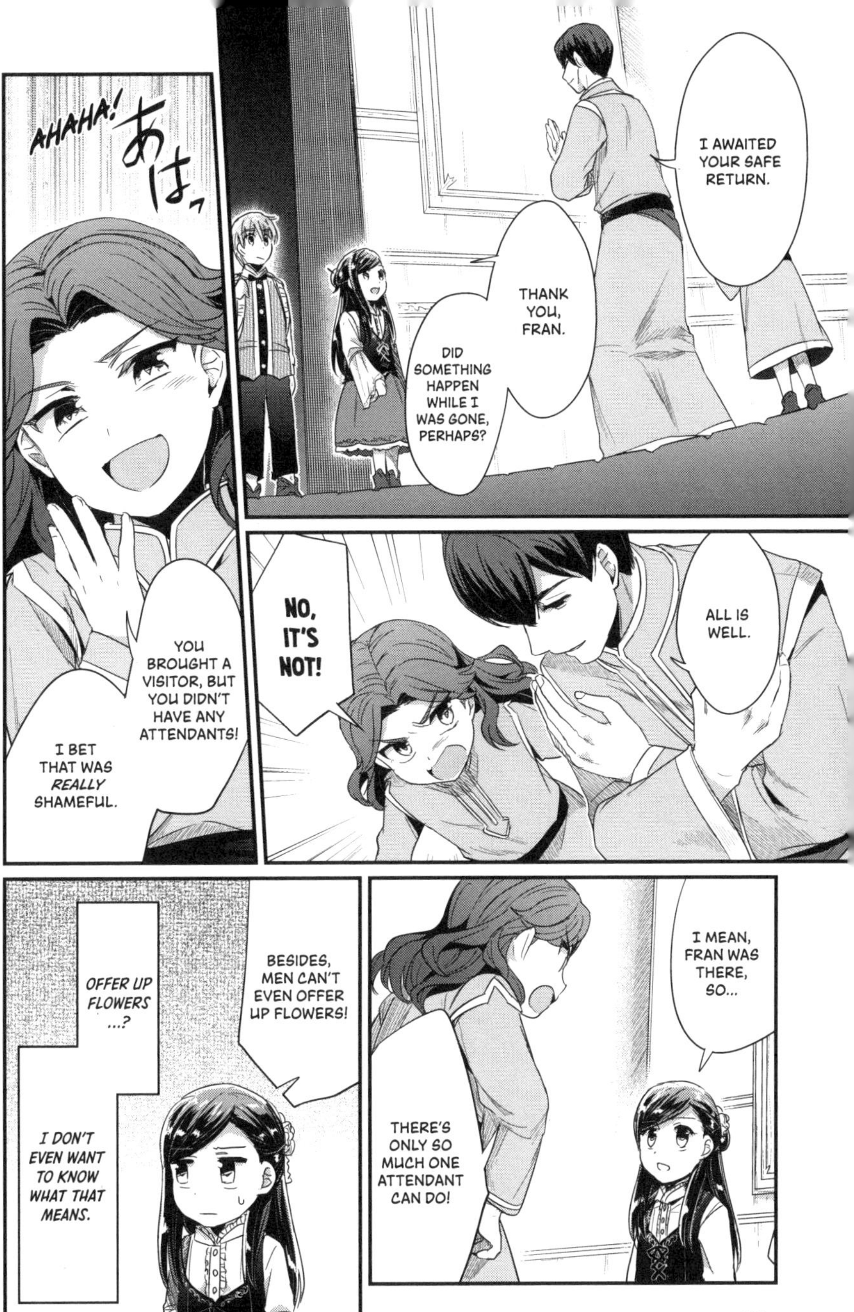
I AWAITED YOUR SAFE RETURN.
THANK YOU, FRAN.
DID SOMETHING HAPPEN WHILE I WAS GONE, PERHAPS?
ALL IS WELL.
NO, IT'S NOT!
AHAHA!
あはっ
YOU BROUGHT A VISITOR, BUT YOU DIDN'T HAVE ANY ATTENDANTS!
I BET THAT WAS *REALLY* SHAMEFUL.
I MEAN, FRAN WAS THERE, SO...
THERE'S ONLY SO MUCH ONE ATTENDANT CAN DO!
BESIDES, MEN CAN'T EVEN OFFER UP FLOWERS!
OFFER UP FLOWERS ...?
I DON'T EVEN WANT TO KNOW WHAT THAT MEANS.

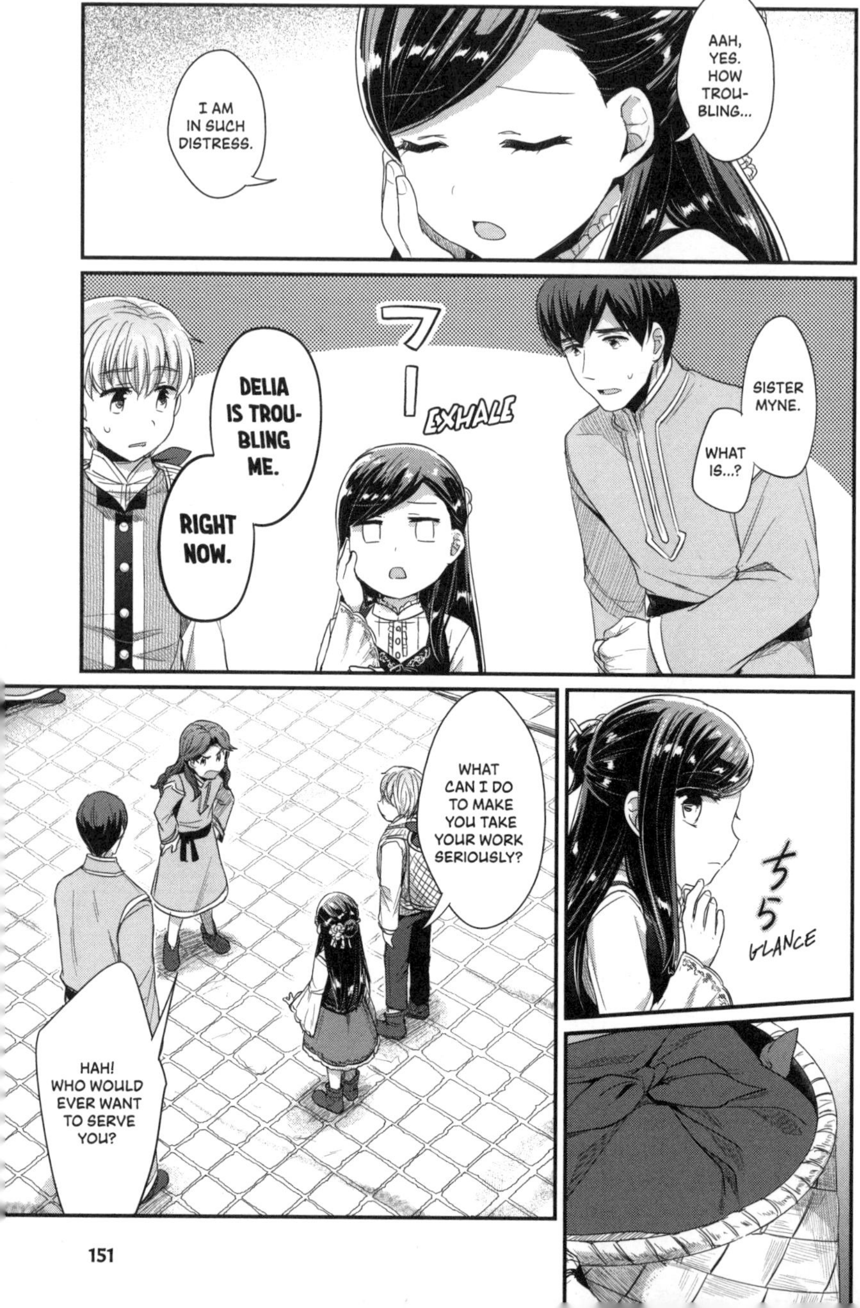
AAH, YES. HOW TROU-BLING...
I AM IN SUCH DISTRESS.
SISTER MYNE.
WHAT IS...?
フー
EXHALE
DELIA IS TROU-BLING ME.
RIGHT NOW.
ちら
GLANCE
WHAT CAN I DO TO MAKE YOU TAKE YOUR WORK SERIOUSLY?
HAH! WHO WOULD EVER WANT TO SERVE YOU?

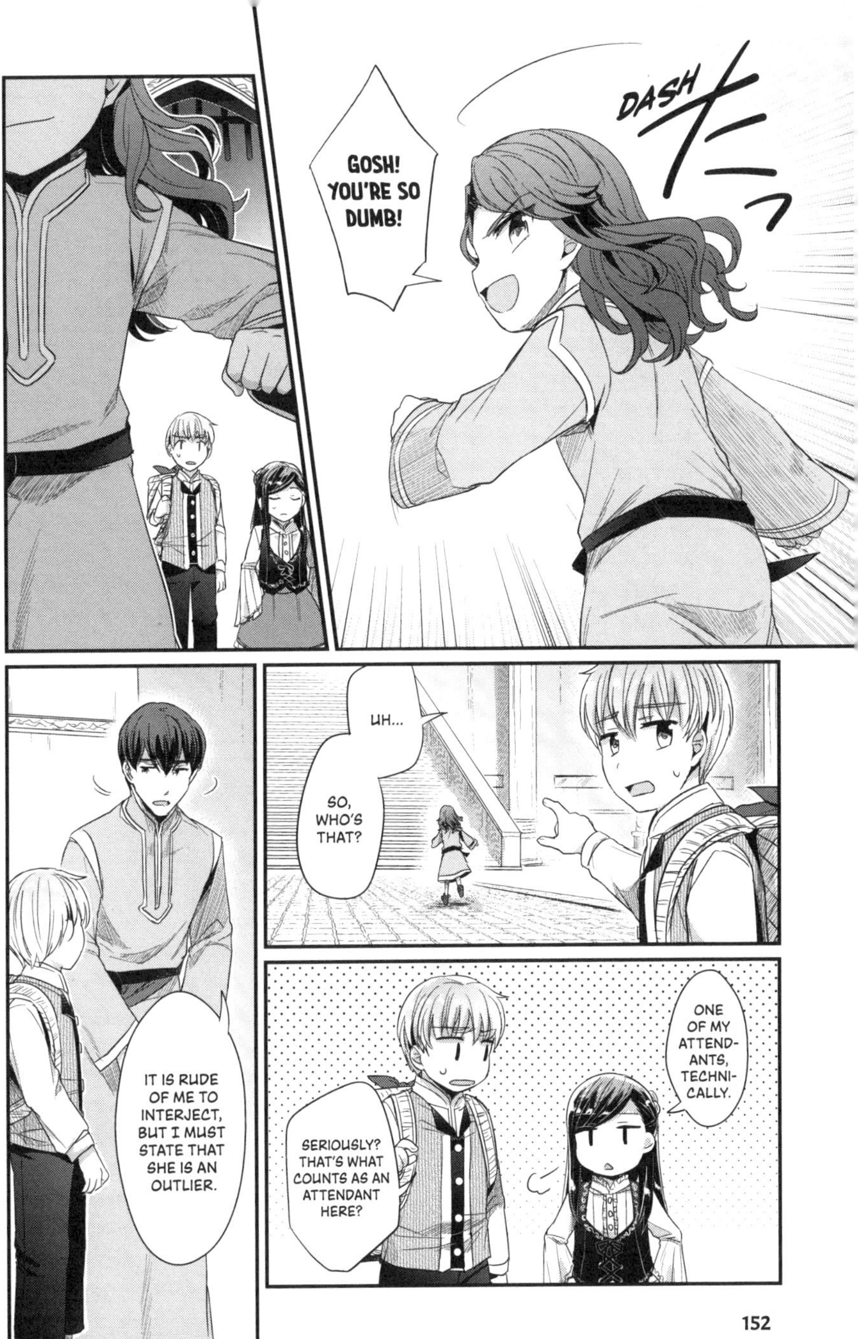
DASH
GOSH! YOU'RE SO DUMB!
UH...
SO, WHO'S THAT?
ONE OF MY ATTENDANTS, TECHNICALLY.
SERIOUSLY? THAT'S WHAT COUNTS AS AN ATTENDANT HERE?
IT IS RUDE OF ME TO INTERJECT, BUT I MUST STATE THAT SHE IS AN OUTLIER.

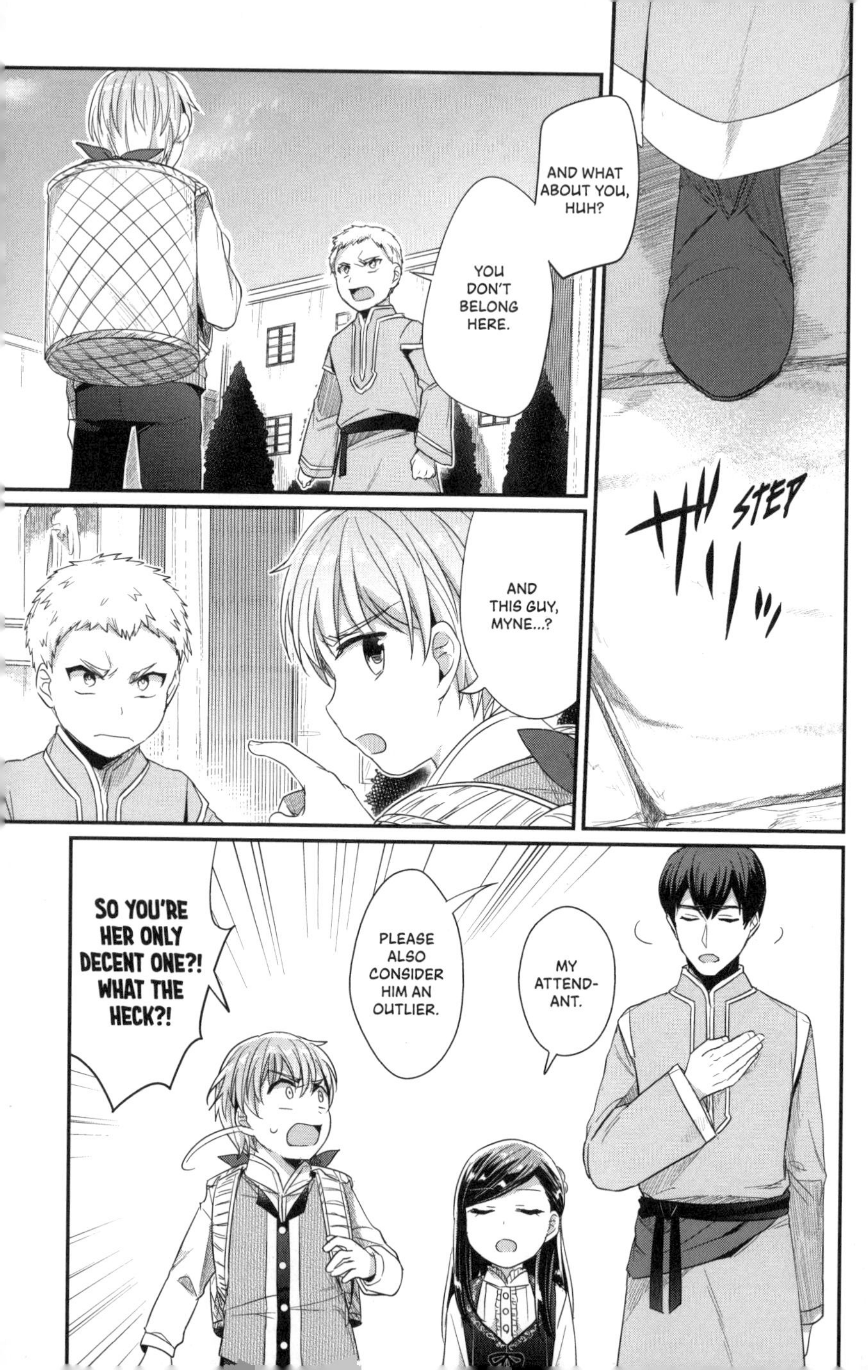

AND WHAT ABOUT YOU, HUH?
YOU DON'T BELONG HERE.
ザリッ
STEP
AND THIS GUY, MYNE...?
MY ATTEND-ANT.
PLEASE ALSO CONSIDER HIM AN OUTLIER.
SO YOU'RE HER ONLY DECENT ONE?! WHAT THE HECK?!

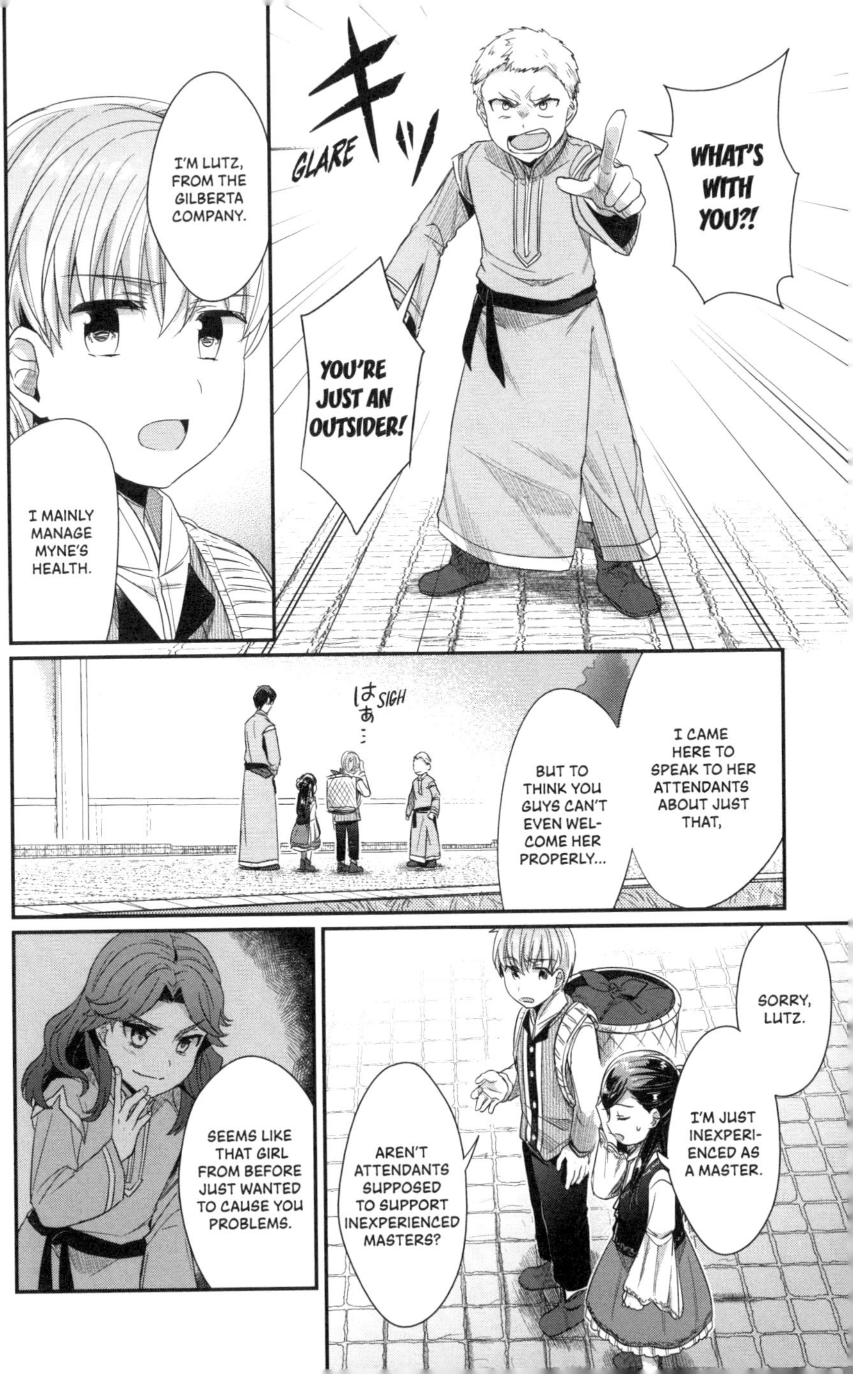

WHAT'S WITH YOU?!
キッ
GLARE
YOU'RE JUST AN OUTSIDER!
I'M LUTZ, FROM THE GILBERTA COMPANY.
I MAINLY MANAGE MYNE'S HEALTH.
はぁ
SIGH
I CAME HERE TO SPEAK TO HER ATTENDANTS ABOUT JUST THAT,
BUT TO THINK YOU GUYS CAN'T EVEN WEL-COME HER PROPERLY...
SORRY, LUTZ.
I'M JUST INEXPERI-ENCED AS A MASTER.
AREN'T ATTENDANTS SUPPOSED TO SUPPORT INEXPERIENCED MASTERS?
SEEMS LIKE THAT GIRL FROM BEFORE JUST WANTED TO CAUSE YOU PROBLEMS.

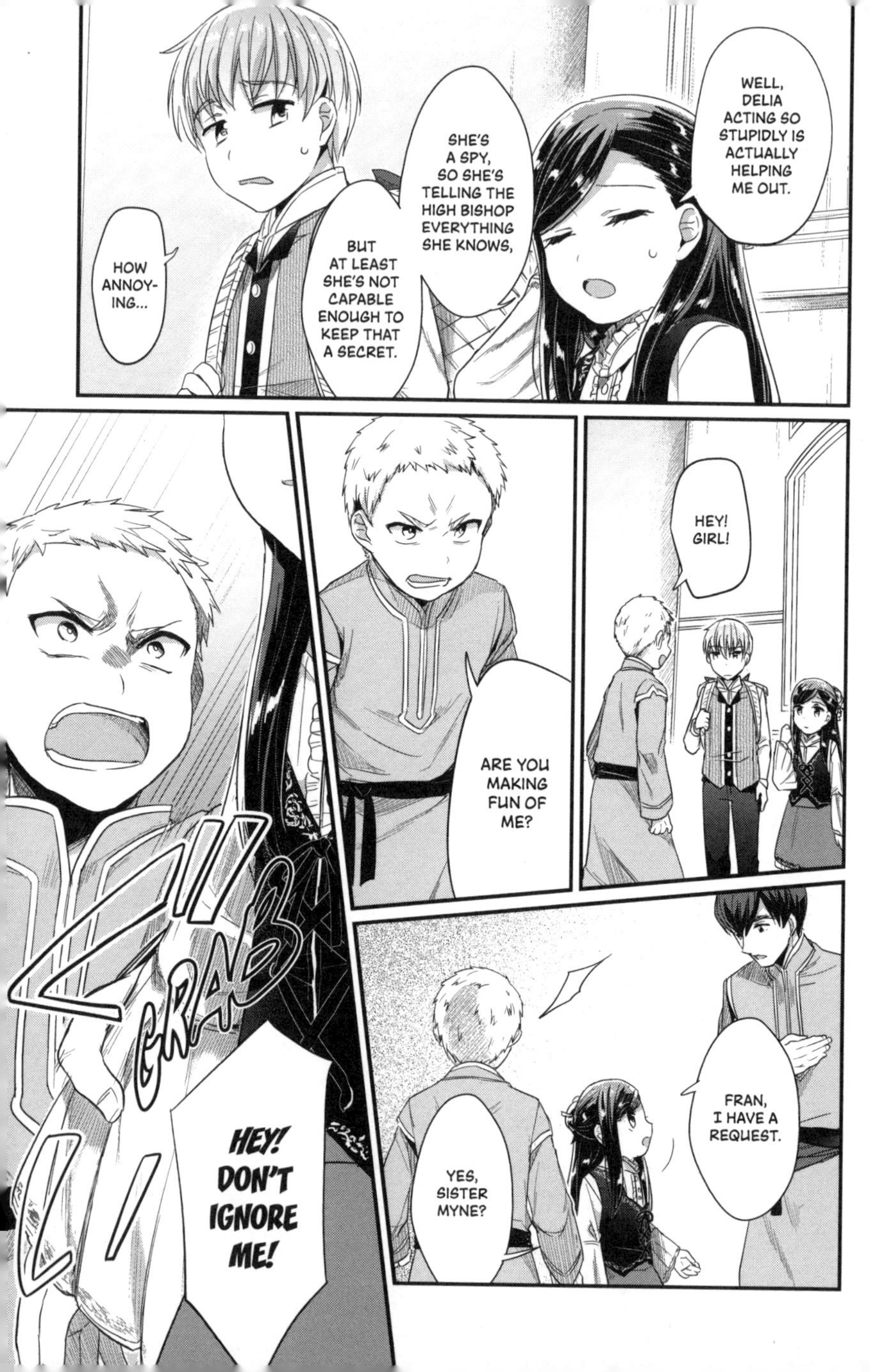
WELL, DELIA ACTING SO STUPIDLY IS ACTUALLY HELPING ME OUT.
SHE'S A SPY, SO SHE'S TELLING THE HIGH BISHOP EVERYTHING SHE KNOWS,
BUT AT LEAST SHE'S NOT CAPABLE ENOUGH TO KEEP THAT A SECRET.
HOW ANNOYING...
HEY! GIRL!
ARE YOU MAKING FUN OF ME?
FRAN, I HAVE A REQUEST.
YES, SISTER MYNE?
GRAB
HEY! DON'T IGNORE ME!

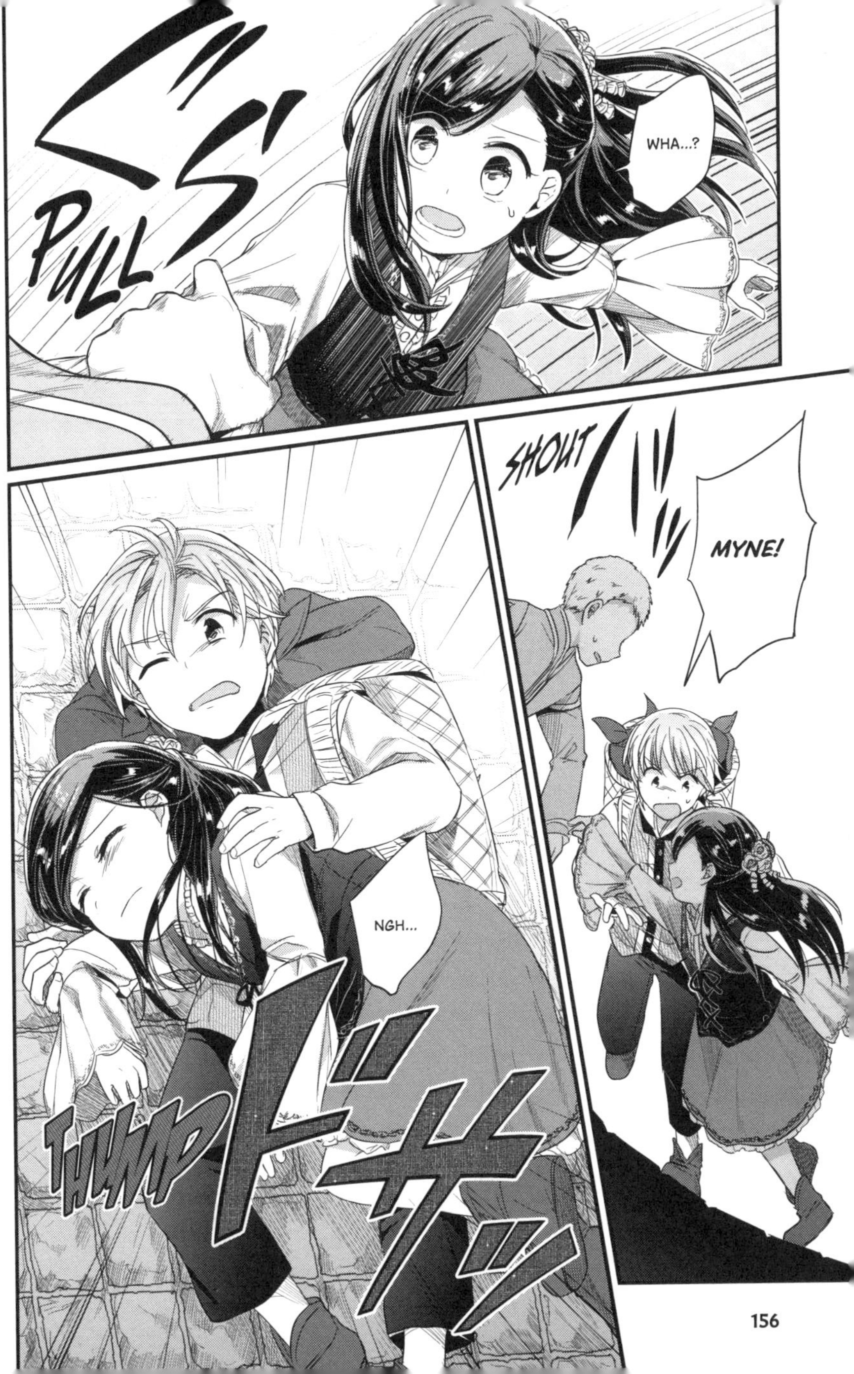
PULL
WHA...?
SHOUT
MYNE!
NGH...
THUMP

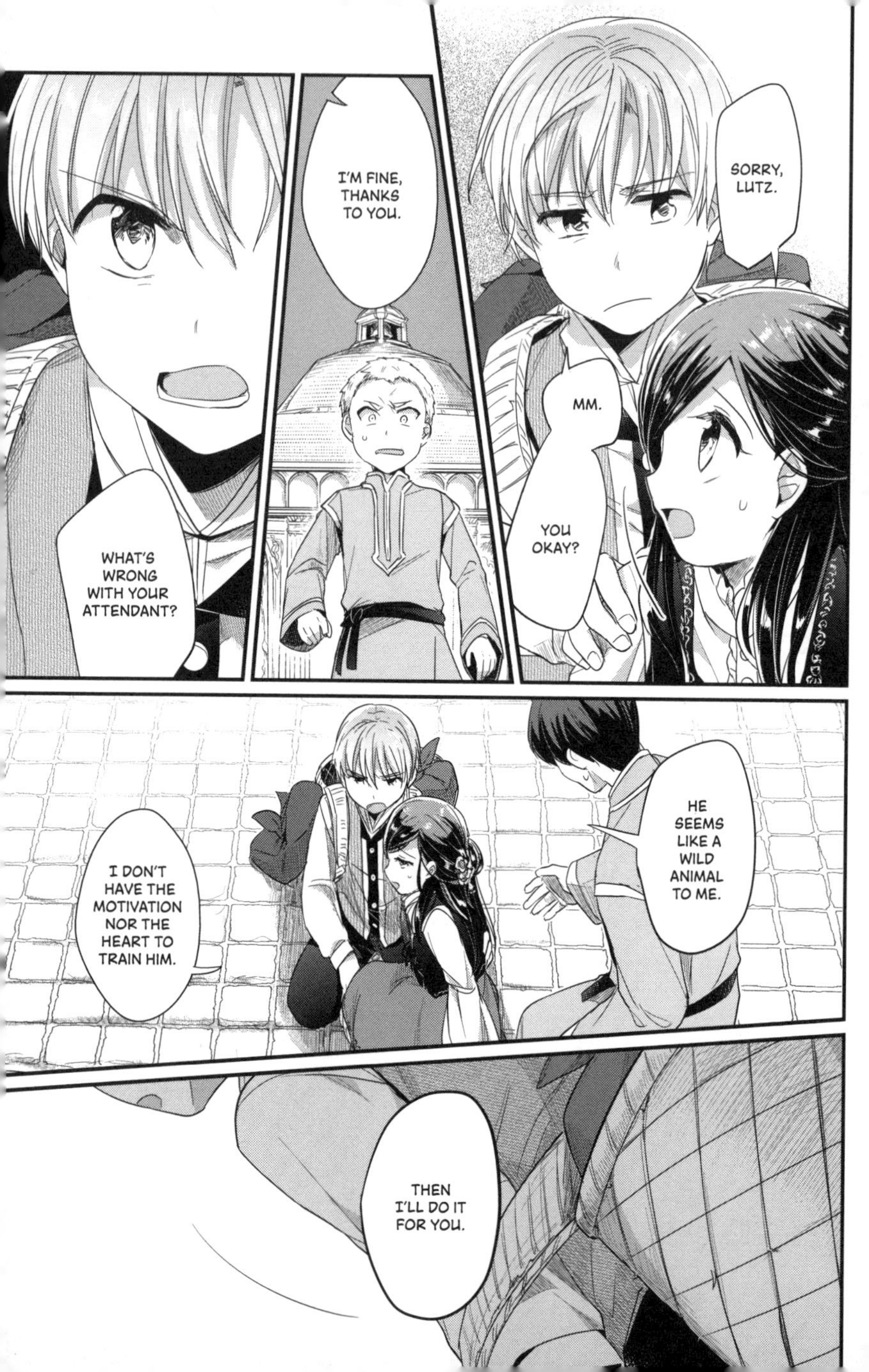
SORRY, LUTZ.
MM.
YOU OKAY?
I'M FINE, THANKS TO YOU.
WHAT'S WRONG WITH YOUR ATTENDANT?
HE SEEMS LIKE A WILD ANIMAL TO ME.
I DON'T HAVE THE MOTIVATION NOR THE HEART TO TRAIN HIM.
THEN I'LL DO IT FOR YOU.

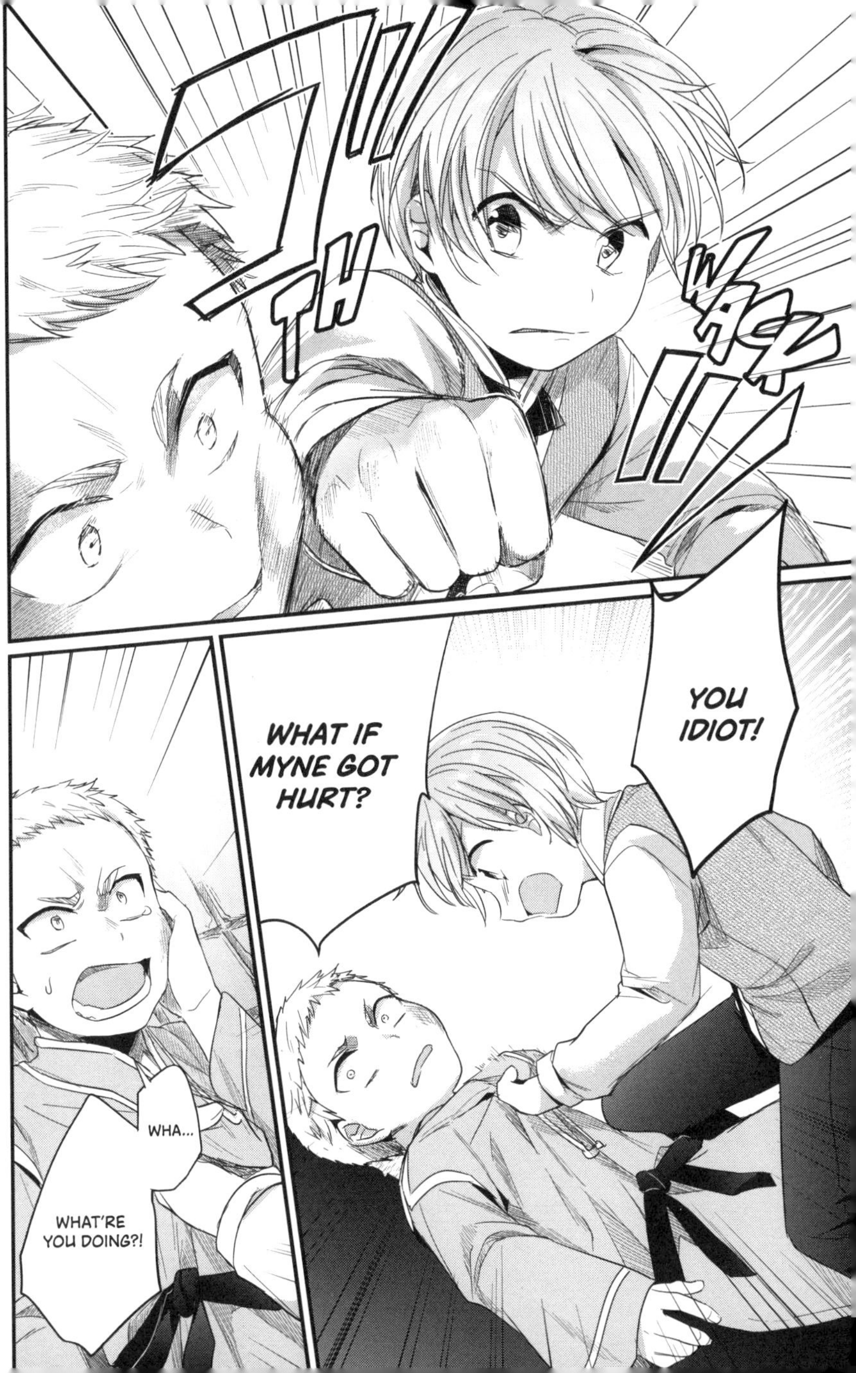
THWACK!!
YOU IDIOT!
WHAT IF MYNE GOT HURT?
WHA...
WHAT'RE YOU DOING?!

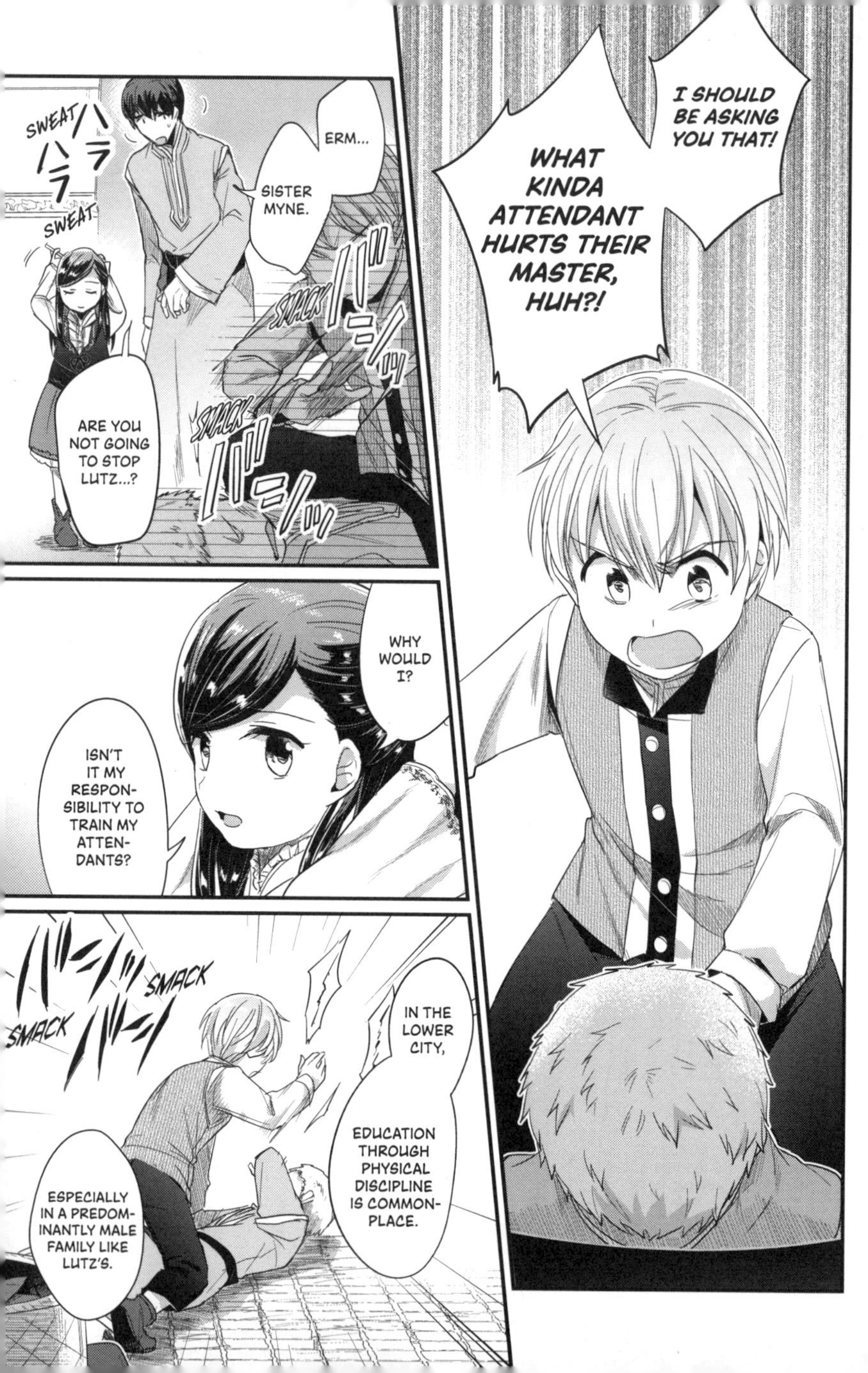
I SHOULD BE ASKING YOU THAT!
WHAT KINDA ATTENDANT HURTS THEIR MASTER, HUH?!
ERM...
SISTER MYNE.
SWEAT
ハラハラ
SWEAT
SMACK
SMACK
ARE YOU NOT GOING TO STOP LUTZ...?
WHY WOULD I?
ISN'T IT MY RESPON-SIBILITY TO TRAIN MY ATTEN-DANTS?
SMACK
SMACK
IN THE LOWER CITY,
EDUCATION THROUGH PHYSICAL DISCIPLINE IS COMMON-PLACE.
ESPECIALLY IN A PREDOM-INANTLY MALE FAMILY LIKE LUTZ'S.

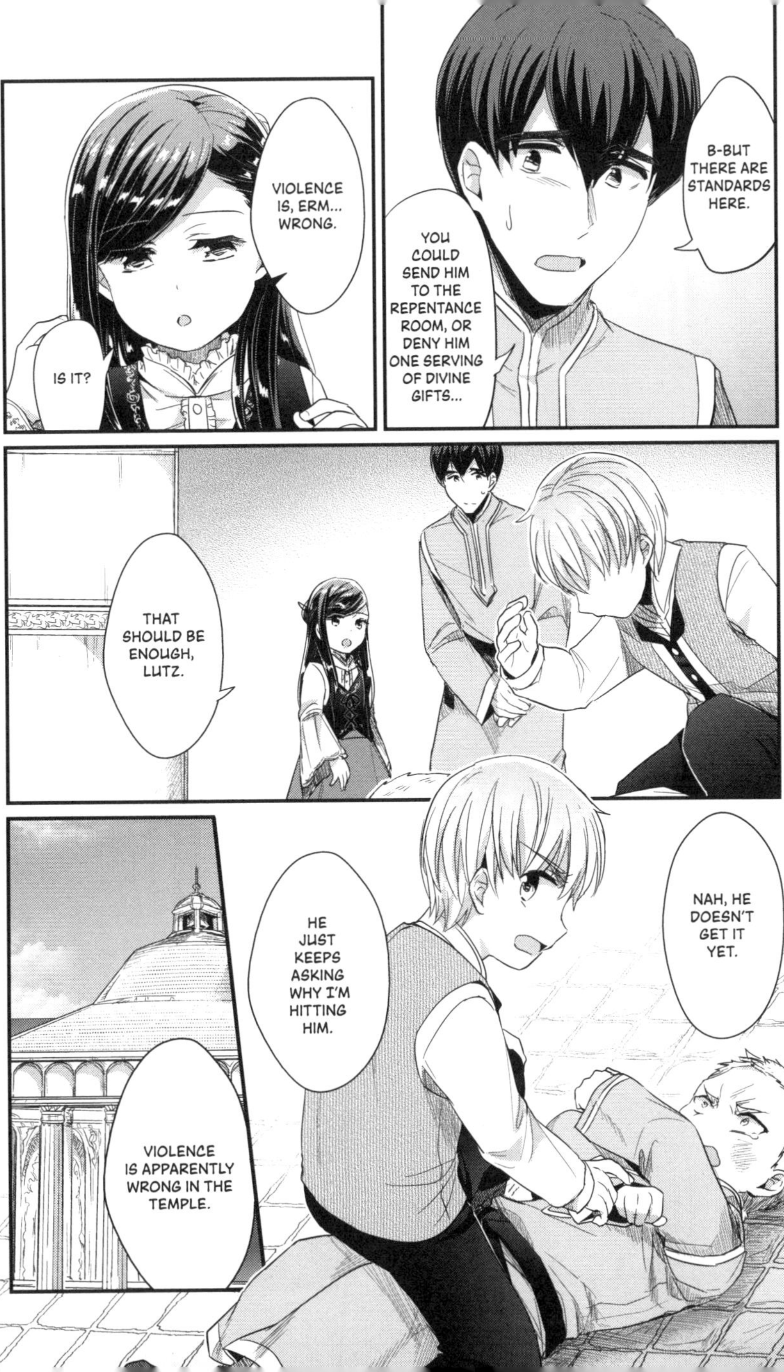
B-BUT THERE ARE STANDARDS HERE.
YOU COULD SEND HIM TO THE REPENTANCE ROOM, OR DENY HIM ONE SERVING OF DIVINE GIFTS...
VIOLENCE IS, ERM... WRONG.
IS IT?
THAT SHOULD BE ENOUGH, LUTZ.
NAH, HE DOESN'T GET IT YET.
HE JUST KEEPS ASKING WHY I'M HITTING HIM.
VIOLENCE IS APPARENTLY WRONG IN THE TEMPLE.

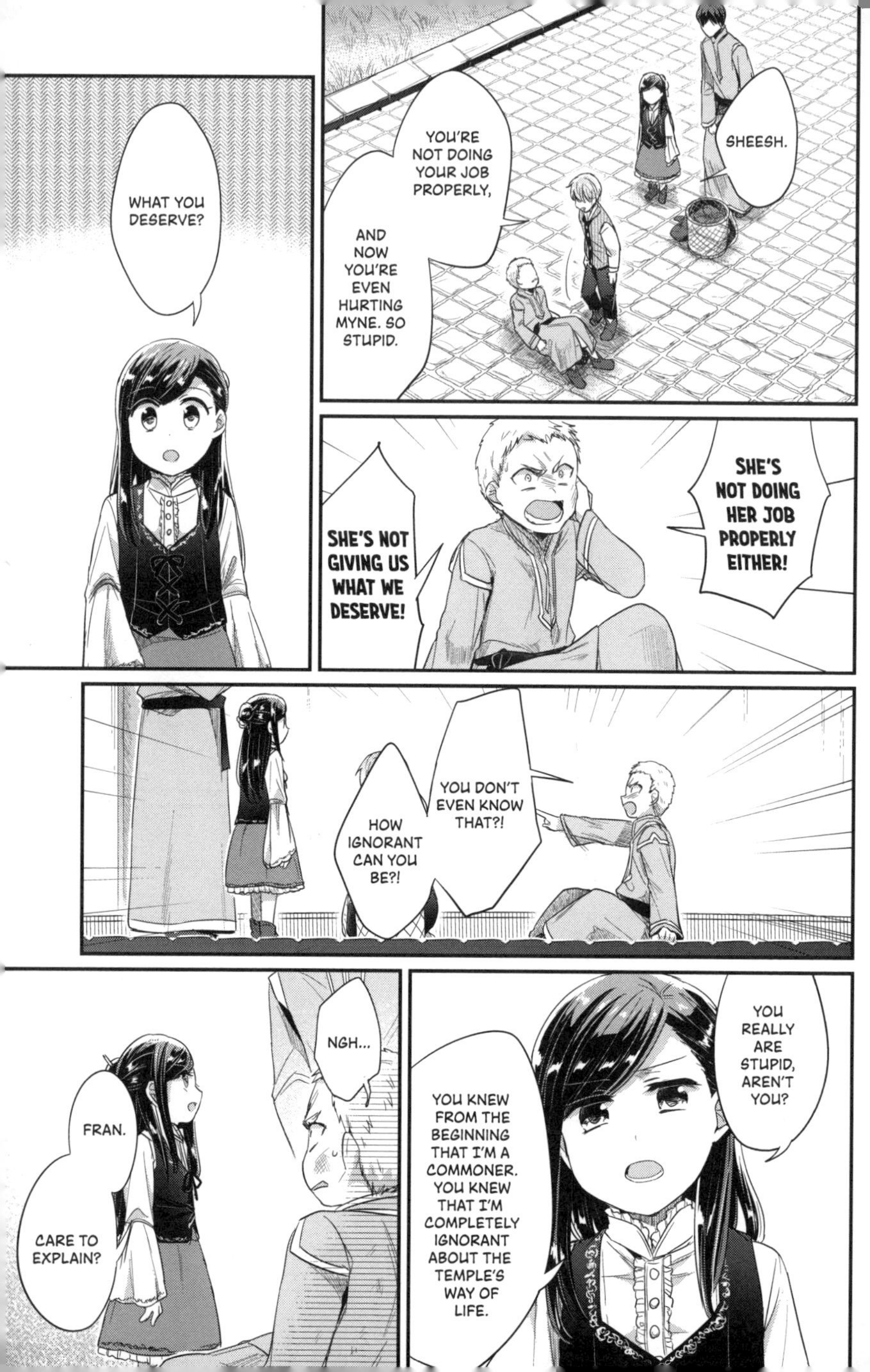
SHEESH.
YOU'RE NOT DOING YOUR JOB PROPERLY,
AND NOW YOU'RE EVEN HURTING MYNE. SO STUPID.
SHE'S NOT DOING HER JOB PROPERLY EITHER!
SHE'S NOT GIVING US WHAT WE DESERVE!
WHAT YOU DESERVE?
YOU DON'T EVEN KNOW THAT?!
HOW IGNORANT CAN YOU BE?!
YOU REALLY ARE STUPID, AREN'T YOU?
YOU KNEW FROM THE BEGINNING THAT I'M A COMMONER. YOU KNEW THAT I'M COMPLETELY IGNORANT ABOUT THE TEMPLE'S WAY OF LIFE.
NGH...
FRAN.
CARE TO EXPLAIN?

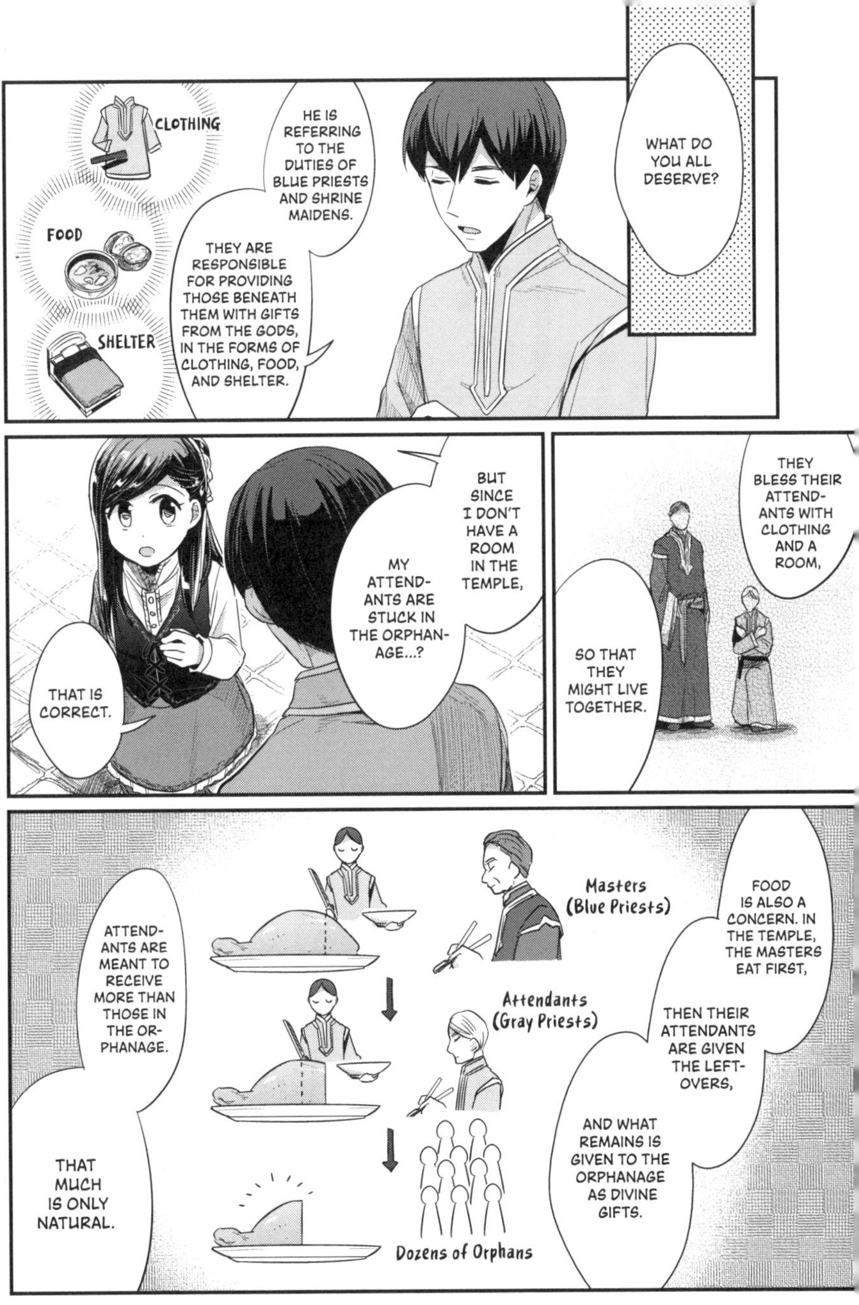
WHAT DO YOU ALL DESERVE?
HE IS REFERRING TO THE DUTIES OF BLUE PRIESTS AND SHRINE MAIDENS.
THEY ARE RESPONSIBLE FOR PROVIDING THOSE BENEATH THEM WITH GIFTS FROM THE GODS, IN THE FORMS OF CLOTHING, FOOD, AND SHELTER.
CLOTHING
FOOD
SHELTER
THEY BLESS THEIR ATTENDANTS WITH CLOTHING AND A ROOM,
SO THAT THEY MIGHT LIVE TOGETHER.
BUT SINCE I DON'T HAVE A ROOM IN THE TEMPLE,
MY ATTENDANTS ARE STUCK IN THE ORPHANAGE...?
THAT IS CORRECT.
FOOD IS ALSO A CONCERN. IN THE TEMPLE, THE MASTERS EAT FIRST,
THEN THEIR ATTENDANTS ARE GIVEN THE LEFTOVERS,
AND WHAT REMAINS IS GIVEN TO THE ORPHANAGE AS DIVINE GIFTS.
Masters (Blue Priests)
Attendants (Gray Priests)
Dozens of Orphans
ATTENDANTS ARE MEANT TO RECEIVE MORE THAN THOSE IN THE ORPHANAGE.
THAT MUCH IS ONLY NATURAL.

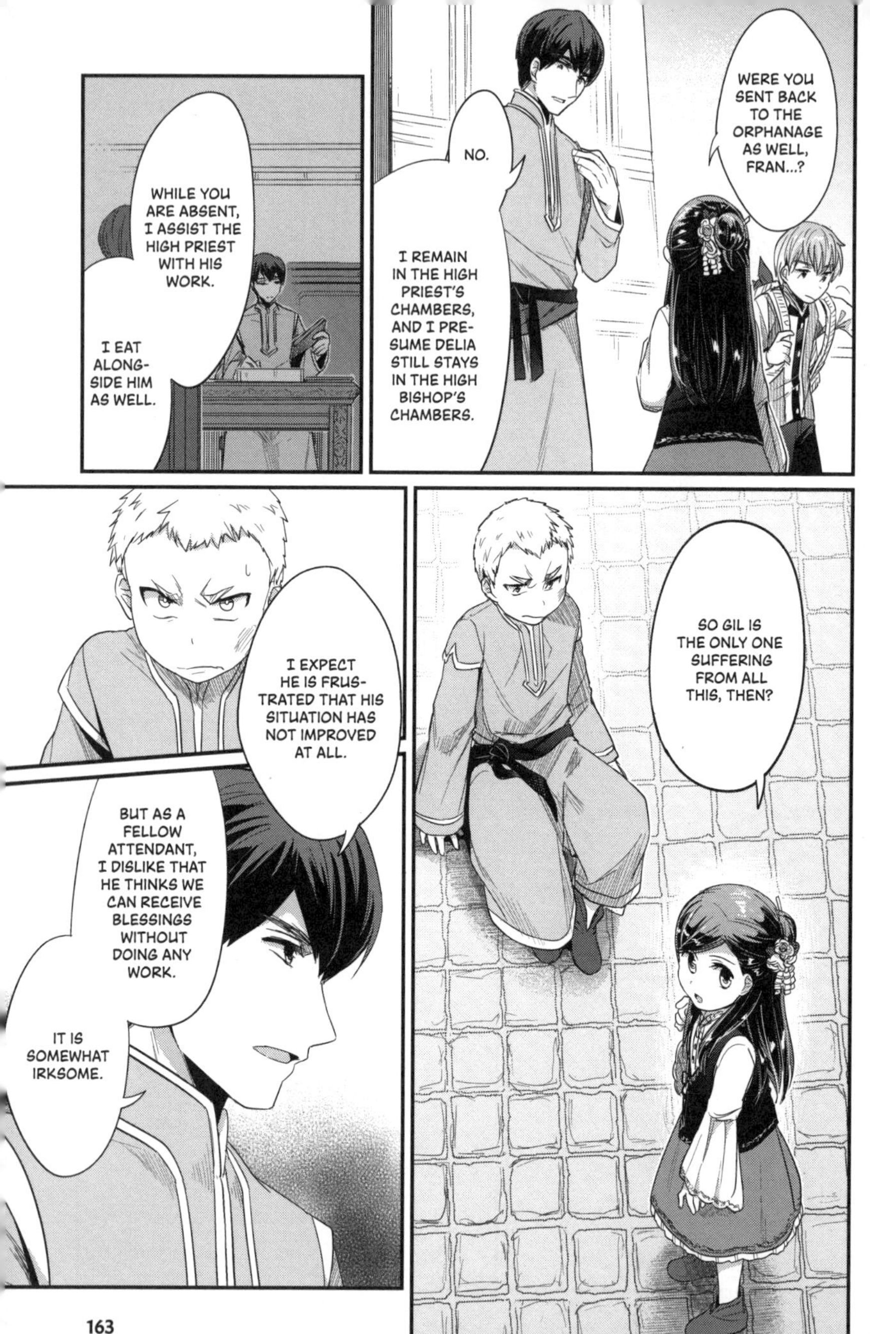
WERE YOU SENT BACK TO THE ORPHANAGE AS WELL, FRAN...?
NO.
I REMAIN IN THE HIGH PRIEST'S CHAMBERS, AND I PRE-SUME DELIA STILL STAYS IN THE HIGH BISHOP'S CHAMBERS.
WHILE YOU ARE ABSENT, I ASSIST THE HIGH PRIEST WITH HIS WORK.
I EAT ALONG-SIDE HIM AS WELL.
SO GIL IS THE ONLY ONE SUFFERING FROM ALL THIS, THEN?
I EXPECT HE IS FRUS-TRATED THAT HIS SITUATION HAS NOT IMPROVED AT ALL.
BUT AS A FELLOW ATTENDANT, I DISLIKE THAT HE THINKS WE CAN RECEIVE BLESSINGS WITHOUT DOING ANY WORK.
IT IS SOMEWHAT IRKSOME.

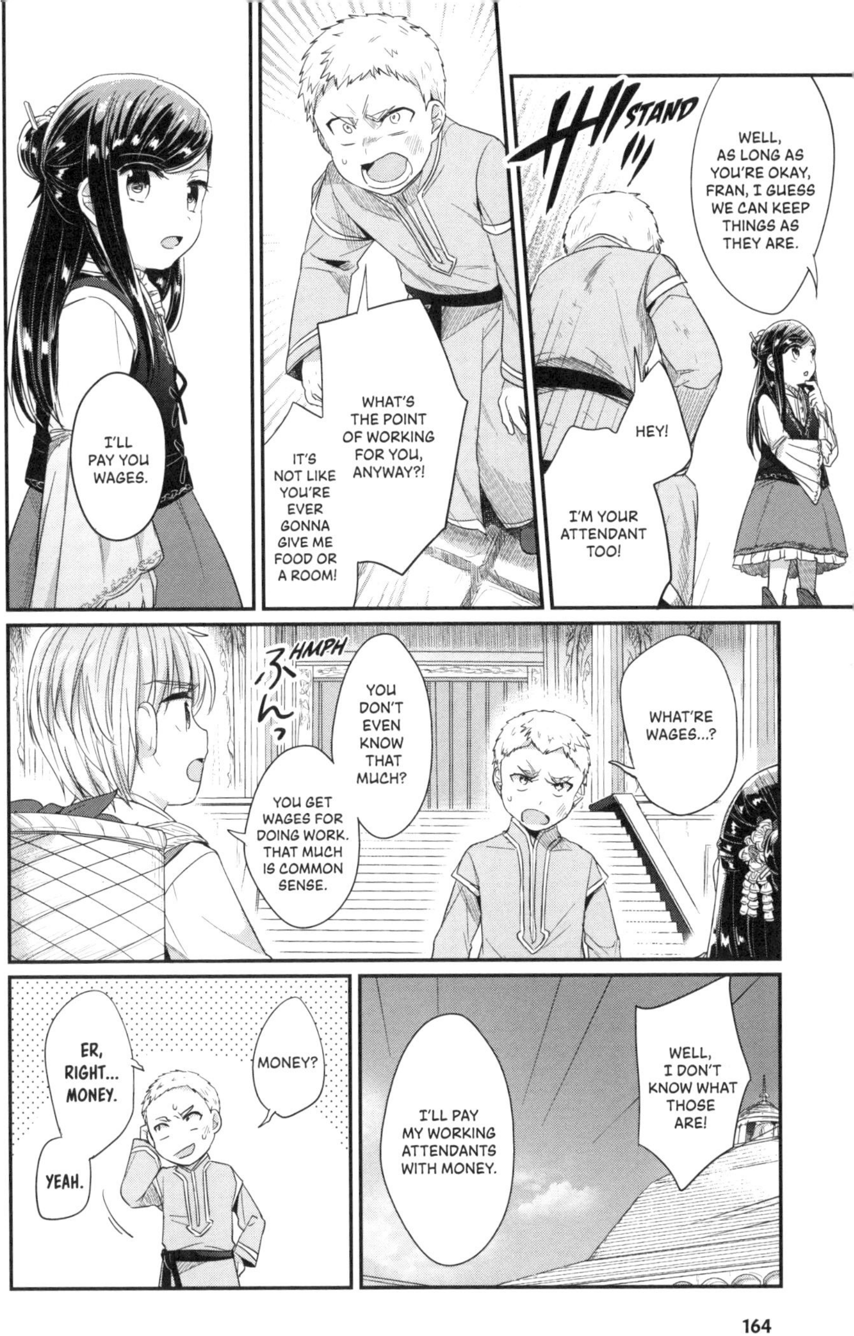
WELL, AS LONG AS YOU'RE OKAY, FRAN, I GUESS WE CAN KEEP THINGS AS THEY ARE.
STAND
HEY!
I'M YOUR ATTENDANT TOO!
WHAT'S THE POINT OF WORKING FOR YOU, ANYWAY?!
IT'S NOT LIKE YOU'RE EVER GONNA GIVE ME FOOD OR A ROOM!
I'LL PAY YOU WAGES.
WHAT'RE WAGES...?
HMPH
ふんっ
YOU DON'T EVEN KNOW THAT MUCH?
YOU GET WAGES FOR DOING WORK. THAT MUCH IS COMMON SENSE.
WELL, I DON'T KNOW WHAT THOSE ARE!
I'LL PAY MY WORKING ATTENDANTS WITH MONEY.
MONEY?
ER, RIGHT... MONEY.
YEAH.

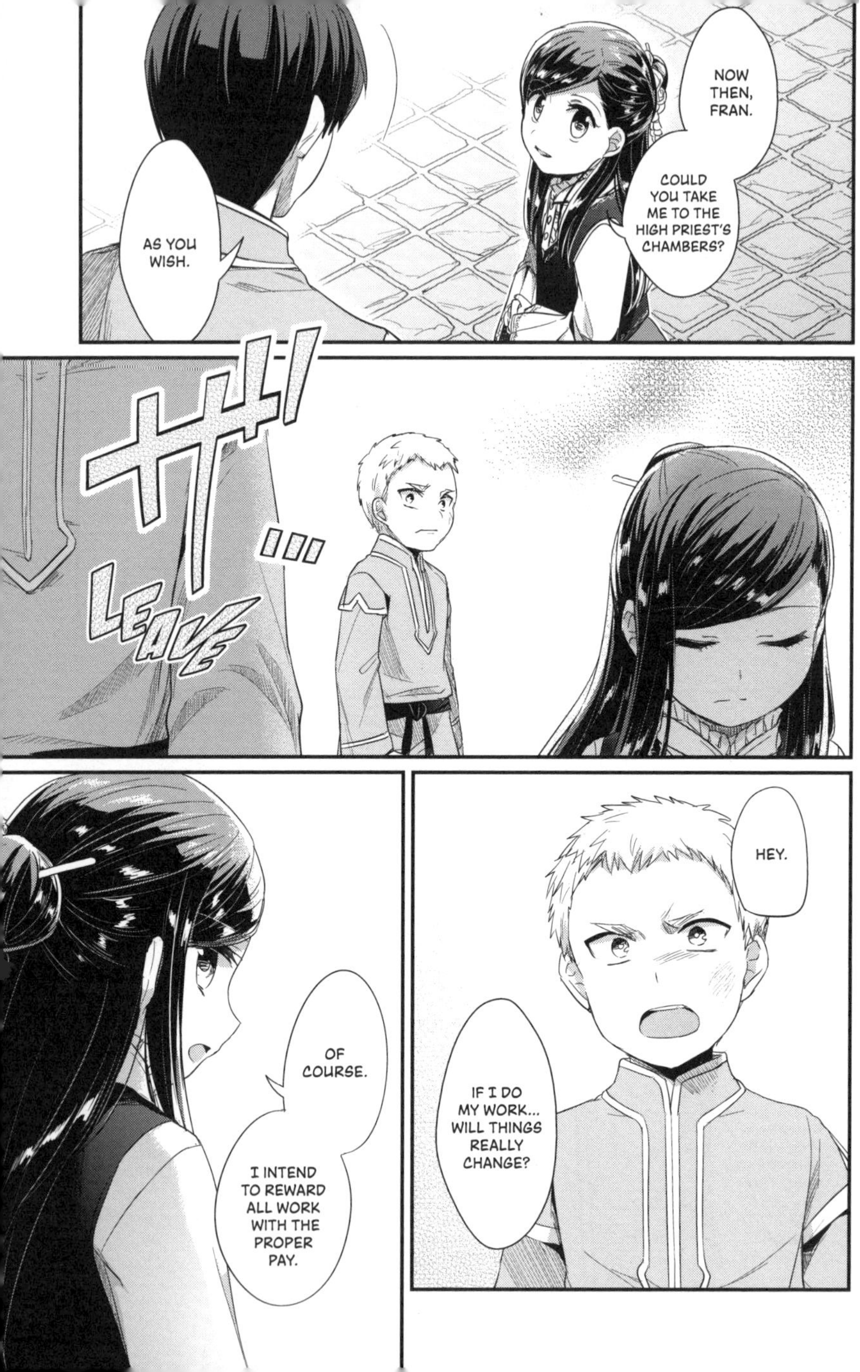
NOW THEN, FRAN.
COULD YOU TAKE ME TO THE HIGH PRIEST'S CHAMBERS?
AS YOU WISH.
サッ!
LEAVE
...
HEY.
IF I DO MY WORK... WILL THINGS REALLY CHANGE?
OF COURSE.
I INTEND TO REWARD ALL WORK WITH THE PROPER PAY.

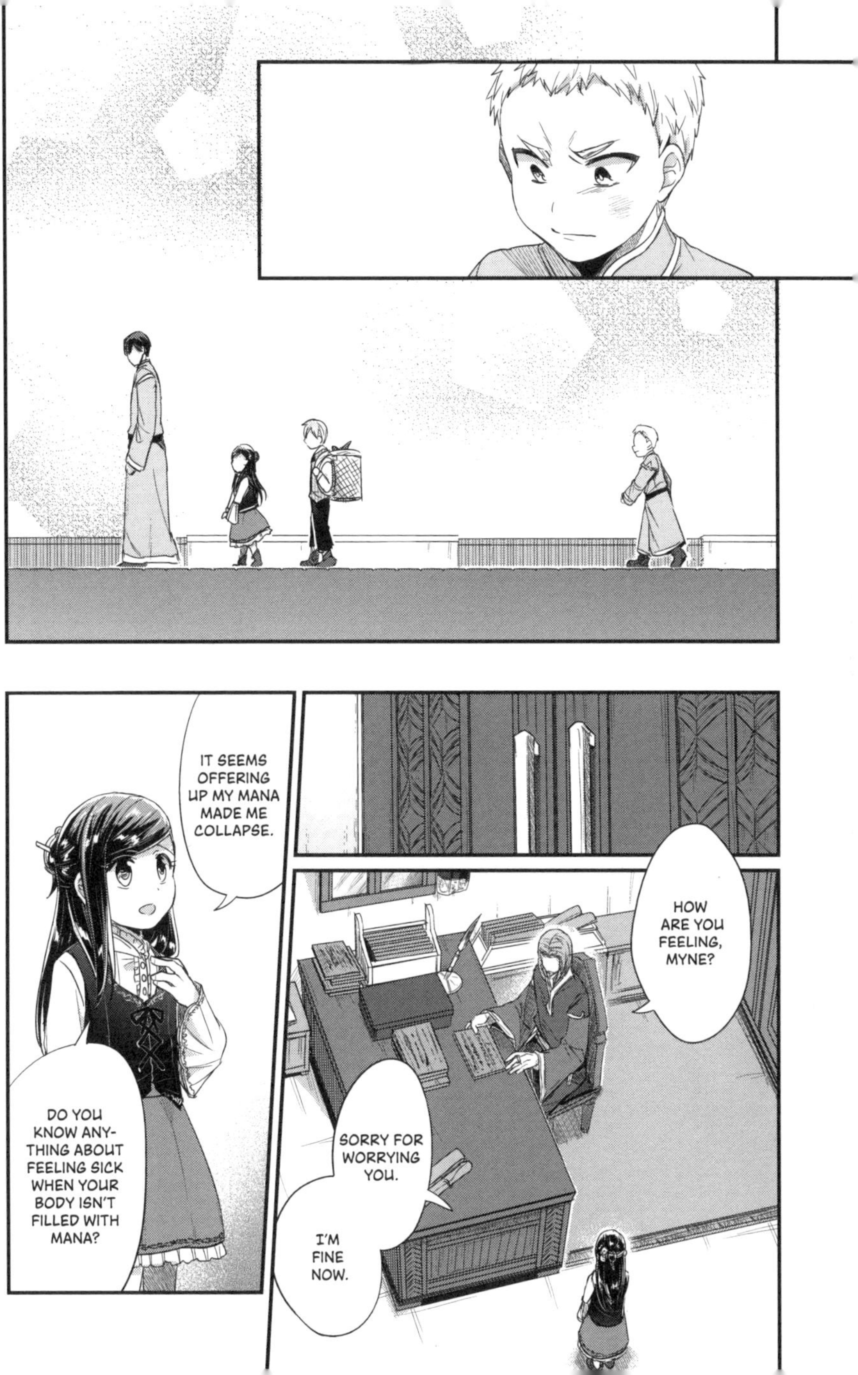
HOW ARE YOU FEELING, MYNE?
SORRY FOR WORRYING YOU.
I'M FINE NOW.
IT SEEMS OFFERING UP MY MANA MADE ME COLLAPSE.
DO YOU KNOW ANY-THING ABOUT FEELING SICK WHEN YOUR BODY ISN'T FILLED WITH MANA?

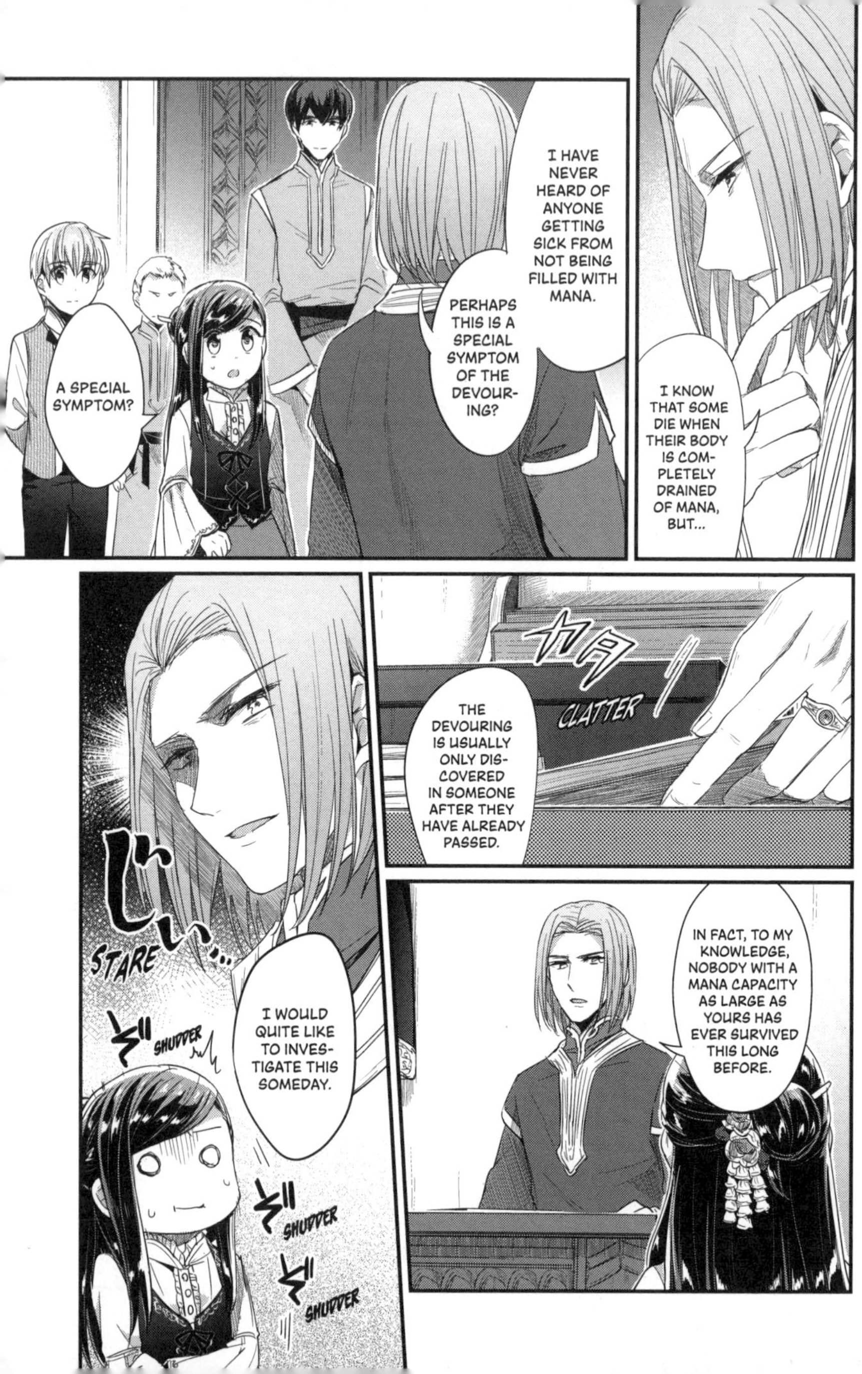
I KNOW THAT SOME DIE WHEN THEIR BODY IS COMPLETELY DRAINED OF MANA, BUT...
I HAVE NEVER HEARD OF ANYONE GETTING SICK FROM NOT BEING FILLED WITH MANA.
PERHAPS THIS IS A SPECIAL SYMPTOM OF THE DEVOURING?
A SPECIAL SYMPTOM?
CLATTER
THE DEVOURING IS USUALLY ONLY DISCOVERED IN SOMEONE AFTER THEY HAVE ALREADY PASSED.
IN FACT, TO MY KNOWLEDGE, NOBODY WITH A MANA CAPACITY AS LARGE AS YOURS HAS EVER SURVIVED THIS LONG BEFORE.
STARE
I WOULD QUITE LIKE TO INVESTIGATE THIS SOMEDAY.
SHUDDER
SHUDDER
SHUDDER

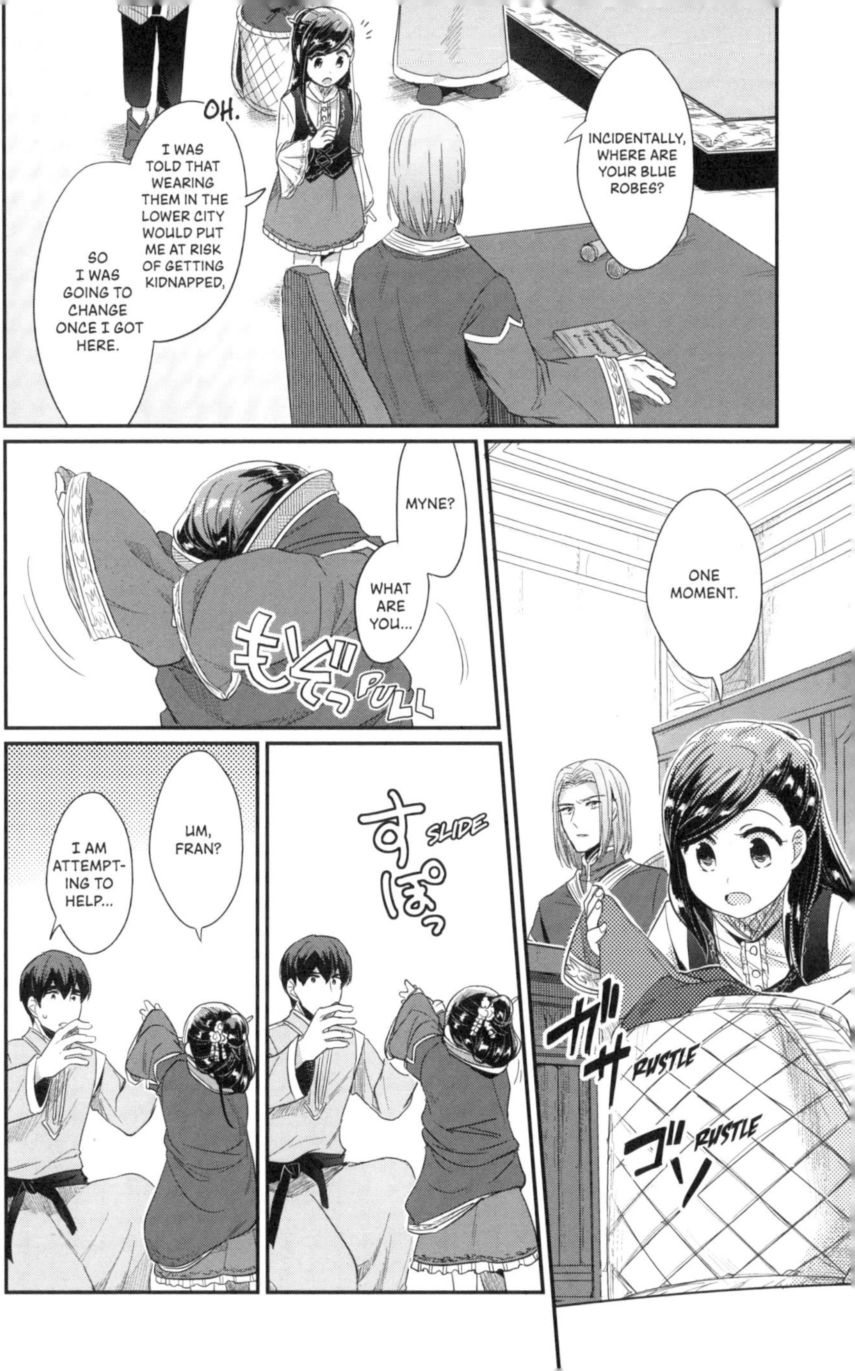
INCIDENTALLY, WHERE ARE YOUR BLUE ROBES?
OH.
I WAS TOLD THAT WEARING THEM IN THE LOWER CITY WOULD PUT ME AT RISK OF GETTING KIDNAPPED,
SO I WAS GOING TO CHANGE ONCE I GOT HERE.
ONE MOMENT.
ガサ RUSTLE
ゴソ RUSTLE
MYNE?
WHAT ARE YOU...
もぞっ PULL
すぽっ SLIDE
UM, FRAN?
I AM ATTEMPT-ING TO HELP...

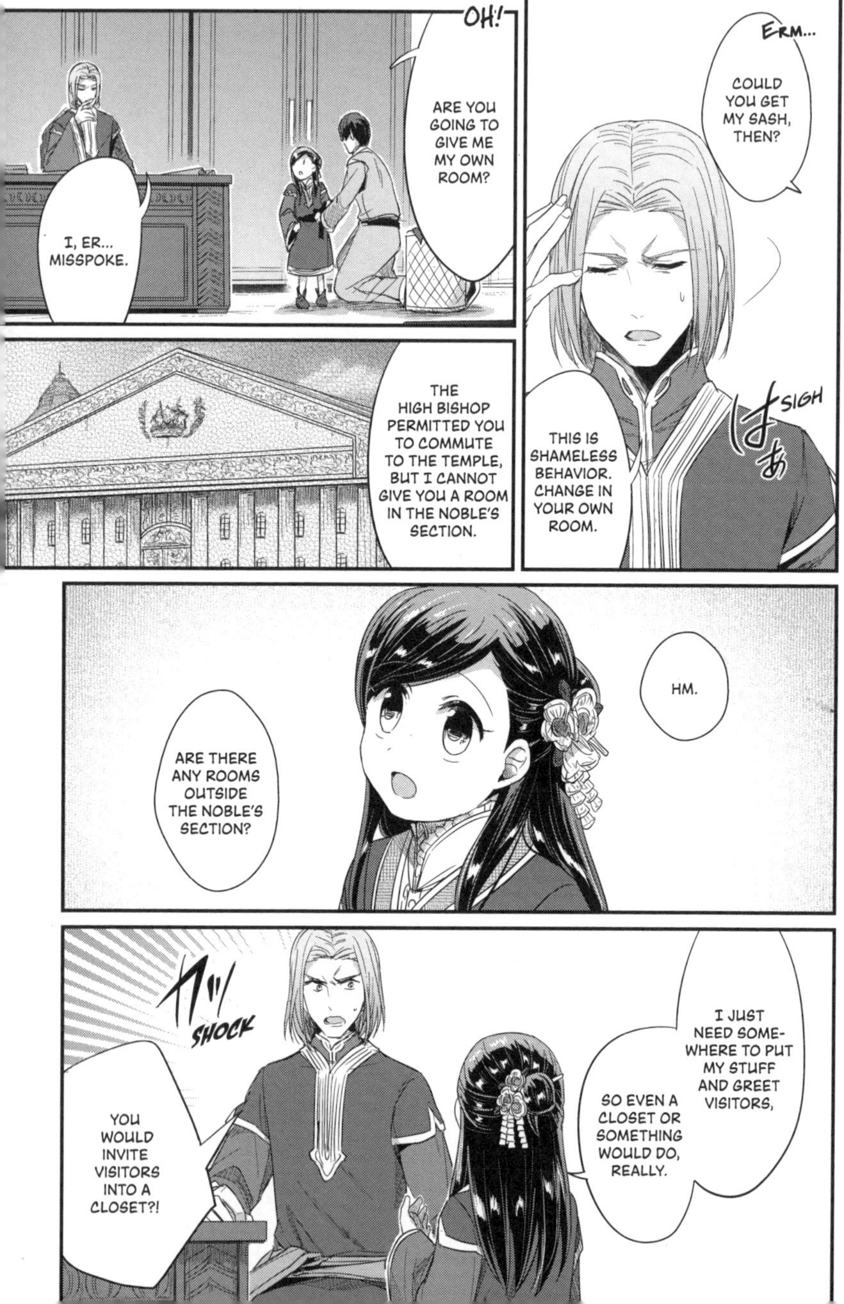
ERM...
COULD YOU GET MY SASH, THEN?
はぁ SIGH
THIS IS SHAMELESS BEHAVIOR. CHANGE IN YOUR OWN ROOM.
OH!
ARE YOU GOING TO GIVE ME MY OWN ROOM?
I, ER... MISSPOKE.
THE HIGH BISHOP PERMITTED YOU TO COMMUTE TO THE TEMPLE, BUT I CANNOT GIVE YOU A ROOM IN THE NOBLE'S SECTION.
HM.
ARE THERE ANY ROOMS OUTSIDE THE NOBLE'S SECTION?
I JUST NEED SOME-WHERE TO PUT MY STUFF AND GREET VISITORS,
SO EVEN A CLOSET OR SOMETHING WOULD DO, REALLY.
ガッ SHOCK
YOU WOULD INVITE VISITORS INTO A CLOSET?!

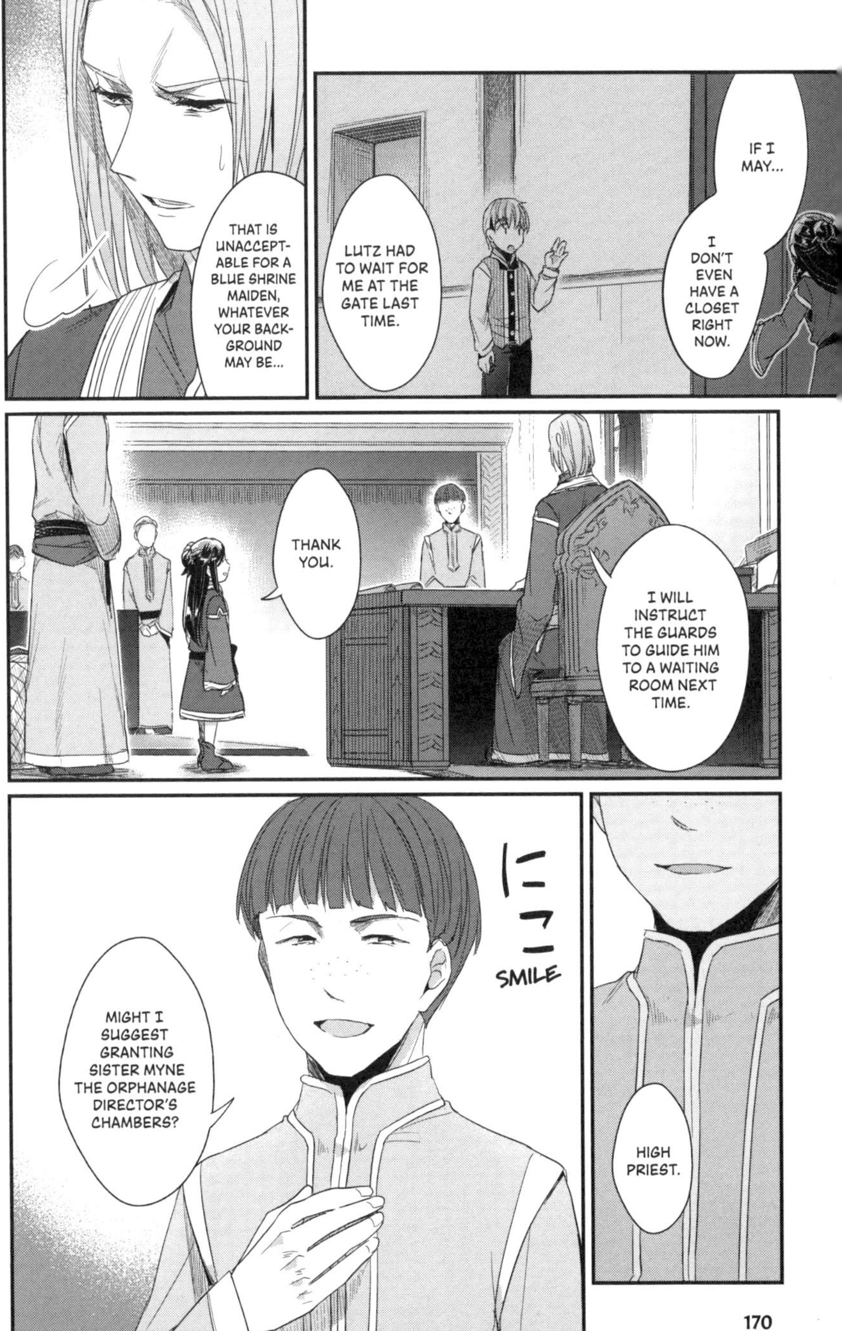
IF I MAY...
I DON'T EVEN HAVE A CLOSET RIGHT NOW.
LUTZ HAD TO WAIT FOR ME AT THE GATE LAST TIME.
THAT IS UNACCEPTABLE FOR A BLUE SHRINE MAIDEN, WHATEVER YOUR BACKGROUND MAY BE...
I WILL INSTRUCT THE GUARDS TO GUIDE HIM TO A WAITING ROOM NEXT TIME.
THANK YOU.
HIGH PRIEST.
にこ
SMILE
MIGHT I SUGGEST GRANTING SISTER MYNE THE ORPHANAGE DIRECTOR'S CHAMBERS?

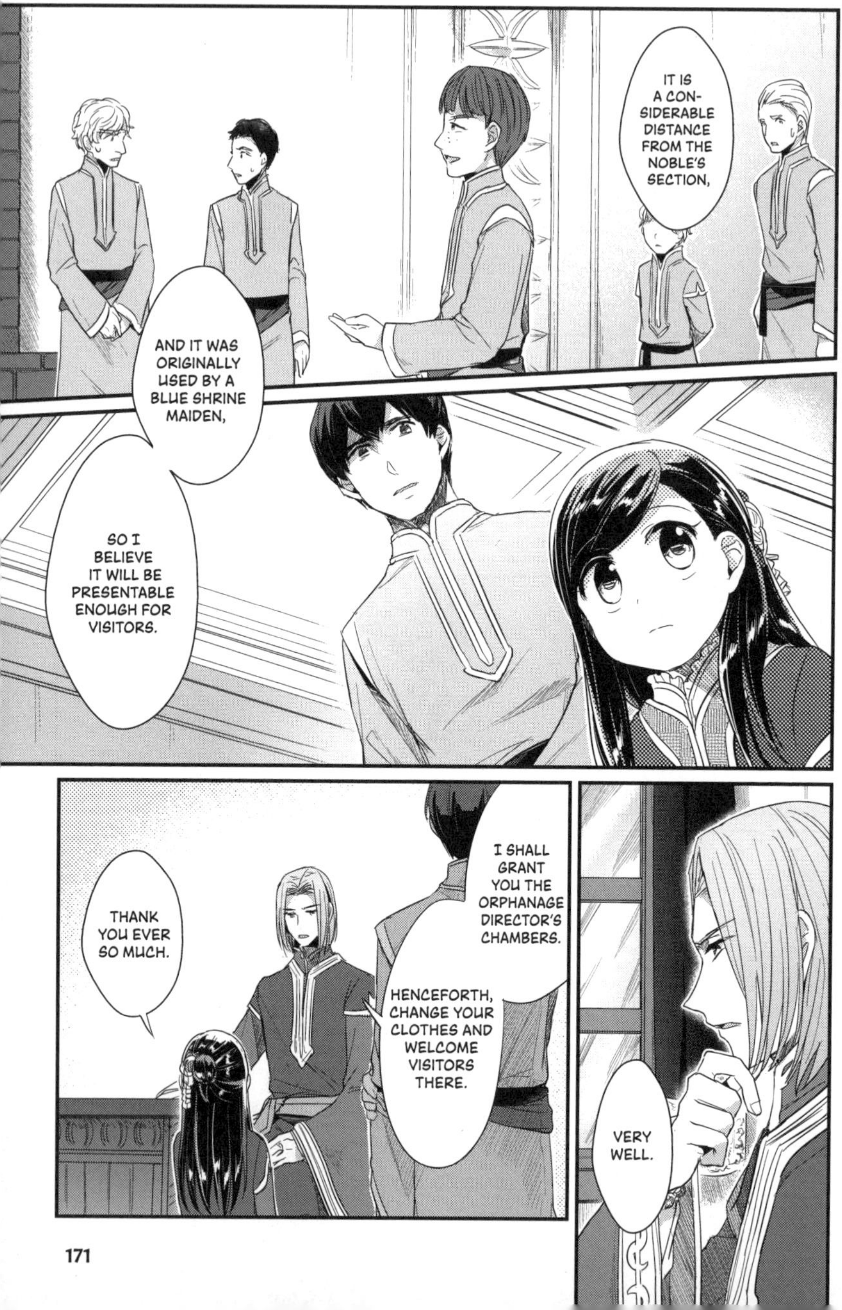
IT IS A CON- SIDERABLE DISTANCE FROM THE NOBLE'S SECTION,
AND IT WAS ORIGINALLY USED BY A BLUE SHRINE MAIDEN,
SO I BELIEVE IT WILL BE PRESENTABLE ENOUGH FOR VISITORS.
VERY WELL.
I SHALL GRANT YOU THE ORPHANAGE DIRECTOR'S CHAMBERS.
HENCEFORTH, CHANGE YOUR CLOTHES AND WELCOME VISITORS THERE.
THANK YOU EVER SO MUCH.

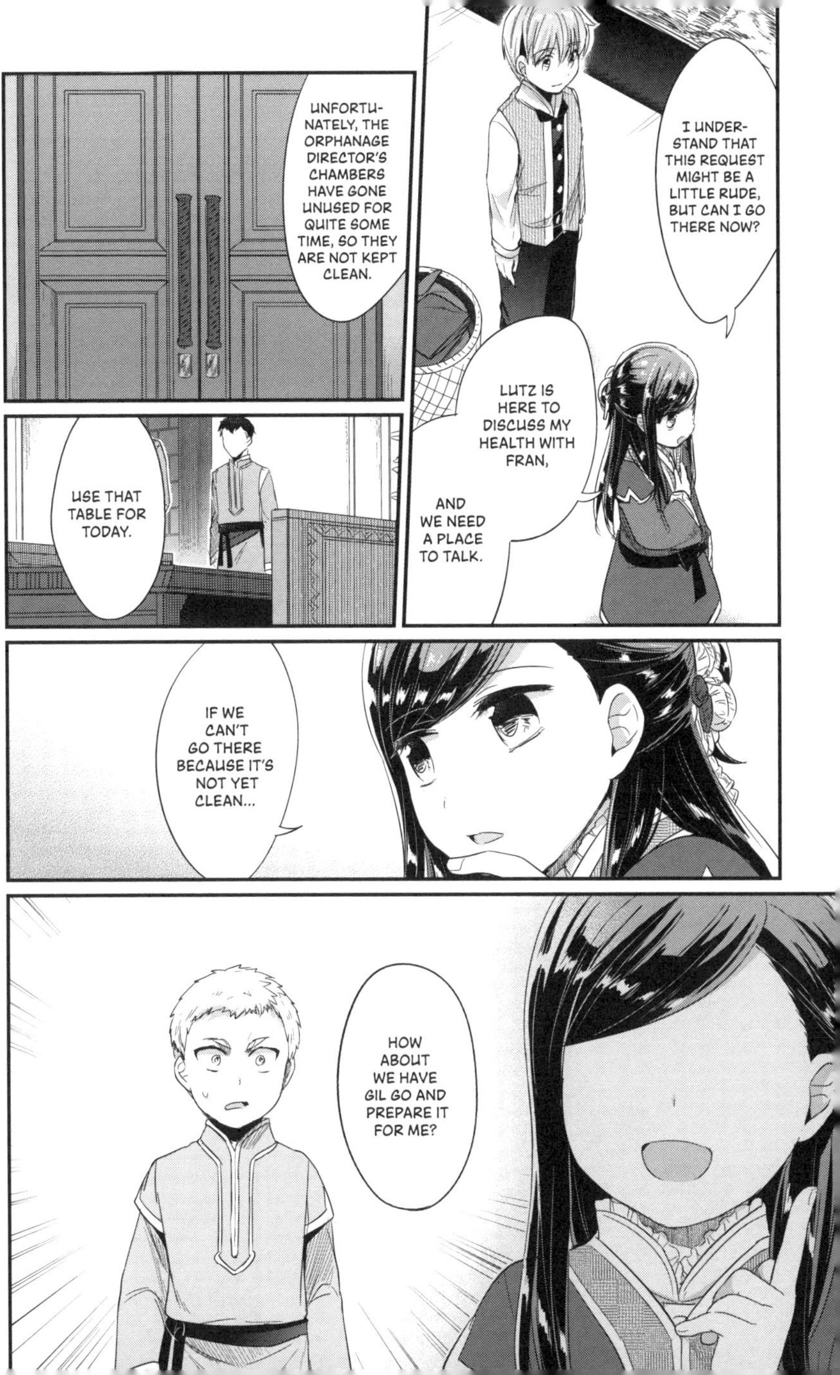
I UNDER-STAND THAT THIS REQUEST MIGHT BE A LITTLE RUDE, BUT CAN I GO THERE NOW?
LUTZ IS HERE TO DISCUSS MY HEALTH WITH FRAN,
AND WE NEED A PLACE TO TALK.
UNFORTU-NATELY, THE ORPHANAGE DIRECTOR'S CHAMBERS HAVE GONE UNUSED FOR QUITE SOME TIME, SO THEY ARE NOT KEPT CLEAN.
USE THAT TABLE FOR TODAY.
IF WE CAN'T GO THERE BECAUSE IT'S NOT YET CLEAN...
HOW ABOUT WE HAVE GIL GO AND PREPARE IT FOR ME?

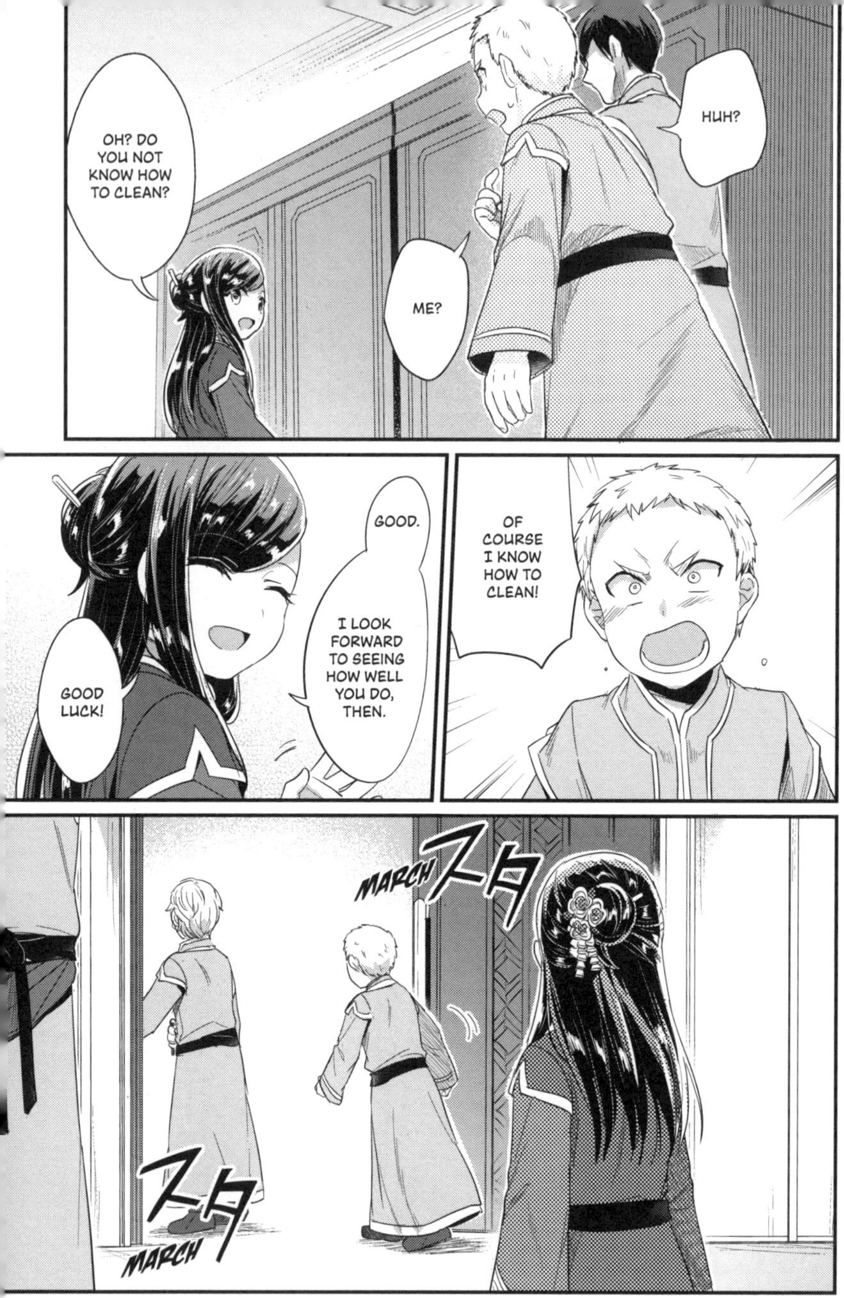
HUH?
OH? DO YOU NOT KNOW HOW TO CLEAN?
ME?
OF COURSE I KNOW HOW TO CLEAN!
GOOD.
I LOOK FORWARD TO SEEING HOW WELL YOU DO, THEN.
GOOD LUCK!
MARCH
MARCH

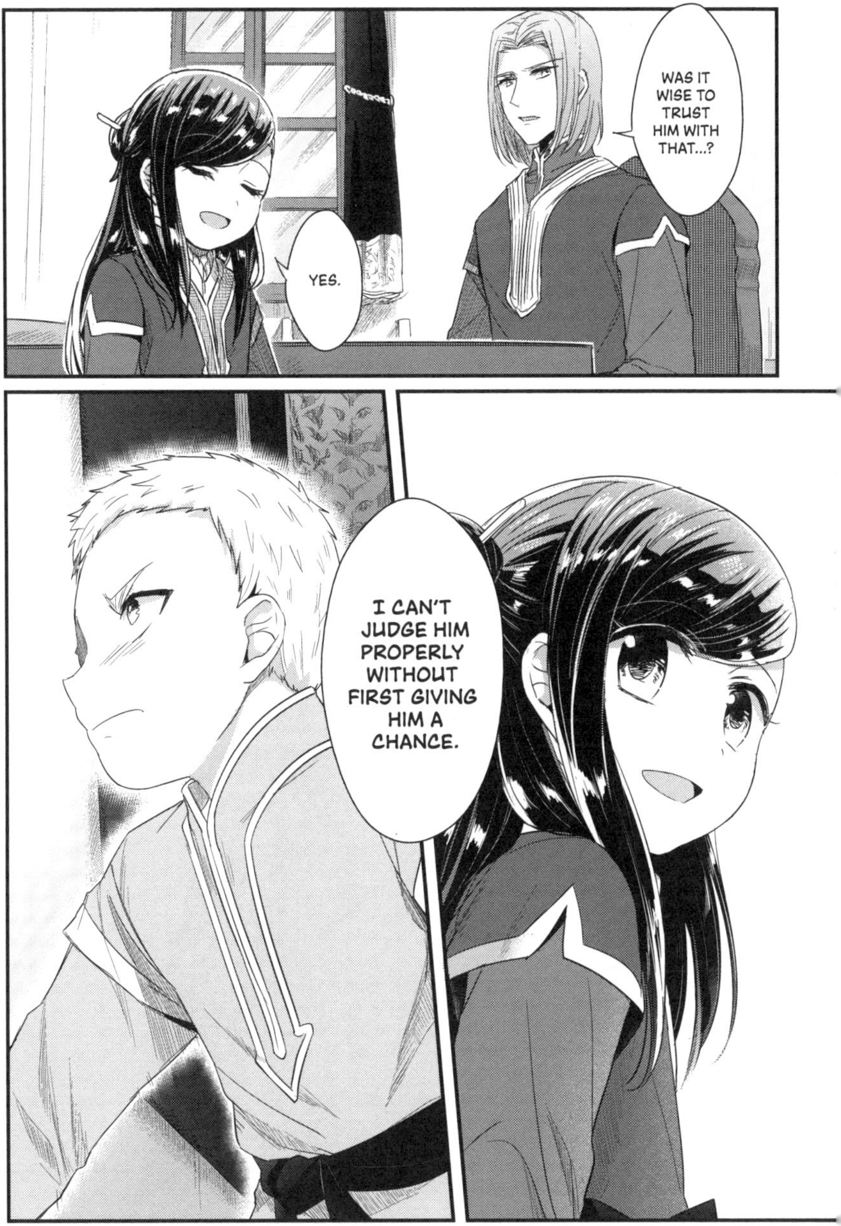
WAS IT WISE TO TRUST HIM WITH THAT...?
YES.
I CAN'T JUDGE HIM PROPERLY WITHOUT FIRST GIVING HIM A CHANCE.

Ch. 4: What They Deserve **End** (To be continued in Volume 2)

ASCENDANCE
OF A
BOOKWORM

I'll do anything to
become a librarian!

Part 2 **I'll even join the
temple to read
books!**

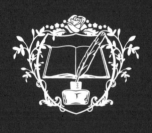

Extra How to Handle the Myne Workshop

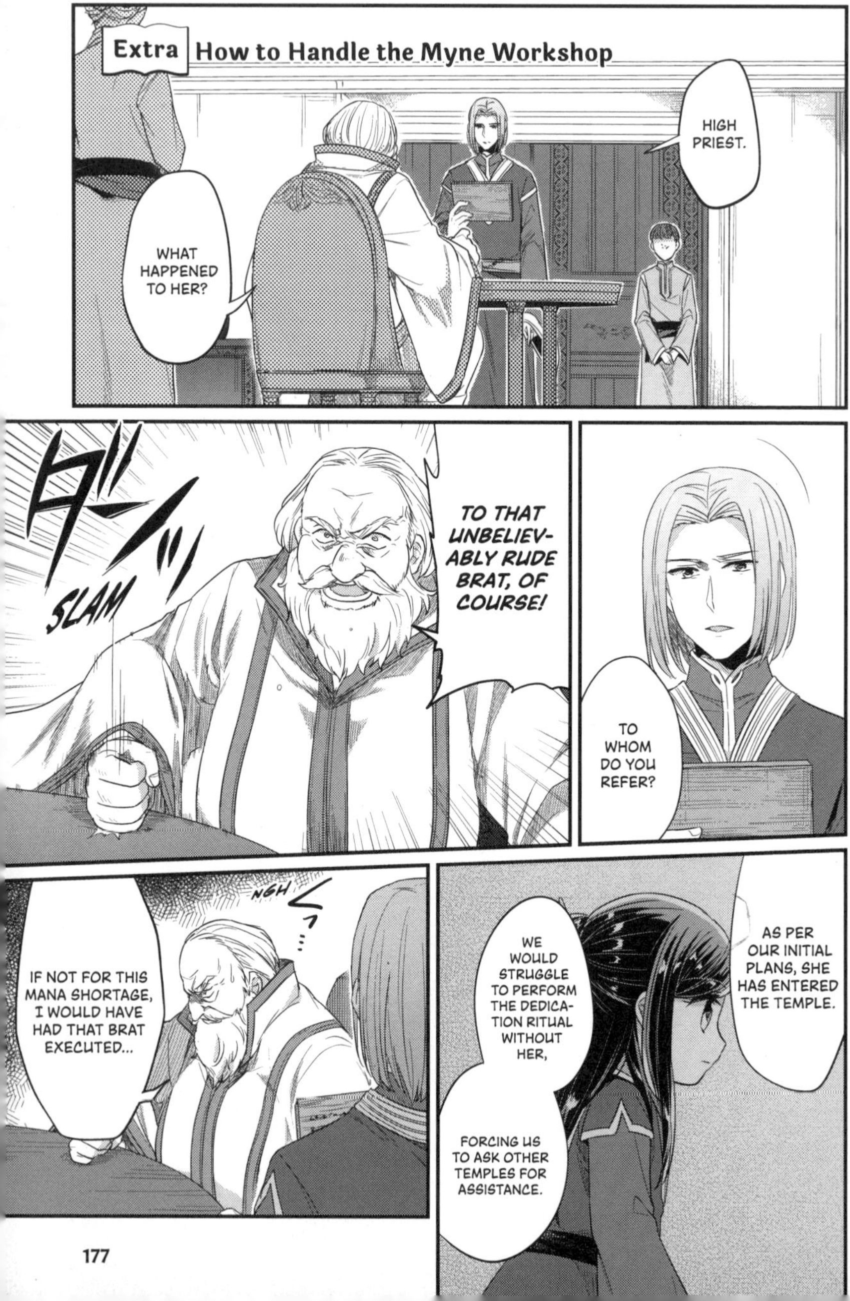
HIGH PRIEST.
WHAT HAPPENED TO HER?
TO WHOM DO YOU REFER?
TO THAT UNBELIEVABLY RUDE BRAT, OF COURSE!
SLAM
AS PER OUR INITIAL PLANS, SHE HAS ENTERED THE TEMPLE.
WE WOULD STRUGGLE TO PERFORM THE DEDICATION RITUAL WITHOUT HER,
FORCING US TO ASK OTHER TEMPLES FOR ASSISTANCE.
NGH
IF NOT FOR THIS MANA SHORTAGE, I WOULD HAVE HAD THAT BRAT EXECUTED...

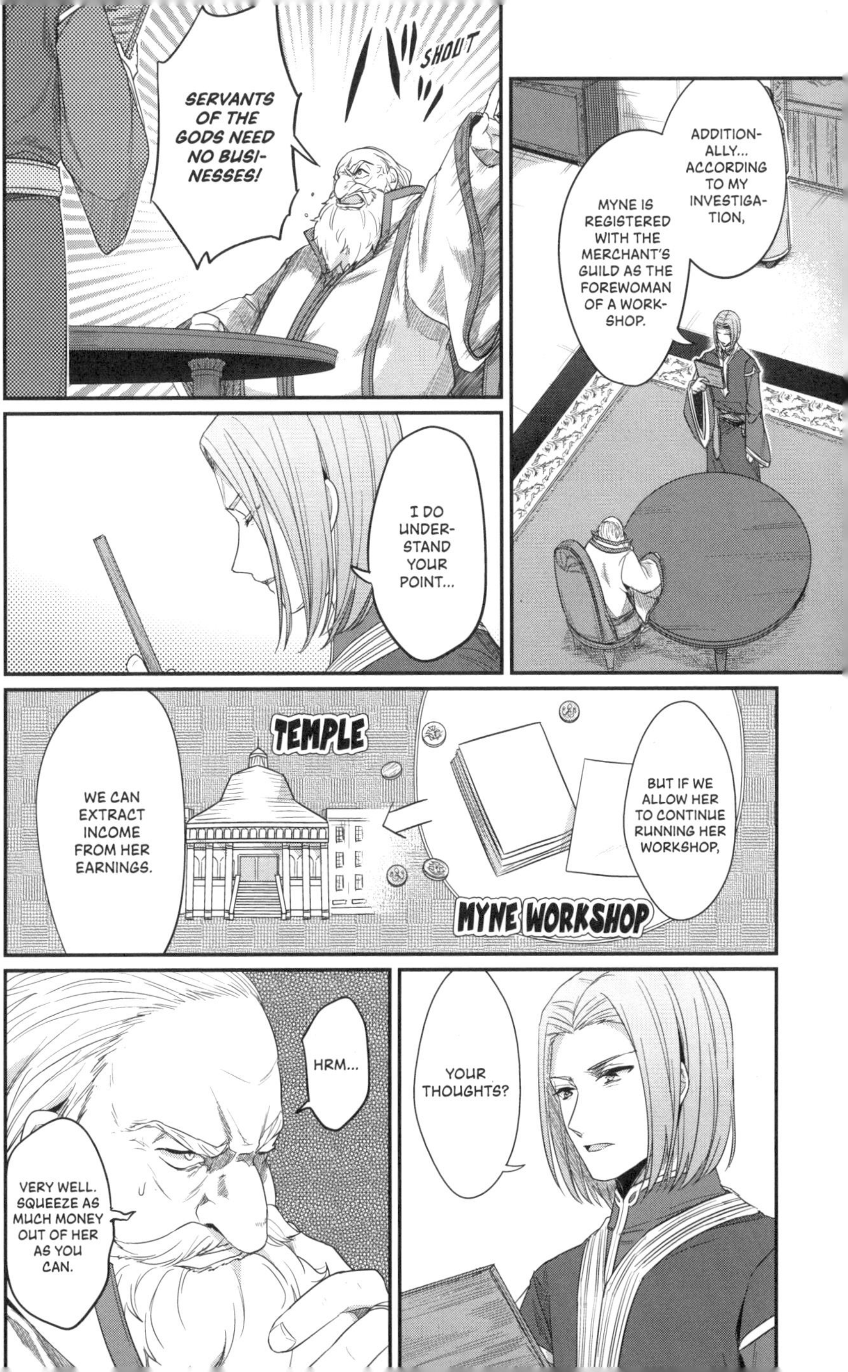
ADDITION-ALLY... ACCORDING TO MY INVESTIGA-TION,
MYNE IS REGISTERED WITH THE MERCHANT'S GUILD AS THE FOREWOMAN OF A WORK-SHOP.
SHOUT
SERVANTS OF THE GODS NEED NO BUSI-NESSES!
I DO UNDER-STAND YOUR POINT...
BUT IF WE ALLOW HER TO CONTINUE RUNNING HER WORKSHOP,
TEMPLE
MYNE WORKSHOP
WE CAN EXTRACT INCOME FROM HER EARNINGS.
YOUR THOUGHTS?
HRM...
VERY WELL. SQUEEZE AS MUCH MONEY OUT OF HER AS YOU CAN.

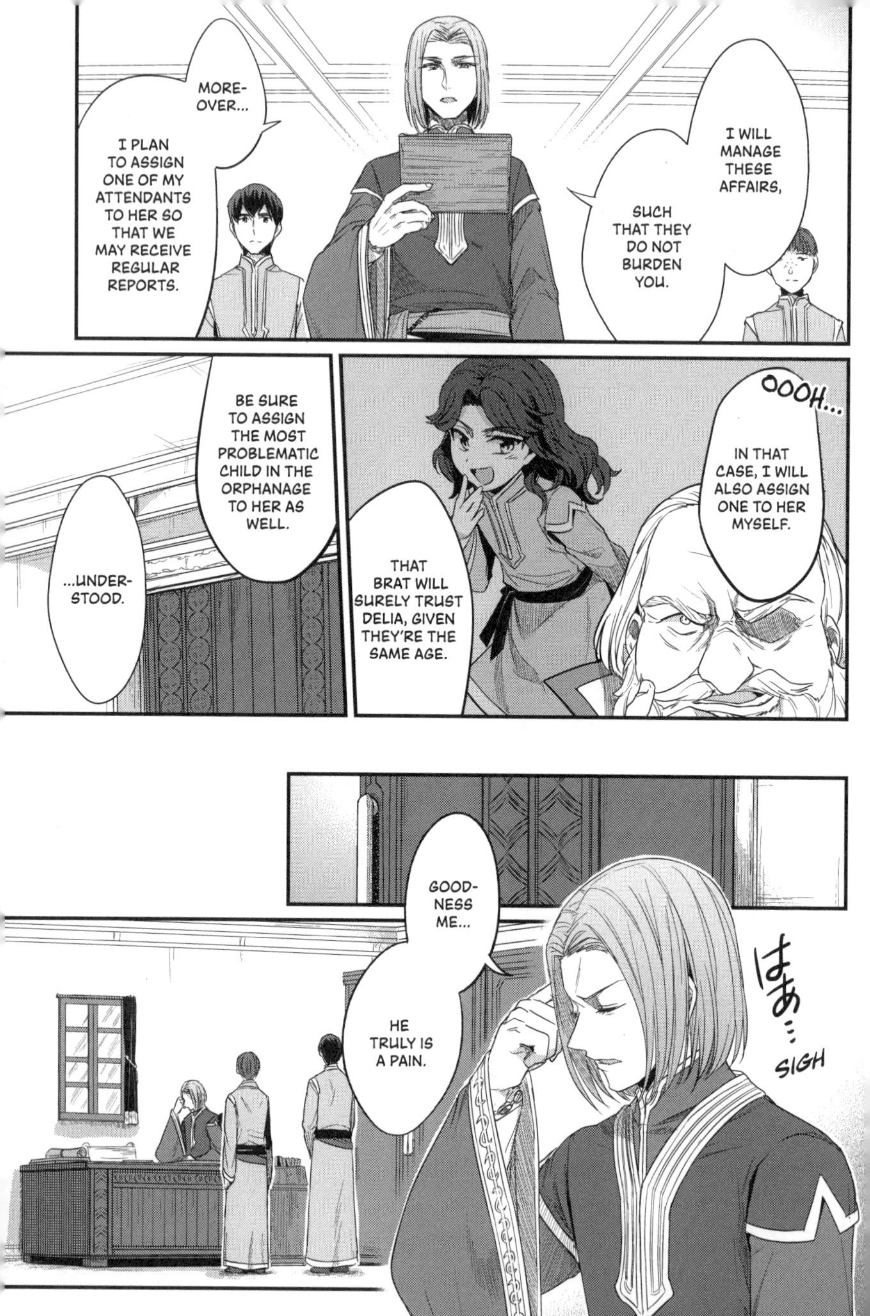
I WILL MANAGE THESE AFFAIRS,
SUCH THAT THEY DO NOT BURDEN YOU.
MORE-OVER...
I PLAN TO ASSIGN ONE OF MY ATTENDANTS TO HER SO THAT WE MAY RECEIVE REGULAR REPORTS.
OOOH...
IN THAT CASE, I WILL ALSO ASSIGN ONE TO HER MYSELF.
THAT BRAT WILL SURELY TRUST DELIA, GIVEN THEY'RE THE SAME AGE.
BE SURE TO ASSIGN THE MOST PROBLEMATIC CHILD IN THE ORPHANAGE TO HER AS WELL.
...UNDER-STOOD.
はぁ…
SIGH
GOOD-NESS ME...
HE TRULY IS A PAIN.

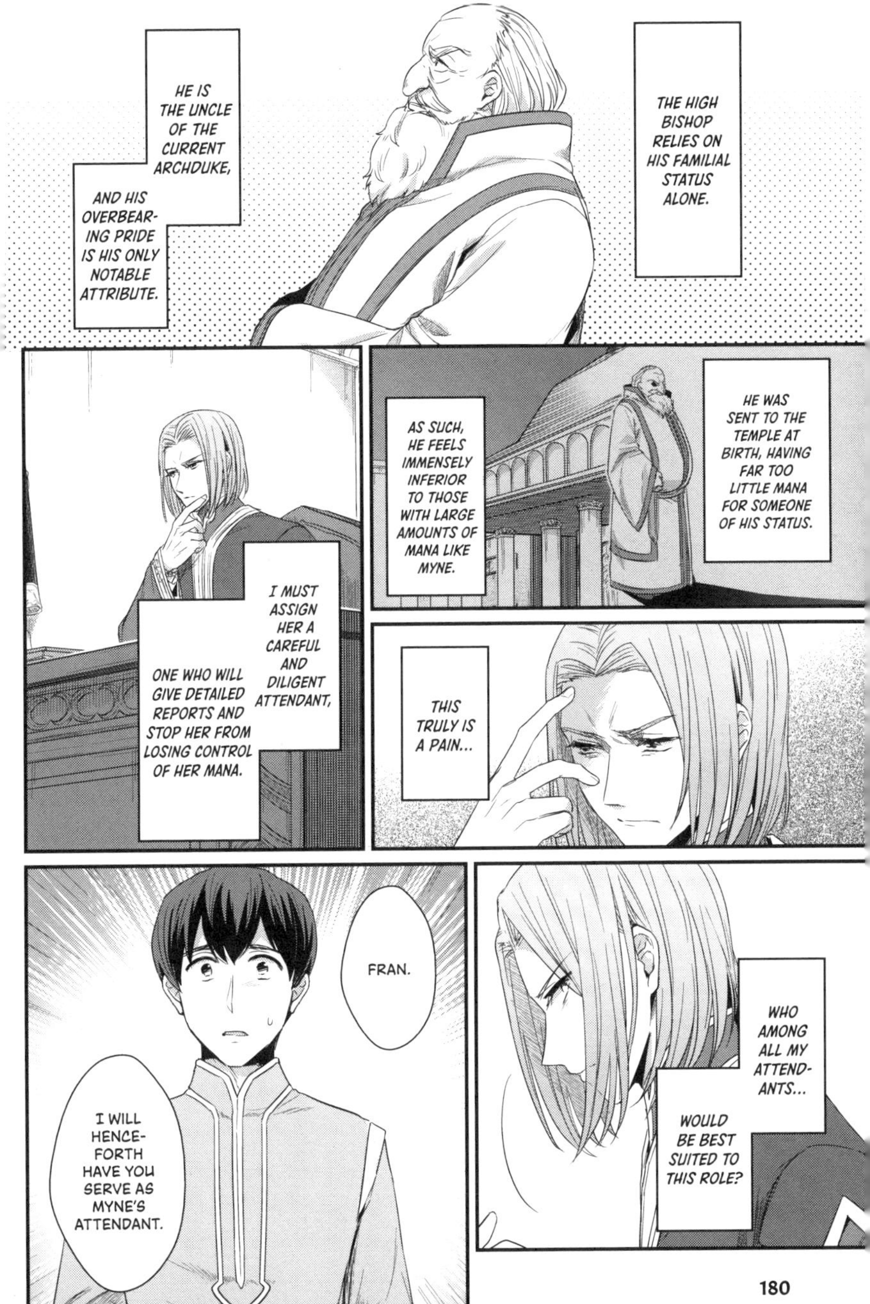
THE HIGH BISHOP RELIES ON HIS FAMILIAL STATUS ALONE.
HE IS THE UNCLE OF THE CURRENT ARCHDUKE,
AND HIS OVERBEARING PRIDE IS HIS ONLY NOTABLE ATTRIBUTE.
HE WAS SENT TO THE TEMPLE AT BIRTH, HAVING FAR TOO LITTLE MANA FOR SOMEONE OF HIS STATUS.
AS SUCH, HE FEELS IMMENSELY INFERIOR TO THOSE WITH LARGE AMOUNTS OF MANA LIKE MYNE.
THIS TRULY IS A PAIN...
I MUST ASSIGN HER A CAREFUL AND DILIGENT ATTENDANT,
ONE WHO WILL GIVE DETAILED REPORTS AND STOP HER FROM LOSING CONTROL OF HER MANA.
WHO AMONG ALL MY ATTENDANTS...
WOULD BE BEST SUITED TO THIS ROLE?
FRAN.
I WILL HENCEFORTH HAVE YOU SERVE AS MYNE'S ATTENDANT.

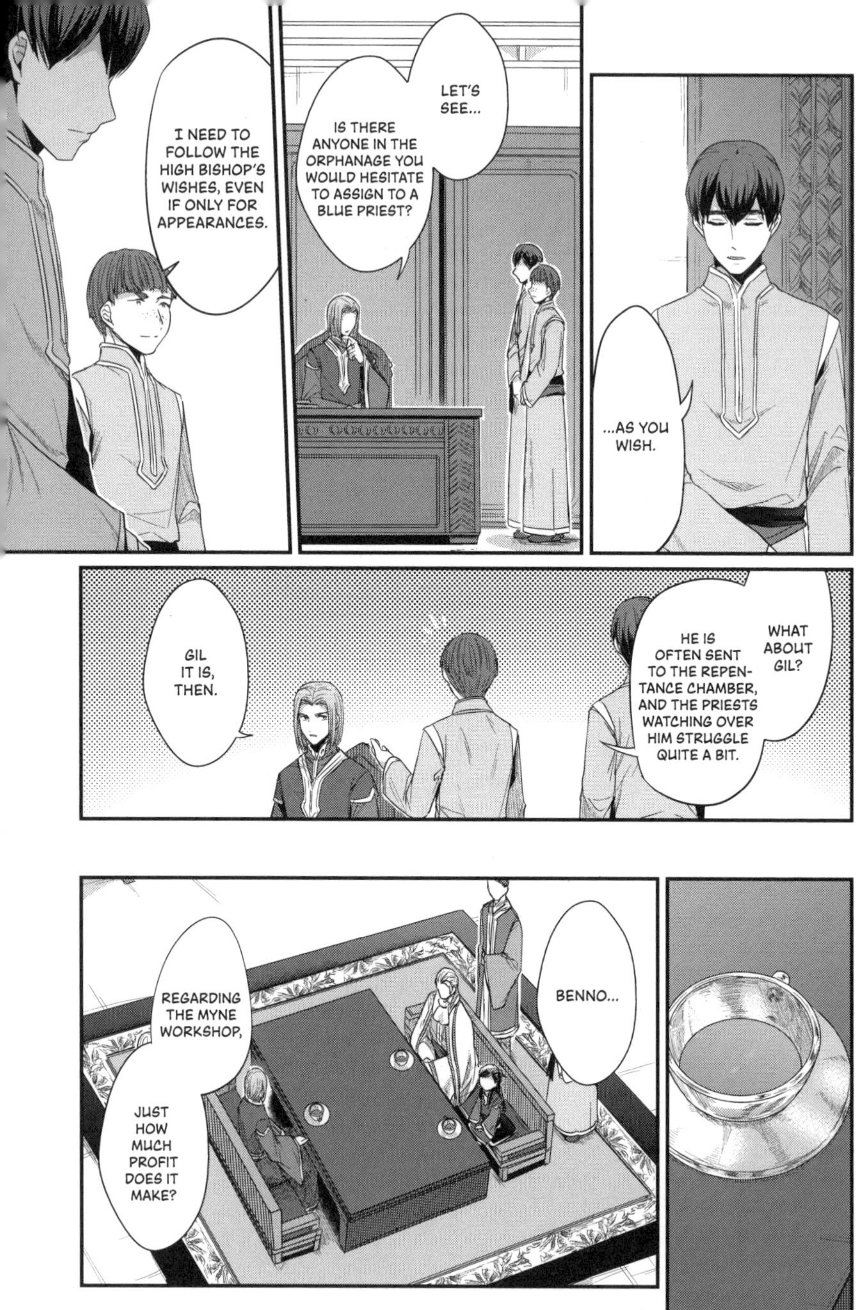
...AS YOU WISH.
LET'S SEE...
IS THERE ANYONE IN THE ORPHANAGE YOU WOULD HESITATE TO ASSIGN TO A BLUE PRIEST?
I NEED TO FOLLOW THE HIGH BISHOP'S WISHES, EVEN IF ONLY FOR APPEARANCES.
WHAT ABOUT GIL?
HE IS OFTEN SENT TO THE REPENTANCE CHAMBER, AND THE PRIESTS WATCHING OVER HIM STRUGGLE QUITE A BIT.
GIL IT IS, THEN.
BENNO...
REGARDING THE MYNE WORKSHOP,
JUST HOW MUCH PROFIT DOES IT MAKE?

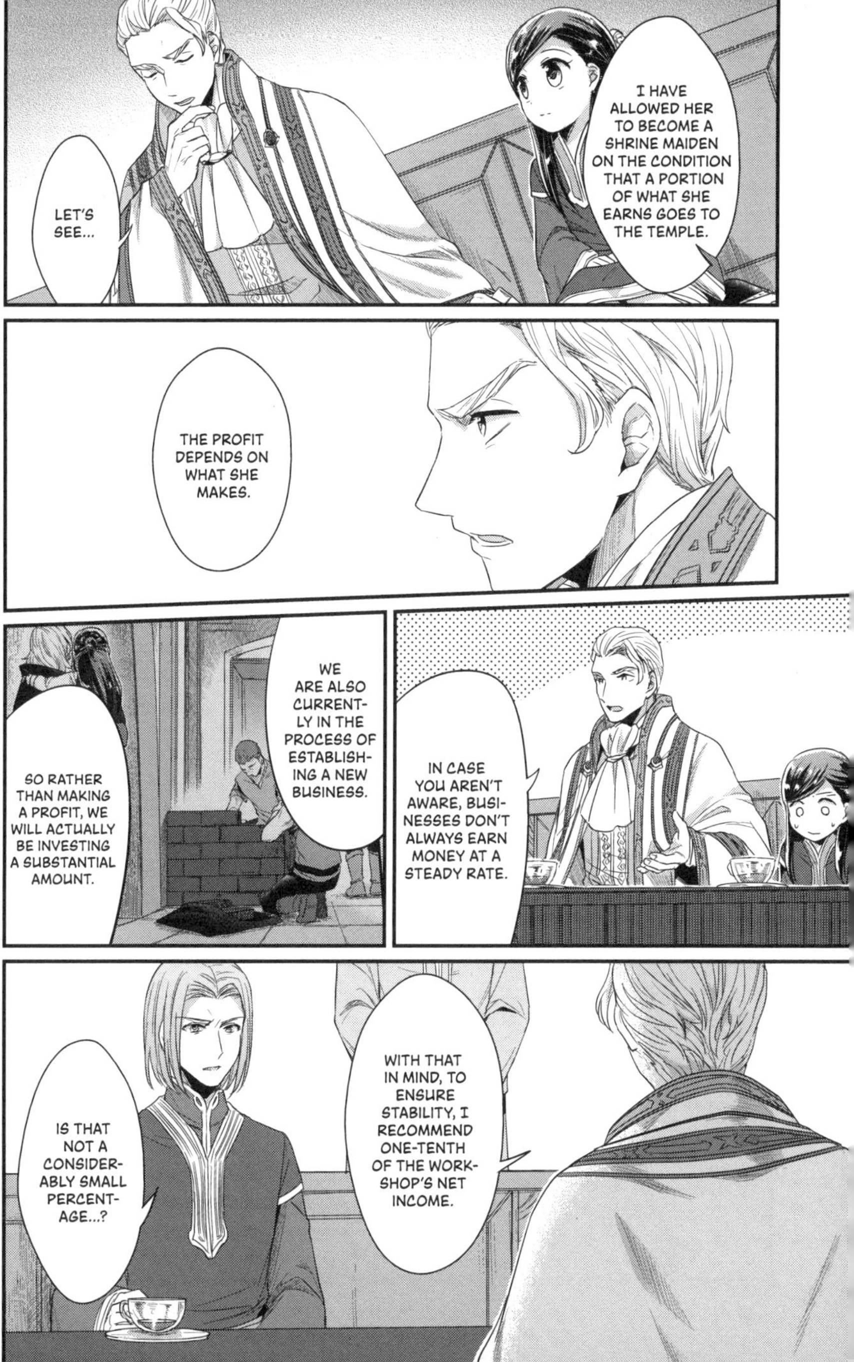
I HAVE ALLOWED HER TO BECOME A SHRINE MAIDEN ON THE CONDITION THAT A PORTION OF WHAT SHE EARNS GOES TO THE TEMPLE.
LET'S SEE...
THE PROFIT DEPENDS ON WHAT SHE MAKES.
IN CASE YOU AREN'T AWARE, BUSI-NESSES DON'T ALWAYS EARN MONEY AT A STEADY RATE.
WE ARE ALSO CURRENT-LY IN THE PROCESS OF ESTABLISH-ING A NEW BUSINESS.
SO RATHER THAN MAKING A PROFIT, WE WILL ACTUALLY BE INVESTING A SUBSTANTIAL AMOUNT.
WITH THAT IN MIND, TO ENSURE STABILITY, I RECOMMEND ONE-TENTH OF THE WORK-SHOP'S NET INCOME.
IS THAT NOT A CONSIDER-ABLY SMALL PERCENT-AGE...?

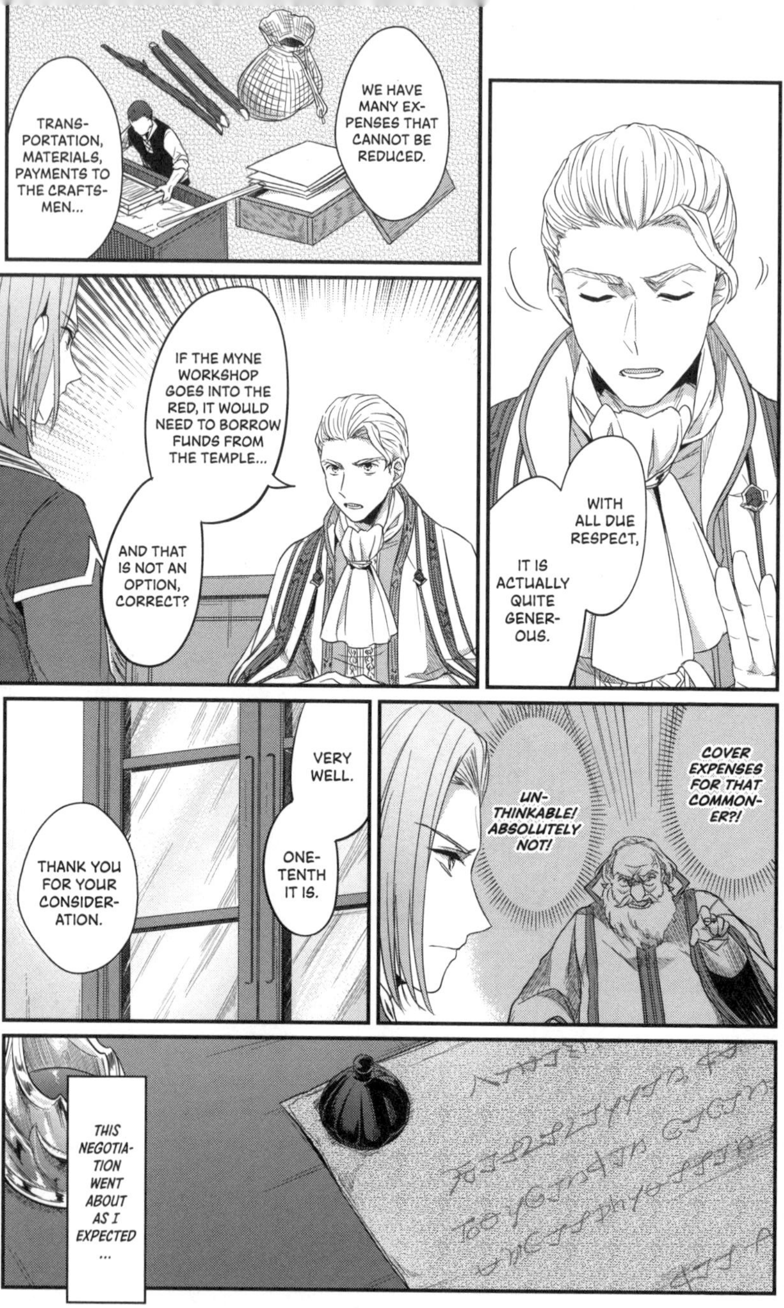
WITH ALL DUE RESPECT,
IT IS ACTUALLY QUITE GENER-OUS.
WE HAVE MANY EX-PENSES THAT CANNOT BE REDUCED.
TRANS-PORTATION, MATERIALS, PAYMENTS TO THE CRAFTS-MEN...
IF THE MYNE WORKSHOP GOES INTO THE RED, IT WOULD NEED TO BORROW FUNDS FROM THE TEMPLE...
AND THAT IS NOT AN OPTION, CORRECT?
COVER EXPENSES FOR THAT COMMON-ER?!
UN-THINKABLE! ABSOLUTELY NOT!
VERY WELL.
ONE-TENTH IT IS.
THANK YOU FOR YOUR CONSIDER-ATION.
THIS NEGOTIA-TION WENT ABOUT AS I EXPECTED...

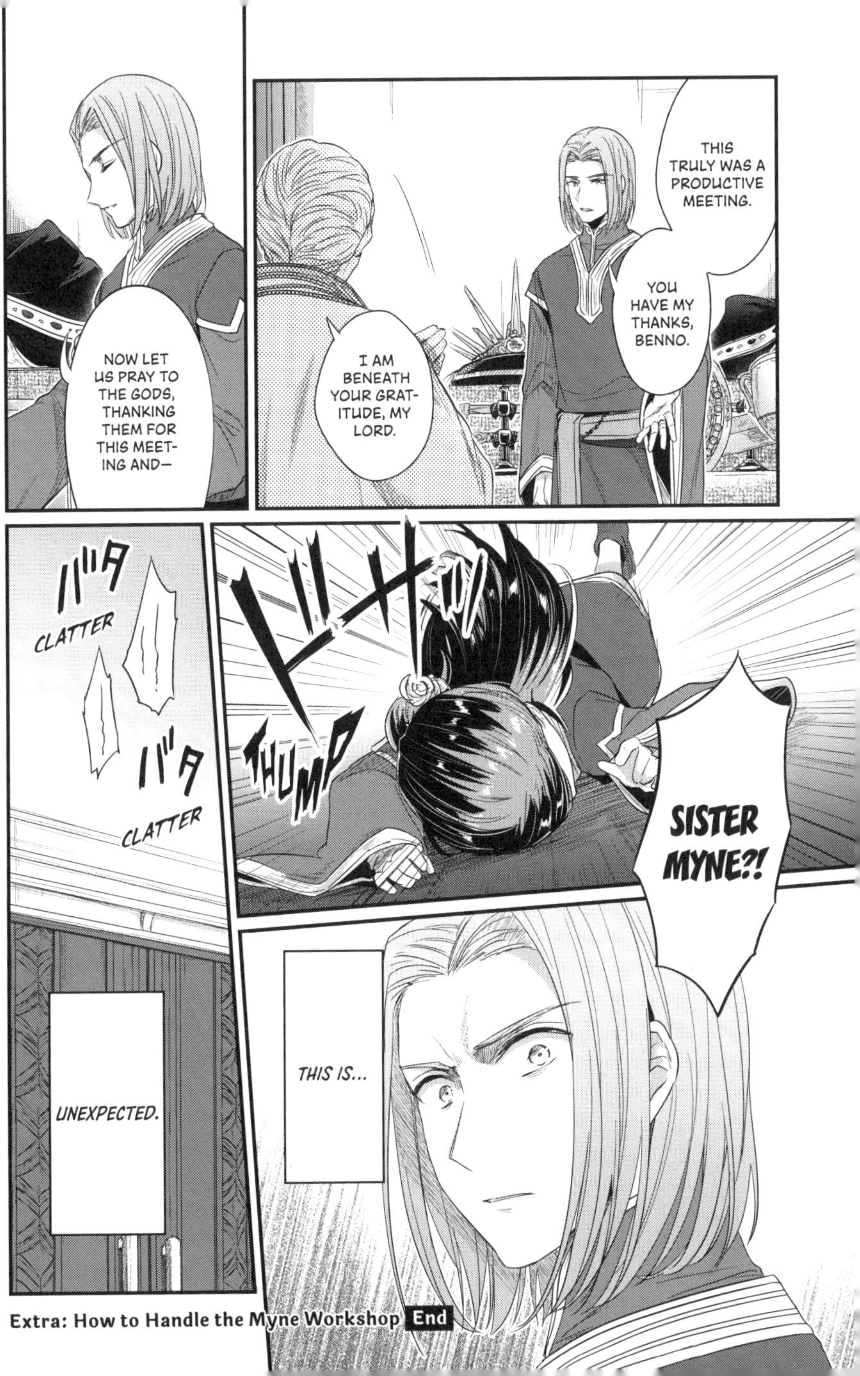
THIS TRULY WAS A PRODUCTIVE MEETING.
YOU HAVE MY THANKS, BENNO.
I AM BENEATH YOUR GRATITUDE, MY LORD.
NOW LET US PRAY TO THE GODS, THANKING THEM FOR THIS MEETING AND—
ドサッ
THUMP
SISTER MYNE?!
THIS IS...
バタ
CLATTER
バタ
CLATTER
UNEXPECTED.

Extra: How to Handle the Myne Workshop **End**

Fran and the Commoner Apprentice Blue Shrine Maiden

Fran and the Commoner Apprentice Blue Shrine Maiden

"Zahm, Lothar—do you have a moment?" Arno called as Lothar and I prepared food in our rooms at the back of the High Priest's chambers. "It has been decided that Fran shall become the head attendant of Sister Myne, a new apprentice blue shrine maiden joining the temple."

"Fran? Serving Sister Myne?" I asked reflexively. Blue priests and shrine maidens entering the temple always chose their attendants from among the gray priests and shrine maidens in the orphanage. At times, an attendant would return to the orphanage after the priest or shrine maiden they served left the temple, and subsequently be assigned to a new one... but I had never heard of an attendant in active duty being moved to serve someone else.

"I imagine he is going to be gathering information and keeping an eye on her, all while keeping her distanced from the High Bishop. This is an order from the High Priest himself."

"I suppose there is no disputing an order... Is this truly wise, though?

This situation simply didn't seem right to me. Sister Myne was an unusual individual who had been given blue robes despite her being a commoner. To be honest, it was hard for me to imagine the current High Bishop ever allowing such a person to remain in the temple.

However, according to the attendants who worked in the High Bishop's chambers, Sister Myne had used her mana to threaten the High Bishop after her father violently beat multiple gray priests, all to force him to accept her as a blue shrine maiden. Rumors of her violent nature were spreading quickly among the gray priests.

"You need not worry about Fran. He will continue living with us despite serving someone else."

"What?"

"Sister Myne shall be commuting from the lower city, and she does not have chambers in the noble section of the temple. Furthermore, she is of poor health, and will only be visiting on days when she is well. On days when she is absent, Fran is going to be working in the High Priest's chambers as usual."

Arno's explanation brought me a little relief. Fran had exceptionally strong feelings of admiration for the High Priest, so it was heartening to know that he would not fully lose his place at his side. And most importantly, if Sister Myne was indeed cruel to Fran, then the High Priest would surely rescue him.

"Still, our own work will become much more difficult without Fran," Lothar said.

The High Priest currently had five attendants: Arno, the head attendant; Lothar; me; Gido; and Fran, who was now assigned to Sister Myne. The dramatic decrease in the number of blue priests in the temple meant that the High Priest had much more work now, so he surely couldn't afford to lose any of us.

Arno fell into thought. "I believe we will need to select new attendants. I will search for good candidates while visiting the orphanage to discuss Sister Myne's apprentice attendant. I expect it will take some time to find one capable of passing the High Priest's trial period, so the sooner we act, the better."

The High Priest was notoriously hard on others, as well as himself. When selecting new attendants, he always put them through an extended trial period, and those who did not satisfy his expectations were swiftly returned to the orphanage. At the time I was selected, four others were sent away.

That said, while the High Priest had high expectations and gave us a considerable amount of work, serving him was a pleasant experience: he did not make unreasonable demands, nor was he violently emotional. His chambers were peaceful as well, completely

free of drama due to the absence of women. I had previously served Brother Shikza who had two gray shrine maidens among his attendants, and moderating their fervent battles for his favor had been exceedingly troublesome.

Sister Myne had come to the temple today. She finished her vows and, after receiving various explanations from the High Priest, headed for the book room with her attendants.

When fourth bell rang, we started clearing away our work to prepare for lunch.

"Zahm, please allow me to help with the preparations," Fran said, returning with us to our rooms at the back of the High Priest's chambers. Gido and Lothar were serving the High Priest today, and those attendants not serving him needed to hurriedly finish their meals while he ate.

"The preparations are already complete," Arno said, answering for me. "You may rest, Fran."

"But I need to do at least some work here to ease my mind. I offered to serve the High Priest his food, but Lothar told me to eat instead."

"Anyone would turn you down when you look that tired. Wouldn't you agree, Zahm?"

"Arno is right," I said. "There will be work for you to do once Sister Myne returns home, so sit down and focus on eating for the time being."

Given how Fran rarely showed any exhaustion in the High Priest's chambers, something must have happened in the book room. I offered him a seat as I finished up the last few preparations.

"O mighty King and Queen of the endless skies who doth grace us with thousands upon thousands of lives to consume, O mighty Eternal Five who rule the mortal realm, I offer thanks and prayers to thee, and do take part in the meal so graciously provided."

We finished the pre-meal prayer and started to eat, which provided me an opportunity to eye Fran carefully and ask whether something had happened in the book room.

"Did something happen with Sister Myne?"

"When Gil told her it was time for lunch, she attempted to Crush him with mana so that he would stop interfering with her reading..."

"Just because he spoke to her?!" I gasped. She was just as violent as the rumors said.

The High Priest had shown no indication of such behavior when we spoke earlier, so I had assumed the High Bishop's attendants were merely exaggerating to damage her reputation. But it seemed Sister Myne truly was a child who flattered the High Priest while treating her attendants harshly. I recalled how erratic and troublesome Shikza had been to deal with and grimaced with displeasure.

"He called out to her multiple times, but she was so focused on her reading that she seemed to not hear him at all," Fran continued. "He ultimately lost his patience and shook her aggressively by the shoulders, so..."

I recalled how Gil had behaved in the High Priest's chambers and nodded; even the most patient of blue priests would get annoyed if their attendants acted so aggressively. Gil was a failure of an attendant, while Sister Myne was a dangerous girl who resorted to violence with mana at the drop of a hat. They would no doubt be clashing every single day from now on.

"It must be taxing being caught between those two, Fran," Arno said with a laugh. "Where is Sister Myne now?"

Fran's gaze moved to the direction of the book room. "She is still reading, and I imagine she will continue doing so until fifth bell when it is time for her to leave. Gil is waiting in the corner of the book room while Delia and I eat."

Gil ate in the orphanage, so his mealtimes weren't the same as those of us attendants. This was convenient, considering that it allowed them to alternate watching over Sister Myne like this.

"Serving someone who would Crush another for simply interrupting their reading time must be miserable. I remember how difficult it was serving the selfish and unpredictable Brother Shikza. Fran, before the High Priest, I recall that you used to serve..."

I quickly trailed off upon seeing Fran and Arno stiffen, both of them having served the former orphanage director Sister Margaret before being moved here. She had committed suicide in her chambers, having been forced to remain in the temple despite so many other blue priests and shrine maidens returning to noble society thanks to the Sovereignty's civil war. As her attendants at the time, they surely both deeply regretted their inability to stop her.

"My apologies. I should not have spoken about her."

At the moment, there were not enough blue priests or shrine maidens for all of the gray priests in the orphanage, leaving a population problem that nobody wanted to address. The orphanage director's chambers remained empty, and there were many dark rumors that Sister Margaret's blood still stained the floor, or that all those who entered would be imprisoned by her mana and prevented from ever leaving the temple again. But this largely had nothing to do with us, since the chambers were far removed from the noble section of the temple.

"Thank you for your concern, Zahm. I must admit, though— I truly am troubled. Sister Myne is so unlike the blue shrine maidens that I'm used to that I have no idea how to serve her. Neither Gil nor Delia are cooperative, either..."

"I will do whatever I can to help, Fran."

Fran had ultimately been assigned to Sister Myne, but it wouldn't have been odd for Gido or me to have been chosen instead. If only she would show a little more concern for him...

That said, I had to admit that the High Priest's selection had been a wise one—despite all the strife she was putting Fran through, he was still doing his best to serve her as diligently as possible. Nobody else would take serving a commoner shrine maiden so seriously. I gave him as much encouragement as I could, then saw him off as he returned to the book room.

It was a little after fifth bell when Fran returned to the High Priest's chambers, looking very pale.

"High Priest, I have a message from Sister Myne. She will soon be arriving with the Gilberta Company to give the temple her donation."

"Without arranging a meeting first...?" the High Priest asked. "Who is with Myne right now?"

Fran apologized with a thoroughly troubled expression. Sister Myne had departed for the Gilberta Company with the boy who had come to greet her. Meanwhile, Gil had returned to the orphanage, and Delia—despite having been entrusted with the same message as Fran—had walked right past the High Priest's chambers and returned to the High Bishop.

"In other words, she is visiting the Gilberta Company without any attendants? Will that not cause problems in the lower city?"

"There is the boy who came to get her. It seems that Sister Myne trusts him deeply, so perhaps he is her attendant in the lower city."

"Now that you mention it, they did say that she had someone who managed her health, or something of the sort."

It would normally be unthinkable for one to visit without first scheduling a meeting or leave without staying in some form of contact with their attendants. I could instantly tell why Fran found Sister Myne so hard to serve.

The High Priest sighed, stopping Fran's apologies with a light handwave. "Her mistake here is not your responsibility, Fran. We have no choice but to teach Myne the noble way of doing things, step by step. Begin preparing for her arrival at once."

At the High Priest's instruction, we began rushing around in preparation of welcoming our visitors. Arno and the High Priest started clearing away boards and documents with important matters written on them, while Lothar checked over the tea stores and Gido went to fetch milk from the kitchen.

"Fran, we should go to the gate to welcome Sister Myne. We do not know when she will arrive, so we must head there at once."

Leaving the preparations to the other attendants, Fran and I exited the High Priest's room. On the way, we enlisted the help of a gray priest who was carrying a box to the orphanage, then began waiting for the carriage to arrive at the front gate.

"...Zahm, would it not be wiser to wait at the back gate leading to the lower city?" Fran asked.

"If she is arriving with a merchant, she will surely arrive at the front gate via carriage. There is no merchant who would visit the High Priest on foot."

"That would normally be the case, but it is impossible for us to predict what Sister Myne might do..."

As I tried to calm Fran down, I started to worry as well. It was then that we received word of the Gilberta Company's carriage arriving at the gate.

"Fran, would you kindly take us to the High Priest?"

When Sister Myne returned to the temple, she seemed completely unlike the person Fran had described earlier. As far as I could tell, at least, she seemed much more like a proper blue shrine maiden than she had been that morning. She spoke politely, held herself with confident grace, and requested Fran's insight rather than progressing

matters purely on her own terms. Fran, too, seemed invigorated by this change: he started to give out brisk orders, truly back in his element.

"As you wish," he said. "We shall divide the luggage among us, but may we first examine what you have brought?"

"We bear gifts of cloth, paper, and rinsham, both to introduce Master Benno and to apologize for the abruptness of our meeting," one of the Gilberta Company's attendants explained. From the way they presented themselves, it seemed they had prior experience doing business with nobles.

"We thank you, but what is rinsham, exactly?"

We would not be able to bring any unknown goods into the High Priest's chambers, and so we could not accept the unfamiliar gift until we knew what its function was.

"It is something resembling liquid soap that makes one's hair glossy. Sister Myne invented it and it is one of our newest products."

Sister Myne's hair was certainly more beautiful than the other blue shrine maidens', so it made sense that it would be a new product. I picked up the luggage alongside the other gray priests, and we walked at the end of the group heading to the High Priest's chambers.

Oh...?

Since we were positioned at the very back, I soon noticed that Sister Myne was falling behind. Fran was walking significantly slower than usual, but even so, he was too fast for her short legs, and the distance between them soon increased to such a point that Sister Myne had to run a little to catch up.

Assuming Fran hadn't noticed this when traveling with her that morning, Sister Myne must have been exerting herself to keep up with him then as well. It would not be strange if she had started to resent him for not carefully considering her needs.

Fran, why are you not noticing this...? Please, I beg of you, turn back just once so that you can see what is happening here.

The merchant looked over at Myne with concern. I debated whether I should call out myself, but he promptly beat me to it.

"At this rate, Myne's going to collapse trying to keep up with you."

Collapse? Just from walking...?

At first, I thought this might be some kind of joke, but Sister Myne was already visibly struggling to breathe. I could tell that Fran simply hadn't been paying enough attention to her.

Perhaps this will drive her to lose her temper again?

After all, she was the kind of person to Crush others simply for informing her of the time. I stiffened, waiting for her to explode... but instead, she defended Fran and gave him a comforting smile.

"You have nothing to worry about," she said.

My eyes widened in disbelief; she was nothing like the person described to me. It was then I realized that I would need to judge her not based on rumors, but through observing her speech and behavior myself.

"That was an unexpected meeting... but it somehow ended without issue," Fran said. "I was concerned for a moment there."

The head of the Gilberta Company knew Sister Myne well, and we had learned much about her during the discussion. According to him, she was for the most part a docile girl who only became merciless when it came to her family, her friends, and books. She was far removed from temple culture and noble society.

What her attendants needed to be aware of more than anything else was her unnatural weakness. I had been frozen with surprise when Sister Myne collapsed at the end of the meeting, only able to watch in a daze as the Gilberta Company merchant carried her away. Fran chased after them in desperation, he seemed a lot more at ease when he returned, so I decided that he did not need my worry.

However...

"Fran, please learn to manage Sister Myne's health as soon as possible. It will surely be bad for all of our hearts if her collapsing becomes a regular occurrence."

"Indeed... I now understand that I had failed on several fronts myself. I intend to learn what I need to know to serve Sister Myne well, as her attendant."

With that, Fran gave a small smile—a bright expression completely unlike the one he had worn during lunch. It had certainly been an unusual day with Sister Myne's abrupt visit and unpredictable behavior, though not a bad one. She had shown that she cared for and was willing to protect Fran, and if they learned to support one another, I was sure that their relationship would only get stronger.

Afterword

To all those who are new to the series and those who read the web or light novels: thank you very much for reading Part 2 Volume 1 of Ascendance of a Bookworm's manga adaptation.

In this new part, the setting moves to the temple, where many new characters pop up all at once. Myne goes nuts when she sees the temple book room, but her commoner upbringing and a variety of tedious formalities mean things aren't going to be easy for her. She is being forced to continue dealing with the High Bishop who she crushed at the end of Part 1, as well as the blue priests connected to the nobility.

The highlight of this volume is likely all the visuals of the temple. Suzuka-san worked together with Namino-san—who is handling Part 3 of the manga adaptation—to design all the specifics, so hopefully you'll be able to enjoy Parts 2 and 3 without any dissonance.

The story being told in manga form means there are background visuals now, making it a lot easier for you all to see that Myne is almost always surrounded by her attendants, as well as how the High Priest's attendants work in his chambers. Drawing all this must be rough on Suzuka-san...

My favorite scene in this volume was Mark freaking out; in fact, I believe this is the first time we've seen him with his eyes open. Haha! Benno's discussion with the High Priest was nice as well. They're Myne's merchant and temple guardians, both struggling with all the chaos she brings.

But more than anything else, there's Fran, whose growth throughout this volume really is the main event. His developing mindset and emotional state can be seen with how his expression changes throughout the book, and no matter how many times I re-read it, I always notice something new.

This volume's short story is from Zahm's perspective. He serves the High Priest alongside Fran. I hope you enjoy seeing how Myne's actions look to a gray priest who doesn't interact with her much.

Finally, Bookworm is going to be getting an anime adaptation! It'd be much easier for you to just watch the PV than for me to try and describe it. It's online and not too hard to find. I hope you enjoy seeing Myne and the others moving around and talking!

Miya Kazuki

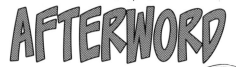

AFTERWORD

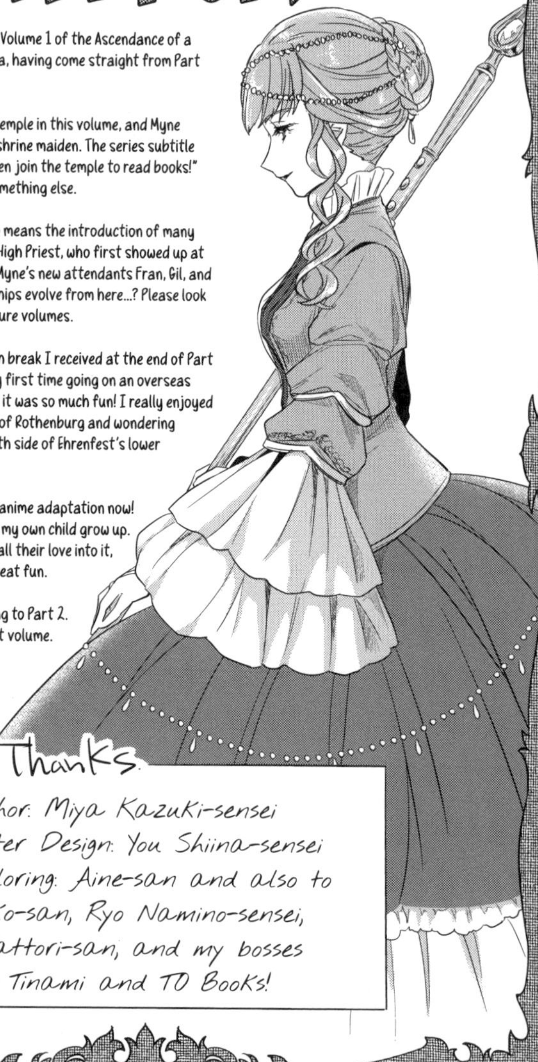

Thank you for buying Part 2 Volume 1 of the Ascendance of a Bookworm manga! I'm Suzuka, having come straight from Part 1 to this.

The setting changes to the temple in this volume, and Myne becomes an apprentice blue shrine maiden. The series subtitle has also changed to: "I'll even join the temple to read books!" Her love for books truly is something else.

A change in environment also means the introduction of many new characters. There's the High Priest, who first showed up at the end of Part 1, as well as Myne's new attendants Fran, Gil, and Delia. How will their relationships evolve from here...? Please look forward to finding out in future volumes.

Oh, and I used the one-month break I received at the end of Part 1 to go to Germany. It was my first time going on an overseas vacation in quite a while, and it was so much fun! I really enjoyed walking through the streets of Rothenburg and wondering whether this is what the north side of Ehrenfest's lower city would look like.

Bookworm is even getting an anime adaptation now! I'm so excited! It's like seeing my own child grow up. The anime staff are pouring all their love into it, so I'm sure it's going to be great fun.

In any case, this is the opening to Part 2. May we meet again in the next volume.

Suzuka

Special Thanks.

Author: Miya Kazuki-sensei
Character Design: You Shiina-sensei
Cover Coloring: Aine-san and also to Sachiko-san, Ryo Namino-sensei, Mio Hattori-san, and my bosses at Tinami and TO Books!

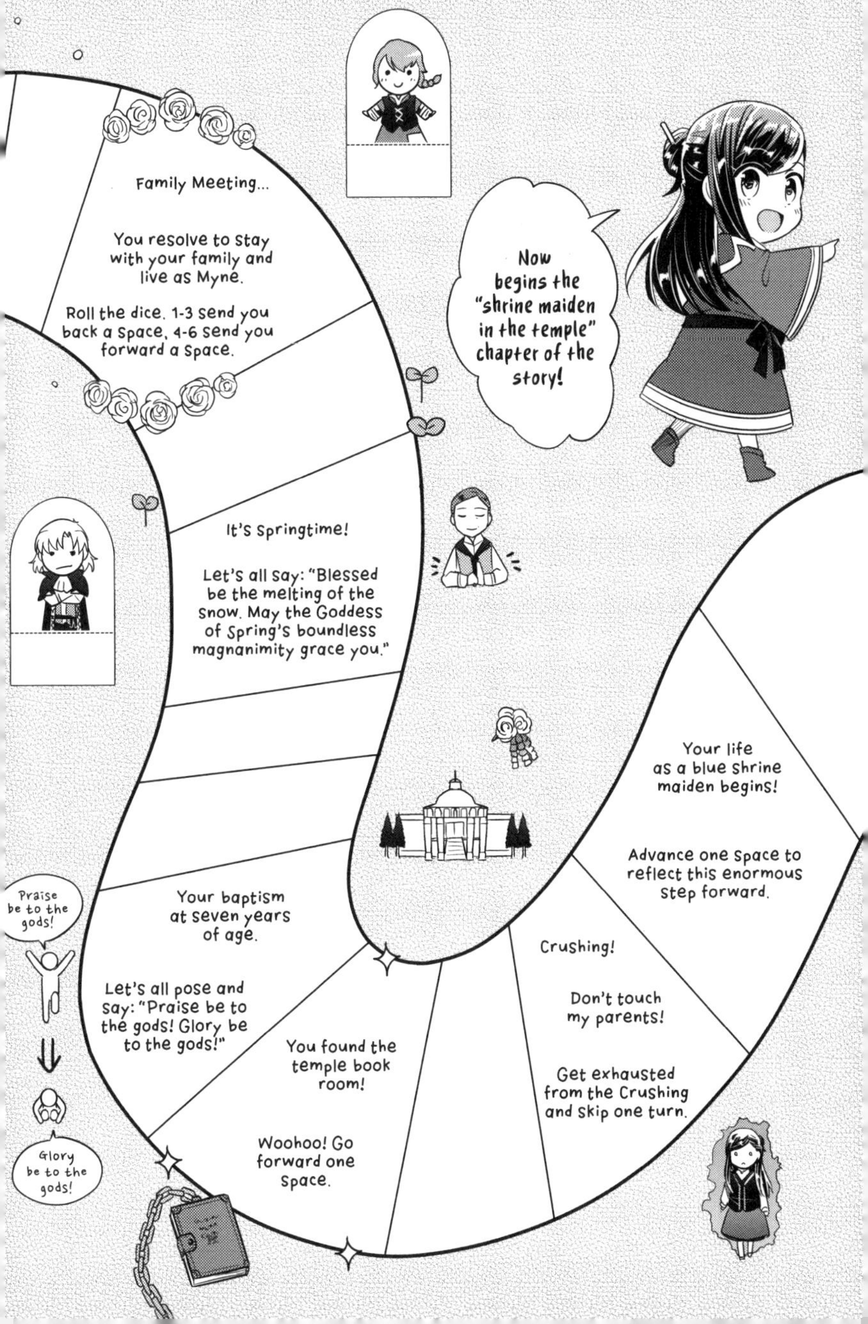

Now begins the "shrine maiden in the temple" chapter of the story!
Family Meeting...
You resolve to stay with your family and live as Myne.
Roll the dice. 1-3 send you back a space, 4-6 send you forward a space.
It's Springtime!
Let's all say: "Blessed be the melting of the snow. May the Goddess of Spring's boundless magnanimity grace you."
Praise be to the gods!
Glory be to the gods!
Your baptism at seven years of age.
Let's all pose and say: "Praise be to the gods! Glory be to the gods!"
You found the temple book room!
Woohoo! Go forward one space.
Crushing!
Don't touch my parents!
Get exhausted from the Crushing and skip one turn.
Your life as a blue shrine maiden begins!
Advance one space to reflect this enormous step forward.

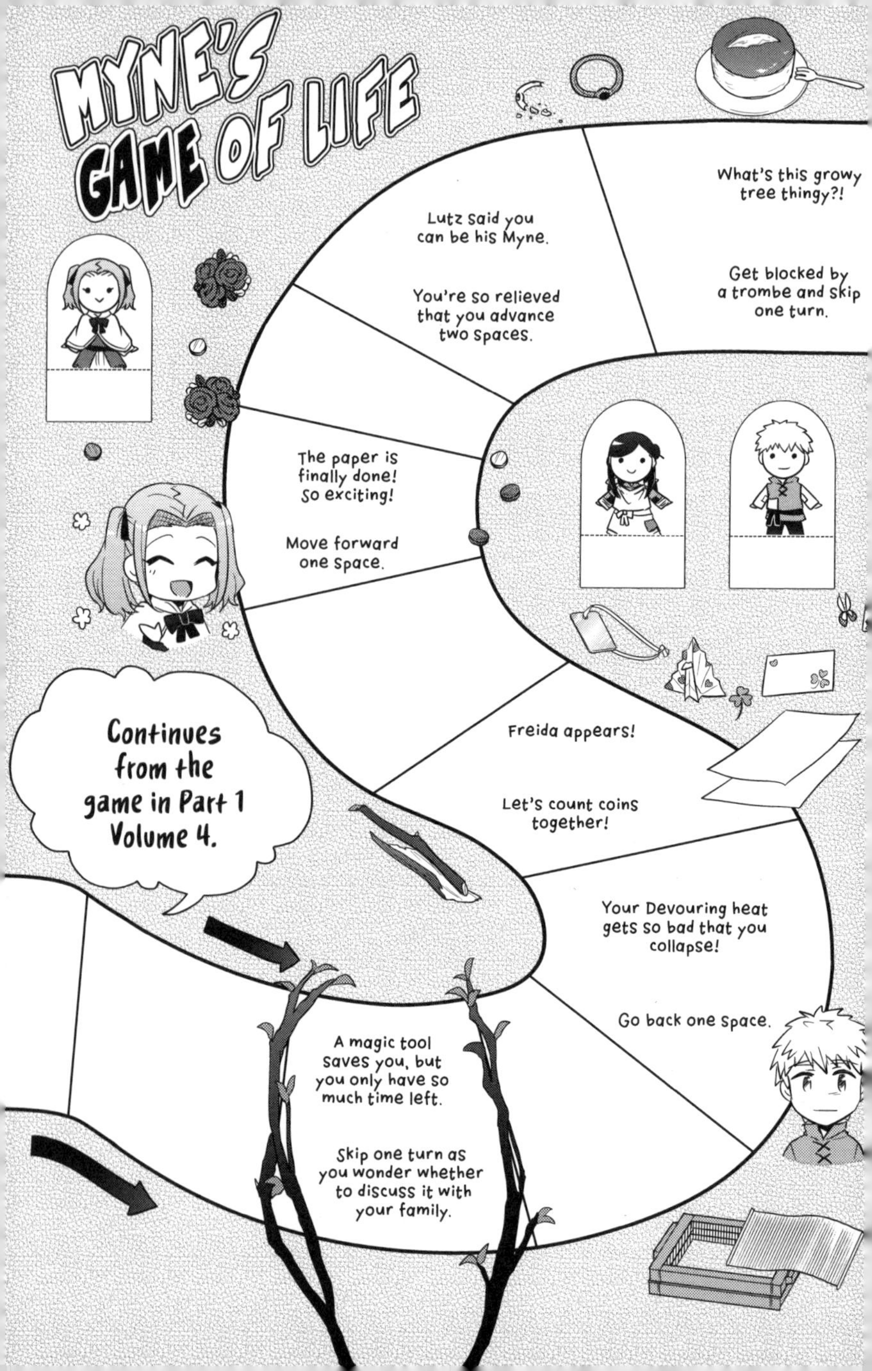
MYNE'S GAME OF LIFE
Continues from the game in Part 1 Volume 4.
What's this growy tree thingy?!
Get blocked by a trombe and skip one turn.
Lutz said you can be his Myne.
You're so relieved that you advance two spaces.
The paper is finally done! So exciting!
Move forward one space.
Freida appears!
Let's count coins together!
Your Devouring heat gets so bad that you collapse!
Go back one space.
A magic tool saves you, but you only have so much time left.
Skip one turn as you wonder whether to discuss it with your family.

ASCENDANCE OF A BOOKWORM (MANGA) PART 2 VOLUME 1
by Miya Kazuki (story) and Suzuka (artwork)
Original character designs by You Shiina

Translated by quof
Edited by Kieran Redgewell
Lettered by Nicole Roderick

First published in Japan in 2019 by TO Books, Tokyo.
Publication rights for this English edition arranged through TO Books, Tokyo.

Find more books like this one at www.j-novel.club!

Managing Director: Samuel Pinansky
Manga Line Manager: J. Collis
Managing Editor: Jan Mitsuko Cash
Managing Translator: Kristi Fernandez
QA Manager: Hannah N. Carter
Marketing Manager: Stephanie Hii

ISBN: 978-1-7183-7257-3
Printed in Korea
First Printing: December 2021
10 9 8 7 6 5 4 3 2 1

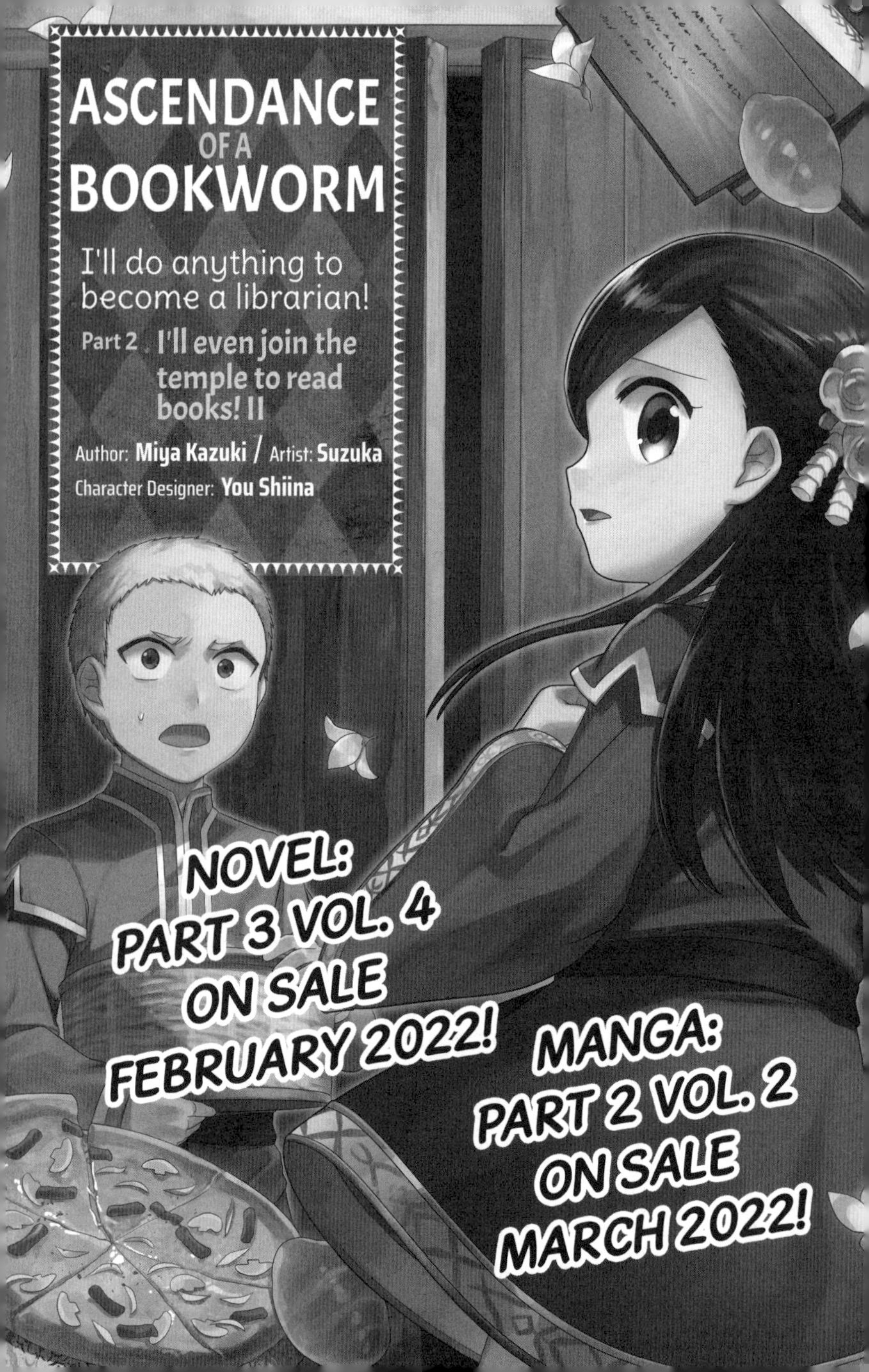
ASCENDANCE OF A BOOKWORM
I'll do anything to become a librarian!
Part 2 I'll even join the temple to read books! II
Author: Miya Kazuki / Artist: Suzuka
Character Designer: You Shiina
NOVEL: PART 3 VOL. 4 ON SALE FEBRUARY 2022!
MANGA: PART 2 VOL. 2 ON SALE MARCH 2022!

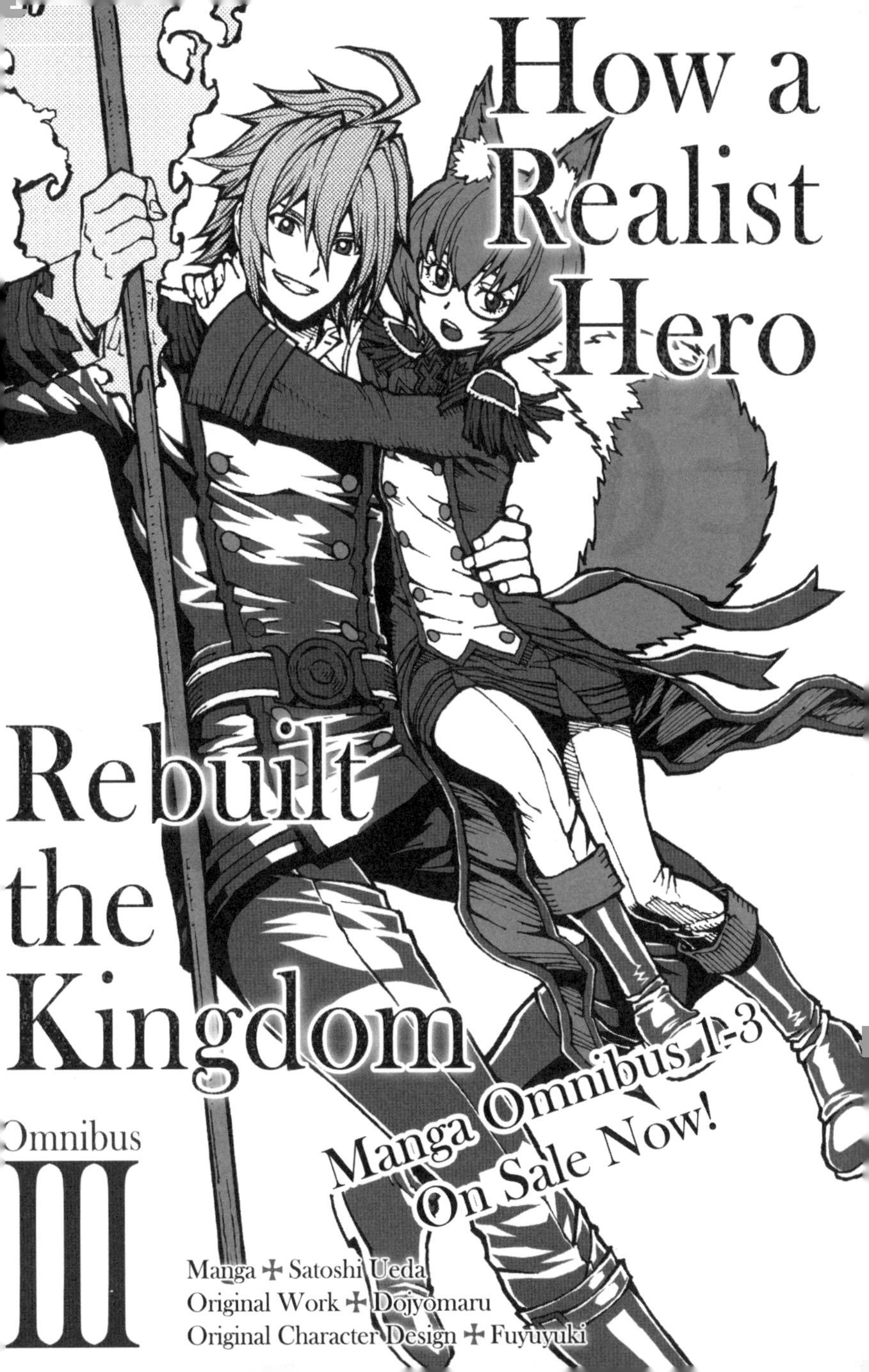
How a Realist Hero Rebuilt the Kingdom
Omnibus III
Manga Omnibus 1-3 On Sale Now!
Manga ✢ Satoshi Ueda
Original Work ✢ Dojyomaru
Original Character Design ✢ Fuyuyuki

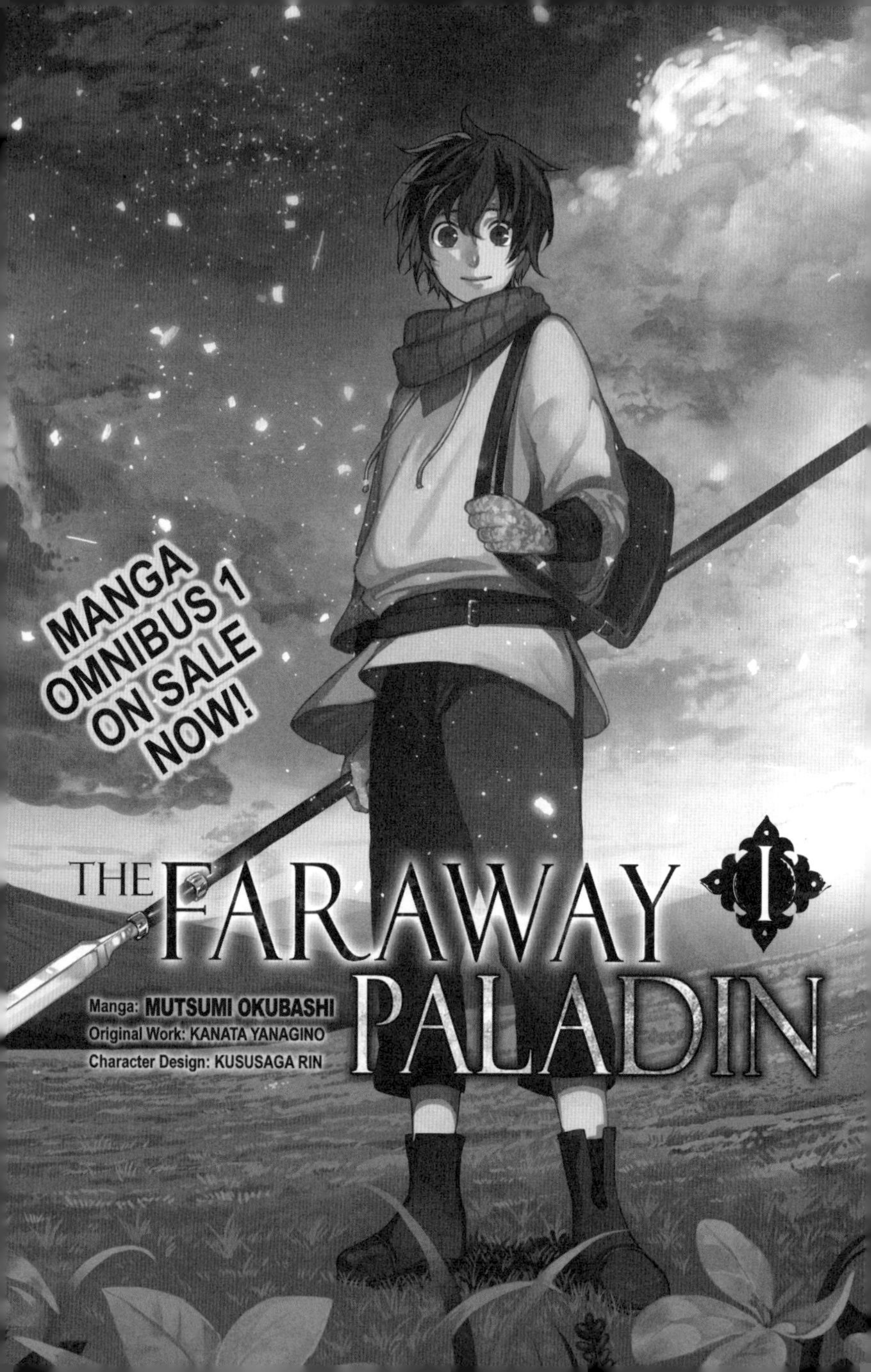

MANGA OMNIBUS 1 ON SALE NOW!
THE FARAWAY PALADIN I
Manga: MUTSUMI OKUBASHI
Original Work: KANATA YANAGINO
Character Design: KUSUSAGA RIN

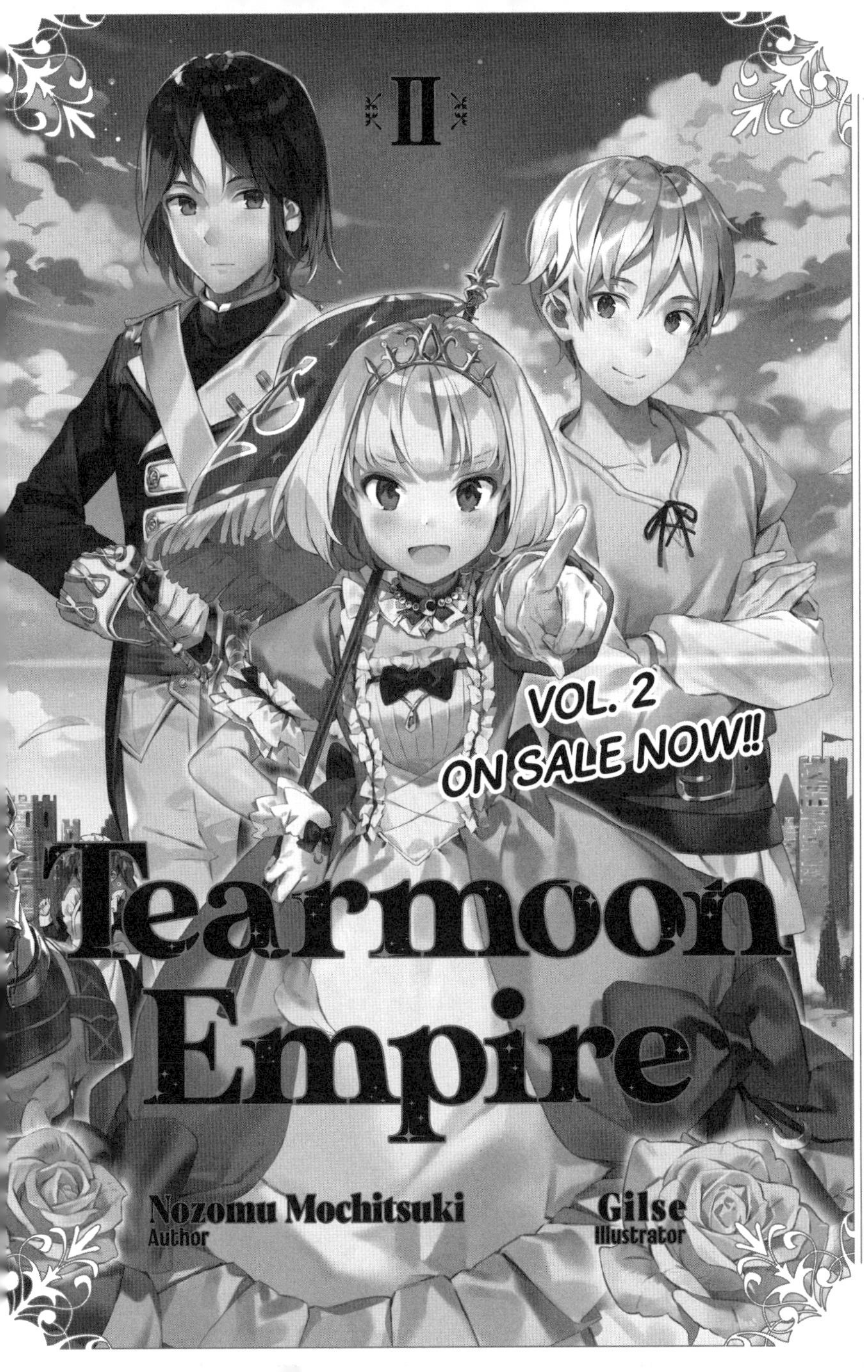
II
VOL. 2
ON SALE NOW!!
Tearmoon Empire
Nozomu Mochitsuki
Author
Gilse
Illustrator

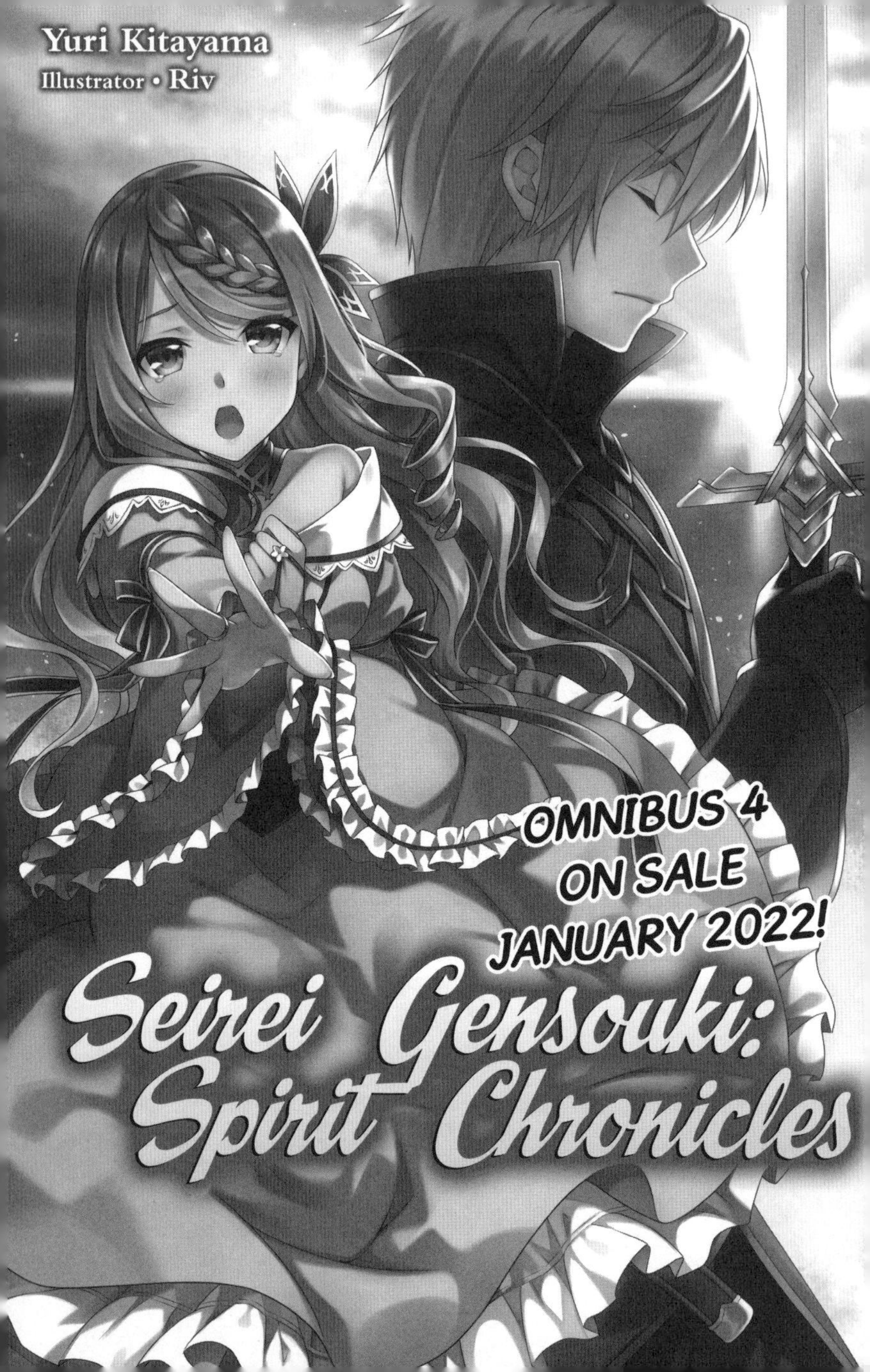
Yuri Kitayama
Illustrator • Riv
OMNIBUS 4
ON SALE
JANUARY 2022!
Seirei Gensouki:
Spirit Chronicles

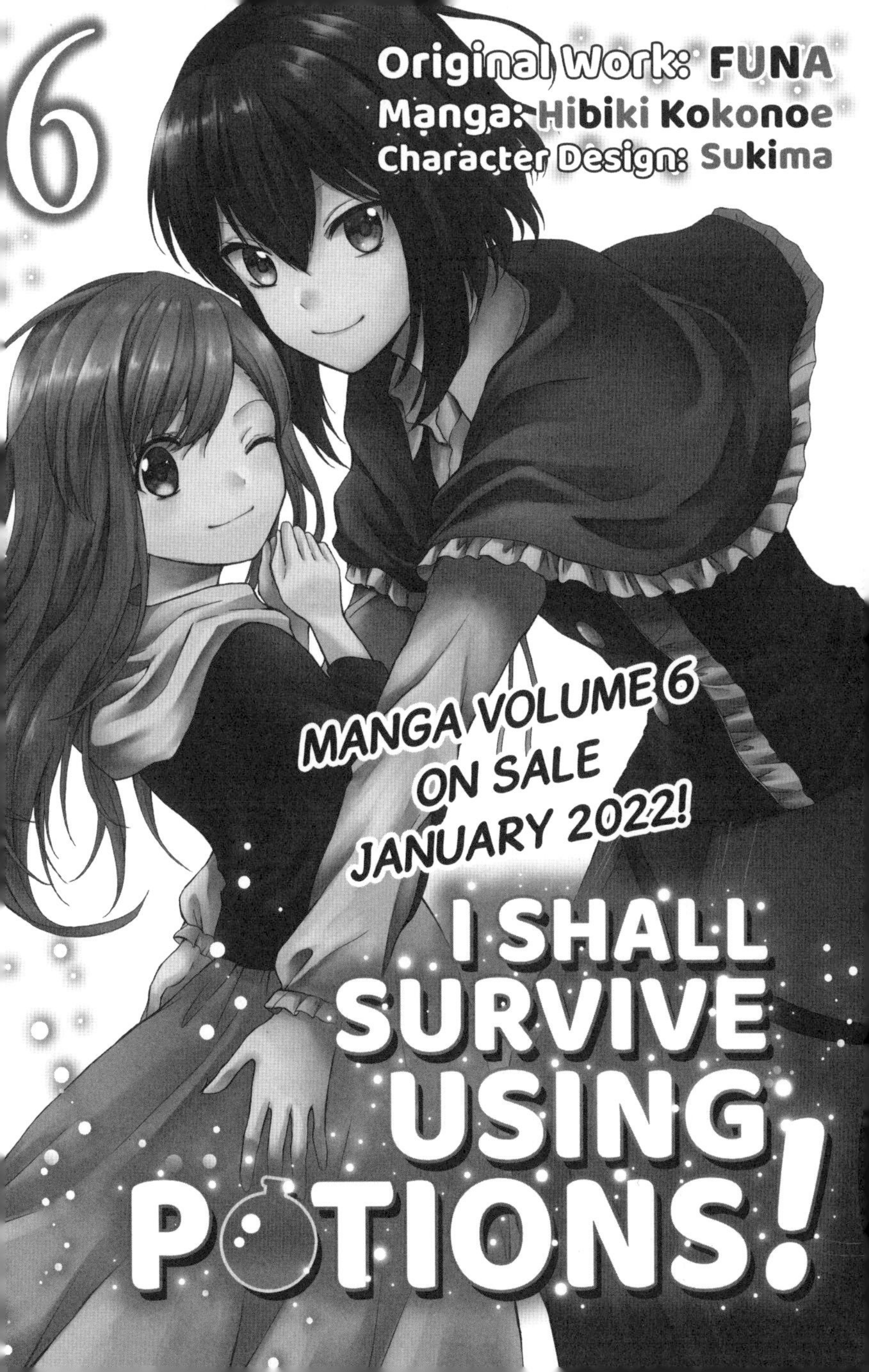
6
Original Work: FUNA
Manga: Hibiki Kokonoe
Character Design: Sukima
MANGA VOLUME 6
ON SALE
JANUARY 2022!
I SHALL
SURVIVE
USING
POTIONS!

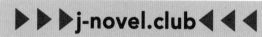

A Lily Blooms in Another World
A Very Fairy Apartment**
A Wild Last Boss Appeared!
Altina the Sword Princess
Amagi Brilliant Park
An Archdemon's Dilemma: How to Love Your Elf Bride*
Animeta!**
The Apothecary Diaries
Are You Okay With a Slightly Older Girlfriend?
Arifureta: From Commonplace to World's Strongest
Arifureta Zero
Ascendance of a Bookworm*
Banner of the Stars
Bibliophile Princess*
Black Summoner*
The Bloodline
By the Grace of the Gods
Campfire Cooking in Another World with My Absurd Skill*
Can Someone Please Explain What's Going On?!
The Combat Baker and Automaton Waitress
Cooking with Wild Game*
Culinary Chronicles of the Court Flower
Deathbound Duke's Daughter
Demon Lord, Retry!*
Der Werwolf: The Annals of Veight*
Discommunication**
Dungeon Busters
The Emperor's Lady-in-Waiting is Wanted as a Bride*
The Economics of Prophecy
The Epic Tale of the Reincarnated Prince Herscherik
The Extraordinary, the Ordinary, and SOAP!
The Faraway Paladin*
Full Metal Panic!
Fushi no Kami: Rebuilding Civilization Starts With a Village
The Great Cleric
The Greatest Magicmaster's Retirement Plan
Girls Kingdom
Grimgar of Fantasy and Ash
Guide to the Perfect Otaku Girlfriend: Roomies & Romance
Her Majesty's Swarm
Holmes of Kyoto
The Holy Knight's Dark Road
How a Realist Hero Rebuilt the Kingdom*
How NOT to Summon a Demon Lord
I Love Yuri and I Got Bodyswapped with a Fujoshi!**
I Refuse to Be Your Enemy!
I Saved Too Many Girls and Caused the Apocalypse
I Shall Survive Using Potions!*
I'll Never Set Foot in That House Again!
The Ideal Sponger Life
If It's for My Daughter, I'd Even Defeat a Demon Lord
In Another World With My Smartphone
Infinite Dendrogram*
Infinite Stratos
Invaders of the Rokujouma!?
Jessica Bannister
JK Haru is a Sex Worker in Another World
John Sinclair: Demon Hunter
Kobold King
Kokoro Connect
Lazy Dungeon Master
The Magic in this Other World is Too Far Behind!*
The Magician Who Rose From Failure
Mapping: The Trash-Tier Skill That Got Me Into a Top-Tier Party*
Marginal Operation**
The Master of Ragnarok & Blesser of Einherjar*
Middle-Aged Businessman, Arise in Another World!
Monster Tamer
My Big Sister Lives in a Fantasy World
My Friend's Little Sister Has It In for Me!
My Instant Death Ability is So Overpowered, No One in This Other World Stands a Chance Against Me!
My Next Life as a Villainess: All Routes Lead to Doom!
Our Crappy Social Game Club Is Gonna Make the Most Epic Game
Otherside Picnic
Outbreak Company
Perry Rhodan NEO
Reborn to Master the Blade: From Hero-King to Extraordinary Squire ♀
Record of Wortenia War*
Reincarnated as the Piggy Duke: This Time I'm Gonna Tell Her How I Feel!
Seirei Gensouki: Spirit Chronicles*
Sexiled: My Sexist Party Leader Kicked Me Out, So I Teamed Up With a Mythical Sorceress!
She's the Cutest... But We're Just Friends!
The Sidekick Never Gets the Girl, Let Alone the Protag's Sister!
Slayers
The Sorcerer's Receptionist
Sorcerous Stabber Orphen*
Sweet Reincarnation**
The Tales of Marielle Clarac*
Tearmoon Empire
Teogonia
The Underdog of the Eight Greater Tribes
The Unwanted Undead Adventurer*
Villainess: Reloaded! Blowing Away Bad Ends with Modern Weapons*
Welcome to Japan, Ms. Elf!*
When the Clock Strikes Z
The White Cat's Revenge as Plotted from the Dragon King's Lap
Wild Times with a Fake Fake Princess
The World's Least Interesting Master Swordsman

* Novel and Manga Editions
** Manga Only
Keep an eye out at j-novel.club for further new title announcements!